Praise for the *STAR WARS*® novels of Timothy Zahn

HEIR TO THE EMPIRE

"MOVES WITH A SPEED-OF-LIGHT PACE THAT CAPTURES THE SPIRIT OF THE MOVIE TRILOGY SO WELL, YOU CAN ALMOST HEAR JOHN WILLIAMS'S SOUNDTRACK."
—*The Providence Sunday Journal*

"A SPLENDIDLY EXCITING NOVEL . . . READ AND ENJOY. THE MAGIC IS BACK."
—*Nashville Banner*

"CHOCK FULL OF ALL THE GOOD STUFF YOU'VE COME TO EXPECT FROM A BATTLE OF GOOD AGAINST EVIL."—*Daily News*, New York

DARK FORCE RISING

"CONTINUES [ZAHN'S] REMARKABLE EXTRAPOLATION FROM GEORGE LUCAS'S TRILOGY."—*Chicago Sun-Times*

"ZAHN HAS PERFECTLY CAPTURED THE PACE AND FLAVOR OF THE *STAR WARS* MOVIES. THIS IS SPACE OPERA AT ITS BEST."
—*The Sunday Oklahoman*

THE LAST COMMAND

"FILLED WITH CHARACTERISTIC *STAR WARS* TECHNOLOGY AND COSMIC BATTLES . . . THE DETAIL AND PLOT DEVELOPMENT FAR EXCEED WHAT ARE POSSIBLE IN A TWO-HOUR MOVIE."
—*The Indianapolis Star*

BY TIMOTHY ZAHN

The Hand of Thrawn:
SPECTER OF THE PAST
VISION OF THE FUTURE

A Star Wars® trilogy:
HEIR TO THE EMPIRE
DARK FORCE RISING
THE LAST COMMAND

The Blackcollar
Cobra
Blackcollar: The Backlash Mission
Deadman Switch
Cascade Point
Cobra Bargain
Cobra Strike
A Coming of Age
Spinneret
Time Bomb & Zahndry Others
Triplet
Warhorse
Distant Friends

Conquerors' Trilogy:
CONQUERORS' PRIDE
CONQUERORS' HERITAGE
CONQUERORS' LEGACY

SPECTER OF THE PAST

TIMOTHY ZAHN

BANTAM BOOKS

NEW YORK • TORONTO • LONDON • SYDNEY • AUCKLAND

This edition contains the complete text
of the original hardcover edition.
NOT ONE WORD HAS BEEN OMITTED.

STAR WARS®: SPECTER OF THE PAST
A Bantam Spectra Book

PUBLISHING HISTORY
Bantam Spectra hardcover edition / December 1997
Bantam Spectra paperback edition / September 1998

ISBN 0-553-29804-6

Published simultaneously in the United States and Canada

PRINTED IN THE UNITED STATES OF AMERICA
OPM   10 9

CHAPTER

1

Slowly, silently, its lights a faint glitter of life amid the darkness, the Imperial Star Destroyer *Chimaera* glided through space.

Empty space. Oppressively dark space. Long, lonely light-years from the nearest of the tiny islands that were the star systems of the galaxy, drifting at the edge of the boundary between the Outer Rim worlds and the vast regions of territory known as Unknown Space. At the very edge of the Empire.

Or rather, at the edge of the pitiful scraps of what had once been the Empire.

Standing beside one of the *Chimaera*'s side viewports, Admiral Pellaeon, Supreme Commander of the Imperial Fleet, gazed out at the emptiness, the weight of all too many years pressing heavily across his shoulders. Too many years, too many battles, too many defeats.

Perhaps the *Chimaera*'s bridge crew was feeling the weight, too. Certainly the sounds of activity going on behind him seemed more muted than usual today. But perhaps it was merely the effect of being out here, so far from anywhere at all.

No, of course that had to be it. The men of the *Chimaera* were the finest the Fleet had to offer. They were Imperial officers and crewers, and Imperials didn't give up. Ever.

There was a tentative footstep at his side. "Admiral?" Captain Ardiff said quietly. "We're ready to begin, sir."

For a moment Pellaeon's mind flashed back ten years, to another very similar moment. Then, it had been Pellaeon and Grand Admiral Thrawn who'd been here on the *Chimaera's* bridge, watching the final test of the prototype cloaking shield Thrawn had recovered from among the Emperor's trophies inside Mount Tantiss. Pellaeon could remember the excitement he'd felt then, despite his misgivings about the insane Jedi clone Joruus C'baoth, as he watched Thrawn single-handedly breathing new life and vigor back into the Empire.

But Mount Tantiss was gone, destroyed by agents of the New Republic and C'baoth's own madness and treason. And Grand Admiral Thrawn was dead.

And the Empire was dying.

With an effort, Pellaeon shook the shadows of the past away. He was an Imperial officer, and Imperials didn't give up. "Thank you," he said to Ardiff. "At your convenience, Captain."

"Yes, sir." Ardiff half turned, gestured to the fighter coordinator in the portside crew pit. "Signal the attack," he ordered.

The officer acknowledged and gestured in turn to one of his crewers. Pellaeon turned his attention back to the viewport—

Just in time to see eight SoroSuub *Preybird*-class starfighters in tight formation roar in from behind them. Cutting tight to the *Chimaera's* command superstructure, they passed over the forward ridgeline, raking it with low-power blaster fire, then split smoothly out in eight different directions. Corkscrewing out and forward, they kept up their fire until they were out of the Star Destroyer's primary attack zone. Then, curving smoothly around, they swung around and regrouped.

"Admiral?" Ardiff prompted.

"Let's give them one more pass, Captain," Pellaeon said.

"The more flight data the Predictor has to work with, the better it should function." He caught the eye of one of the crew pit officers. "Damage report?"

"Minor damage to the forward ridgeline, sir," the officer reported. "One sensor array knocked out, leaving five turbolasers without ranging data."

"Acknowledged." All theoretical damage, of course, calculated under the assumption that the Preybirds were using full-power capital-ship turbolasers. Pellaeon had always loved war games when he was younger; had relished the chance to play with technique and tactics without the risks of true combat. Somewhere in all those years, the excitement had faded away. "Helm, bring us around twenty degrees to starboard," he ordered. "Starboard turbolasers will lay down dispersion fire as they make their next pass."

The Preybirds were back in tight formation now, once again approaching their target. The *Chimaera*'s turbolasers opened up as they came, their low-level fire splattering across the Preybirds' overlapping deflector shields. For a few seconds the opponents traded fire; then, the Preybirds broke formation again, splitting apart like the fingertips of an opening hand. Twisting over and under the *Chimaera*, they shot past, scrambling for the safety of distance.

"Damage report?" Pellaeon called.

"Three starboard turbolaser batteries knocked out," the officer called back. "We've also lost one tractor beam projector and two ion cannon."

"Enemy damage?"

"One attacker appears to have lost its deflector shields, and two others are reading diminished turbolaser capability."

"Hardly counts as damage," Ardiff murmured. "Of course, the situation here isn't exactly fair. Ships that small and maneuverable would never have the kind of shields or firepower we're crediting them with."

"If you want fairness, organize a shockball tournament," Pellaeon said acidly. "Don't look for it in warfare."

Ardiff's cheek twitched. "I'm sorry, sir."

Pellaeon sighed. The finest the Imperial Fleet had to

offer . . . "Stand by the cloaking shield, Captain," he ordered, watching the faint drive glows as the Preybirds regrouped again in the distance. "Activate on my command."

"Yes, Admiral."

There was a sudden flare of drive glow, partially eclipsed by the Preybirds themselves, as the enemy kicked into high acceleration. "Here they come," Pellaeon said, watching as the single glowing dot rapidly resolved itself into eight close-formation ships. "Lock Predictor into fire control. Stand by cloaking shield."

"Predictor and cloaking shield standing by," Ardiff confirmed.

Pellaeon nodded, his full attention on the Preybirds. Nearly to the point where they'd broken formation last time . . . "Cloaking shield: *now.*"

And with a brief flicker of bridge lighting, the stars and incoming Preybirds vanished as the cloaking shield plunged the *Chimaera* into total darkness.

"Cloaking shield activated and stabilized," Ardiff said.

"Helm, come around portside: thirty degrees by eight," Pellaeon ordered. "Ahead acceleration point one. Turbolasers: fire."

"Acknowledged," an officer called. "Turbolasers are firing."

Pellaeon took a step closer to the viewport and looked down along the *Chimaera*'s sides. The faint blasts of low-level fire were visible, lancing a short distance out from the Star Destroyer and then disappearing as they penetrated the spherical edge of the Star Destroyer's cloaking shield. Blinded by the very device that was now shielding it from its opponents' view, the *Chimaera* was firing wildly in an attempt to destroy those opponents.

Or perhaps not quite so wildly. If the Predictor worked as well as its designers hoped, perhaps the Empire still had a chance in this war.

It was a long time before the *Chimaera*'s turbolasers finally ceased fire. Far too long. "Is that it?" he asked Ardiff.

"Yes, sir," the other said. "Five hundred shots, as pre-programmed."

Pellaeon nodded. "Deactivate cloaking shield. Let's see how well we did."

There was another flicker from the lights, and the stars were back. Mentally crossing his fingers, Pellaeon peered out the viewport.

For a moment there was nothing. Then, from starboard, he spotted the approaching drive glows. Seven of them.

"Signal from Adversary Commander, Admiral," the comm officer called. "Target Three reports receiving a disabling hit and has gone dormant; all other targets have sustained only minimal damage. Requesting orders."

Pellaeon grimaced. One. Out of eight targets, the *Chimaera* had been able to hit exactly one. And that great feat had required five hundred shots to achieve.

So that was that. The wonderful Computerized Combat Predictor, touted by its creators and sponsors as the best approach to practical use of the cloaking shield, had been put to the test. And to be fair, it had probably done better than simple random shooting.

But it hadn't done enough better. Not nearly enough.

"Inform Adversary Commander that the exercise is over," Pellaeon told the comm officer. "Target Three may reactivate its systems; all ships are to return to the *Chimaera*. I want their reports filed within the next two hours."

"Yes, sir."

"I'm sure they'll be able to improve it, Admiral," Ardiff said at Pellaeon's side. "This was just the first field test. Surely they'll be able to improve it."

"How?" Pellaeon retorted. "Train the Predictor to be omniscient? Or simply teach it how to read our enemies' minds?"

"You only gave it two passes to study the targets' flight patterns," Ardiff reminded him. "With more data, it could have better anticipated their movements."

Pellaeon snorted gently. "It's a nice theory, Captain, and under certain controlled situations it might even work. But combat is hardly a controlled situation. There are far too many variables and unknowns, especially considering the hundreds of alien species and combat styles we have to contend with. I knew from the beginning that this Predictor idea was probably futile. But it had to be tried."

"Well, then, we just have to go back to mark zero," Ardiff said. "Come up with something else. There have to be practical uses for this cloaking shield device."

"Of course there are," Pellaeon agreed heavily. "Grand Admiral Thrawn devised three of them himself. But there's no one left in the Empire with his military genius."

He sighed. "No, Captain. It's over. It's all over. And we've lost."

For a long moment the low murmur of background conversation was the only sound on the bridge. "You can't mean that, Admiral," Ardiff said at last. "And if I may say so, sir, this is not the sort of thing the Supreme Commander of Imperial forces should be talking about."

"Why not?" Pellaeon countered. "It's obvious to everyone else."

"It most certainly is not, sir," Ardiff said stiffly. "We still hold eight sectors—over a thousand inhabited systems. We have the Fleet, nearly two hundred Star Destroyers strong. We're still very much a force to be reckoned with."

"Are we?" Pellaeon asked. "Are we really?"

"Of course we are," Ardiff insisted. "How else could we be holding our own against the New Republic?"

Pellaeon shook his head. "We're holding our own for the simple reason that the New Republic is too busy right now with internal squabbling to bother with us."

"Which works directly to our advantage," Ardiff said. "It's giving us the time we need to reorganize and rearm."

"Rearm?" Pellaeon threw him a quizzical frown. "Have you taken even a cursory look at what we're working with here?" He gestured out the viewport at the Preybirds, disappearing now beneath the edge of the *Chimaera*'s hull as they headed for the Star Destroyer's hangar. "Look at them, Captain. SoroSuub Preybirds. We're reduced to SoroSuub Preybirds."

"There's nothing wrong with the Preybirds, sir," Ardiff

said stubbornly. "They're a quite capable midsize starfighter."

"The point is that they're not being manufactured by the Empire," Pellaeon said. "They're being scrounged from who knows where—probably some fringe pirate or mercenary gang. And they're being scrounged precisely because we're down to a single major shipyard and it can't keep up with demand for capital ships, let alone starfighters. So tell me how you plan for us to rearm ourselves."

Ardiff looked out the viewport. "It's still not yet over, sir."

But it was. And down deep, Pellaeon was sure Ardiff knew it as well as he did. A thousand systems left, out of an Empire that had once spanned a million. Two hundred Star Destroyers remaining from a Fleet that had once included over twenty-five thousand of them.

And perhaps most telling of all, hundreds of star systems that had once maintained a cautious neutrality were now petitioning the New Republic for membership. They, too, knew that the outcome was no longer uncertain.

Grand Admiral Thrawn could perhaps have breathed the remaining sparks into an Imperial victory. But Grand Admiral Thrawn was gone.

"Have the navigator plot a course for the Bastion system, Captain," Pellaeon said to Ardiff. "Send transmissions to all the Moffs, instructing them to meet me at Moff Disra's palace. We'll leave as soon as the Preybirds are aboard."

"Yes, Admiral," Ardiff said. "May I tell the Moffs what the meeting is about?"

Pellaeon looked out the viewport at the distant stars. Stars that the Empire had once called theirs. They'd had so much . . . and somehow it had all slipped through their fingers. "Tell them," he said quietly, "that it's time to send an emissary to the New Republic.

"To discuss the terms of our surrender."

CHAPTER

2

The *Millennium Falcon*'s console gave a final proximity beep, jolting Han Solo out of a light doze. Uncrossing his arms, he stretched tired muscles and gave the displays a quick look. Almost there. "Come on, Chewie, look alive," he said, giving the Wookiee beside him a couple of quick slaps with the back of his fingertips.

Chewbacca came awake with a jolt, rumbling a question. "We're here, that's what," Han told him, widening his eyes a second to clear them. Getting a grip on the hyperdrive levers, he watched the timer count down. "Stand by the sublight engines. Here we go."

The counter went to zero, and he eased the levers forward. Outside the *Falcon*'s canopy, the mottled sky of hyperspace turned to starlines, which collapsed into stars, and they were there. "Right on target," he commented, nodding toward the bluish-red planetary half circle ahead of them.

Beside him, Chewbacca growled. "Yeah, well, it's always crowded around Iphigin," Han said, eyeing the hundreds of tiny drive glows moving around the planet like some crazy multrille dance. "Main transfer point for this sector and at least two others. Probably why Puffers set up the meeting for here—you don't start shooting if some of your own stuff might get in the way."

Chewbacca growled in annoyance. "Well, excuse me,"

Han apologized sarcastically. "President Gavrisom, then. Didn't know you were such a big fan."

There was a beep from the comm. Slapping a massive hand at the switch, Chewbacca roared out an acknowledgment.

"Hey, Chewie," Luke Skywalker's voice came over the speaker. "You're right on schedule. The *Falcon* must be running smoothly for a change."

"Nothing broken but the comm switch," Han grumbled, throwing a scowl at the Wookiee. "Chewie just tried to flatten it. Where are you, Luke?"

"Just coming in nightside," Luke said. "What's wrong with Chewie?"

"Nothing much," Han said. "Small difference of political opinion, that's all."

"Ah," Luke said knowingly. "Been calling President Gavrisom 'Puffers' again, have you?"

"Now, don't *you* start," Han growled, glaring at the comm speaker.

Chewbacca rumbled a question. "Well, for one thing, he never seems to do anything except talk," Han said.

"That's what Calibops are best at," Luke pointed out. "Face it, Han: words are the tool of the task these days."

"I know, I know," Han said, making a face. "Leia's been pounding it into me forever." His voice drifted into an almost unconscious parody of his wife's. "We're not the Rebel Alliance anymore, with a handful of people running the whole show. We're negotiators and arbitrators and we're here to help system and sector governments be all nice and friendly to each other."

"Is that really the way Leia put it?"

"So I paraphrased a little." Han frowned out the *Falcon*'s canopy, glanced back at his displays. "Is that you in the X-wing?"

"That's me," Luke confirmed. "Why? You think I've forgotten how to fly one?"

"No, I just thought you usually used one of the academy's Lambda shuttles these days."

"That's because I'm usually flying with other people,"

Luke said. "Students and such. Artoo was with me on Yavin doing some data sifting, so when your call came we just hopped in the old snubfighter and headed out. What's this all about?"

"What's it always about at this end of the Core?" Han countered sourly. "The Diamala and Ishori are at it again."

Luke sighed, a faint hiss on the speaker. "Let me guess. Commerce and resource-sharing dispute?"

"Close," Han said. "This time it's shipping security. The Diamala don't like having to rely on local patrol ships when they're coming into Ishori ports. The Ishori, on the other hand, don't want armed Diamala ships coming into their systems."

"Sounds typical," Luke said. "Gavrisom have any ideas on how to solve this one?"

"If he did, he didn't mention them," Han said. "He just called me on Wayland and said to flare it on over here. Help them be all nice and friendly to each other, I guess."

"Gavrisom asked *you* to arbitrate?"

Han pursed his lips. "Well . . . not exactly. He kind of thinks Leia's here with us."

"Ah."

"Look, Luke, I *am* official liaison to the Independent Shippers Association," Han reminded him testily. "It's not like I haven't done this sort of thing before. And Leia hasn't had any kind of real vacation in a long time—she and the kids need some time off together. And just for once, I'm not going to let her get dragged away on some stupid diplomatic thing, especially when she's supposed to be on a leave of absence. She deserves better."

"I can't argue with that," Luke conceded. "It's not like her last few times away from the Presidency have been exactly restful. Though personally, I can't imagine Wayland being very high on anyone's list of resort spots."

"You'd be surprised," Han said. "It's not like when we went tromping through the forest on the way to Mount Tantiss. Not with all the Noghri who've settled there."

"I'll take your word for it," Luke said. "So what can I do to help?"

"I've got a plan worked out," Han said. "You know how Diamala get when they think: all icy calm and unemotional, right? Well, that's kind of like your deep Jedi stuff, so you can go talk to their delegation. The Ishori are just the opposite—they can't discuss anything without getting all worked up and screaming their heads off at each other."

"But they don't mean anything by it," Luke put in. "It's all hormonal—a 'fight or think' response, I think it's called."

"Yeah, I know, I know," Han said, feeling a flicker of annoyance at the lecture. Jedi Master or not, Luke still didn't have half of Han's experience in flying around the galaxy and dealing with other species. "Point is, they can shout all they want without bothering a Wookiee any. So Chewie will talk to *their* group. Then the three of us get together, we come up with a fix, and we're done."

"It's an inventive approach—I'll give it that much," Luke said, his tone thoughtful. "Personally, I'd still rather have Leia here. She's got a genuine gift for conciliation."

"All the more reason for us to take this one for her," Han said darkly. "The way things are going out there, Gavrisom and the High Council could have her running around stomping out these scrub fires for the rest of her life."

"The New Republic does seem to be having more than its share of growing pains," Luke agreed soberly. "Maybe it's a normal adjustment to the collapse of Imperial domination."

"That, or what's left of the Empire is stirring the soup," Han said with a grimace. "Come on, let's get down there. The sooner we get started, the sooner we can go home."

They put down in a double-sized docking bay that had been cleared for them in the capital city's north spaceport complex. Han and Chewbacca were standing at the foot of the *Falcon*'s landing ramp, talking to a triad of white-maned Diamala, as Luke maneuvered his X-wing to an only slightly out-of-practice landing.

And even before he cut the repulsorlifts, he could sense that there was trouble.

"You stay with the ship, Artoo," he ordered the droid as he popped the canopy and took off his flight helmet. "Keep an eye on things, okay?"

Artoo gave an affirming warble. Dropping his helmet and gloves onto the seat, Luke vaulted lightly over the X-wing's side to the ground and walked over to the group waiting by the *Falcon*. The three Diamala, he noted uneasily, were watching him closely . . . and their expressions did not strike him as particularly friendly.

"Greetings," he said, nodding politely, as he reached Han's side. "I'm Luke Skywalker."

The Diamal standing closest to Han stirred. "We greet you in return, Jedi Master Skywalker," he said, his voice flat and emotionless, his leathery face unreadable. "But we do not welcome you to this conference."

Luke blinked. He glanced at Han, caught the tightness in the other's face and thoughts, then looked back at the Diamal. "I don't understand."

"Then I will make it clearer," the alien said, his left ear twitching once. "We do not wish you to be part of these negotiations. We do not intend to discuss any of this matter with you. We would prefer, in fact, that you leave this system entirely."

"Now, wait a minute," Han put in. "This is my friend, all right? I asked him here, and he's come a long way to help."

"We do not wish his help."

"Well, *I* wish it," Han shot back. "And I'm not going to tell him to leave."

There was a moment of awkward silence. Luke kept his eyes on the Diamala, wondering if he should unilaterally solve the disagreement by simply leaving. If they really didn't want him here . . .

The head Diamal twitched an ear again. "Very well," he said. "The Jedi Master may stay. But only as your adviser, to be absent from actual negotiations. The Diamala will not discuss these matters in his presence."

Han grimaced, but he nodded. "If that's the way you want it, fine. Why don't you show us to our quarters, and we'll get started."

The Diamal gestured, and one of his companions handed Chewbacca a datapad. "You have been given a suite in the spaceport control complex," he said. "The map will show you the way. The Ishori are already assembled in the meeting chamber. We will begin when you are ready."

In unison, the three aliens turned and headed across the landing bay toward one of the stairways leading out. "Well, that was interesting," Luke said quietly as he watched them go. "Any idea what that was all about?"

"Yeah," Han said. "Well, sort of."

"Sort of? What does that mean?"

Han threw Luke a sideways look, his expression and thoughts both oddly troubled. "Look, let's forget it for right now, okay? They don't—well, they don't like you. Just leave it at that."

Luke gazed at the backs of the departing Diamala, watching their shimmering manes fluttering slightly in the breeze. He didn't have to leave it at that, of course; he could stretch out right now with the Force and draw out the necessary knowledge. Surely whatever the problem was had to be some kind of misunderstanding, and he could hardly help clear it up unless he knew what it was. Yes, that was what he should do.

And yet . . .

He looked at Han. Han was looking back at him, the troubled expression still on his face. Perhaps wondering if Luke would do exactly that.

No. As Han had asked, he would let it go. For now. "All right," he said. "What's the new strategy?"

"Chewie and me'll handle the talks," Han said, turning to face the Wookiee. Even with his expression hidden, there was no mistaking the flicker of quiet relief in his emotional state. "If you don't mind waiting until we're finished, maybe you can help us figure out how to settle the deal."

"Sure." Luke looked in the direction the Diamala had

gone. "He said I could be your adviser. So I guess I'll advise."

He looked back to find Han studying his face. "You don't like this, do you?" the older man said.

Luke shrugged. "Well, it's not exactly the high point of my day," he conceded. "It's always a little embarrassing to offer to help someone and get turned down. But I suppose a little embarrassment never hurt anyone."

"Yeah," Han said. "Sometimes it even helps."

It was, Luke thought, a rather odd thing to say. But before he could ask about it, Han had stepped to Chewbacca's side and taken the datapad the Diamal had given him. "You figured out where we're supposed to go?" he asked.

The Wookiee rumbled an affirmative, pointing a shaggy finger at the datapad display. "Yeah, okay," Han said, handing the datapad back. "Lead the way." He threw Luke a lopsided grin. "There's nothing like a Wookiee to get people to move out of the way."

"You realize there's one other possibility," Luke said quietly as they set off across the docking bay. "They may be trying to split us up for some kind of attack."

Han shook his head. "I don't think that's it."

"I'd still like to keep an eye on your meetings," Luke persisted. "I should be able to follow your presence from wherever they put us. That way, I can get there right away if you need me."

"Just my presence, though, right?"

Luke frowned at him. "Of course. I wouldn't try to read your mind without permission. You know that."

"Yeah," Han said. "Sure."

As it turned out, it wasn't necessary for Luke to use the Force in order to keep track of the proceedings. Their Iphigini hosts had somehow learned about the restrictions the Diamala had put on his attendance, and by the time Han and Chewbacca began the negotiations they had a monitor line set up between Luke's suite and the conference room, allowing him to directly watch the meeting.

It took him two hours to realize that the talks were getting nowhere. It was another hour before Han came to the same conclusion. Or at least was willing to admit it out loud.

"They're crazy," Han growled, tossing a handful of datacards onto a low center table as he and Chewbacca joined Luke in the suite. "The whole bunch of them. Completely crazy."

"I wouldn't say crazy," Luke told him. "Stiff-faced stubborn, maybe, but not crazy."

"Thanks," Han growled. "That's real helpful."

Chewbacca rumbled a warning. "I am *not* losing my temper," Han informed him stiffly. "I am under perfect control."

Luke looked at his friend, carefully hiding a smile. It was like the old Han again, the brashly confident smuggler he and Obi-Wan had first met back in the Mos Eisley cantina. Charging cheerfully into unknown situations, and more often than not finding himself up to his neck in trouble. It was nice to know that even as a respectable family man and responsible official of the New Republic, Han hadn't lost all of the recklessness that had once driven his friends almost as crazy as it had the Imperials. Up to his neck in trouble was where Han functioned best. Perhaps, through sheer habit, it was where he was most comfortable.

"All right," Han said, dropping into a chair across the table from Luke. "Let's think this through. There's got to be a way out."

"How about trying a third-party approach?" Luke suggested. "Maybe the New Republic could run security for Diamalan freighters when they're in Ishori systems."

Chewbacca rumbled the obvious problem. "Yes, I know we don't have a lot of ships to spare," Luke said. "But the High Council ought to be able to scrounge up something."

"Not enough to do any good," Han said, shaking his head. "The Diamala do an awful lot of shipping, and I don't think you realize how thin our hardware is spread out there."

"It would still be cheaper in the long run than whatever it would cost to pull the Diamala and Ishori apart if they start shooting at each other again," Luke argued.

"Probably," Han conceded, toying with one of the data-cards. "Problem is, I don't think the Diamala would accept the offer even if we had the ships to spare. I don't think they're ready to trust anyone else with their security."

"Not even the New Republic?" Luke asked.

Han shook his head, his eyes darting surreptitiously to Luke's face for a moment, then just as quickly shifting away. "No."

Luke frowned. In that moment he'd caught another flicker of the same troubled mood he'd felt back by the *Falcon*. "I see."

"Yeah," Han said, all brisk business again. "Anybody got any other ideas?"

Luke glanced at Chewbacca, searching for a diplomatic way to say this. But there really wasn't one. "You know, Han, it's not too late to bring Leia in on this. We could call Wayland and ask the Noghri to bring her here."

"No," Han said firmly.

Chewbacca growled agreement with Luke. "I said no," Han repeated, glaring at the Wookiee. "We can handle this ourselves."

There was a trill from the console built into the table. Luke looked at Han, but he was still engaged in a glaring contest with Chewbacca. Reaching out with the Force, he keyed the switch. "Skywalker," he said.

On the hologram pad in the middle of the table the quarter-sized image of a young Iphigini appeared, his braided lip-beard not quite covering up the throat insignia of the Iphigin Spaceport Directorate. "I apologize for disturbing your deliberations, Jedi Skywalker," he said, his voice far more melodious than the craggy face and physique would have suggested. "But we've received notification from New Republic Commerce that a Sarkan freighter is on its way here under a Customs Red alert."

Luke looked at Han. *Customs Red*: a warning that there was illegal and highly dangerous cargo aboard. "Did Commerce identify the captain and crew?"

"No," the Iphigini said. "A follow-up transmission was promised, but it has not yet arrived. The suspect freighter is already approaching Iphigin, and we have dispatched the bulk of our inner-system customs frigates and patrol craft to intercept. It was thought that as New Republic representatives, you and Captain Solo might wish to observe the procedure."

There was a sudden change in Han's emotions. Luke looked over, to see his friend gazing thoughtfully off into space. "We appreciate the invitation," he said, looking back at the hologram. "At the moment, though—"

"Where's this Sarkan coming in from?" Han interrupted.

"Sector Three-Besh." The Iphigini's image was replaced by a schematic of Iphigin and the space around it. A red dot blinked a few degrees off a line connecting Iphigin to its sun; nearly twenty blinking green dots were converging on it from the planet and nearby space. "As you can see, we have attempted to send a force adequate to overcome any resistance."

"Yeah," Han said slowly. "And you're sure it's a Sarkan?"

"Its transponder ID has been checked," the Iphigini told him. "The ship itself is a Corellian Action-Keynne XII, rarely seen in this part of the Core except under Sarkan authority."

Luke whistled soundlessly. He'd been given a tour of an Action-Keynne XII once, and had come away thoroughly impressed by both the touches of inner luxury and the multiple tiers of outer weaponry. Designed to transport the most valuable of cargoes, it very nearly qualified as a capital warship.

Which was probably why the Iphiginis were sending so many ships to intercept it. If its captain decided not to cooperate, the Iphiginis were in for a fight.

"Sounds like a Sarkan, all right," Han agreed, his voice a

little bit too casual. "You go ahead and do your intercept. Maybe we'll come up later and have a look."

"Thank you, Captain Solo," the Iphigini said. "I will alert the officials that you will be joining them. Farewell."

The hologram vanished. "Don't count on it," Han muttered, gathering up the datacards from where he'd tossed them on the table and thumbing rapidly through them. "Chewie, get over to that console—see if you can pull up a full listing of the traffic pattern out there."

"What's going on?" Luke asked, frowning at Han and trying to read his mood. Suddenly all the earlier frustration was gone, leaving a sort of sly excitement in its place. "You know who the smuggler is?"

"He's not a smuggler," Han said. He found the card he was looking for and slid it into his datapad. "You got it, Chewie? Great. Punch it into the hologram pod over here."

Chewbacca growled acknowledgment, and a more complete Iphigin schematic appeared over the table. Han peered at it, then looked down at the datapad in his hand. "Great. Okay, come here and give me a hand with this."

"What is it?" Luke asked.

"This is the ground station list and the orbit data for their Golan I Defense Platform," Han told him, waving the datapad as Chewbacca lumbered to his side again. "Let's see . . ."

For a minute the two huddled close together, peering alternately at the hologram and Han's datapad and conversing in low tones. Luke studied the schematic, watching the color-coded freighters and other ships moving in and out and wondering what this was all about.

"Okay," Han said at last. "That's where they'll come in. So all we need to do is sit somewhere in the middle of that cone and wait. Great. Get down to the *Falcon* and get 'er ready. I'll be right there."

Chewbacca rumbled an acknowledgment and headed out the door at a fast Wookiee trot. "Do I get to know what's going on?" Luke asked.

"Sure," Han said, gathering up the datacards and packing them away again. "We've got pirates on the way."

"Pirates?" Luke blinked. "Here?"

"Sure. Why not?"

"I didn't think pirate gangs operated this far into the Core, that's all," Luke said. "So the Sarkan is just a feint?"

"Yeah," Han said, getting to his feet. "Only he doesn't know it. It's an old trick: you call an alert on some ship coming in sunside, then hit a nightside target while Customs is busy half a planet away. The only tricky part is making sure the ground and orbit defenses can't get to you. Plus figuring out how to fake the alert in the first place. Come on, let's go."

"Shouldn't we alert the Iphigini first?" Luke asked, reaching for the comm.

"What for?" Han said. "You and Chewie and me ought to be able to handle it."

"What, a whole pirate gang?"

"Sure, why not? The only gangs working this sector are small ones—two or three ships, tops." Han's lip twitched. "Actually, you probably won't even need us."

"I appreciate your confidence," Luke said icily. "But I'd just as soon not take them all on myself, thank you."

Han held up his hands. "Hey. No offense."

"None taken." Luke gestured to the hologram and the patrol ships weaving their net around the incoming Sarkan freighter. "And I still think we ought to call in the Iphigini."

"We can't," Han said. "The pirates probably have a spotter already here. Any sign of an alert, and they'll just call off the raid. We'd end up looking stupid, and Diamalan opinion of the New Republic would sink a little deeper. The High Council will have my hide if that happens."

Luke sighed. "Things were a lot easier when Alliance military activity wasn't always getting tangled up in politics."

"Tell me about it," Han growled. "Look, we've got to get going. You in or out?"

Luke shrugged. "I'm in," he said, pulling out his comlink. "Artoo?"

·   ·   ·

R2-D2 didn't like it. Not a bit. The words scrolling across the X-wing's computer display made that very clear indeed.

"Oh, come on, Artoo," Luke chided. "We went all the way through a war together, against the most powerful military machine the galaxy has ever seen. You're not going to tell me you're afraid of a couple of patched-up pirate ships, are you?"

The droid grunted indignantly. "That's better," Luke said approvingly. "Just keep an eye out. We'll be fine."

Artoo warbled again, clearly not convinced, and went silent. Luke peered out the X-wing's canopy, trying to shake away his own collection of nagging doubts. The odd discomfort that kept surfacing in Han's emotions—the unexplained Diamalan refusal to allow him at the negotiations—all of it just added to the strange restlessness that had been simmering and growing in him over the past few weeks.

He'd talked to Leia twice about it, hoping her insight and experience could help him bring the vague glimmerings into sharper focus. But the best she'd been able to do was suggest that it was some kind of subconscious prodding from the Force itself. Something Luke was supposed to do, she hypothesized, or perhaps something he wasn't supposed to do.

At her urging, he'd been spending more time lately in meditation, hoping that immersing himself in the Force would help. So far, though, there had been no results.

"Luke?" Han's voice said into his helmet. "Where are you?"

Luke shook his thoughts back to the task at hand. "I'm above you and a little to portside," he said. "I don't see anything out here that looks like a pirate ship. You?"

"Not yet," Han said. "Don't worry; when they get here, you'll know it."

"Right." Turning his head slowly, Luke looked around at the drive glows and running lights of the various freighters.

And then suddenly they were there.

Only it wasn't just two or three ships. Dropping in from

lightspeed were no fewer than eight ships, all unmarked, all bristling with turbolaser batteries.

Behind Luke came a startled shrill. "Easy, Artoo," Luke soothed the droid. "Give me a readout on them."

Artoo beeped uncertainly, and a list appeared on Luke's sensor scope. Two mangled-looking Corellian gunships, an old but impressively big *Kaloth* battlecruiser with an equally old KDY a-4 ion cannon welded awkwardly to its bow, and five *Corsair*-class assault starfighters. The whole group of them were in encirclement formation, closing on a pair of medium transports a few kilometers below and ahead.

Transports bearing New Republic insignia.

"Han?" Luke called.

"Yeah, I see them," Han said tightly. "Okay. What do you want to do?"

Luke looked out at the incoming pirates, a sudden tightening sensation in his stomach. There were many options, of course. He could reach out with the Force and damage the ships' control surfaces, crippling them. He might even be able to wrench off whole hull plates or deform the weapons emplacements, tearing them apart with the Force alone. Or he could simply reach inside to the crews' minds, turning them into helpless observers or even forcing them to surrender. For a Jedi Master with the Force as his ally, there were no limits. No limits at all.

And then, abruptly, he stiffened, his breath seeming to freeze in his throat. There in front of him, starkly visible against the blackness of space, he could see the faint images of Emperor Palpatine and Exar Kun, two of the greatest focal points of the dark side he'd ever had to face. They were standing there before him, gazing back at him.

And laughing.

"Luke?"

Han's voice made him start; and as he did so, the images vanished. But the icy horror stayed behind. *Something he wasn't supposed to do . . .*

"Luke? Hey, look alive, pal."

"I'm here," Luke managed. His mouth, he discovered, was suddenly very dry. "I—you'd better take charge, Han."

"You all right? Can you fly?"

Luke swallowed. "Yes. I'm fine."

"Sure," Han said, obviously not convinced. "Look, you'd better hang back. Chewie and me'll handle this."

"No," Luke said. "No, I'm with you. Just tell me what you want me to do."

"Well, if you're sure you're up to it, you can run me some cover," Han said. "First thing is to take out that ion cannon."

Luke took a deep breath, settling his mind and stretching out to the Force. Two ships against eight. It was like the old days, when the Rebel Alliance was struggling against the awesome power of the Empire. He hadn't been nearly as strong in the Force then. Hardly strong enough, in fact, to enhance his natural combat and flying abilities.

And yet, somehow, the memories of those days felt strangely clean. Cleaner than his mind had felt for a long time.

Something he wasn't supposed to do . . .

All right, he told the memories. *Let's call this a test.* "Go ahead," he told Han. "I'm right behind you."

It was unclear in that first minute whether the pirates, concentrating on their intended prey, had even noticed the old YT-1300 freighter and the X-wing flying alongside it. It was abundantly clear, though, that a sudden attack from outside their encirclement ring was the last thing they were expecting. The *Falcon* shot between two of the Corsairs without drawing any fire at all until it was well past them. They got a single ineffective turbolaser salvo off before Luke slid in behind them, dropping a proton torpedo each into their drive sections. A brilliant double flash, and they were effectively out of the fight.

The X-wing shot between them, curving up out of the crippled ships' line of fire. The battlecruiser was starting to turn its turrets toward them—

There was a sudden warning squeal from behind him. "I see them, Artoo," Luke said, throwing the X-wing into a stomach-twisting spiral out and away from the battlecruiser just as two of the three remaining Corsairs shot past. A burst of light caught the edge of his eye as he turned, and he twisted back around to see the bow of the battlecruiser flash into shrapnel. "Han? You okay?"

"Sure," Han's voice came back. "I got the ion cannon, but it got a shot off at one of the transports first. Don't know if they're disabled or not. You?"

"No problems yet," Luke said. His danger sense flickered, and he dropped the X-wing into another twist as a withering pattern of laser fire cut through the spot he'd just vacated. Swinging up and around, he settled in behind one of the attacking Corsairs. It was a long time since he'd done this kind of thing on any sort of regular basis, but he didn't seem nearly as rusty as he'd feared he would be. "These things are better armored than TIE fighters, but they're not nearly as maneuverable."

The words were barely out of his mouth when he nearly had to eat them. Abruptly the Corsair in front of him cut sharply to starboard, twisting out of Luke's line of fire and trying to swing in behind him. Clenching his teeth, Luke matched the maneuver, and for a few seconds they chased each other around in a tight circle, each trying for a clear shot. Luke won by a single heartbeat, and the Corsair flashed into flame and debris.

From his comm came an anxious Wookiee snarl. "I'm okay, Chewie," Luke said, stretching out to the Force for calm. That one had been a little too close. "You two still all right?"

"So far," Han put in. "Watch it—they're probably getting mad now."

Luke smiled lopsidedly and took a quick look around. The last two Corsairs were heading full-throttle toward him, but he had a few seconds yet before he had to do anything about them. In the near distance he could see the battlecruiser, firing furiously at the much smaller *Falcon* skimming like a stingfly across its hull, systematically taking out turbolaser emplacements as it went. To one side, the two gunships were exchanging fire with the New Republic transports, which were clearly better armed than they had first appeared. The rest of the freighter traffic around them was understandably vacating the area just as fast as they could.

He frowned, focusing again on the battlecruiser. With his decision to back away from using the full power of the Force against the pirates much of the confusion and tension in his mind seemed to have cleared away.

And now, in that silence, he could sense something strange about the big ship out there. A strangeness he hadn't felt for a long time . . .

Artoo shrilled a warning. "Right," Luke said, shaking the feeling away. The two Corsairs were coming in fast, the wingman to portside and slightly behind the leader. "Here's the plan," he told the droid. "On my signal, run full power to the top starboard engine and to both portside braking vents. After four seconds cut the vents and throw half power to all engines. Got it?"

The droid whistled acknowledgment. Resting his thumbs on the proton torpedo triggers, Luke watched the Corsairs streaking toward him, stretching out through the Force to touch the minds of the two crews. Not to control or twist, but merely watching the texture of their thoughts. Holding course, he waited . . . "Now," he called to Artoo.

The droid's warble was swallowed up by the sudden roar of the drive; and a second later the X-wing was spinning wildly around its center of mass. Eyes half-closed, Luke let the Force guide the timing of his shot—

And then he was jammed back into his seat as the X-wing took off on a new trajectory, straightening reluctantly out of its spin. Blinking against his sudden dizziness, Luke looked around for the Corsairs.

The gambit had worked. Concentrating on his Gandder's spin, trying to anticipate the direction he would take when he popped out of it, they'd probably never even noticed the incoming proton torpedoes until it was too late.

"Luke?" Han's voice came over the comm. "Looks like they're pulling out."

Sternly addressing his rebellious inner ear, Luke brought the X-wing around again. The battlecruiser was driving for deep space, the two gunships right behind it. One of the gunships, he noted, was showing considerable damage. "Artoo, give me a damage assessment," Luke said, switching his comm control to one of the official New Republic frequencies. "Transports, this is New Republic X-wing AA-589," he said. "What's your situation?"

"Looking a lot better than it was a few minutes ago," the reply came back promptly. "Thanks for the assist, X-wing. You or your friend need any help?"

Artoo's damage assessment came up on the computer screen. "No, I'm fine," Luke said. "Han?"

"No problems here," Han said. "We'll give you an escort down if you want."

"Sounds good to me," the transport captain said. "Thanks again."

The transports turned back toward Iphigin. Swinging the X-wing toward their vector, Luke switched back to the private frequency. "Just like old times," he said wryly to Han.

"Yeah," Han said, his voice sounding distracted. "You catch any insignia or markings on any of those ships?"

"There wasn't anything on the Corsairs," Luke said. "I didn't get close enough to the others to see. Why? You think they might not have been pirates?"

"Oh, they were pirates, all right," Han said. "Problem is, most pirates like to splash blazing claws or fireballs all over their ships. Try to scare the target into giving up without a fight. Usually the only reason they'd cover down is if they were working for someone else."

Luke looked out his canopy at the lights of the rest of the freighters around them, slowly and gingerly settling back into a normal traffic pattern again. A hundred exotic cargoes, from a hundred different worlds . . . and yet the pirates had chosen to hit a pair of New Republic transports. "Privateers, then," he said. "Hired by the Empire."

"I'd say that's a good bet," Han agreed grimly. "I wonder which gang they were."

"Or where the Empire's getting the funds to hire them," Luke said slowly. Stretching out with the Force, he brought back the memory of the odd sensation he'd picked up from the battlecruiser. "I remember Leia telling me what privateers cost, back when the Alliance was hiring them to hit Imperial shipping. They don't come cheap."

"Not good ones, anyway." Han snorted. "Not that this batch was anything special."

"I'm not so sure," Luke said, focusing his full attention on the memories. It was indeed something he'd felt before . . .

And then it clicked into place. "I may be wrong, Han," he said, "but I think there was a group of clones aboard that battlecruiser."

For a long moment the comm was silent. "You sure?"

"The sense was the same one I got when we were chasing Grand Admiral Thrawn's clone warriors around the *Katana*."

Han hissed thoughtfully into the comm. "Terrific. I wonder where the Empire's been hiding clones for the past ten years. I thought they'd pretty much thrown all of them at us already."

"I thought so, too," Luke said. "Maybe they've got a new cloning facility going."

"Oh, *that's* a cheerful thought," Han grumbled. "Look, let's take care of one crisis at a time. We'll finish up here and then turn Intelligence loose on it."

"I was under the impression that Intelligence wasn't having much luck pinning down these gangs."

"They're not," Han admitted. "Neither are my contacts with the Independent Shippers."

"Sounds like we need someone better connected with the fringe." Luke hesitated. "Someone like Talon Karrde, for example."

There was a brief silence from the other end. "You didn't say that like you meant it," Han suggested. "Trouble?"

"No, not really," Luke said, wishing now he'd kept quiet. "It's just—no, nothing."

"Let me guess. Mara?"

Luke grimaced. "It's nothing, Han. Okay? Just let it go."

"Sure," Han assured him. "No problem. Soon as we finish up here, you can go on back to Yavin and forget about it. Chewie and me can get word to Karrde. Okay?"

"Okay," Luke said. "Thanks."

"No problem. Let's go talk to the Diamala some more. See if any of this might have changed their attitude toward New Republic protection."

"We can try." Luke hesitated. "Han, what is it about me the Diamala don't like? I really need to know."

There was a short pause. "Well, to put it in a sprey-shell . . . they don't trust you."

"Why not?"

"Because you're too powerful," Han said. "At least, according to them. They claim that Jedi who use as much power as you do always end up slipping over to the dark side."

An unpleasant sensation settled into the pit of Luke's stomach. "You think they're right?" he asked.

"Hey, Luke, I don't know about any of that stuff," the other protested. "I've seen you do some pretty wild things, and I'll admit it sometimes worries me a little. But if you say you've got it under control, hey, that's good enough for me. You sure weren't getting all flashy out here just now."

"No, I wasn't," Luke agreed, a little defensively. Because Han was right; he had indeed gotten a little flashy at other times in the past. Many times, in fact.

But only when it was necessary, and only to accomplish some great and noble goal. His power in the Force had saved his life numerous times, and Han's life, and the lives of countless others. In none of those instances had he had any other choice.

And yet . . .

Luke stared out the canopy at the distant stars. And yet there was Obi-Wan Kenobi, his first teacher in the Force. A powerful Jedi, who'd nevertheless allowed himself to be cut down on the first Death Star rather than sweep Vader and the stormtroopers away with a wave of his hand.

And there was Yoda, who had surely had as deep an understanding of the Force as anyone in recent history. If

Luke's own current level of knowledge was any indication, Yoda could surely have defeated the Emperor all by himself. Yet he'd chosen instead to leave that task to Luke and the Rebel Alliance.

And there was Callista. A woman he'd loved . . . who had run away from him because his power had somehow intimidated and frightened her.

"Look, Luke, it might not mean anything," Han's voice came into his thoughts. "You know how alien minds work sometimes."

"Yes," Luke murmured. But it was clearly not something to be dismissed out of hand. It was a question he needed to study, and to meditate on, and to discuss with his family and closest friends.

He shuddered, that horrifying vision of a laughing Emperor flickering across his memory. And he'd better do it fast.

But as Han had said, one crisis at a time. Pulling up the X-wing's nose, he eased into escort formation beside the transports and headed in.

CHAPTER

3

For a long moment Leia Organa Solo just stood there, the restless breezes of the Wayland forest rustling through her hair, staring at the gold-colored protocol droid twitching nervously in front of her. There were, she reflected distantly, very few things in the galaxy anymore that could shock her speechless. Han Solo, her husband and father of her three children, was apparently still one of them. "He did *what*?"

It was a rhetorical question, of course. Possibly a way of confirming to herself that her voice still functioned. C-3PO either didn't realize that or else didn't want to risk guessing wrong. "He and Chewbacca have gone to Iphigin, Your Highness," the droid repeated, his voice miserable. "Several hours ago, shortly after you left on your tour. I tried to stop them, but he wouldn't listen. Please don't deactivate me."

Leia took a careful breath, stretching out to the Force to calm herself—apparently, she looked angrier than she actually was—and tried to think. Han would be on Iphigin by now, probably already engaged in a dialogue with the Diamalan and Ishori delegations. She could have her honor guard fly her there in one of their ships, calling ahead and telling Han to declare a recess until she arrived. The children she could leave here; the rest of the Noghri could look after them until she and Han returned. Alternatively, she could get in touch with President Gavrisom and have him send someone else out there to take over.

But either approach would make Han's effort an obvious and embarrassing false start, hardly the sort of thing that would bolster the already low opinion the Diamala had of New Republic capabilities. In fact, depending on how seriously the Diamala chose to take it, it could easily make things worse than if she just left Han alone.

Besides, he was a hero of the Rebellion, and both the Diamala and Ishori appreciated that sort of thing. And after years of watching her handle this sort of negotiation, he must surely have picked up a trick or two.

"Oh—one other thing," Threepio spoke up hesitantly. "Captain Solo also made one other call before he and Chewbacca left. I believe it was to Master Luke."

Leia smiled wryly, her first real smile since Threepio had broken the news. She should have guessed that Han hadn't just rushed in on this thing alone. He'd conned Luke into going with him.

Threepio was still standing there looking nervous. "It's all right, Threepio," she soothed him. "Once Han gets an idea in his head, there's no stopping him. He and Luke should be able to handle things."

The droid seemed to wilt with relief. "Thank you, Your Highness," he murmured.

Leia turned away from him and looked back across the clearing. Her youngest son, Anakin, was crouched down beside one of the slender airspeeders the group had just arrived in, and even at this distance she could hear the mix of seriousness and excitement in the eight-year-old's voice as he discussed the finer points of design with the Noghri pilot. Standing a little way to one side beside the Mobquet speeder bikes that had flown escort for them, the twins Jacen and Jaina were watching with the air of stressed patience that came naturally of being a whole year and a half older and wiser than their younger brother. Grouped around the children and vehicles were the short gray figures of their Noghri escort, the bulk of their attention directed outward. Even here at the edge of a Noghri settlement, they were continually on the alert for danger. Beyond them, rising above the forest, Leia could see the top of Mount Tantiss.

"Welcome back, Lady Vader," a gravelly Noghri mew came from beside her.

"Oh, my!" Threepio said, jerking back.

Only long experience—and her strength of calmness in the Force—kept Leia from doing the same. Even when they weren't particularly trying to be quiet, Noghri were next to impossible to hear. One of the many reasons why Grand Admiral Thrawn, and Darth Vader before him, had so coveted their services as private Death Commandos for the Empire.

Had coveted that service so much, in fact, that they'd deliberately destroyed the Noghri homeworld of Honoghr, keeping the Noghri at a perpetual edge of disaster. A disaster that had been carefully structured to keep them in eternal servitude.

Leia had helped them discover the truth about the Empire's deceit. But though it had brought the Noghri firmly onto the side of the New Republic, it had in many ways been a hollow victory for all concerned. Despite the effort that had been put into the New Republic's restoration project over the past ten years, hopes were steadily fading that Honoghr could ever be truly brought back to life. And though the Noghri seemed reasonably content with their new settlements here on Wayland, Leia could hear the quiet sadness in their voices whenever they spoke of home.

Alderaan, her own homeworld, had been shattered to dust before her eyes by the first Death Star. Honoghr, brown and dead, had been destroyed more subtly but no less thoroughly. Unknown numbers of others, all across the galaxy, had been ravaged by the war against the Empire.

Some of those wounds would take a long time to heal. Others never would.

"I greet you, Cakhmaim clan Eikh'mir," she said to the Noghri standing beside her. "I trust all is well?"

"All is well and quiet," Cakhmaim said gravely, giving her the Noghri bow of respect. "With perhaps one small exception."

"I know," Leia said. "Han and Chewie took off while we were on the tour."

Cakhmaim frowned. "Was he not to leave?" he demanded, his voice suddenly darker. "He told us he was summoned."

"No, it's all right," Leia said quickly. Relations between Han and the Noghri had never been quite as relaxed as she might have liked, and she had no desire to add this incident onto anyone's grudge list. "He should have talked to me first, but it's all right. He probably just didn't want me worrying about New Republic politics for a while."

Cakhmaim peered up at her. "If I may say so, Lady Vader, I must concur with Han clan Solo in this thought. Reports from your honor guard make it clear that you spend too little time in needed relaxation."

"I can't argue with that," Leia admitted. "It comes of having both a family and a job to do, and a limited number of hours per day to share between them. Maybe now that Ponc Gavrisom's taken over the Presidency for a while, things will be easier."

"Perhaps," Cakhmaim said, not sounding any more convinced of that than Leia herself felt. "Still, while the Noghri people live, you shall always have a place of refuge among us. You and your children and their children. Always."

"I appreciate that, Cakhmaim," Leia said, and meant it. There were very few places in the galaxy where she could feel as safe, both for herself and her children, as she did inside a Noghri settlement. "But you mentioned a problem. Tell me."

"I now hesitate to involve you, Lady Vader," Cakhmaim said uncertainly. "You came here for relaxation, not to settle disputes. Further, I would dislike to take you away from your firstsons and firstdaughter."

"The children are doing fine right where they are," Leia assured him, looking back at the group. Anakin was halfway underneath the airspeeder now, with a pair of Noghri legs sticking out alongside his. The twins still had that strained-patient look as they talked quietly together, but Leia could see Jaina's hand fondly stroking the saddle of one of the speeder bikes. "Anakin has inherited his father's love of puzzles," she told Cakhmaim. "And the twins aren't nearly as bored as they might pretend. Tell me about this dispute."

"As you wish," Cakhmaim said. "Please come with me."

Leia nodded. "Threepio, you might as well stay here."

"Certainly, Your Highness," the droid said, a definite note of relief in his voice. Threepio hated disputes.

The two of them walked a short distance through the trees to a second clearing, this one the main part of the Noghri's Mount Tantiss settlement. Clustered together were perhaps thirty houses, built to the same basic design of the homes Leia had seen on Honoghr, though modified by the differences in local building materials. In the middle was the longer, somewhat taller *dukha* clan center.

Other Noghri settlements on Wayland had transported their ancient clan *dukhas* from Honoghr, making them the honored focal points of their villages on this world just as they had been back home. But the Mount Tantiss settlement had a specific mission to perform; and part of that mission was to never forget what the Empire and Emperor had taken from the Noghri people. Their clan center, freshly built from local lumber and stone, was a permanent and graphic reminder of that loss.

The *dukha* door was flanked by a pair of straight-backed Noghri children, performing their door-warder duties with the seriousness of generations of custom and ritual. One of them pulled open the door, and Cakhmaim and Leia stepped inside.

The clan center consisted of a single large room, roofed with heavy wooden beams, with walls on which the history and genealogy of the settlement had begun to be carved. Two-thirds of the way back was the thronelike High Seat, the only chair in the room.

And seated on the floor at the foot of the High Seat, dressed in dirt-stained clothing, was a Devaronian. "Ah," he said, favoring Cakhmaim with a thin smile as he got to his feet. "My kindly host. I hope you brought food; I am beginning to get hungry." He shifted his attention to Leia. "And you, I take it, are the wandering decision-maker I was promised?"

"This is New Republic High Councilor Leia Organa Solo," Cakhmaim identified her, his voice edged with knives. "You will speak to her with respect."

"Of course," the Devaronian said dryly, touching the rightmost of his two forehead horns with the fingertips of his right hand. "I would never speak otherwise to an official of the New Republic."

"Of course not," Leia said, matching his tone as she stretched out toward him with the Force. Male Devaronians were avid travelers and a common sight in the spaceports of the galaxy, but there had been few if any of them in the Rebel Alliance and she had never had much personal contact with the species. "And your name?" she asked, trying to get a reading on his thoughts and emotions.

"I am Lak Jit, Councilor. A simple seeker of knowledge and truth."

Leia smiled. "Of course," she said, focusing a bit harder on his thoughts. There was no change she could detect that would indicate a lie, but given her unfamiliarity with the species that didn't mean much. More than likely it was no more than a bending or embellishment of the truth, anyway. "Tell me about this dispute, Cakhmaim."

"This alien was discovered near Mount Tantiss by one of the cleansing teams," Cakhmaim said, his gaze hard on the Devaronian. "He had been digging through the soil in the fault line area and had found six datacards. When the team attempted to take them from him, he claimed possession under the Debble Agreement."

"Really," Leia said, eyeing the Devaronian with new interest. The Debble Agreement was a slice-of-the-moment compromise deal she'd worked out between the Noghri cleansing teams, who had sworn to eradicate every memory of the Emperor's presence on Wayland, and Garv Debble, a New Republic archaeologist who had insisted that items plundered from other worlds should be returned to their proper owners. The agreement had been informal and reasonably private, hardly something a casual treasure hunter would know about. "Tell me, Lak Jit, how did you come to know about the Debble Agreement?"

"Quite honestly, Councilor, I assure you," the Devaronian said. "I am associated with a human who I believe has had some dealings with the New Republic. Talon Karrde."

"I see," Leia said, keeping her voice and face expressionless. To say that Talon Karrde had had dealings with the New Republic was to vastly understate the case. Smuggler chief and information broker, with an organization that stretched across the known galaxy, Karrde had reluctantly thrown in with the New Republic during the massive Imperial counteroffensive led by Grand Admiral Thrawn. More than that, he'd put together an unlikely coalition of fellow smugglers that had played a significant role in stopping Thrawn's advance and ultimately defeating him. The coalition had drifted apart over the years, but Leia had made an effort to keep somewhat in touch with Karrde himself.

A presence brushed at the back of her mind, and she turned as Jacen came into the room. "Mom, when are we going to the mountain?" he asked, throwing an incurious look at the Devaronian. "You said we'd be going to see the mountain after the other tour."

"We'll go soon, honey," Leia said. "Just a little business to clear up first."

Jacen frowned. "I thought we weren't going to have any business here."

"It'll just take a minute," Leia assured him.

"But I'm bored," he insisted. He looked at Lak Jit again, and Leia could sense the effort as the child reached out with his limited abilities in the Force. "Are you my mom's business?" he asked.

"Yes," Lak Jit said with another thin smile. "And she is right: it will only take a minute. Councilor Organa Solo, it should be clear that historical datacards are precisely the sort of thing the Debble Agreement was created to protect. Therefore—"

"We have only your statement that the datacards are

historical," Cakhmaim put in. "We must study them ourselves."

"Agreed," Leia said before the Devaronian could object.
Unfortunately, that kind of examination could take hours,
and the children were waiting. "Here's the offer, Lak Jit. I'll
take the datacards, paying you five hundred now as earnest
money. After I've examined them, the New Republic will
pay you whatever they're worth."

"And who will decide that value?" Lak Jit demanded.

"I will," Leia said. "Or, if you prefer, I can take the
datacards back to Coruscant and ask Councilor Sien Siev or
another historical expert to evaluate them."

"And if I refuse?"

Leia nodded toward Cakhmaim. "Would you prefer I
let the Noghri set the price?"

Lak Jit grimaced, an expression that came across as just
another Devaronian smile, only thinner. "I seem to have no
alternative." He stepped forward, thrusting out a stack of
datacards. "Here, then. Evaluate. Since you have not
brought me food, would you and your hosts object if I went
and foraged while you work?"

"You said just a minute, Mom," Jacen spoke up.

"Quiet, Jacen," Leia said, gingerly taking the stack of
datacards and doing a quick count of the edges. Six of them,
all right, as filthy and dirt-stained as Lak Jit's clothing.
They'd probably been blown out of Mount Tantiss with the
general cloud of debris when Chewbacca and Lando Calrissian set off the base's power reactor, and had been lying
buried in the Wayland soil ever since.

Lak Jit cleared his throat. "May I—?"

"Yes, go," Leia cut him off. She hadn't realized
Devaronians foraged for food, and she certainly wasn't interested in the details. "Jacen, be quiet. It'll just be another
minute. I promise."

"Please be quick," Lak Jit said, and disappeared out the
door.

"Mom—"

"If you're bored, why don't you ask Cakhmaim to
show you the history they're carving in the walls here," Leia

suggested, gingerly brushing at the dirt covering the top datacard. "Or go join the Noghri children in their fighting class. I think Mobvekhar was going to be teaching them leverage holds today."

Jacen sniffed. "Jedi don't need that stuff. We have the Force."

"You're not a Jedi yet," Leia reminded him, giving him a stern look. She wasn't exactly happy about this interruption in their vacation either, but all his whining was accomplishing was to drag it out further. "If you were, you'd know that just because you have the Force doesn't mean you can ignore the condition of your physical body. The Noghri combat classes are good exercise."

"So's hiking up the mountain," Jacen countered. "So when are we going?"

"When I'm done," Leia said firmly, finishing her cleanup job and peering at the datacard's label. *Listings of the Fourth Pestoriv Conference*, it said. Nothing important there, one way or the other: the Pestoriv Conferences had been completely open, and just as completely documented.

Unless the Emperor had had his own private version of what had gone on there. Something to check out later, though the datacard would have to be thoroughly cleaned before she would be willing to risk it in her datapad. Shifting the datacard to the bottom of the stack, she peered at the label of the second. Equally innocuous: something about Ri'Dar mating dances. The third datacard—

She stared at the label, a sudden chill running straight through her. Four words, with the dirt already brushed off. *The Hand of Thrawn.*

"Mom?" Jacen asked, his voice not much above a whisper. Young and inexperienced in the Force, he nevertheless was keenly attuned to his mother, almost as closely attuned as he was to his sister Jaina. "What's wrong?"

Leia reached out to the Force, calming herself. "I'm all right," she told her son. "Something on this card just startled me, that's all."

Jacen craned his neck to look. " 'The Hand of Thrawn.' What does that mean?"

Leia shook her head. "I don't know."

"Oh." Jacen frowned up at her. "Then how come you were so scared?"

It was a good question, Leia had to admit. Could the simple if unexpected appearance of Thrawn's name really have thrown her so hard? Even coupled with her memories of his near victory, it didn't seem likely. "I don't know that, either, Jacen," she said. "Maybe I was just remembering the past."

"Or seeing into the future," Cakhmaim said softly. "The *Mal'ary'ush* has great powers, secondson of Vader."

"I know," Jacen said gravely. "She's my mom."

"And don't you forget it," Leia admonished him mock-severely as she ruffled his hair. "Now be quiet a minute and let's see what this is all about." Pulling her datapad from her pouch, suddenly not caring at all about possible dust contamination, she slid the datacard in.

"What does it say?" Cakhmaim asked quietly.

Leia shook her head. "Nothing," she told him. "At least, nothing legible." She tried a different section of the card, then another. "Looks like the whole datacard has been scrambled. I guess ten years of exposure will do that. Maybe the experts on Coruscant can—"

She broke off. Jacen's face and thoughts— "Mom!" he blurted. "Jaina and Anakin!"

"It's Lak Jit," Leia snapped, stretching out through the Force and catching the sudden flash of fright from her children. She caught a secondhand image of the Devaronian charging through the clearing and a sudden cloud of billowing white smoke—"Cakhmaim!"

But Cakhmaim was already through the door, screaming the alert in the warbling Noghri combat code. Jamming the datapad and datacards back into her hip pack, Leia grabbed Jacen's hand and followed Cakhmaim outside, clearing the doorway just as an answer trilled through the trees. "They are unharmed," Cakhmaim said, his tone icy with grim relief. "The Devaronian has stolen a speeder bike."

All around them, armed Noghri were pouring out of the houses in response to Cakhmaim's alert. "Which way was he going?" Leia asked, heading across the settlement. On both sides of them, Noghri were falling into escort positions; ahead, through the trees, she could see glimpses of the smoke as it dispersed. Stretching out through the Force, she sent reassurance to her children.

Cakhmaim warbled again, was answered as they reached the edge of the settlement. "Unknown," he reported. "They could not see his departure."

Most of the smoke had cleared by the time they reached the clearing a minute later. Of the nine Noghri Leia had left there, six remained, pressing in a tight defensive circle around the children. "Jaina, Anakin," she breathed, dropping to one knee beside them and giving them each a quick but tight hug. There was no need to ask if they were all right; her Jedi senses had already confirmed that. "Khabarakh, what happened?"

"He surprised us, Lady Vader," the Noghri said, his face set in the quiet agony of a warrior who has failed his duty. "He walked casually into the clearing and dropped his digging tool onto the ground between us. Part of the handle was a disguised smoke grenade, which exploded with the impact. We could hear him as he activated one of the speeder bikes, but I would not allow any to try to seek him out in the smoke. Should I have acted differently?"

"No," Cakhmaim said firmly. "The machine is of no consequence. Only the safety of the Lady Vader's first-children is important. Your honor is not compromised, Khabarakh clan Kihm'bar."

Jaina tugged at Leia's sleeve. "Why did he run, Mother? Was he afraid of the Noghri?"

"In a way, honey, yes," Leia said grimly. Suddenly, with the clear vision of hindsight, the whole deception was obvious. Pulling the Devaronian's datacards from her hip pack, she fanned them in her hands.

All of them, as she'd already noted, had dirty edges. On one, though, it was only the edges that were dirty.

"Lady Vader?"

Leia turned. From the brush at the edge of the clearing, two Noghri were helping up a dazed-looking Threepio.

"Oh, my," the droid breathed. "I must have taken a bad step."

"Threepio!" Anakin squealed, ducking between his mother and Cakhmaim and racing across to help. "You all right?"

Threepio briefly examined his arms. "I appear to be undamaged, Master Anakin, thank you," he assured the child.

"We've got to find him," Leia said, turning back to Cakhmaim and Khabarakh and holding up the clean datacard. "He's still got one of the datacards he found at the mountain."

"I will send out more searchers," Cakhmaim said, pulling out a comlink. "Perhaps I can also arrange an unexpected surprise for our thief."

"Your Highness?" Threepio called. "I don't know if this is of any use to you—or indeed whether or not you already know it—but before I tripped and fell—"

"Speak quickly," Cakhmaim snapped.

Threepio shrank back slightly. "I observed the stolen speeder bike leave in that direction." He pointed.

"Hey, yeah," Anakin said. "Threepio was outside the smoke!"

"He's making for the northern side of Mount Tantiss," Cakhmaim said decisively. "Undoubtedly where his ship is located. Khabarakh, your group will take the airspeeders and remaining speeder bikes and pursue. I will take the Lady Vader and her firstchildren back to the settlement."

"Just the children, Cakhmaim," Leia corrected, heading for one of the airspeeders. "I'm going with Khabarakh."

Thirty seconds later the group was airborne. "Do we have any idea where his ship might be?" Leia asked as the vehicles tore across the landscape.

"The Myneyrshi will know," Khabarakh said. "They watch all movements near the forbidden mountain. Perhaps that is the surprise Cakhmaim spoke of."

Leia pulled out a set of macrobinoculars from the airspeeder's storage compartment, and for a few minutes she scanned across the forest below and ahead. Nothing. "He's probably staying right down at ground level," she said.

"That will slow him," Khabarakh said. "Still, if we cannot locate his ship, he will likely be able to lift off before we reach him."

And unless the Noghri airspeeders were lucky enough to be right on top of him at the time, the Devaronian would be out of their firing range in a matter of seconds. Pressing her face tighter against the macrobinoculars, Leia stretched out as hard as she could through the Force, trying to locate Lak Jit's presence.

There was nothing she could detect from the forest ahead of them. But even as she tried to focus her thoughts more tightly, she caught a flicker of something else nearby. Something unexpected, yet definitely familiar, and coming steadily closer. Lowering the macrobinoculars, she half closed her eyes and tried to focus on the sensation—

"Hold on!" Khabarakh snapped, and the airspeeder curved sharply around to the left. Leia grabbed for a handhold, nearly losing her grip on the macrobinoculars. Ahead and below them, an old Gymsnor-2 freighter had appeared above the trees. Half closing her eyes again, she stretched out toward the freighter, finally catching the Devaronian's presence. "That's him," she confirmed. "Can we stop him?"

"We will try," Khabarakh said.

Leia grimaced. *Do; or do not. There is no try.* Luke had quoted that Jedi dictum to her over and over during her training.

And it was quickly becoming clear that here, too, there was no try. Even with the airspeeders running full throttle, the Gymsnor was steadily pulling away from its pursuers. Ahead of it, there was nothing: no ships, no hills, no obstacles of any sort, nothing that would slow it down. Already it was above the speeder bikes' maximum height limit; a few minutes more and it would be leaving the airspeeders behind, as well.

There was a sudden gravelly mewing of Noghri words from the comm speaker. Khabarakh answered; and abruptly the airspeeders slowed. Leia turned to him, opening her mouth to ask why they were giving up the chase—

And with a terrific roar, a spaceship shot past them on their right, heading straight for the Gymsnor.

"Khabarakh!" Leia snapped, wincing as the airspeeder bucked in the other ship's slipstream.

"It is all right, Lady Vader," Khabarakh assured her. "It is an ally."

"An ally?" Leia repeated, frowning at the newcomer. A Corellian Action VI bulk freighter, by the looks of it. Nearly four times the size of Lak Jit's ship to begin with; and if the rate it was closing on the Devaronian was any indication, it had undergone a substantial engine upgrade.

Lak Jit had apparently come to a similar conclusion. Banking hard to the right, he dipped back down toward the trees and then cut sharply up and around, settling into a new vector and clawing hard for space.

It was a maneuver that Leia had seen used time and again in the war against the Empire, and it was one that nearly always worked against a larger and more ungainly pursuer. But in this case, it didn't. Almost before Lak Jit had even begun his turn, the Action VI was moving to counter; and by the time the Gymsnor had straightened out, the larger ship was right back on top of him, forcing him to abandon his climb or risk a midair collision. Slowly but inexorably, the Devaronian was being forced down.

"Well done," Khabarakh said.

"Yes," Leia murmured . . . and finally she understood the odd sensation she'd felt a few minutes ago. "So this is the surprise Cakhmaim promised."

"Yes," Khabarakh said. "The *Wild Karrde*, with your allies Talon Karrde and Mara Jade aboard." He eyed her, almost furtively. "I trust you are not displeased?"

Leia smiled tightly. Talon Karrde: genteel smuggler chief, onetime ally of the New Republic, considered untrustworthy by the majority of the High Council. Mara Jade: former agent of the Emperor, Karrde's second-in-command, and aside from Leia herself, Luke's first attempt at teaching the ways of the Force. Also considered untrustworthy. "No, Khabarakh, I'm not displeased at all," Leia assured him. "Like the Noghri, I too remember the past."

• • •

The Gymsnor squatted in the clearing, canted slightly to one side on a crumpled landing skid, its hatchway open and surrounded by a group of Noghri. "I wouldn't have believed you could force a ship down like that," Leia commented, running a critical eye over the freighter. "Not without wrecking half of it in the process."

Beside her, Talon Karrde shrugged modestly. "Cakh-maim said 'relatively undamaged,' " he told her. "We do try to please."

"And you generally succeed," Leia agreed. A pair of Noghri appeared at the hatchway, conversed briefly with the others standing guard outside, then disappeared back inside. "I'm glad you happened to be on Wayland. What are you doing here, anyway?"

"Business," Karrde told her. "I've been experimenting with hiring Noghri to help protect my contact people in some of the more dangerous or unsavory parts of the galaxy."

Leia frowned. "I hadn't heard anything about this."

"We've been keeping it quiet," Karrde said. "I'm not exactly welcome on Coruscant these days; and given your close ties with the Noghri, we didn't want your reputation and influence damaged by association."

"I appreciate your concern," Leia said. "But I can take care of my own reputation, thank you. And as far as New Republic hospitality goes, there are still quite a few of us who haven't forgotten your part in stopping Grand Admiral Thrawn."

"I don't think any of the High Councilors or Senators have actually forgotten," Karrde countered, an uncharacteristic touch of bitterness seeping into his voice and mood. "The point is that many of them resented my organization's assistance even at the time we were providing it."

Leia looked up at him, noting the hard set of his face and the equally hard edge to his emotions. She'd been aware that official ties between Karrde's smuggler friends and the New Republic had been growing more and more distant over the past few years, but she hadn't realized he felt this strongly about it. "I'm sorry," was all she could think of to say. "What can I do to help?"

He waved the offer away, and as he did so the bitterness faded into a kind of wry resignation. "Don't try," he said. "Smugglers are part of the fringe, just like mercenaries and con men and pirates. Try to defend us, and all you'll accomplish will be to get muddied alongside us."

"As I've already said, my reputation is my own concern."

"Besides which," Karrde continued quietly, "drawing any attention to me at this point would also put the Noghri at risk. Or don't you think some in the High Council would consider hiring themselves out to a smuggler to be an unacceptable activity?"

Leia grimaced. But he was right; and with the Noghri still under their self-imposed cloud of penance for their years of service to the Empire, the clan dynasts would be extremely sensitive to any such charges. "I'm sorry," she said again.

"Don't be," Karrde advised her. "If the New Republic doesn't need me, I certainly don't need it, either. Ah—here we go."

Leia looked back at the freighter. A new group had exited the hatchway: three Noghri, a sullen-looking Lak Jit, and Mara Jade, her red-gold hair glistening in the sunlight. In her hand was a dirt-stained datacard. "Incidentally, what ever happened with Mara's independent trading company?" Leia asked. "I heard it had failed, but never heard why."

"It didn't fail; it was simply closed down," Karrde said. "Actually, it was never meant to be anything permanent—I wanted her to have some experience running a small company directly, so we set her up with one. All part of the process of grooming her to take over my organization someday."

The group crossed the clearing to where Karrde and Leia were waiting. To Leia's complete lack of surprise, the Devaronian got in the first word. "I vehemently protest this treatment," he bit out, his eyes and horns glistening with anger. "I have committed no crime that would permit you, Councilor Organa Solo, to open fire on me and to cause damage to my ship. Rest assured that I will be lodging formal complaints with the New Republic High Council and Senate, the Ojoster Sector Assembly, the Corellian Merchants' Guild—"

"And your employer, Talon Karrde?" Karrde suggested mildly.

"Certainly: and Talon Karrde," Lak Jit agreed. "I demand the immediate return of my property—"

He broke off, his eyes focusing on Karrde for the first time. Leia stretched out with the Force, and caught the sudden startled burst of recognition. "You are—?"

"Yes," Karrde confirmed, his voice suddenly cold. He held out a hand, and Mara put the datacard into it. "Tell me, where were you taking this?"

"I was going to bring it to you, of course," Lak Jit said.

Leia looked at Mara, standing a little behind the Devaronian, her hand resting casually on the lightsaber attached to her belt. The other woman returned Leia's look, a knowing and slightly cynical half smile on her face. Clearly, both of them had caught the quaver in Lak Jit's thoughts. Mara shifted her eyes back to Karrde, tilted her head fractionally to the left. "That's lie number one, Lak Jit," Karrde told the Devaronian, lifting a finger. "One more, and I'll inform the Corellian Merchants' Guild you're illegally using their name." The temperature of his voice dropped still lower. "Third lie puts you in trouble with *me*. Now. Where were you going?"

The Devaronian seemed to shrink. "To sell the datacard," he muttered. "To those who would pay the most." He looked furtively at Leia. "Much better than she would have."

"And who are these generous people?" Karrde asked.

Lak Jit twitched his horns left, then right: the Devaronian equivalent of a shrug. "You'll know as soon as you read it. Be careful when you do—I nearly destroyed my datapad trying. It's extremely dirty."

"Yes, I noticed." Karrde looked at Mara. "You've checked his entire ship?"

"The Noghri are still poking around, but this is definitely the card," Mara said.

"All right." Karrde looked back at the Devaronian. "As soon as they're finished, you can leave. Depending on what we find in the datacard, you may or may not still be associated with my organization. Your usual contact will let you know."

Lak Jit bowed elaborately. "As always, a most generous master," he said, not quite enough sarcasm in his tone to take offense at. He looked at Leia. "There was, I believe, mention of five hundred in earnest money?"

Leia and Karrde exchanged incredulous glances. "I think you forfeited any claims to that when you threw the smoke grenade at my children," she told the Devaronian. "We'll still pay you whatever we decide these datacards are worth, but now you'll have to wait."

"They *may* pay you," Karrde amended. "I may consider taking any such payment as my fee for helping keep you here."

Lak Jit smiled thinly. "As I said, a most generous master."

"Just be thankful you didn't try this on a Hutt," Karrde countered. "Get going."

The Devaronian bowed again and headed back toward his ship, the three Noghri trailing along with him. "Yours, I believe," Karrde said, handing Leia the datacard. "We have facilities for cleaning it aboard the *Wild Karrde*, if you'd care to avail yourself of them."

"Which would allow you a chance to read it over my shoulder?" Leia suggested dryly.

Karrde smiled. "We could consider it my fee. Unless you don't think we've earned it?"

Leia shook her head in mock-resignation. "Sometimes I forget what dealing with you is like, Karrde. Lead on."

* * *

The last readable page scrolled a second time across the display, giving way to the randomly scattered bits and blanks of the ruined sections of the datacard. Carefully, Leia set the datapad down on a corner of Karrde's desk, feeling her heart pounding in her throat. Suddenly the private office, which had seemed so snug and warm only minutes ago, felt very cold.

A movement caught her eye as she stared into the distance: Karrde, now seated in the high-backed chair on the other side of the desk, reaching over to the datapad. "Well," he said soberly as he swiveled the device around to face him. "At least we now know why our Bothan friend Fey'lya was so anxious that Mount Tantiss be thoroughly destroyed."

Leia nodded silently, that scene from ten years earlier flashing back to mind. Councilor Borsk Fey'lya, standing outside the *Wild Karrde* in the Imperial City on Coruscant, all but pleading with Karrde to fly Leia to Wayland to help Han and the others destroy the Emperor's Mount Tantiss storehouse. Warning darkly that there were things in that storehouse that, if found, could bring disaster to the Bothan people and the galaxy.

Lak Jit had found it. And Fey'lya had been right.

"I don't suppose there's any chance the record is a forgery," Karrde said, gazing thoughtfully at the datapad. "Something the Emperor might have created with an eye to someday blackmailing the Bothans."

"I doubt it," Leia said. "The royal library on Alderaan had a great deal of information on the attack that burned off Caamas. Details that were never made public knowledge."

"It's hard to believe anything about Caamas could have been kept secret," Karrde said. "The outrage at the time was certainly widespread enough. Worse even than when your own Alderaan was destroyed."

Leia nodded mechanically, her mind's eye drawn unwillingly back to the horrifying holo images she'd seen as a child in the history records. The destruction of Caamas had happened before her time, but the pictures were as vivid as if she'd witnessed the aftermath of the event in person.

The attack had been sudden and thorough, with a viciousness that had made it stand out even against the widespread devastation of the Clone Wars that had preceded it. Perhaps that was what the attackers had banked on, that a populace weary of war would be too emotionally drained to even notice, much less care about the fate of a single world.

But if that was indeed their strategy, it turned out to be a serious miscalculation. The Caamasi had been a good and noble people, with an artistic bent and a gentle wisdom that had won them a deep respect even among their adversaries. Their unwavering belief in peace through moral strength had been a strong influence on the political philosophies of many worlds, including Alderaan, while their firm support of the principles of the Old Republic had made them a rallying point for all such supporters during the political chaos of that era.

It was still not known who the attackers had been who had come out of nowhere to systematically and ruthlessly burn off the planet. None of the Caamasi's political opponents had claimed credit—indeed, all of them had joined in the universal condemnation, at least verbally—and the Caamasi's surviving records of the battle were too badly damaged to be of any use in identification.

But with Lak Jit's datacard, at least one piece of the puzzle had now been solved.

"They were an almost universally beloved people." Leia sighed, bringing her attention back to the present. "Still are, those few who are left." She blinked back tears. "You wouldn't have known, but there was a large Caamasi refugee group on Alderaan when I was growing up, living in the South Islands in secret under my father's protection. They were hoping that someday when they were strong enough they could return to Caamas and try to rebuild."

"Interesting," Karrde murmured, absently stroking his beard. "As it happens, I did know about that group—I used to smuggle in foodstuffs and medicines they needed that were on Alderaan's forbidden-import list. I always wondered why your customs people never seemed to notice me."

"My father didn't want anything official showing up in any import records," Leia said. "He'd always suspected Palpatine's involvement in Caamas's destruction, either directly or through intermediaries, especially when it became clear as to the direction Palpatine was trying to twist the Republic. The Caamasi would never have stood for it, and they would have been much quicker to recognize and respond to the threat than we on Alderaan were."

"Hence, they had to be eliminated," Karrde said heavily. "As you say, obvious in hindsight." He gestured toward the datapad. "But I would never have guessed there were Bothans involved."

"It's going to surprise everybody," Leia said, wincing. "And it couldn't have come at a worse time. With tensions and brush wars cropping up all over the New Republic, I'm not at all sure we're in any shape to deal rationally with something like this."

There was a flicker of presence from outside the office, and she turned as the door slid open. "The alert's out," Mara said, coming into the office and sitting down next to Leia. "All our ships and ground stations, and I got word to Mazzic's and Clyngunn's people, too. If Lak Jit gets near any of them, we'll have him." She nodded at the datapad. "Was there anything else on the datacard?"

"Nothing readable," Leia told her. "Maybe the techs on Coruscant can pull something more out of it. I doubt it, though."

"We were just trading bits and pieces of information on Caamas and the aftermath," Karrde said. "You wouldn't happen to have anything to add, would you?"

Mara threw him a cool look. "You mean like the names and clans of the Bothans who sabotaged Caamas's planetary shield generators?"

"That would be a good start," he agreed.

Mara snorted gently. "I'll bet it would. Unfortunately, I don't know anything more than what's on that datacard. Less, actually, since I didn't know there were any Bothans involved. Don't forget, Caamas was long gone by the time the Emperor found me and trained me to be his Hand."

"He never mentioned the attack?" Leia asked. "Bragged or gloated about it? Anything?"

Mara shook her head. "Not to me. The only time he even mentioned the Caamasi was once when he was convinced they were stirring up Bail Organa against him and was thinking about sending me to do something about it. But then he changed his mind."

Leia felt her heart tighten inside her. "He must have decided he had something better to use as an object lesson. The Death Star."

For a long minute no one spoke. Then Karrde stirred. "What are you going to do with the datacard?" he asked.

With an effort, Leia pushed back the memories of her shattered home and lost family and friends. "I don't have any choice," she told him. "Lak Jit's already read it, and he's bound to spread the story, out of spite if nothing else. All I can do is try to get word back to Coruscant before that happens. At least give the High Council some time to prepare for the uproar."

Karrde looked at Mara. "What's our schedule look like?"

"Busy," she said. "But we've got time to drop her off first."

"If you'd like a ride, that is," Karrde said, turning back to Leia. "Though with Solo and the Wookiee off somewhere in the *Falcon* I suppose you don't really have much choice."

Leia made a face. "Was I the last one on the planet to find out Han had left?"

Karrde smiled. "Probably. But then, information is my business."

"I remember when it used to be mine, too," Leia said with a sigh. "Yes, I'd be very grateful for a ride. Do you have room for my children and Khabarakh's team?"

"I'm sure we can squeeze them in," Karrde assured her, reaching across his desk to the comm. "Dankin? Get us ready to fly. We'll be picking up Councilor Organa Solo's children and honor guard at the Noghri's Mount Tantiss settlement and then heading out."

He got an acknowledgment and switched off. "Cakhmaim said Lak Jit found six datacards," he said, eyeing Leia closely. "Was there anything of this magnitude on any of the others?"

"There was one that might be," Leia said mechanically, a sudden thought jabbing like a blade into her. Mara Jade, once a secret and powerful agent of the Emperor's . . . known only as the Emperor's Hand.

She turned to look at Mara, found those brilliant green eyes gazing with equal intensity back at her. The Emperor's Hand. The Hand of Thrawn . . .

A memory sparked: ten years ago, soon after the birth of Jacen and Jaina, the two women facing each other in a small room in the Imperial Palace. Leia, staring into those same green eyes as Mara calmly announced her intention to kill Leia's brother Luke.

Even then, she'd recognized Mara's abilities in the Force. Now, with practice and some of Luke's own training, those powers were even more in evidence. She could feel Mara's thoughts probing at her own, testing her mind and trying to discern what it was that was suddenly troubling her. And it occurred to her—or was perhaps wordlessly suggested—that Mara with her unique Imperial background might already know who or what was meant by the Hand of Thrawn.

But she couldn't ask her. Not now. Mara and Karrde she considered friends; but this was something that the High Council of the New Republic should hear about first. "I can't say anything about it," she told them. "Not yet."

"I understand," Karrde said, his eyes flicking thoughtfully between the two women. He knew that something was going on beneath the surface, but was too polite to press the point. Besides, he'd be able to find out about it later from Mara, anyway. "No harm in asking."

He lowered his eyes to the datapad. "It does occur to me, though, that we might be worrying more than necessary about this whole Caamas thing. That was a long time ago, and it could be that no one will care anymore who was to blame."

Leia shook her head. "I don't believe that for a minute."

"Neither do I," Mara said.

Karrde grimaced. "No. Neither do I."

CHAPTER

4

He laid it out for them; all of it, in complete and painful detail. And when he had finished, they were, as he'd expected, outraged.

"You must be joking, Admiral Pellaeon," Moff Andray said, his voice icy.

"I agree," Moff Bemos said, fingering the massive codoran ring on his finger. "We are the Empire, Admiral. The Empire does not surrender."

"Then the Empire dies," Pellaeon said bluntly. "I'm sorry, Your Excellencies, but that is the end line of all this. The Empire is beaten. With a negotiated peace treaty, we can at least—"

"I've heard enough," Moff Hort spat, sweeping his datacards off the table into his hand with a grand gesture and pushing back his chair. "I have important business waiting for me back at my sector."

"As do I," Moff Quillan joined in, standing up with him. "If you ask me, a man like this has no business leading our military forces—"

"Sit down," a quiet voice ordered. "Both of you."

Pellaeon focused on the man who'd spoken, seated at the far end of the table from him. He was short and slender, with receding silver hair, piercing yellow-flecked blue eyes, and clawlike hands that were far stronger than they looked.

His face was lined with age and bitterness, his mouth twisted with cruelty and smoldering ambition.

He was Moff Disra. Chief administrator of Braxant sector, ruler of the new Imperial capital planet code-named Bastion, and their host here in the conference room of his palace. And of all the eight remaining Moffs, the one Pellaeon trusted the least.

Quillan and Hort were looking at Disra, too, their intended grand exit suddenly faltering into uncertainty. Hort made as if to speak; then, silently, both of them resumed their seats.

"Thank you." Disra shifted his gaze to Pellaeon. "Please continue, Admiral."

"Thank you, Your Excellency." Pellaeon looked around the table. "I don't blame any of you for being upset with my recommendation. I don't make it lightly. But I see no other way. With a negotiated treaty, we can at least hold on to the territory we still have. Without one, we will certainly be destroyed."

"*Can* we hold on to our territory, though?" Moff Edan asked. "The New Republic has perpetuated the lie that we rule by terror and force. Won't they insist on our destruction, treaty or not?"

"I don't think so," Pellaeon said. "I believe we can convince even the most rabid of them that the worlds currently under Imperial rule remain with us by their own choice."

"Not all of them do," Moff Sander rumbled. "Some in my sector would leave in a moment if offered the choice."

"Certainly we'll lose some systems," Pellaeon said. "But on the opposite side, there are undoubtedly systems currently within New Republic borders whose inhabitants would prefer to live under Imperial law if given that same choice. As matters stand, there's nothing we can do about such systems—we don't have the ships or manpower necessary to defend them, nor could we maintain supply routes to them. But under a peace treaty such systems could be invited to rejoin."

Quillan snorted under his breath. "Ridiculous. Do you

really believe the New Republic would just meekly release their stolen systems back to us?"

"On the contrary, Quillan: they'd have no choice in the matter," Moff Vered put in dryly. "Their sole claim to authority is that the systems of the New Republic willingly accept their authority. How could they then turn around and forbid systems to renounce that authority?"

"Exactly," Pellaeon said, nodding. "Especially with all the small conflicts that have flared up recently. Forbidding systems to leave the New Republic would be handing us a major propaganda weapon. The Almania incident is certainly still fresh enough in their minds."

"Still, if things are so unstable there, why do we need to do anything at all?" Bemos suggested. "If we bide our time, there's a fair chance the New Republic will disintegrate on its own."

"I'd say the chances are better than just fair," Andrey said. "That was the whole philosophic basis for the Emperor's New Order in the first place. Alone of all those in the Imperial Senate, he understood that so many diverse species and cultures could never live together without a strong hand governing them."

"I agree," Pellaeon said. "But at this point the argument is irrelevant. The New Republic's self-annihilation could take decades; and long before they destroyed themselves they would have made sure to grind the remnants of the Empire to dust." He lifted his eyebrows. "All of us, needless to say, would be dead. Killed in battle, or else executed under their current concept of justice."

"After being paraded as war prizes before crowds of cheering subhumans," Sander muttered. "Probably stripped and staked out—"

"There's no need to be so graphic, Sander," Hort growled, throwing the other Moff a glare.

"The point needs to be made," Sander countered. "The Admiral is right: this is precisely the right time to open negotiations. While they can be persuaded that cessation of hostilities is in their own best interests."

The debate ran on for another hour. In the end, showing the same deep reluctance Pellaeon himself felt, they agreed.

The lone guard standing in front of the ornate double doors leading to Moff Disra's private office was tall, young, and strongly built—the very antithesis, Pellaeon thought irreverently as he approached him, of Disra himself. "Admiral Pellaeon," he identified himself. "I wish to see Moff Disra."

"His Excellency left no word—"

"There are surveillance holocams all along this corridor," Pellaeon interrupted him brusquely. "He knows I'm here. Open the doors."

The guard's lip twitched. "Yes, Admiral." He took two steps to his side; and as he did so the double doors swung ponderously open.

The room was fully as ornate as the doors that sealed it, with the kind of luxury Pellaeon hadn't seen in a Moff's palace since the height of the Empire's power. Disra was seated at a glassy white desk in the center of the room, a youngish military aide with short-cropped dark hair and wearing major's insignia standing behind him. The aide had a pack of datacards in his hand; apparently, he'd either just arrived or had been preparing to leave.

"Ah—Admiral Pellaeon," Disra called, beckoning him forward. "Do come in. I'd have thought you'd have been busy organizing your peace envoy."

"We have time," Pellaeon said, glancing around the room as he walked toward the desk, mentally adding up the values of the various furnishings. "According to our Intelligence reports, General Bel Iblis won't be arriving at the Morishim starfighter base for another two weeks."

"Of course," Disra said sarcastically. "Surrendering to Bel Iblis is for some reason more palatable than humiliating yourself before anyone else of that rabble?"

"I have a certain respect for General Bel Iblis, yes," Pellaeon said, stopping a meter away from the desk. It was made of culture-grown ivrooy coral, he noted; from the color, probably of pre-Clone Wars origin. Expensive. "You seem rather bitter at the prospect of peace."

"I have no aversion to peace," Disra countered. "It's the thought of groveling that turns my stomach."

The aide cleared his throat. "If you'll excuse me, Your Excellency," he murmured, laying his stack of datacards on the desk and turning to go.

"No, stay, Major," Disra said, holding up a hand to stop him. "I'd like you to hear this. You know my aide, Admiral, don't you? Major Grodin Tierce."

The corner of Tierce's mouth might have twitched. Pellaeon couldn't tell for sure. "I don't believe we've met," he said, nodding politely to the major.

"Ah. My mistake," Disra said. "Well. We were discussing capitulation, I believe?"

Pellaeon glanced back at Tierce. But after that maybe-twitch the major's face had gone impassive, giving no clue to his thoughts. "I'm still open to suggestions, Your Excellency."

"You already know my suggestions, Admiral," Disra bit out. "To send in teams to help foment the rising tide of interplanetary and intersector conflict within the New Republic. To use this cloaking shield of yours to plant forces where they'll be able to take full advantage of such clashes. To expand our military forces wherever and however we can, using whatever means are available."

Pellaeon felt his lip twist. They'd been over this same ground time and again. "We are the Imperial Fleet," he told Disra stiffly. "We do not hire mercenaries and pirate gangs from the fringe to fight our battles for us."

"I suggest you reread your history, Admiral," Disra shot back. "The Empire has always made use of such scum. Moffs have hired them, so have Grand Moffs—even the Lord Darth Vader himself, when it suited his purposes. And so have the senior officers of your precious and righteously upstanding Fleet. Don't come on all over-sanctimonious with me." He flicked his fingers impatiently. "I'm quite busy, Admiral, and you have groveling to prepare for. Was there something you wanted?"

"One or two things, yes," Pellaeon said, making a supreme effort to hold on to his temper. "I wanted to talk to you about those SoroSuub Preybirds you've been supplying to the Fleet."

"Yes," Disra said, leaning back in his chair. "Excellent little starfighters, aren't they? Not quite the same psychological presence as TIE fighters, perhaps, but perfectly adequate in their own way."

"Adequate enough that I wondered why we hadn't seen more of them over the years," Pellaeon said. "So I did some checking. It turns out that SoroSuub never really got the Preybird project going, but wound up shutting down the line after only a few production models. Which leads to an interesting question: where are you getting them from?"

"I don't see why the source should matter to anyone, Admiral," Disra said. "As long as they show the traditional SoroSuub quality—"

"I want to know who the Empire is doing business with," Pellaeon cut him off. "Who *I* am doing business with."

Under the silver eyebrows, Disra's eyes seemed to flash. "A group of private investors bought up the Preybird production line and restarted it," he growled. "I have a business agreement with them."

"Their names and systems?"

"It's a group of *private* investors," Disra repeated, enunciating the words carefully as if talking to a young child.

"I don't care," Pellaeon said, matching the other's tone. "I want their names, their home systems, and their corporate connections. And the means you're using to finance this deal."

Disra drew himself up. "Are you suggesting there's anything improper about any of this?"

"No, of course not." Pointedly, Pellaeon let his gaze sweep across the room. "Certainly a man of your obvious means has access to a great number of financial resources." He looked back at the Moff. "I merely wish to make sure the entire Empire is benefiting from the deal."

He'd rather expected Disra to take offense at that. But

the Moff merely smiled. "Rest assured, Admiral," he said softly. "The entire Empire will indeed benefit."

Pellaeon stared at him, feeling a slight frown creasing his forehead. There was something in that expression he didn't care for at all. Something ambitious, and vaguely sinister. "I want the names of your investment group."

"I'll have the list transmitted to the *Chimaera*," Disra promised. "Now if you'll excuse me, Major Tierce and I have work to do."

"Of course," Pellaeon said, trying to put a touch of condescension into his voice. The Supreme Commander of Imperial forces should not leave the impression that he could be summarily dismissed that way. Not even by a Moff. Not unless he himself chose to go. "Good day, Your Excellency."

He turned and headed back toward the double doors. Yes, he would have Intelligence look into the names of Disra's private investment group, all right— he'd put Commander Dreyf and his team on it immediately. And while he was at it, he'd have them look into the Moff's personal finances as well. There might be some very interesting connections there to be dug up.

But in the meantime, he had a diplomatic mission to prepare. And, with luck, a war to bring to an end.

The double doors closed behind Pellaeon, and for a moment Disra permitted his face to show a small portion of the contempt he felt for the departing Admiral. Contempt for Pellaeon as a man and an Imperial officer. Contempt for his inability to win against this motley collection of alien-loving Rebels. Contempt for his faceless attitude of appeasement.

The moment passed. There were more pressing matters to deal with right now, matters that required a clear mind. Besides, if things went as planned Pellaeon would very soon be reduced to an irrelevancy. Swiveling his chair halfway around, he peered up at Major Tierce. "Interesting conversation, wouldn't you say, Major?" he inquired mildly. "Tell me, what were your impressions?"

With obvious effort, Tierce dragged his eyes from the doors where Pellaeon had exited. "I'm sorry, Your Excellency, but I really don't know," he said. His shoulders were curled slightly with the humility of a man who knows his limits, his expression earnest but simple. "I'm just a Fleet adjutant. I don't know much about these political things."

It was an extremely competent bit of role-acting, Disra had to admit, one which had apparently fooled dozens of civilian and military commanders over the past fifteen years, including Disra himself. But he knew better now . . . and the performance was about to come to an abrupt end. "I see," Disra said. "Well, then, let's leave politics out of it and have the military opinion of a military officer. You heard my suggestions as to how the Empire can avoid this capitulation the Admiral seems to want so badly. Comments?"

"Well, Your Excellency, Admiral Pellaeon *is* the Supreme Commander," Tierce said reluctantly. The stolid expression was still there, but Disra could now see a hint of tightening around the eyes. Did he suspect that Disra knew? Probably not. Not that it mattered. "I would presume he knows best our strategic situation," Tierce went on. "Again, I'm afraid my own knowledge of grand strategy is also very limited."

"Ah." Disra shook his head, reaching down to the side of the desk to touch the personal-coded switch grown into the ivrooy there. There was a click, and the hidden drawer built into the bottom of the writing surface slid open. "You disappoint me, Major," he said, fingers ruffling through the half-dozen datacards there, his eyes steady on Tierce's face. "I would have assumed the Emperor would have insisted on only the best."

No mistake this time: Tierce's eyes definitely tightened. But he wasn't ready yet to give up the charade. "The Emperor, Your Excellency?" he asked, blinking with bewilderment.

"Only the best," Disra repeated, selecting one of the datacards and holding it up for Tierce's inspection, "to serve in his Royal Guard."

Disra had expected the other to pull a burst of surprise

or bewilderment from his acting repertoire. But Tierce just stood there, his eyes locked on Disra's twinlike turbolaser batteries. Disra held the gaze, forcing back a sudden twinge of doubt. If he'd miscalculated—if Tierce decided his continued anonymity was important enough to murder an Imperial Moff for—

Tierce exhaled softly, the hiss of a poisonous snake. "I suppose there's no point in making loud noises of protest, is there?" he said. He straightened up from his usual slouch—

And Disra found himself pressing involuntarily back in his chair. Suddenly the diffident and marginally competent Major Tierce who'd served as his military aide for eight months was gone.

In his place stood a warrior.

Disra had once heard it said that a discerning person could always recognize an Imperial stormtrooper or Royal Guardsman, whether he stood before you in full armor or lay dying on a sickbed. He'd always discounted such things as childish myths. He wouldn't make that mistake again.

"How did you identify me?" Tierce asked into the silence.

It took Disra another moment to find his voice. "I did a search of the main Imperial records library after it was moved here to Bastion," he said. "Duplicates of the Emperor's private records are also stored there. I was able to find a way to access them."

Tierce lifted an eyebrow. "Really. Those files were supposed to be absolutely secure."

"There's no such thing as absolute security," Disra said.

"Apparently not," Tierce said. "Well. What now?"

"Not what you're expecting," Disra assured him. "I have no intention of denouncing you as a deserter or whatever it is you're worried about, even presuming I could find anyone with the appropriate authority to denounce you to. The Empire can hardly afford to waste its best people." He cocked an eyebrow. "Speaking of which, I have to ask. How did you escape the destruction of the second Death Star?"

Tierce shrugged, a fractional lift of the shoulders. "For the simple reason that I wasn't there. We of the Royal Guard were periodically rotated to regular stormtrooper units to keep us in fighting trim. I was on Magagran at the time, out in the Outer Rim, helping to break up a Rebel cell."

"And the rest of your unit was destroyed?"

"By a single Rebel cell?" Tierce snorted contemptuously. "Hardly. No, we completed our mission and were ordered back. There were all sorts of rumors raging around at the time as to whether or not the Emperor had died at Endor, so as soon as we got within range of Coruscant I jumped ship and went to see if there was anything I could do to salvage the situation."

Disra felt his lip twist. "I remember those months. Pure chaos, with the Rebels gathering pieces that might as well have been handed to them on serving trays."

"Yes," Tierce said, his voice and face bitter. "It was as if the whole Empire was unraveling from the top down."

"Perhaps it was," Disra agreed. "Pellaeon mentioned once that Grand Admiral Thrawn had a theory about that."

"Yes: that the Emperor had been using the Force to drive his troops," Tierce said. "I remember similar discussions aboard the *Chimaera*. Perhaps he was right."

Disra frowned. "You were on the *Chimaera*?"

"Of course," Tierce said. "What better place for a Royal Guardsman than at the side of a Grand Admiral? About a month after he returned from his service in the Unknown Regions, I was able to arrange a transfer to the *Chimaera*'s stormtrooper detachment."

"But then—?" Disra floundered.

"Why did he die?" Tierce's jaw tightened. "Because I guessed wrong. I was expecting an attack on the Grand Admiral when we encountered unexpected numbers at the Bilbringi shipyards. But I was expecting it in the form of a commando team boarding the *Chimaera* in the confusion of battle. Luke Skywalker had penetrated the ship that way once before, to rescue the smuggler Talon Karrde, and I thought they might try it again. So I put my stormtrooper unit on station near the hangar bays."

"Ah." Disra nodded, a stray bit of history from that battle falling into place. "So it was your unit that intercepted and killed the Noghri traitor Rukh after he murdered the Grand Admiral?"

"Yes. For what cold comfort that was."

"Um." Disra eyed him. "Did Thrawn know about you?"

Tierce shrugged again. "Who could ever tell what a Grand Admiral knew or didn't know? All I can say is that I never identified myself to him, and he never confronted me with my past."

"Why didn't you identify yourself?" Disra asked. "I'd have thought a Royal Guardsman would be entitled to certain—ah—special assignments."

"Don't ever suggest such a thing again, Disra," Tierce said, his voice quiet and deadly. "Don't even think it. A Royal Guardsman never seeks special privileges. Ever. His entire goal in life is to serve the Emperor, and the New Order he created. His goal in life, and his desire in death."

"Yes," Disra murmured, taken aback in spite of himself. It was becoming increasingly clear that the reputation of the Royal Guard—a reputation he'd always assumed to be the spun-frosting product of the Emperor's propagandists—had in fact been quite honestly earned. "I beg your pardon, Guardsman."

"Major," Tierce corrected. "Just Major. The Royal Guard no longer exists."

"Again, your pardon, Major," Disra said, a touch of annoyance seeping through the awkwardness. He had intended to stay on top of this conversation; yet, at every turn, it seemed, he was losing control of it. "And I am to be addressed as 'Your Excellency.' "

Tierce frowned, and for a painful moment Disra held his breath. Then, to his relief, the other's lip twitched into an ironic smile. "Of course," he said dryly. "Your Excellency. Have you properly satisfied your curiosity, Your Excellency?"

"I have," Disra said, nodding. "The past is past, Major. Let us now consider the future. You heard my suggestions to Admiral Pellaeon. What do you think?"

Tierce shook his head. "The Admiral is right: it won't work. The numbers are too heavily slanted against us."

"Not even with the New Republic busy with dozens of internal conflicts?"

"No." Tierce gestured at Disra's desk. "Not even with the interesting report filed under 'Lak Jit' on the third data-card down."

"Oh?" Disra frowned, pulling out the datacard from the stack Tierce had brought in. All these reports were supposed to be private, encrypted with a special Imperial code reserved for top Intelligence officers and the Moffs themselves. Obviously, Disra wasn't the only one who'd been doing some high-level slicing. Sliding the datacard into his reader, he keyed for decryption.

It was an Intelligence report, purchased from a Devaronian freelancer named Lak Jit, concerning the discovery in the Mount Tantiss ruins of a partial record of the destruction of Caamas. "This is perfect," he told Tierce as he skimmed through it. "Exactly what we need."

Tierce shook his head. "Certainly it's useful. But it's not enough."

"Ah, but it is," Disra said, feeling a tight smile tugging at his lips as he reread the crucial parts of the report. "I don't think you fully understand the political situation the New Republic finds itself in these days. A flash point like Caamas—especially with Bothan involvement—will bring the whole thing to a boil. Particularly if we can give it the proper nudge."

"The situation among the Rebels is not the issue," Tierce countered coldly. "It's the state of the Empire *you* don't seem to understand. Simply tearing the Rebellion apart is not going to rebuild the Emperor's New Order. We need a focal point, a leader around whom the Imperial forces can rally. Admiral Pellaeon is the closest thing we have to such an authority figure, and he's obviously lost the will to fight."

"Forget Pellaeon," Disra said. "Suppose I could provide such a leader. Would you be willing to join us?"

Tierce eyed him. "Who is this 'us' you refer to?"

"If you join, there would be three of us," Disra said.

"Three who would share the secret I'm prepared to offer you. A secret that will bring the entire Fleet onto our side."

Tierce smiled cynically. "You'll forgive me, Your Excellency, if I suggest you couldn't inspire blind loyalty in a drugged bantha."

Disra felt a flash of anger. How dare this common soldier—?

"No," he agreed, practically choking out the word from between clenched teeth. Tierce was hardly a common soldier, after all. More importantly, Disra desperately needed a man of his skills and training. "I would merely be the political power behind the throne. Plus the supplier of military men and matériel, of course."

"From the Braxant Sector Fleet?"

"And other sources," Disra said. "You, should you choose to join us, would serve as the architect of our overall strategy."

"I see." If Tierce was bothered by the word 'serve,' he didn't show it. "And the third person?"

"Are you with us?"

Tierce studied him. "First tell me more."

"I'll do better than tell you." Disra pushed his chair back and stood up. "I'll show you."

Judging from Tierce's lack of reaction, the supposedly secret corridor between the private office and Disra's quarters came as no surprise to the former Guardsman. The camouflaged doorway halfway along it, however, did. "Installed by the palace's previous owner," Disra explained as they walked down a narrow passageway to an equally narrow turbolift car. "It goes down fifty meters. From there you can then go either to the torture chamber beneath the dungeon level or to a secret exit tunnel in the hills to the north. I've sometimes wondered which direction he used the most."

"Which are we using today?" Tierce asked as the turbolift car started down.

"The one to the torture chamber," Disra said. "It's the most private and secure place in the palace. Or anywhere on Bastion, for that matter. The third person of our group is waiting there."

The car stopped and the door slid open. Two narrow, rough-carved tunnels branched off the open space in front of the turbolift; brushing aside a stray strand of cobweb, Disra led the way down the rightmost corridor. It ended in a dusty metal door with a wheel set into its center. Gripping the edges of the wheel, Disra turned; and with a creak that echoed eerily in the confined space the door swung open.

The previous owner would hardly have recognized his onetime torture chamber. The instruments of pain and terror had been taken out, the walls and floor cleaned and carpet-insulated, and the furnishings of a fully functional modern apartment installed.

But for the moment Disra had no interest in the chamber itself. All his attention was on Tierce as the former Guardsman stepped into the room.

Stepped into the room . . . and caught sight of the room's single occupant, seated in the center in a duplicate of a Star Destroyer's captain's chair.

Tierce froze, his eyes widening with shock, his entire body stiffening as if a power current had jolted through him. His eyes darted to Disra, back to the captain's chair, flicked around the room as if seeking evidence of a trap or hallucination or perhaps his own insanity, back again to the chair. Disra held his breath . . .

And then, abruptly, Tierce straightened to parade-ground attention. "Grand Admiral Thrawn, *sir*," he said with laser-sharp military formality. "Stormtrooper TR-889, reporting for duty."

Disra shifted his attention to the room's occupant as he rose slowly to his feet. To the blue skin, the blue-black hair, the glowing red eyes, the white Grand Admiral's uniform. The glowing eyes met Disra's; then he turned back to Tierce. "Welcome back to duty, stormtrooper," he said gravely. "However, I'm afraid I must tell you"—he glanced again at Disra—"that I'm not who you think I am."

The first hint of a frown crept across Tierce's face. "Sir?"

"Allow me," Disra said. Stepping across the room, he took hold of the white uniform sleeve and pulled the man a step closer to Tierce. "Major Tierce: allow me to present my associate Flim.

"A highly talented con artist."

For a long minute the room was filled with a brittle silence. Tierce stared at the white-uniformed impostor, disbelief and disappointment mixing with anger and betrayal in his face. Disra watched the play of emotions, his pulse pounding unpleasantly in his neck. If Tierce let his pride take charge here—if he chose to take offense at the deception they'd just played on him—then neither Disra nor Flim would be leaving this room alive.

Tierce turned his gaze onto Disra, the emotional turmoil retreating behind a mask of stone. "Explain," he said darkly.

"You said yourself the Empire needed a leader," Disra reminded him. "What better leader could we have than Grand Admiral Thrawn?"

Slowly, reluctantly, Tierce looked back at the false Grand Admiral. "Who are you?" he demanded.

"As His Excellency told you, my name is Flim," the other said. His voice was subtly changed, his manner no longer the powerful, almost regal air of a Grand Admiral. Precisely the same transformation, Disra realized suddenly, as the one Tierce himself had gone through a few minutes ago up in the private office, except in reverse.

Perhaps Tierce recognized that, too. "Interesting," he said, taking a step forward and peering closely at Flim's face. "It's uncanny. You look exactly like him."

"He should," Disra said. "It took me nearly eight years of searching to find someone who could pull off such a masquerade. I've been planning this a long time."

"So I see." Tierce gestured. "How do you do the eyes?"

"Surface inserts," Disra said. "Self-powered to provide the red glow. The rest is just skin and hair coloring, plus a remarkable voice control and natural acting ability."

"I've done many such impersonations," Flim said. "This is just one more." He smiled. "Though with considerably greater potential for reward."

"It's remarkable," Tierce said, looking back at Disra.

"There's only one problem. Thrawn is dead, and everyone knows it."

Disra lifted his eyebrows. "Ah, but do they? He was reported dead, certainly, but that may or may not mean anything at all. Perhaps he was merely comatose from Rukh's knife wound. Perhaps he was taken to some secret place where he has spent the long years in recovery." He nodded toward Flim. "Or perhaps it was actually an impostor like Flim who died on the *Chimaera*'s bridge. You said you were expecting an attack on him at Bilbringi; perhaps Thrawn was, too, and made private arrangements of his own."

Tierce snorted. "Farfetched."

"Of course," Disra agreed. "But that doesn't matter. All we need to do is present Thrawn, and wishful thinking will do the rest. The entire Empire will rush to believe in him, from Admiral Pellaeon on down."

"Is that your plan, then?" Tierce asked. "To present the Grand Admiral to Pellaeon, reinstate him aboard the *Chimaera*, and use him as a rallying point for the Empire?"

"Basically," Disra said, frowning. "Why?"

For a moment Tierce was silent. "You said you had other resources besides the Braxant Sector Fleet," he said. "What are they?"

Disra glanced at Flim. But the con man was merely looking interestedly at Tierce. "I have an arrangement with the Cavrilhu Pirates," he told the Guardsman. "They're a large and highly sophisticated group working out of—"

"I'm familiar with Captain Zothip's gang," Tierce said. "Not particularly sophisticated, to my mind, but certainly large enough. What sort of arrangement?"

"One of interlocking interests," Disra said. "I use Imperial Intelligence reports to locate useful New Republic shipments, which Zothip then attacks. He gets whatever booty he can; we get further destabilization of our enemy."

"And a share of the SoroSuub Preybirds being turned out by Zothip's production line?" Tierce suggested.

Disra pursed his lips. Either Tierce knew a great deal more than he should about the Moff's secrets, or he was a lot sharper than Disra had expected. Either way, he wasn't sure he liked it. "We're getting all the Preybirds, actually," he said. "Zothip has all the starfighters he needs."

"How are you paying for them?"

"With the kind of expert assistance Zothip can't get anywhere else," Disra said, favoring the other with a sly smile. "I'm loaning him some very special warrior-advisers: groups of Thrawn's own Mount Tantiss clones."

He had the satisfaction of seeing Tierce's jaw drop a fraction. "There are still some of them left?"

"There are whole nests of them left," Disra told him sourly. "Our clever little Grand Admiral scattered groups all over the New Republic under deep cover. What he intended to do with them I don't know; there wasn't anything in his records specifically concerning—"

"You found Thrawn's records?" Tierce cut him off. "His personal records, I mean?"

"Of course," Disra said, frowning slightly. For an instant there had suddenly been something electric in the Guardsman's expression. "How else do you think I knew how to find where he'd hidden all those clones?"

The flash of interest had already vanished behind Tierce's mask. "Of course," he said calmly. "What else was in there?"

"There was the outline of a grand strategy," Disra said, watching him closely. But whatever had sparked that flicker was buried again. "His plans for the next five years' worth of campaigns against the New Republic. Incredibly detailed; unfortunately, at this point, also completely useless."

"I'd be careful about dismissing anything Thrawn ever did as completely useless," Tierce reproved him mildly. "Anything else?"

Disra shrugged. "Personal memoirs and such. Nothing that struck me as militarily interesting. You're welcome to look through them later if you want."

"Thank you," Tierce said. "I believe I will."

"I take it," Flim put in, "that you're considering something more ambitious than simply using my Thrawn as a rallying point?"

Tierce inclined his head slightly to the con man. "Very

perceptive, Admiral," he said. "Yes, I think we can do better
than that. Much better, in fact. Is there a computer terminal
down here?—ah; excellent. I'll need the datacards we left on
your desk, Your Excellency. Would you mind getting
them?"

"Not at all," Disra murmured. "I'll be right back."

Already busy at the computer terminal, Tierce didn't
bother to answer. For a moment Disra gazed at the back of
his head, wondering if he might possibly have miscalculated.
Major Tierce, former Royal Guardsman, would be a useful
servant. He would not be an appreciated master.

But for right now, they all needed each other. Swallow-
ing his words, and his pride, Disra stepped out into the tunnel and headed back toward the turbolift.

CHAPTER

5

Councilor Borsk Fey'lya looked up from the datapad, his violet eyes dilated, his cream-colored fur flattened tightly against his body. "So it has finally come to light," he whispered.

"Yes, it has," Leia said. "And it demands an explanation."

Fey'lya shook his head. "There is nothing to explain," he said softly. "It is true."

"I see," Leia said, feeling a heaviness settle across her shoulders. She hadn't realized how hard she'd been hoping that Karrde had been right about the Caamas record being a forgery. "You're certain?"

"Yes," Fey'lya said, his gaze drifting away from Leia to the datapad again.

"Then you know who was involved."

"No," Fey'lya said. "That is the core of the problem, Councilor Organa Solo. And the reason we have been silent over this for so long. We know only what you now know: that a group of Bothans helped agents of Senator Palpatine gain access to the Caamas shield generators. We don't even know the clan involved, let alone the specific individuals."

"Did you try to find out?" Leia asked bluntly.

Fey'lya's fur rippled. "Of course we did. But Palpatine had covered his trail far too well. It was only long after the event, in the early days of the Rebellion, that the chief clan leaders even became aware of Bothan complicity at Caamas. It was our shock at that revelation, in fact, that moved us to dedicate our people to the Rebel Alliance and Palpatine's downfall. But the trail was by then too old to follow."

Leia sighed. "I understand."

"You believe me, don't you?" Fey'lya persisted. "You must believe me."

For a moment Leia didn't speak. Gazing into his face, reaching out with the Force, she searched as best she could for any hint of deception. But if it was there, she couldn't find it. "I believe you're telling the truth, at least as far as you know it," she told the Bothan. "Unfortunately, I'm not the only one you'll have to convince."

Fey'lya shivered, random clumps of his fur stiffening across his body. "No," he agreed soberly. "There will be many who will believe we are merely protecting the criminals in the name of Bothan solidarity."

Leia picked up the datapad, suppressing a grimace. He was certainly right about that. The Bothan approach to interstellar politics was far more biting and pop-and-topple than many in the New Republic cared for. Even species who thought nothing of all-out physical combat between themselves generally tried to moderate their approach when dealing with outsiders. The fact that the Bothans were either unable or unwilling to do likewise had earned them more than their fair share of ill will in diplomatic circles. "I agree," she said. "All the more reason to get this resolved as quickly as possible."

"But how?" Fey'lya asked. "The Bothans have searched long and hard for a list of those responsible, both in the official clan libraries on Bothawui as well as on all our colony worlds and enclaves. It simply doesn't exist."

"It existed here," Leia pointed out, pulling the datacard from the datapad. "I'm convinced it did. We can see if the techs can reconstruct it; if they can't, we'll just have to locate another copy somewhere. At least now we know what to look for."

"We can try," Fey'lya said doubtfully. "But in the meantime, what do you plan to do?"

Leia fingered the datacard. "I can't just forget the whole thing, Councilor Fey'lya—you have to understand that. I have to at least take it to the rest of the High Council. But I'll do what I can to persuade President Gavrisom that it shouldn't be made public. At least not until the techs have had time to see what they can do with the ruined sections."

"I see," Fey'lya said, his fur and emotions both rippling. "Whether the techs will keep silent is of course another question. More important, what about the smuggler Talon Karrde? You said he also knows."

"He's given his promise that he won't say anything," Leia told him. "And he has a message out to the rest of his people to watch for the Devaronian who found the datacard. Maybe they can catch up with him before he tells anyone else."

Fey'lya sniffed. "You really think he hasn't already told others? After the way you and Karrde treated him?"

"We did what we deemed necessary at the time," Leia said, sternly ordering down her sudden flash of annoyance with the Bothan. "Would you rather he had left Wayland with the datacard?"

"To be blunt: yes," Fey'lya said stiffly. "Clearly, we were his intended recipients. He would have demanded a tremendous sum of money from us, and we would have paid him, and it would have been over."

Leia sighed. "It wouldn't have been over, Councilor. It won't be over until the whole truth is known and those responsible punished."

"That is indeed all that is left to us now," Fey'lya said, standing up. "Thank you for your courtesy in giving me this private briefing, Councilor Organa Solo. I will go now to prepare my defense."

"You're not on trial here, Councilor," Leia reminded him.

Fey'lya's fur flattened. "I will be," he said softly. "As will the entire Bothan race. You will see."

•   •   •

The Dona Laza tapcafe was about as crowded as Shada
D'ukal had ever seen it, packed almost literally wall-to-wall
with beings of a dozen different species and every social class
from lower-middle on down. "Popular place tonight," she
commented to her boss, sitting close beside her at the table.

"It's their turn at the floating Boga Minawk tournament," Mazzic explained, idly stroking the back of Shada's
hand. "You wouldn't believe how crazy they go for the
game around here."

"You suppose that's why he chose this place?" Shada
asked. "Because of the crowd?"

"Don't worry, Cromf will bring him in okay," Mazzic
soothed her. "Pass him enough money and he becomes positively reliable. Especially when the second half of the payment doesn't come until delivery."

Shada looked at the beings pressing around their table.
"I'm more concerned about whether we'll be able to pull
him out of here quietly with this many people watching."

"There's no rush on that," Mazzic said. "Considering
all the trouble we've gone to, we ought to at least hear this
deep dark secret he wants to tell us. After that, we can see
about putting the restraints on him."

Shada looked at him out of the corner of her eye.
"Karrde won't be happy about that," she warned. "He was
very specific about Lak Jit not talking to anyone."

"We're not on Talon Karrde's paylist," Mazzic reminded her tartly. "What with Cromf's finder's fee, we're
not going to break even on this as it is. If this little secret has
any market value, we deserve to get a cut of it."

Shada turned away from him, a wave of blackness flowing over her already dark mood. That was always what it
came down to in the world of smuggling: profit, and more
profit, and doing whatever scheming and back-blading it
took to get as much of it as possible. Concepts like loyalty
and honor—

"Oh, come on, Shada," Mazzic chided, stroking her

hand again. "These bursts of personal guilt have got to stop. This is how the game is played. You know that."

"Sure," Shada murmured. She knew, all right. What hurt the most was that for the past twelve years she'd been a willing participant in it. Willing, and very able.

Sometimes, late at night, she wondered what had happened to the galaxy. Or perhaps it was just her.

At the near edge of the crowd a young Garoos appeared, easing himself and his loaded tray gingerly between a pair of loud and wildly gesticulating Ishori. He made it without spilling the drinks, and wilted into the seat across from Mazzic. "Wheh!" he half-whistled, picking up one of the four drinks from the tray, his purple-tinged gillis flaps undulating rhythmically as he breathed. "Dint think I was gon make it."

"And a fine job you did, too, Cromf," Mazzic assured him, selecting two of the other glasses and setting one in front of Shada. "Any sign of our quarry yet?"

"I dint see him," Cromf said, sipping carefully at his drink and looking nervously around him. One ear cluster opened briefly as someone nearby gave a raucous laugh, then closed down again. "I dont like this, Maz'k. Too man' here watch."

"Don't worry," Mazzic soothed. "You just get him to the table. We'll do the rest."

Beside Shada's left ear, one of the decorative lacquered needles twisted into her hair gave two soft clicks. "Signal from Griv," she told Mazzic. "Possible make."

"Good," Mazzic said. "Go get him, Cromf—side entrance. Concentrate on the other half of your finder's fee."

The Garoos half-whistled as he got up from the table and disappeared again into the crowd. Shada took a deep breath, settling into combat mode, and gave the area around them a final examination. If the Devaronian smelled trouble and tried to bolt, he would probably head to his left . . .

And then Cromf was back, a horn-headed Devaronian in tow. "Wheh!" he half-whistled, sitting down beside Mazzic. "Crowd in here. This Lak Jit. This smug' Maz'k."

"Pleased to meet you, Lak Jit," Mazzic said, offering

him the fourth glass from the tray. "You drink Vistulo brandale, I trust?"

"When someone else is paying," Lak Jit said, taking the seat across from Mazzic. "I want you to know first, Mazzic, that though what I am about to tell you is true, I know I cannot ask for money in exchange. I no longer have tangible proof, only the evidence of my own eyes."

"I understand," Mazzic said, setting his hand down in the center of the table. He withdrew it, revealing the short stack of high-denomination coins. "Still, a respectable gentleman should be willing to pay for value received."

Lak Jit smiled his thin Devaronian smile and reached for the coins—

And found his wrist locked solidly in Mazzic's grip. "For value received," Mazzic reminded him coldly. Reaching out with the other hand, he slid the stack of coins back to the edge of the table in front of him. "Now," he said, releasing the Devaronian's wrist. "Let's hear what you have."

Lak Jit hunched forward to lean across the table. "Understand that what I am about to tell you is both private and exclusive," he murmured. "No one else outside the New Republic government knows this."

"Of course," Mazzic said dryly, his tone making it clear to Shada that he didn't believe that any more than she did. The Devaronian had probably already sold this same "exclusive" information to a half-dozen other people. "Let's hear it."

Lak Jit glanced around and hunched a little closer. "It concerns Caamas," he said. "There exists evidence that it was indeed agents of the then Senator Palpatine who engineered its destruction."

Beneath the table, Shada felt her hand curl into a hard fist. Caamas. It had been a long time since she'd thought about that world. A long time since she'd tried to block its name and the childhood memories it evoked of her own world of Emberlene from her mind. Now, suddenly, it was all coming back.

She wouldn't have expected Mazzic to be equally moved. And he wasn't. "Hardly groundbreaking news," he said with a shrug. "That's been the leading theory practically since the last Caamasi firestorm burned itself out."

"But this is proof," Lak Jit insisted. "A record recovered from the Emperor's personal storehouse on Wayland."

"A document you don't happen to have."

"But there's more," the Devaronian hissed, leaning forward until his horns were almost touching Mazzic's forehead. "We now know how it was that the planet was so easily destroyed. The shield generators were deliberately sabotaged." He jabbed a finger onto the table for emphasis. "By a group of Bothans."

Mazzic shot Shada a glance. "Really," he said, his voice still nonchalant but with a definite note of interest beneath it. "You know their names?"

"Unfortunately not," Lak Jit said. "That part of the document was too badly damaged for my humble datapad to read." He leaned back again in his chair. "But I suggest it doesn't matter. Either way, the Bothans are in for an exceedingly rough time. A clever businessman should be able to make a profit from knowledge of such imminent instability." He gestured to the stack of coins in front of Mazzic. "Wouldn't you agree?"

"I would indeed," Mazzic said, looking at Shada and twitching an eyebrow. "Very well. Shada, would you assist our friend?"

"No need," Lak Jit said. Leaning forward over the table again, he reached out for the coins—

And rising half from her seat, Shada jabbed the knuckles of her right hand at the base of his leftmost horn.

He went down without a whimper, dropping face first onto the table, his leftmost horn almost but not quite knocking over Mazzic's drink. A Barabel and a couple of Duros glanced over and then looked away; passed-out customers were apparently a common sight at the Dona Laza. "Wheh!" Cromf wheezed, staring bulge-eyed at the limp form. "Is he not—?"

"Of course not," Mazzic said, reaching over to tap the needle-shaped signaler in Shada's hair three times. "No one's paying us to kill anyone."

Pushing his way through the crowd, Griv appeared at the table. "Ready?" he asked.

"Ready," Mazzic nodded, scooping up the stack of coins. He handed Cromf four of them, dropped the rest into his inside pocket. "Get him out to the speeder."

Griv hoisted the Devaronian to his shoulder and pushed his way back into the crowd. "Well, that was a waste of time," Mazzic commented, standing up and courteously offering Shada a hand. "Maybe we can bargain up Karrde's bounty a little. Try to at least come out even."

"We're not going to do anything with this?" Shada asked.

"Don't be silly," he chided, taking her arm and guiding her into the crowd. "Who's going to care about a planet destroyed almost half a century ago?"

Shada's stomach tightened. Caamas . . . and Emberlene. "No one," she agreed bitterly. "No one at all."

It took a while—at least two complete read-throughs each, Disra estimated as he slowly paced the floor behind his ivrooy desk, trying to look impatient rather than apprehensive. But eventually the last of the four Imperial captains finished reading and lifted his eyes from his datapad. "With all due respect, Your Excellency, I find this proposal incredible," Captain Trazzen of the *Obliterator* said, his soft voice belying his reputation for viciousness. "Surely you realize that you can't simply pull four Imperial Star Destroyers out of a sector fleet and expect the remaining forces to adequately defend their territory."

"I agree," Captain Nalgol of the *Tyrannic* put in, fingering the Kuat family crest ring he always wore. "In addition—and also with due respect—I would go so far as to question your authority to even order these two missions. All incursions into New Republic space are supposed to be under the direct command of Supreme Fleet Commander Pellaeon."

"Perhaps," Disra said. "Perhaps not. We'll put that aside for a moment. Are there other questions?"

"I have one," Captain Dorja of the *Relentless* spoke up. "This mission to Morishim that you want me to go on. What exactly is this courier ship I'm being asked to intercept?"

Disra lifted his eyebrows. "Being 'asked,' Captain? Being *'asked'*?"

"Yes, Your Excellency," Dorja said stiffly. "Captain Nalgol is correct: you are supreme commander of the Braxant Sector Fleet only with regard to operations within Braxant sector. Missions to Morishim and Bothawui do not fall under this authority."

"I see." Disra looked at the fourth captain. "You've been rather quiet, Captain Argona."

"The *Ironhand* is of course under your command, Your Excellency, and we'll go wherever you send us," Argona said quietly. "At the same time, I have to concur with Captain Trazzen's assessment. Sending away four of the sector fleet's thirteen Star Destroyers is not something to be done lightly."

"Especially with three of them on this long-term mission to the Bothawui system," Trazzen added. "The nature of which, I remind you, precludes any chance of a quick recall."

"Indeed," Argona said. "You'd have to physically send couriers out there to contact us. In an emergency, the extra days that would cost could prove disastrous."

"Nothing worthwhile is ever gained without risk," Disra said coldly. "I'm beginning to think that perhaps a wrong choice has been made in offering these missions to you. If you'd prefer to bow out of a history-making military campaign—"

"No."

The voice had come from the direction of Disra's secret passageway. The captains turned—

And Grand Admiral Thrawn stepped into the office.

There was a gasp from someone, choked off into a stunned silence. "Excuse me, Admiral?" Disra asked carefully.

"I said they will not be excused from this mission, Your Excellency," Thrawn said, his voice calm and cool as he walked to the desk and sat down in Disra's chair. "I had my reasons for choosing these particular Star Destroyers and their captains. Those reasons have not changed."

For a moment his glowing eyes focused on the captains as they stood at obviously confused attention before him, measuring and evaluating each in turn. Then, leaning back in his seat, he smiled slightly. "Observe, Your Excellency," he said, looking up at Disra and waving a hand at the officers. "Utterly stunned by my unexpected appearance; yet already they are largely recovered. Quick and flexible minds, combined with utter loyalty to the Empire. That is the combination I need. The combination I will have."

"Of course, Admiral," Disra said.

Thrawn turned his attention back to the captains. "You have questions, of course," he said. "Unfortunately, the one foremost in all your minds cannot at this time be answered. As I make preparations to return to open command, the method which allowed me to survive the assassination attempt ten years ago must remain confidential. I must also ask that for the moment my return be kept a secret, to be shared only with your senior officers, and that only after you've left Imperial space. Other than that—" He cocked his head slightly to the side. "I believe there were some questions about command authority?"

"No questions, Admiral," Trazzen said, his voice almost reverent. "Not anymore."

"Good." Thrawn cocked a blue-black eyebrow at Nalgol. "I take it from your expression, Captain Nalgol, that you don't concur with your colleague?"

Nalgol cleared his throat self-consciously, his finger squeezing his ring as if trying to extract confidence from the carved crest. "I certainly don't question your authority, Admiral Thrawn," he said. "But I would very much appreciate some clarification. I'm familiar with the Bothawui system, and I can think of no reason why it should be of any serious military value to the Empire. Certainly not worth tying up three Star Destroyers for."

"Your evaluation is quite correct," Thrawn agreed. "It's not the system itself that interests me, but events which in the near future will be taking place over the Bothan homeworld. Events which I intend to turn to the Empire's advantage."

"Yes, sir," Nalgol said. "But—"

"In time, all will be clear," Thrawn said. "For now, I must ask that you trust my judgment."

Nalgol drew himself to his full height. "Always, Admiral." He stepped forward and offered his hand across the desk. "And if I may say so, welcome back. The Empire has sorely missed your leadership."

"As I have missed the privilege of command," Thrawn said, rising to his feet and gripping the proffered hand briefly. "The refitting of your three Star Destroyers is already under way, and should be completed within two days." He shifted his attention to Dorja. "As for your mission, Captain Dorja, the Imperial courier you're to intercept at Morishim is scheduled to leave in twenty hours. Will you have enough time to return to the *Relentless* and reach the system ahead of it?"

"Easily, Admiral." Dorja's lip twitched in what passed for a smile with him these days. "And if I may, sir, I'd like to echo Captain Nalgol's sentiments. I'm honored to once again serve under your direct command."

Disra looked at Dorja, his chest suddenly feeling tight. Dorja had served directly under Thrawn?

"I'm pleased to once again lead you, Captain," Thrawn said gravely. "During my time on the *Chimaera* I often felt that you had more leadership potential than circumstances allowed you to develop. Perhaps we'll have the opportunity now to judge that evaluation."

Dorja fairly glowed. "I'll do my best to prove you right, sir."

"I can ask no more than your best," Thrawn said. "And will accept nothing less," he added, looking at each of the captains in turn. "You have your orders. Dismissed."

"Yes, Admiral," Trazzen said for all of them. They turned and left, with what seemed to Disra to be a markedly more spirited step than that with which they'd entered the office half an hour earlier. The double doors swung ponderously shut behind them—

"A fine group of gentlemen," Flim declared, digging a finger into the collar of his white Grand Admiral's uniform. "A bit gullible, perhaps, but fine gentlemen all the same."

"Oh, they're fine, all right," Disra snarled, glaring at the secret door the con man had made his grand entrance through. "They're also extremely dangerous. Tierce? Where are you?"

"Right here," Tierce said, stepping out of the secret door. "What's the matter?"

"What's the *matter*?" Disra snapped. "Bad enough that three of the four captains you picked for these missions aren't particularly loyal to me. But someone who served directly with Thrawn? Are you insane?"

"Don't be insulting," Tierce said coldly, joining the others by the desk. "I had to bring in someone like Dorja on this. A junior student of tactics could tell you that."

"I don't think tactically," Disra shot back. "At least, not according to you. That's why your expertise is so necessary, remember?"

"Calm down, Your Excellency," Flim interjected, carefully popping the glowing surface insert out of his left eye. "Sooner or later, it was inevitable that I face someone who personally knew Thrawn. What better time or place than here, where all four of them could have been dealt with quietly and discreetly if necessary?"

"Exactly," Tierce said. "And as to my choice of commanders, those not personally loyal to you are precisely the ones we need to work Flim's magic on."

"And have you considered what they might do once they're out of range of that magic?" Disra countered. "What if they decide they're not really convinced after all and do some checking?"

"Oh, they're going to," Tierce assured him. "That was why I wanted Nalgol to be in this first group. He comes from a long line of Kuat nobility, and I knew he'd be wearing his poison injector ring."

Flim paused midway through popping out the other surface insert. "His *what*?"

"His poison injector ring," Tierce repeated. "Poisoning one's enemies is a centuries-old tradition there. Oh, relax—Nalgol hasn't carried any poison in that ring for years."

"I'm glad *you* think so," Flim said irritably, examining his hand closely where Nalgol had gripped it. "It wasn't *your* hand he came over and—"

"I said relax," Tierce said again, and this time there was an edge to his voice. "He wasn't putting anything in. He was taking something *out*."

"A small skin sample, to be exact," Disra said, finally catching on. "Which he'll undoubtedly take straight over to the archives to compare against the genetic profile in Thrawn's ID records."

"Exactly," Tierce said. "And once he's convinced—and he'll certainly share his findings with the others—there will be literally nothing they won't do for us."

"I wondered why you were so insistent we get those ID records altered last night," Disra said. "Not exactly a large margin of error built into that operation."

"Especially considering the two of us were taking all the risks," Flim seconded, still cradling his hand. "You weren't even in the room with us."

"Calm down, both of you," Tierce said, a hint of contempt in his tone. "There's a long way yet to go on this. I hope you're not losing your nerve already."

"Don't worry about our nerve, Major," Disra bit out. "You just worry about this strategy of yours actually working."

"It will," Tierce assured him. "Trust me. Whatever the preliminary skirmishes, the opening battle of the Rebellion's final civil war will be fought over Bothawui. The Caamas Document will insure that. We want to orchestrate the details of that blow-up as best we can; and we want an Imperial presence at Bothawui to make sure the damage to both sides is as extensive as possible."

"Well, whatever we do, we'd better do it quickly," Disra warned. "Pellaeon's already three-quarters of the way to making my connection to the Cavrilhu Pirates and their associates. If he does a check and finds my sector fleet missing four Star Destroyers, he's going to be all over me."

"There's not much we can do about the timetable," Tierce reminded him. "The three heading to the Bothawui system won't be in attack position for several weeks."

"Then perhaps we should scrap the comet aspect," Disra said. "They can form up around some other marker."

"There isn't one," Tierce said patiently. "At least, nothing that would be safe for them to use. You'll just have to use your native charm to keep Pellaeon at bay."

"I'll do my best," Disra said sarcastically. "And what sort of charm would you suggest I use on Captain Zothip?"

"What's wrong with Captain Zothip?" Flim asked.

"Major Tierce called and told him we were cutting off their supply of clones," Disra growled. "Zothip is rather upset."

"We've been through this once already," Tierce said with an air of strained patience. "We need those clones ourselves now. Zothip has no cause to complain—he's benefited well enough from having them aboard his ships. Anyway, what are you worried about? That he'll come here and demand satisfaction?"

"You don't know Zothip," Disra said heavily.

"He's scum from the fringe," Tierce said, dismissing the pirate with a twist of his lip. "Buy him off or calm him down—I don't care which."

"I'm less worried about Zothip than I am about your attitude," Disra countered. "From now on, major decisions like this are going to be made jointly. I won't have you tearing down things I've built and then handing me the pieces to put back together."

For a long moment Tierce just looked at him. "Let's get one thing straight right now, Disra," he said at last, his voice icy smooth. "I'm in command of the military aspects of this operation. All of them. That's what you offered me, and that's what I'm taking. Your part right now—your only part right now—is to supply the ships and men I need, and to handle any political aspects that crop up."

Disra glared again at him. But it was a glare whose edge he could feel blunting. Just what sort of monster had he created here? "Is that all I am to you?" he asked Tierce quietly. "Your supply officer?"

Tierce smiled, a cold twitch of the corner of his lip. "Afraid you've lost control of this scheme you've created? Don't be. My goal here—my only goal—is to avenge the Emperor's death and wipe the Rebellion off every map of the galaxy. After that, my job is done. Ruling the new Empire that emerges will be entirely up to you."

For a moment Disra eyed him, trying to read past his stony expression, trying not to let wishful thinking color his judgment. If the man was lying . . .

No. Tierce was a soldier; an uncommonly good one, but a soldier nonetheless. He had nowhere near the political skills or experience Disra himself possessed. Even if he grew to like the taste of power, he would still need Disra after the fighting was over.

"Most triumvirates are unstable, Your Excellency," Flim spoke up. "I know; I've seen many of them rise and collapse among pirate and smuggler organizations in the fringe. But this one is different. None of us can make it work without both of the others."

"He's right," Tierce agreed. "So shut up your whining and do your part. Or it'll be penal colonies for all of us."

"Agreed," Disra said reluctantly. "My apologies, Major. It won't happen again."

"Good," Tierce said briskly. "Back to business. I'm going to need a copy of the decryption algorithm you used to slice into the Emperor's and Thrawn's private records."

Disra frowned. "What for?"

"So that I can pull a complete list of the sleeper cells Thrawn planted around the Rebellion," Tierce explained. "We're going to need all the trained Imperial soldiers and pilots we can get our hands on."

That seemed reasonable enough. "All right," Disra said. "But I can pull the list for you."

"It would be useful if I could get into those files myself whenever I needed to," Tierce pointed out.

"It would also be useful for me to know a few things that you don't," Disra countered. "For the sake of balance and all."

Tierce shook his head. "Fine. Go ahead and play your little games. Just get me that list."

Disra inclined his head in an ironic bow. "Immediately, Major."

No, there would be no more outbursts, Disra decided as he walked back across the office to the secret tunnel. But that didn't mean he wouldn't keep a close eye on his partners in this triumvirate. And if they both still needed him, the time might well come when he no longer needed them.

It was something to think about.

CHAPTER

6

She was short, she was furry, she was loud, and she was determined to sell him a melon. "Sorry," Wedge Antilles said, moving away as best he could in the press of the crowded Morishim marketplace, holding his hands palms outward in front of him. "Not interested in wk'ou melons today, thanks."

Either the female Morish didn't understand Basic or else she wasn't ready to concede defeat quite yet. She followed along with him behind her produce table, paralleling his retreat, thrusting the double-bulbous, pale red melon toward him and jabbering away nonstop in her own language. "Not today," Wedge repeated firmly, looking around and trying to catch a glimpse of any of his Rogue Squadron teammates in the crowd of shoppers. Janson and Tycho were supposed to know a little of the Morish language, but neither of them was anywhere to be seen.

But there was a gap freshly opened up in the pedestrian traffic pattern beside him. "Maybe tomorrow," he called to the wk'ou seller, and made his escape.

"For a big bad X-wing warrior, you're sure rotten at saying no," Janson's voice said from behind him.

"I didn't buy it, did I?" Wedge countered, turning to face his grinning teammate. "Where were you when I needed you?"

"Oh, I caught most of the show," Janson said, grinning a little wider. "I especially liked the part where you gave her that palms-outward sign."

Wedge felt his eyes narrow. "That doesn't mean 'no' here?"

"Not quite," Janson said, clearly enjoying himself. "It means you don't want it at that price but that she might want to try a better offer."

"Oh, well, thanks for telling me that going in," Wedge growled. "No wonder she wouldn't leave me alone."

"It's a big galaxy," Janson said philosophically. "There's so much out there to learn. Come on—I ran into an old friend of yours over here."

"As long as he doesn't try to sell me something," Wedge grumbled as Janson led the way through the shoppers. "Any word from the base?"

"Hardly," Janson said over his shoulder. "The meeting only started half an hour ago. With a general of Bel Iblis's standing, they probably haven't even gotten through the preliminary compliments yet. Here we go. Hey—General!"

A few people away a distinguished-looking man in a black cloak turned around—

"Well, well," Wedge said, easing through the passersby and offering his hand. "General Calrissian."

"It's just plain Calrissian now," Lando Calrissian corrected, tucking the wk'ou melon he was carrying under one arm and gripping Wedge's hand. "My military days are long behind me. Good to see you again, Wedge."

"You, too," Wedge said. "What are you doing in this part of the galaxy?"

"Hoping for a chance to talk to General Bel Iblis," Lando said, nodding his head back toward the pyramidal launch towers of the New Republic Starfighter Base rising up behind the city. "We have got to do something about the pirate activity we've been getting out near Varn."

"Been hitting your ore shipments, have they?" Wedge asked.

"That, and scaring away potential customers," Lando

said. "I don't know if you knew I added a casino and observation gallery to the *Deep Pockets*."

"Sounds like a really big draw," Janson said dryly.

"You'd be surprised how interesting underwater mining is to watch," Lando told him. "Actually, at full capacity the casino could probably pay the overhead for the whole operation all by itself. But not if everyone's afraid to come there."

"Pirate gangs have been coming out of the stonework just about everywhere," Wedge agreed. "Even in the Core systems. Have you tried talking to Coruscant?"

"Till my voice gave out," Lando said sourly. "Didn't gain me a thing. The bureaucratic bit-sorters there are as bad as the ones we had under the Empire."

Janson snorted. "Some of them are the same ones."

"This latest policy reorganization should help," Wedge said, trying to steer the conversation away from what was a permanent sore point for him and his Rogue Squadron comrades. "Shifting the bulk of political power back down to system and sector levels is definitely the way to go. The Empire already proved the centralized approach doesn't work."

He looked up at the clear blue sky overhead. "Funny, isn't it, how things wind up. I remember when being in a system this close to the edge of Imperial space meant you slept in your X-wing. Instead, here we are, strolling along like we were on Svivren or Ord Mantell."

"I wouldn't get too overconfident if I were you," Janson warned. "The Empire isn't exactly dead yet. They could still deliver a pretty good punch if they wanted to."

"And they've looked like they were ready to throw in their cards before," Lando added. "Remember what things were like just before Grand Admiral Thrawn came back from wherever it was he'd been hiding?"

"Wedge?" a voice called over the din. "Hey—Wedge!"

Wedge peered over the crowd, caught a glimpse of tousled light brown hair, and lifted a hand. "Over here."

"Who's that?" Lando asked, craning his neck to peer over the crowd.

"His name's Tycho Celchu," Wedge told him. "One of

my Rogue Squadron people. I don't know if you ever met him."

Tycho reached them. "Hey, Wedge, you've got to come hear this guy," he said, his voice and face dark. "Come on—he's over here."

He led them through the marketplace to a small booth with a wizened Morish hunched over it. "Here he is," Tycho said, gathering the others in front of the booth. *"W'simi p'rotou?"*

"M'rish'kavish f'oril," the Morish wheezed. *"M'shisht C'aama', por kri'vres'mi B'oth."*

Janson whistled softly. "What is it?" Wedge asked.

"He says new information's just been dug up about the destruction of Caamas," Tycho said grimly. "And that it was the Bothans who were responsible."

Wedge stared at Tycho. "You must be joking," he said.

"Do I look like I'm joking?" Tycho bit out, a fire in his blue eyes. "Figures, doesn't it? Endor, Borleias, and now this."

"Take it easy," Wedge said, putting some parade-ground steel into his voice. "Borleias wasn't really the Bothans' fault."

Tycho's shoulders shifted uneasily. "Not all of it, anyway," he conceded grudgingly.

Wedge looked at Lando. "Have you heard anything about fresh Caamas information?"

"Not a whisper," Lando said, eyeing the Morish suspiciously. "Ask him where he heard it."

"Right." Tycho spoke to the Morish again, got an answer. "He says it came from the Old Recluse," he translated. "He lives up in a cave in the High Tatmana. Apparently knows everything about what goes on in the galaxy."

Wedge turned and looked up at the Tatmana Mountains, rising in a saw-toothed crest in the distance on the opposite side of the city from the New Republic base. On the face of it, it was absurd to think that some old native hermit would have any idea what was even going on in the city down here, let alone in the larger galaxy above his mountains.

But on the other hand, Wedge had hung around Luke

Skywalker long enough to know that there were a lot of unexplainable things in the galaxy. Maybe this Old Recluse was one of those latent Force-users Luke was always trying to find.

And it wasn't like they were exactly busy right now, anyway. "Ask him where we can find this Old Recluse," he instructed Tycho.

"You going up there?" Lando asked as Tycho began talking to the Morish again. "What in the worlds for?"

"Curiosity," Wedge told him. "We've got time—the general won't be needing us for at least a few more hours. You coming?"

Lando sighed. "Lead the way."

Leaning slightly into the steady wind, the three X-wings settled smoothly onto the bluff overlooking the city. "Easy for *you*," Lando muttered under his breath, mentally gauging the chunk of space they'd left him to put the *Lady Luck* down onto. It would be tight, but pride alone dictated he not back out now. Muttering some more, he eased the yacht down toward the bluff.

It was indeed a tight squeeze, made all the trickier by the wind. But he managed it without too much trouble and, more important, without any embarrassment. Dropping the engines into their standby settings, he climbed down the ladder just aft of the cockpit bridge and headed for the yacht's hatchway.

Wedge, Janson, and Tycho were waiting for him at the foot of the *Lady Luck*'s ramp. "Chilly up here," he commented, gripping the edge of his cloak to keep it from flapping. "I hope the Old Recluse's cave is heated."

"At least it'll be out of this wind," Janson agreed, pointing toward a narrow, two-meter-high crack in the cliff face. "That must be it. Let's go."

The cave was much deeper than Lando would have guessed from the relatively small size of the entrance. It was also surprisingly warm. "Looks like a glow up ahead,"

Wedge said, his voice sounding odd in the enclosed space.
"Around that bend."

"I wonder if we should announce ourselves," Lando
said, glancing around uneasily. Flying in cramped spaceships
had never bothered him in the least, but walking down a
narrow passageway with the top of a mountain weighing
down on him was something else entirely.

Or maybe it was that the place reminded him too much
of the inside of Mount Tantiss. Either way, as they rounded
the corner, he found his right hand resting on the grip of his
holstered blaster.

Which made the scene that opened up in front of them
just that much more anticlimactic. Sitting at the back of a
widened section of the cave was a single ancient Morish,
even older than the one they'd talked to at the booth, medi-
tatively plucking the stretched wires of some kind of musical
instrument. To his right was a squat military-surplus worklight; to his left, an antique wood brazier. On both sides of
the cave, only vaguely touched by the worklight's glow,
were a collection of objects that were apparently the Old
Recluse's household goods. At his back, not quite covering
the cave's back wall, was a hand-decorated curtain of heavy-
looking cloth.

If the Old Recluse was surprised to see them, he didn't
show it. He studied them for a moment in silence as they
stepped to within a couple of meters of him, then dropped
his gaze back to his instrument and muttered something in
his own language.

"He's greeting us," Tycho translated. "Sort of. He also
demands to know what we want."

"Tell him we've heard he knows something about the
destruction of Caamas," Wedge said. "We'd like to hear
more."

"He'll want money," Janson warned.

"Right," Tycho agreed. "Try offering him fifty."

The Morish stirred. "Three hundred," he said in clear
and nearly unaccented Basic. "This story is worth three hundred."

"Well, well," Wedge said dryly. "So much for local

color. I thought they probably spoke more Basic than they were letting on. I'll give you one hundred."

"Three hundred," the Old Recluse insisted. "Or no story."

"One-fifty," Wedge offered. "New Republic currency. All I have on me."

"Three hundred. No less."

"I'll cover it," Lando spoke up, looking around the cave. There was something odd about this place. Something that was triggering some very unpleasant memories . . .

"All right," Wedge sighed. "Three hundred it is. But this had better be worth it."

"It is," the Old Recluse assured him. "As the dark battle fleet assembled outside Caamas—"

And suddenly it clicked in the back of Lando's mind. Stepping around behind the brazier, he got a grip on the edge of the curtain—

"*Ka'alee!*" the Morish screeched, tossing aside his musical instrument and lunging toward the worklight. His hand darted beneath it—

"Freeze it!" Wedge snapped. All three Rogue Squadron pilots had dropped into combat crouches, blasters in their hands and steady on the Morish. "Bring your hand out," Wedge ordered. "Empty."

Slowly, glaring at them, the Old Recluse pulled his hand back out. Janson circled over to the worklight and crouched down beside it, coming up with a small but nasty-looking blaster. "All right," Wedge said as Janson returned to Tycho's side. "Now you just sit there and be good. And keep your hands where we can see them." Holstering his blaster, he walked around behind his teammates and came over to Lando. "What did you find?"

"The source of his omniscience," Lando said grimly, pulling the curtain aside. "Take a look."

Wedge whistled softly under his breath; and even Lando, who had more or less known what to expect, had to admit he was impressed. Crammed into a wide floor-to-ceiling crack in the back wall of the cave was a fully functioning Imperial communications center, complete with encrypt/decrypt modules, the input jacks for a variety of droids and sensor feeds, a space/planetary monitor module, and a self-contained Generations III power generator. "Well, well," Wedge commented. "Nice find, Lando. What tipped you off?"

"The smell," Lando told him, an involuntary shiver running through him. "Dusty electronics have a smell like nothing else in the universe. The Spaarti cylinder chamber in the Mount Tantiss storehouse was reeking with it."

"Probably set this place up just before we took Morishim back from them," Janson suggested. "Must have used it to spy on the base."

"And for propaganda and incitement of the locals," Wedge said, pushing aside the curtain for a closer look. "There's a direct feed to the Imperial news service here. *And* a direct feed to Coruscant Hourly."

"Might be interesting to have someone go back through the recent history records," Lando said. "See if we can spot their hand in events."

"Yes," Wedge agreed. "They must have abandoned it in a hurry to have left this much stuff behind . . ."

He trailed off, frowning at the space monitor display. "Tycho, get out to your X-wing and give the base a call. Looks like we've got a Corellian Corvette coming in. Broadcasting an Imperial ID—"

Abruptly he stiffened. "Belay that," he snapped, dropping the curtain and charging past the Old Recluse. "Get to your fighters—double-time."

The others fell into step behind him, the group disappearing around the bend in the tunnel. "What is it?" the Old Recluse demanded anxiously. "You—human—what is it?"

A single look at the display was all Lando needed. "It's an Imperial Star Destroyer," he said. "It dropped in right behind the Corvette.

"Heading this way."

"Lando?" Wedge's voice came from the *Lady Luck*'s console. "You reading me?"

"Loud and clear," Lando said, making one last adjustment to the speaker control.

"Stay close," Wedge warned. "This freq-mixing trick won't work against their jamming if we get too far apart."

"Got it," Lando said, eyeing the confused readouts from his comm board. His comm system was pretty much state-of-the-art, with a few exotic add-ons besides, but it wasn't really set up to deal with New Republic military frequencies and encrypts. But so far the jury-rig he'd thrown together on the fly seemed to be holding. "What's happening?"

"I got through to the base while you were getting set up," Wedge said. "The rest of Rogue Squadron's on the way, along with every starfighter the base can scramble."

A couple of wings of X-wings and A-wings, against an Imperial Star Destroyer. Terrific. "What about the *Peregrine* and the Assault Frigate that Admiral Vriss came in with?"

"The *Peregrine*'s on its way, but it's having to come from around the far side of the planet," Wedge said, an edge of contempt creeping into the cool professionalism in his voice. "The Assault Frigate, unfortunately, is going to be out of it. Apparently, they let the systems drop a little too far past standby."

"Sloppy," Lando grunted. "Who's in command?"

"A committee of Bagmims," Wedge told him. "The crew is mostly Bagmims, humans, and Povanarians."

"Bagmims are pretty good fighters when they get riled."

"They should have stayed more riled, then," Wedge said. "Right now, they're just a waste of air."

"Too late to worry about it now," Lando said, carefully refraining from reminding Wedge about his own earlier comments on how much more relaxed things had become. "What's the plan?"

"We try to slow them down," Wedge said. "The *Peregrine*'s on its way, and the general's got two Star Cruisers coming from Haverling. Until they get here, we're on our own."

The three X-wings and the yacht rose above the curve of Morishim's horizon; and there they were: the awe-inspiring

bulk of the Imperial Star Destroyer with the Corvette leading it toward the planet.

And then Lando frowned. "Wedge?"

"I see it," Wedge murmured. "Rogue Seven, give me a
fast analysis."

"No mistake, Rogue Leader," Tycho's voice came
promptly. "Those aren't accidental misfires—the Star Destroyer's definitely targeting the Corvette. The Corvette's
running flank speed, with full aft deflector shields. She's being chased, all right."

"They're jamming her transmissions, too," Janson
added. "Course projection shows she's making straight for
the edge of the base's energy shield. Looks like we've got a
theft-and-defection on our hands."

"Could be," Wedge said cautiously. "It could also be a
trick to get us to let an unexamined ship in under the energy
shield."

"So what do we do?" Janson asked.

"Let's try running a little interference," Wedge said.
"Rogue Two, Rogue Five: cut in around the Corvette's starboard side and see if you can draw some of the Star Destroyer's attention. I'll take the other side. Watch out for
tractor beams—they may try to pull the Corvette in."

"Copy, Rogue Leader."

The two X-wings swerved smoothly away from Wedge
and Lando. "What about me?" Lando asked.

"Better stay back here," Wedge told him, putting on a
burst of speed of his own. "That yacht isn't designed for this
sort of maneuvering. Anyway, we may need you to act as
relay between us and our reinforcements."

The words were barely out of his mouth when there was
a sort of muffled flash from the Corvette, accompanied by a
cloud of debris. "Topside sensor group's been hit," Janson
reported. "Internal fire—probably going to have to shut
down the main reactor core."

Which meant no drive, no shields, and no hope of escape. Lando swore under his breath, keying his secondary
comm system to scan across the channels. Static hissed out at
him at each of the frequencies the Imperials were jamming.

"Tractor beam activated," Tycho said tightly. "Making connection . . . they've got her."

"Incoming to aft," Janson cut in. "The rest of Rogue Squadron, plus three wings of A-wings and two of X-wings. ETA, about four minutes."

Wedge's sigh was a softer echo of the jamming hiss. "Too little, too late," he said reluctantly. "Break off. There's nothing we can do to help them now."

Lando looked out at the Corvette, tapping a frustrated fist gently against the edge of his control board. Muzzled and helpless both, the Corvette would be taken or destroyed without anyone knowing who they were or what they were doing here.

Unless . . .

"Wedge?" he called. "I've got an idea. Fire up all the transmission frequencies the three of you can handle—full power, with all the encryption you can put on them. Maybe we can dilute their jamming enough to at least get something out of the Corvette."

"Worth a try," Wedge said. "Let's do it, Rogues."

Lando swiveled around to the comm board, keying in one of those exotic add-ons he'd spent all that good money for. This probably wouldn't work. Almost certainly wouldn't work, in fact; and the effort alone might easily irritate the Imperials into taking a lethal swipe at him. But at least it was doing *something*. He stared at the comm readings, holding his breath . . .

And then, to even his gambler's amazement, there was a flicker of something through the static. "Keep it up," he shouted to Wedge and the others, keying madly at the board. The flicker strengthened, faded, strengthened again . . .

It cut off suddenly. Lando looked up just in time to catch a final glimpse of pseudomotion as the Star Destroyer vanished into hyperspace. "Well, that's that," Tycho said.

"I wasn't watching," Lando said. "Did they take the Corvette with them?"

"Pulled it into the bay and took straight off," Wedge told him. "You get anything?"

"I don't know." Lando keyed for replay. "Let's see."

There was a burst of static; and then, almost buried beneath the hissing, a few faint words could be heard. "—is Colo . . . . zh Ver . . . . ecial envoy fro . . . . miral . . . . on, sent here . . . . . ontact Gen . . . . . . el Iblis concern . . . . ego . . . . ce tre . . . be . . . . Empire and New Repub . . . . under atta . . . . traitorous ele . . . . the Empire . . . . do not expect . . . . . urvive. If the New Re . . . . to hold su . . . . ions, Adm . . . . Pel . . . . at the aban . . . . mining cent . . . . itiin in . . . . nth to meet wi . . . . peating: This is . . . . . nel Me . . . . Vermel . . ."

The recording ended. "Not much there," Wedge commented.

"No," Lando conceded. "What now?"

"You'd better head back and get that recording to General Bel Iblis," Wedge said. "I think we'll stay out here a little while longer."

"In case this was just the first act?" Lando suggested.

"You never know."

Lando gazed out at where the Corvette had lost its race for safety, an unpleasant chill running up his spine. The whole thing was very similar—disturbingly similar, in fact—to the race Princess Leia Organa's consular ship had lost to Darth Vader's Star Destroyer above the planet Tatooine nearly two decades ago. It had been a pivotal point in the struggle against the Empire's tyranny, though no one had known it at the time.

And now, here over Morishim, the same scene had just been played out again. Could there have been something of equal consequence behind it? "Wedge?"

"Yes?"

"There weren't, by any chance"—Lando hesitated, afraid this was going to sound silly—"any escape pods jettisoned from the Corvette?"

"Actually, that's the first thing I thought of," Wedge told him soberly. "But no, there weren't."

"Didn't think so," Lando said, shaking away the memories of the past. History never truly repeated itself, after all. Odds were that Janson had already called it: a simple theft-and-defection.

The odds also were that none of them would ever know for sure.

Officially, the planet was named Muunilinst; unofficially, it was known to many as Moneylend. And if Bastion was the political center of the Empire, Muunilinst was its financial core.

The reasons for its status were many and varied, a long history that dated back well into the days of the Old Republic. The fact that it still retained its role in these darker times was as much a triumph of inertia and habit as it was the two Golan III Defense Platforms tracing their lazy orbits high overhead.

Standing at the conference-room window, Pellaeon glanced up as one of the platforms passed in front of Muunilinst's sun, momentarily dimming its light. Back when the Imperial capital was moved to Bastion, he remembered, Moff Disra had tried to get those two Golan IIIs transferred there as well, arguing that the Empire's governmental center deserved the protection more than the credit shufflers did. It had been one of Disra's rare miscalculations, and one of his most embarrassing political defeats.

Behind Pellaeon, someone coughed discreetly. "Yes?" Pellaeon asked, turning again to face the table.

All six of the senior officers gathered around the table were looking back at him. "I presume, Admiral," High General Sutt Ramic said quietly, "that this is not simply a trial suggestion. You and the Moffs have already agreed on this offer, haven't you?"

For a moment Pellaeon studied the other's face. General Ramic, commander of one of the Golans up there, was the senior man of the Muunilinst defense setup, in experience and respect as well as in rank. If he chose to resist the proposed peace agreement, the others would most likely fall in line behind him.

But no. The question hadn't been a challenge, merely a question. "The Moffs have approved it, yes," he said. "For what it's worth, they were no more pleased by the idea than any of the rest of us are."

"I thought you were the one who made the proposal," General Jaron Kyte put in, his voice and eyes dark with suspicion. "How can you say now that you oppose it?"

"I didn't say I opposed it," Pellaeon corrected him. "I said I didn't like it. But in my professional judgment, we simply have no other options left."

"I was under the impression we had revolutionary new systems and equipment ready to come on-line," Ramic said.

With perfect timing one of the lights on Pellaeon's comm blinked on. "Some of those systems haven't proved as workable as their designers had hoped," Pellaeon said, stepping to his seat and leaning over to tap the confirmation button. "As for the equipment, some of it has been tainted by decidedly treasonous activity." Across from Pellaeon the conference door slid open—

And a lean man wearing the traditional Muunilinsti banker's shawl and pendant stepped inside.

His reaction to the roomful of officers might have been interesting, but Pellaeon wasn't watching him. His eyes were instead on the officers themselves, as their expressions of surprise or indignation at his veiled accusation were interrupted by this unexpected intrusion. They turned, most of them obviously irritated, to see who it was who had presumed to intrude on Fleet business.

And midway down the left side of the table, General Kyte twitched.

It wasn't a big reaction, little more than a twitch of the head and a flicker of shock across his face before he got himself back under control. But set against the backdrop of the others' more or less indifferent curiosity, it stood out like the guidelight on a landing bay.

"Ah, Lord Graemon," Pellaeon said, focusing on the

banker at last. "Thank you for coming. If you'll wait in the other room there, I'll be with you shortly."

"As you wish, Admiral Pellaeon," Graemon said. His eyes, Pellaeon noted, flicked once to Kyte as he crossed to the inner chamber and disappeared inside.

"And what was that all about?" Ramic asked.

The man was shrewd, all right; clearly, he'd recognized that the banker's interruption wasn't entirely a coincidence. "I was speaking of treason," Pellaeon said, waving a hand toward the inner chamber. "Lord Graemon is one of the threads in that web."

A fresh ripple of surprise ran around the rest of the table, but Ramic himself didn't even twitch. "You can prove this?" he demanded.

"Enough of it," Pellaeon said. "He's one of the money men helping funnel Imperial funds to a consortium that's building the Preybirds that are now supplementing the more traditional TIE-class starfighters aboard our ships."

"I don't see any treason in that," someone snorted. "Seems to me that the Empire's getting its money's worth with those Preybirds."

"The treason is in the fact that the deal has been made outside proper channels," Pellaeon said. "And in the fact that certain high Imperial officials are siphoning off a significant percentage of those funds for their own personal gain."

Deliberately, he turned his gaze on Kyte. "And in the fact that the deal includes the supplying of Imperial equipment and personnel to various pirate gangs."

Kyte held his gaze without flinching, but his face paled just noticeably. Pellaeon knew, all right; and now Kyte knew that he knew.

"And how do you expect your treaty with the New Republic to stop this?" Ramic asked.

"Cooperation and open lines of communication would enable us to track down the participants more efficiently," Pellaeon said. "And those participants would no longer be able to pretend they were merely doing the Empire's business in their own, shall we say, creative way."

"Then you suspect some in the Fleet are involved?" one of the others asked.

"I don't suspect," Pellaeon said. "I know."

For a long moment no one spoke. Pellaeon let the silence linger and harden, then gestured to the datapads in front of them. "But that's not the issue here today. The issue is the proposed peace treaty, and whether you will support it. I suggest we adjourn for an hour so that you'll have time to consider all the ramifications. Discuss it among yourselves if you like; I'll be here if you have any questions you wish to ask privately."

He looked at each of them in turn. "At the end of that hour we'll reconvene, and I'll expect your answers. Any final questions? Very well, then; dismissed."

He turned again to the window, his back to the table, as they gathered their datapads and datacards and exited quietly from the room. The door slid shut, and Pellaeon took a careful breath. "Your comments?" he asked, turning around again.

Ramic hadn't moved from his seat. "I disagree completely," the high general said bluntly. "The New Republic is going to self-destruct—you know it and I know it. The only questions are how violent the explosion will be and whether the trigger will be this Caamas thing we keep hearing about or something else. There's no need for us to humiliate ourselves in front of aliens and alien-lovers this way."

"I understand your position," Pellaeon said. "Is that your final word?"

Ramic's thin lips compressed briefly. "I don't support your treaty, Admiral," he said, standing up. "But I'm an Imperial officer, and I will obey my superiors. You and the Moffs have agreed; if and when the order to cease hostilities is given, I will obey it."

Some of the weight on Pellaeon's shoulders eased a bit. "Thank you, General," he said quietly.

"Thank my family and its history of proud service," Ramic countered. "They're the ones who installed the sense of duty and loyalty in me." He dropped his gaze to the table and set about gathering together his datacards. "Do you think the New Republic will accept your offer of a meeting?"

"We'll find out soon enough," Pellaeon said. "Colonel Vermel should be reaching the Morishim system just about now."

"Yes," Ramic murmured. He started for the door; paused and turned back. "You're certain there are pirate gangs involved in all this?"

"There's no doubt at all," Pellaeon assured him. "From what I've been able to piece together, they're being hired to attack specified New Republic shipments. They get the booty; the Empire gets a degree of confusion and consternation in the New Republic; and the shadow partners, knowing which shipments are going to be hit, make money on the business and commodity exchanges."

Ramic shrugged. "Aside from that last, it sounds like perfectly reasonable privateer activity."

"Perhaps," Pellaeon conceded. "The problem is that the ultimate decisions on which shipments are to be hit are coming from the shadow partners, not the High Command or Imperial Intelligence. And there are also strong indications that the sleeper cells Grand Admiral Thrawn set up are being raided to provide crewers for the gangs."

"If those alleged sleeper cells really exist," Ramic rumbled. "I've never been convinced of that myself."

"If the troopers aren't from the sleeper cells, then the conspirators are getting them from somewhere else," Pellaeon said. "The only other choice is that they're siphoning them off from the regular line forces."

Ramic's face hardened. "If they're doing that, I'll personally help you flay the perpetrators. We don't have enough troopers and crewers as it is." His eyes narrowed slightly. "And which of us do you suspect of being in on it with Lord Graemon?"

"General Kyte was the only one who reacted to his entrance," Pellaeon said. "As such, he's my prime suspect. With luck, he may panic and lead my Intelligence team to some of the others involved."

"Kyte won't panic," Ramic said. "But he might think it wise to alert them."

"Either way will suit me," Pellaeon said. "Now, if you'll excuse me, I need to spend a few minutes with Lord Graemon."

"Pulling on another thread of the web?"

Pellaeon smiled grimly. "Something like that. I'll see you and the others in an hour."

"Very well, sir." For a moment Ramic studied his face. "I'd advise you to be careful, though. Every web has something nasty in the middle . . . and whoever's in the middle of this one could well decide that with a peace treaty in the works the Empire doesn't need a Supreme Fleet Commander anymore. Especially one who's pulling pieces out of his web."

Pellaeon looked over at the room where Lord Graemon waited. "Yes," he said quietly. "That thought has occurred to me."

The secret door slid open, and Disra looked up as Tierce strode into the room. "Well?" he demanded. "Did you get through to Dorja?"

"Finally, yes." Tierce nodded. "He reports the mission was more or less successful."

" 'More or less'?"

Tierce shrugged. "Dorja said he had full-spectrum jamming going from the moment he emerged from hyperspace, but that some of Colonel Vermel's signal might have gotten through before they took his Corvette aboard."

Disra hissed between his teeth. "Sloppy."

"That observation has already been expressed to him by our Grand Admiral," Tierce said. "Apparently there were some X-wings and an unidentified yacht off Morishim that happened to be hanging around the Corvette's incoming vector when he dropped out of hyperspace."

Disra snorted. "In my experience, X-wings don't just 'happen' to hang around places."

"I agree," Tierce said. "My guess is that they spotted the

incoming ships somehow and went out to take a look. Possibly using the old Imperial spy center we abandoned on the surface, though how they would have located it I don't know."

"Did Dorja have any idea how much of Vermel's message might have gotten through?"

"A few words at the most," Tierce assured him. "And that assumes one or more of the nearby ships even had the right equipment, which is unlikely."

Disra pondered. "Yes," he conceded. "And even if they did, a few words aren't going to grab anyone's attention. No one who counts, anyway."

"Especially considering how many other crises are about to come down on their heads," Tierce agreed.

"Right," Disra said. "What did you have Dorja do with the ship and crew?"

"He's currently en route back here, doing a quick interrogation on the way. Most of the crew, I suspect, will have had no idea what Vermel's mission was; those we can bring back into service with vague intimations that Vermel was up to some sort of treason. As for Vermel himself—" He shrugged. "I thought we'd lock him up somewhere quiet for the moment. We might find a use for him later."

"Sounds reasonable," Disra said. "Any word from Trazzen and the others?"

"We've received their last scheduled report," Tierce said. "They'll be out of contact from now on until summoned."

"Um," Disra grunted. Everything seemed to be going according to plan.

And yet, this whole thing with Vermel and his possibly leaked message bothered him somehow. Surely no one could have caught any of it; and even if they had, surely they would dismiss it out of hand as smugglers or a simple theft-and-defection attempt gone bad. "It occurs to me, Major," he said slowly, "that perhaps we ought to push up our timetable a little. Just in case."

There was a long moment of silence. "I suppose that would be possible," Tierce said. "But I really don't think it's necessary. No one's going to pay any attention to the incident over Morishim."

Disra stared hard at him. "You're certain of that?"

Tierce smiled thinly. "I guarantee it."

The recording ran through to the end for the third time, and finally General Garm Bel Iblis shut it off. "About as clear as roiled mud," he commented to Lando. "Still, I would have bet you couldn't have gotten even this much through all that jamming. Very nicely done."

"I just wish we'd gotten more," Lando said. "Janson figured it was probably a theft-and-defection gone wrong."

"Yes, it does look that way," Bel Iblis said, fingering his mustache thoughtfully. "But somehow I don't think it was."

Lando eyed him. "Then what was it?"

"I don't know yet," Bel Iblis said. "But consider the facts. The Empire hasn't got nearly enough Imperial Star Destroyers left to waste one on a simple chase mission. *And* they wanted him taken alive; *and* they wanted to make sure he didn't talk to anyone."

"And he knew you were here," Lando pointed out. "You can almost hear the words 'General Bel Iblis' in there."

"Yes," Bel Iblis agreed. "Though keeping track of my whereabouts is no big deal anymore. We don't keep things nearly as secret as we did even five years ago."

He swiveled over his computer and began punching keys. "It seems to me you can also hear the name 'Vermel' mentioned. If I remember right, there was an Imperial officer of that name on Admiral Pellaeon's staff."

Lando looked out the viewport at the curve of the planet below, and at the distant flares of the X-wings still circling around in the distance. "Seems to me that would add weight to the defection theory," he suggested. "They wouldn't want to kill someone of that rank out of hand, and they certainly wouldn't want us to know he'd tried it."

"Perhaps." Bel Iblis peered at the display. "Yes, there he is. Colonel Meizh Vermel."

Lando spread his hands. "There it is, then."

Bel Iblis fingered his mustache again. "No," he said slowly. "My instincts still say no. Why use a Corellian Corvette if you were going to defect? Why not something faster or more heavily armed? Or requiring a smaller crew, unless all hundred-odd crewers were defecting together?"

"I don't know."

"I don't know either." Bel Iblis slid out the datacard of Lando's recording. "But I think I'll make a few copies of this and see if I can find out."

Lando cocked an eyebrow. "In all your copious spare time?"

The general shrugged. "I've been needing a hobby anyway."

CHAPTER

7

The Grand Convocation Chamber of the New Republic Senate had been completed only three months earlier, its construction stepped up out of necessity after Kueller's bombs had weakened the structure of the old Senate Hall beyond repair. And while there were still bits of trim and scrollwork left to be finished, the overall effect was every bit as impressive as its designers had promised. The old arrangement—with the delegates' seats arranged in concentric semicircles, descending inward toward a raised dais—had been replaced by a series of variably sized, variably shaped blocks of seats, connected to each other by short stairways or ramps that had been arranged at apparent random, yet which maintained a consistent grace and style. Separating the seat groups were clear glass panels, or carved lattices, or merely short railings and a meter or two of vertical height, as the designers' fancy had taken them. Each block of seats had an unobstructed view of the central dais, as well as a display that could be adjusted to show either a closer view of the dais or any of the other blocks of seats in the chamber.

In many ways the place reminded Leia of the magnificent Corioline Marlee theater back on Alderaan, a renowned palace of the arts that had always been synonymous in her mind with courtesy, culture, and civilization. It had been her secret hope that the Grand Chamber's similar design would help encourage those same qualities in the Senators who assembled there.

But for today, at least, that was clearly not going to be the case.

"Let me be certain I understand you, President Gavrisom," a rough Opquis voice called over the chamber's sound system. "You're telling us that the Bothans were the key to the destruction of Caamas and the near genocide committed against the Caamasi people. Yet at the same time you tell us you will not seek justice for this heinous act?"

"That is not at all what I have told you, Senator," President Ponc Gavrisom said mildly, twitching his tail once and resettling it against his hind legs. "Allow me to repeat. A small group—a *small* group—of as yet unidentified Bothans were involved in that tragedy. If and when we are able to learn their names, we will certainly dispense in full measure the justice I know we all seek. Until then, though, it simply cannot be done."

"Why not?" an alien with shaggy blue-green hair and a long, thin face demanded. A Forshul, Leia tentatively identified her, representing the eighty-seven inhabited worlds of Yminis sector in the Outer Rim. "Councilor Fey'lya does not deny Bothans were involved. Very well, then: let them be duly punished for this monstrous blot on galactic civilization."

Leia glanced across the dais at Borsk Fey'lya, seated at the far end of the curved row of High Councilors. The Bothan's expression and fur were under rigid control, but her Jedi senses had no trouble picking up the turmoil of anxiety behind his face. He'd had, she knew, a long conversation with the heads of the Combined Clans back on Bothawui just prior to this meeting. From the hardness of his expression, she guessed the conversation hadn't gone well.

"I understand your feelings, Senator," Gavrisom said. "However, I must point out that the legal guidelines of the New Republic are not the same as the traditional codes of Forshuliri justice." He unfolded his wings from across his long back and brought them in front of him. The prehensile feathertips touched one of the keys on the lectern, and a section of New Republic criminal law appeared on the display above his head. "Those guidelines do not allow us to penalize the entire Bothan people for the crimes of a few."

"And why do we not know the identities of those supposed few?" the Ishori Senator called out. "I see Councilor Fey'lya seated to your right. What has he to say about all this?"

Gavrisom turned his head to look over his withers at Fey'lya. "Councilor Fey'lya, do you wish to respond?"

Visibly bracing himself, the Bothan rose to his feet. "I understand the anger this revelation has elicited from many of you," he said. "I assure you that we of the Bothan clan leadership feel the same anger, and the same desire that the perpetrators of this terrible crime be brought to justice. And rest assured that if we knew exactly who those perpetrators were, we would long ago have dealt with them. The problem is that we do not."

There was a short, warbling scream. Reflexively, Leia jumped, belatedly identified the blood-chilling sound as the Ayrou equivalent of a skeptical snort. "Do you expect us to believe—?"

"President Gavrisom, I would ask you to once again remind the Senator from Moddell sector to shut up that noise!" another Senator interrupted angrily. "The harmonics have already caused me to lose two eggs this session, and if I cannot bear my yearly hatchlings on schedule, I will lose both my status and any possibility of reappointment by my sector assembly."

"Speaking for myself, that would be a relief," someone else put in before Gavrisom could respond. "Some of us are exceptionally tired of your precious eggs being used as an excuse for everything you don't like—"

Gavrisom's wingtips touched a key, and the voice was cut off as the sound system shut down. For another minute angry voices continued to be heard, echoing indistinctly from various quarters of the chamber, before finally falling reluctantly silent as the participants realized that none of their verbal jabs was getting through to the designated recipients. Gavrisom waited another few seconds before turning the sound system back on. "The prologue to the New Republic charter," he said quietly, "exhorts all member worlds to behave toward one another in an acceptable and civilized manner. Shall the members of this Senate be held to a lesser standard?"

"You speak of civilization, President Gavrisom," a tall Bagmim said darkly. "How can we of the New Republic Senate consider ourselves civilized if we do not show our repugnance for the horrible crime committed against the Caamasi?"

Leia cleared her throat. "May I remind the Senate," she said, "that whatever part any group of Bothans might have played, there is no indication any of them participated in the actual destruction of Caamas. *That*, it seems to me, should be the focal point of our outrage and justice."

"Do you seek then to excuse the Bothans?" a Senator she didn't recognize demanded.

"Besides which, the actual perpetrators were undoubtedly agents of then Senator Palpatine," someone else added from the opposite side of the chamber. "All such agents have surely been destroyed during our onerously long war against the Empire."

"Are you certain of that?" another voice chimed in. "We are still learning the full depth of Emperor Palpatine's deceptions against the peoples of the galaxy. Who is to say his agents don't yet walk among us?"

"Are you accusing one of *us*?"

"If you claim the title, what is that to me?" the other shot back. "There are still rumors of Imperial agents scattered among us—"

Again Gavrisom touched the cutoff switch, and again the debate was reduced to distant voices shouting uselessly at each other. Leia listened to the budding argument fade away, for the umpteenth time thanking the Force that she was at least temporarily no longer the one in charge of this madhouse.

The voices faded away into a tense silence. Gavrisom touched the key again. "I'm sure the Senator from Chorlian sector was speaking only figuratively," he said with his usual unflappable poise. "At any rate, this debate has already passed the point of usefulness and will therefore be suspended for now. If the document which Councilor Organa Solo brought back can be reconstructed to the point where names can be discovered, we will reopen the discussion. Until then, there are many other matters which require our attention."

He glanced at his display, then looked up to his right. "We will begin with the report of the Economics Committee. Senator Quedlifu?"

The Economics Committee report was longer than usual, with two bills being submitted to the full Senate for consideration. That in itself was fairly unusual: with each Senator limited to introducing one bill per year, and a straight up-down vote required to get that bill out of committee, most of the proposed legislation never found the support necessary to make it to the full Senate. Only a small fraction of those few, moreover, ever survived the Senate's scrutiny to actually become law.

Which was precisely how the system was supposed to work. With nearly a thousand Senators already—and with each one representing fifty to two hundred entire worlds—there was no possible way Coruscant could truly look after the interests of all the beings making up the New Republic. This latest modification of the Senate had reduced its role to little more than providing for the common defense and mediating disputes between member sectors. The more commonplace day-to-day governing was handled at the sector, system, planetary, regional, district, and local levels.

A few of the Senators, remembering the glory days of the Old Republic, occasionally grumbled about the Senate being reduced to what they saw as little more than an elaborate debating society. For the majority, though, the more vivid memory was that of Coruscant's domination during the dark days of the Empire. A relatively weak central government was exactly what they wanted.

As it turned out, the Economics Committee was the only one with any bills to introduce or, for that matter, anything really new to report. Gavrisom cycled through the rest of the committees with practiced ease and dispatch, bringing the meeting to a close less than two hours after it had begun.

And yet, even as Leia joined the flow of beings exiting from the chamber, she suspected that none of the Senators or High Councilors would be occupied with business as usual this afternoon. Caamas would be the thought on everyone's mind. Caamas, and justice.

Or perhaps vengeance.

"Your Highness?" a tentative voice called through the rumble of conversation.

Leia paused and lifted a hand. "Over here, Threepio."

"Ah," the droid said, making his tentative way across the traffic flow toward her. "I trust the assembly went well?"

"As well as can be expected, under the circumstances," Leia told him. "Any messages from the techs about the datacard?"

"I'm afraid not," Threepio said, sounding regretful. "But I do have a message from Captain Solo. He has returned, and will be waiting for you."

Leia felt her heartbeat pick up. "Did he say anything about his mission to Iphigin?"

"I'm afraid not," Threepio apologized again. "Should I have asked him?"

"No, that's all right," Leia assured him.

"He did not seem inclined to be overly conversational," the droid mused. "He may not have answered even if I had asked."

Leia smiled. "Probably not," she agreed, a hundred fond memories of her husband flashing through her mind. She'd been planning to head straight to her office to sift through some of the mountain of datawork waiting on her desk. Now, suddenly, she decided it could wait. Han would be waiting for her in their quarters—

"Councilor Organa Solo?" a voice said from her side.

Leia turned, a sinking feeling settling into her. The voice and mental profile . . .

And she was right. It was indeed Ghic Dx'ono, the Ishori Senator. "Yes, Senator Dx'ono?"

"I would speak with you, High Councilor," the other said firmly. "In your office. Now."

"Certainly," Leia said, her feeling sinking a little further. The alien's emotions indicated disquietude, but that was all she could read from it. "Come with me."

Together they made their way across the flow of beings, Threepio struggling to keep up, and into the curved side corridor where the members of the High Council had their offices. Leia caught a glimpse of Fey'lya as he disappeared into his office; then they rounded the curve—

Leia stopped short, a soft gasp escaping her lips before she could stop it. Preoccupied with her thoughts, and with Dx'ono's somewhat overpowering presence beside her, she hadn't extended her senses ahead down the corridor. Three people were standing outside her office door: one of Dx'ono's aides, and two slender beings completely shrouded in hooded cloaks.

"They wish to speak with you," Dx'ono said gruffly. "Will you speak with them?"

Leia swallowed, her memories flashing back to her childhood on Alderaan and the time her adoptive father Bail Organa had permitted her to go with him on a private trip to the South Islands . . .

"Yes," she told Dx'ono quietly. "I will be honored to speak with your Caamasi friends."

The way Senate meetings usually went, Han had expected to be stuck hanging around Leia's office for at least another hour before she returned. It was therefore to his mild surprise that he'd barely gotten comfortable in his wife's inner office when a flicker of displaced air pressure announced that the door from the outer office had just opened.

He swiveled his feet off the corner of her desk and

landed them quietly on the floor, getting up just as quietly from her chair and padding his way to the door that separated the sections of the office. In the old days, he would have tried to surprise her by jumping out and giving her a big hug and kiss. But her increasing Jedi skills had long since made trying to sneak up on her a pretty futile exercise.

Besides which, embarrassing her with some silly schoolkid prank would make her madder at him than she probably already was over the Iphigin thing. Especially if she'd brought company with her.

She had. With his ear pressed against the door, he could hear at least two other voices besides Leia's.

For a moment he stood there, waiting to see if she would either bring her visitors in or else invite him out to greet them. She certainly knew by now that he was in here. Unless she'd rather he keep out of sight completely . . .

And then, across the room at her desk, the intercom display abruptly came on.

"—understand that we have no desire to make trouble for anyone," someone was saying. "We do not wish vengeance, and it is far too late for justice."

Frowning, Han crossed back to the desk. So okay. Leia wanted him to listen in on the conversation, but didn't want him out there. Or didn't want whoever it was knowing they were being listened to.

And then he got his first close look at the display, and suddenly he understood her reticence. There were two Ishori out there . . . and two Caamasi.

"It is not a question of vengeance," one of the Ishori insisted. Probably a full Senator, Han decided, if the elaborate tangle of his shoulder clasp was any indication. "And it is never too late for justice."

"Yet what purpose would this so-named justice serve?" one of the Caamasi countered quietly. "Our world is destroyed, and we are few and scattered. Would punishing the Bothans miraculously make all right again?"

"Perhaps it would," the Ishori said, his voice starting to rise. Thinking hard and fast, with that trademark Ishori anger coming along with it. Han grimaced, the memory of his botched negotiation attempts at Iphigin nagging painfully at him. "If the Bothans were declared guilty and forced to make reparations—"

At the other side of the board, the comm pinged. Leia's private comm channel, Han noted with annoyance. Just when the conversation out there was starting to get interesting; but it was probably one of the kids, and he really ought to answer it. Flicking the intercom channel to record the rest of the conversation going on out there—which was probably illegal, but he didn't care—he muted the speaker volume and hit the comm key.

It wasn't the kids, or Winter, or even one of the Noghri. "Hello, Solo," Talon Karrde said. "I didn't expect to find you on this channel."

"Likewise," Han said, frowning at the smuggler. "How did you get this frequency?"

"Your wife gave it to me, of course," Karrde said, managing to look roguish and innocent at the same time. "I gave her a ride back here from Wayland in the *Wild Karrde*. I thought you knew."

"Yeah, I got a quick message from her about that," Han said. "I didn't know you'd conned her out of her private frequency, though."

Karrde smiled, then sobered. "We're all suddenly sitting on some highly explosive matters, my friend," he said. "Leia and I decided it might be useful for me to be able to contact her, shall we say, discreetly. Has she told you yet about the Caamas datacard we brought back from Wayland?"

Han's eyes flicked to the intercom display and the two Caamasi. "No, I haven't had a chance to talk to her since I got back," he said. "But as it happens she's got a pair of Caamasi in the outer office right now. Along with a couple of Ishori."

Karrde hissed softly between his teeth. "So the Ishori are getting involved. Which means the Diamala will undoubtedly be coming in on the other side."

"Oh, undoubtedly," Han agreed. "The other side of what?"

"I don't suppose it's much of a secret anymore," Karrde

said. "At least not on the exalted levels you circle in these days. I'm sure Leia will fill you in later, but the bottom line is that we've discovered it was a group of so far unidentified Bothans who sabotaged Caamas's shields on the eve of its destruction."

Han felt his stomach tighten. "Great," he growled. "Just great. There aren't enough people out there who hate the Bothans already. This is just what we need."

"I agree," Karrde said. "I hope the Senate is up to the task of keeping this under some semblance of control. The main reason I called was to tell Leia that our friend Mazzic has caught Lak Jit, the Devaronian who actually found the datacard. We've got him locked away, and I'll keep him there as long as she wants me to. Unfortunately, it appears he's already spread the news as far as his little feet and the flow of credits would take it. I don't think there's any chance of keeping this a private matter within the New Republic hierarchy."

"Yeah, well, things were going along too smooth anyway," Han said sourly. "Thanks."

"Anytime," Karrde said blandly. "You know I'm always at your service."

"That's good," Han said. "Because I've got another problem I'd like you to tackle."

"Certainly. Cash or account?"

"We had a little run-in with some pirates off Iphigin," Han said, ignoring the question. "Good-sized crowd: they had a *Kaloth* battlecruiser, a couple of Corellian gunships, and some Corsair starfighters."

"Well-equipped group," Karrde agreed. "On the other hand, you'd be a fool to hit a place like Iphigin without enough firepower to handle the job."

"It still surprised me a little," Han said. "But here's the kicker. Luke says the battlecruiser had clones aboard."

Karrde's expression didn't change, but the lines at the corners of his eyes tightened noticeably. "Does he, now," he said. "Any idea what kind of clones?"

"He didn't say," Han said. "You ever hear of a pirate gang running with cloned crewers?"

"Not that I can recall," Karrde said, stroking his beard thoughtfully. "My guess would be that they're leftovers from that big Imperial offensive ten years ago. Grand Admiral Thrawn had Mount Tantiss long enough to have turned out quite a lot of them."

"So what are they doing with a pirate gang?" Han persisted. "Don't you think that what's left of the Empire would want to keep them for themselves?"

"Point," Karrde conceded. "On the other hand, maybe they've decided it's more effective to hire them out to one or more gangs as advisers or elite warriors. Perhaps in exchange for a hand in choosing their targets, or else a share of the plunder."

"Could be," Han said. "It could also be that some pirate group's found its own supply of cloning cylinders."

Karrde's lip twitched. "Yes," he agreed grimly. "That could conceivably be the case."

"So what are we going to do about it?"

"I suppose I'd better look into it," Karrde said. "See what I can find out." He lifted an eyebrow slightly. "Cash or account?"

Han rolled his eyes. Every time he thought Karrde might actually be on the edge of doing something noble and self-sacrificing, the other always found a way to remind Han that his relationship with the New Republic was strictly professional. "I give up," he said. "What's it going to take to bring you over to our side, anyway?"

"Oh, I don't know," Karrde said consideringly. "What did it take to lure *you* away from the carefree life of an independent trader?"

Han made a face. "Leia," he said.

"Exactly," Karrde said dryly. "Now, if she had a sister—I don't suppose she does?"

"Not that I know of," Han said. "Though with the Skywalker family you never know."

"I won't hold my breath," Karrde said. "We'll do this on account, then. We can set the price later."

"You're all heart."

"I know," Karrde said. "Who shall I report to, you or Luke?"

"Better make it me," Han said. "Luke may be out of touch; he's gone off on a little pirate hunt of his own."

"Really," Karrde said, frowning. "Who's he going after, if I may ask?"

"The Cavrilhu gang. He got the location of one of their bolt-holes from New Republic Intelligence—it's an asteroid cluster in the Kauron system—and he decided to sneak in and take a look around."

"I see," Karrde said. "Too late to call him back, I suppose?"

"Probably," Han said. "Don't worry, Luke can take care of himself."

"That wasn't the part I was worried about," Karrde said. "I was thinking more along the lines that his sudden appearance might chase them underground where we can't get at them at all."

"Well, if they scare that easily, they can't be much of a threat, can they?" Han suggested.

"I suppose that's one way of looking at it." Karrde paused, and a shadow seemed to pass over his face. "Speaking of Luke, how is he doing these days?"

Han studied the smuggler, trying to decipher his suddenly changed expression. "All right, I guess," he said cautiously. "Why?"

"A feeling," Karrde said. "Mara's been oddly restive lately, and seemed a bit touchy for a while after we ran into Leia on Wayland. I thought it might have something to do with him."

"Funny you should bring that up," Han said, scratching his chin thoughtfully. "I got that same feeling about Luke the last time I mentioned Mara to him. Coincidence?"

"Perhaps," Karrde said. "On the other hand, they're both rather strong in the Force. Maybe there's something going on there that they're both sensing."

"Could be," Han said slowly. Though that wouldn't explain the other stuff Luke seemed to have been going through at Iphigin. Would it? "These clones, maybe?"

Karrde shrugged. "I'll try to talk to her about it. Maybe find a way to get the two of them together."

"Yeah, it's been a while since they've talked," Han agreed. "I'll try to work on Luke at this end when he gets back."

"Good," Karrde said. "In the meantime, I'd better get on this pirate matter. Tell Leia good-bye for me, if you would, and tell her I'll be in touch."

"Sure," Han said. "Happy hunting."

Karrde smiled, and the display went blank.

Han leaned back in his chair, gazing darkly at nothing in particular. Caamas. It was, as he'd said to Karrde, all that the New Republic needed right now.

Because it wasn't just Caamas, though Caamas by itself was certainly bad enough. The bigger problem was that dragging Caamas back into the light again was going to dredge up memories of a thousand other atrocities that had been inflicted by one group or another over the years. Old grudges, old feuds, old conflicts—the galaxy was riddled with them. It was what had made it possible for people like Karrde—and him and Chewie, for that matter—to make a good living at smuggling. There were so many sides of so many conflicts for smugglers to sell stuff to.

For the last couple of decades the need for a common resistance to the Empire had kept most of those resentments buried under the surface. But not anymore. The Imperial threat was so small now as to be laughable. If this Caamas thing got all those old problems boiling to the surface again . . .

He started as the door to his left hissed open. "Hi," Leia said softly as she came into the room.

"Oh. Hi," Han said, scrambling to his feet and throwing a belated look at the intercom display. Engrossed first with Karrde and then with his own thoughts, he hadn't even noticed Leia's guests departing. "Sorry—I got distracted."

"That's all right," Leia said, stepping into his arms for a quick hug.

Or not so quick. She remained there, pressing close to him, holding him tightly. "I just talked to Karrde," Han said, her hair tickling his lips. "He told me what you found out about Caamas."

"We're in trouble, Han," Leia said, her voice muffled by his shirt. "They don't realize it yet, most of them. But this could be the biggest threat the New Republic has ever faced. It could literally tear us apart."

"It'll be okay," Han soothed her, feeling just a tiny bit smug despite the seriousness of the moment. Most of the Senators in there hadn't spotted the danger of the Caamas thing, but he had. "We got through that Almania rebellion okay, didn't we?"

"It isn't the same," Leia said. "Kueller was a troubled man lashing out around him, and the New Republic was trying to stop him without looking to everyone like we were becoming a new version of the Empire. What Caamas is going to do is polarize good, honest people, all of whom genuinely want justice but differ violently as to what that justice should consist of."

"It'll still be okay," Han insisted, taking her by her upper arms and pushing her far enough away to peer sternly into her eyes. "Let's not give up before we even get started, okay?"

He stopped, a sudden horrible suspicion digging into him. "Unless," he added slowly, "it's already over. Do you know something I don't?"

"I don't know," Leia said, her eyes slipping away from his gaze. "I'm sensing something about the coming days. A—I don't know—a crisis point, I suppose, where something vitally important could go either of two ways."

"About Caamas?" Han asked.

"I don't know," Leia sighed. "I've tried meditating, but so far I haven't been able to get anything more. All I know is that it started when I met Karrde on Wayland and we read the Caamas datacard."

"Mm," Han said, wishing now that he'd tried to talk Luke out of his private pirate hunt. He might have been able to help Leia focus this feeling of hers. "Well, don't worry, you'll get it. A little quiet time—a little husbandly affection—and it'll pop right out at you."

Leia smiled at him, some of the tension leaving her face as she did so. "Is that what you want right now? A little wifely affection?"

"First thing I want is to get you out of here," Han told her, taking her arm and starting her toward the door. "You need some peace and quiet; and once the kids get back from their classes, there'll be precious little of either. Let's grab it while we can."

"Sounds good to me," Leia sighed. "I don't imagine they're doing anything out there right now except arguing about justice and revenge. They can do that without my help."

"Sure," Han said. "Nothing important's going to happen in the galaxy for the next hour."

"You sure?"

Han squeezed her arm reassuringly. "I absolutely guarantee it."

There was a flicker from the bridge lights, and through the viewports the mottled sky of hyperspace faded away.

But not into the usual pattern of starlines. This time when the mottled sky vanished, it vanished into total blackness.

And into total blindness.

For a long moment Captain Nalgol gazed out the *Tyrannic*'s viewport at the emptiness, fighting against the queasy feeling of vulnerability. True, jumping his Imperial Star Destroyer while cloaked had brought them into the Bothawui system completely blind and deaf, which was a potentially disastrous position for a combat ship to be in. But in this case, of course, the cloaking shield also worked the other way, concealing them from their enemies. Still, all other things being equal, it wasn't a trade-off he would have voluntarily chosen to make.

"Report from the hangar bay," the fighter control officer called. "Scout ships are away."

"Acknowledged," Nalgol said, scanning as much of the blackness out there as he could see without moving his head—it wouldn't look good for the bridge crew to see him looking back and forth at nothing. He caught a glimpse of one of the drive flares coming out from beneath the hull; and then the scout crossed the cloaking shield boundary and vanished.

He took a deep breath, wondering yet again what in the Empire he and the others were doing here. Sitting there in Moff Disra's office with Trazzen and Argona and Dorja, it had all sounded reasonable enough. Out here in the wilds of the Bothawui system, millions of kilometers from anywhere, it didn't seem nearly as clever anymore.

On the other hand, how many of Grand Admiral Thrawn's schemes had ever looked even vaguely reasonable until they were sprung on the enemy?

Nalgol snorted under his breath. He'd never served directly beneath Thrawn, or any of the Emperor's other Grand Admirals for that matter, so he'd never been able to form a personal opinion of their skills. Still, even viewed from the edges of Thrawn's war machine where the *Tyrannic*'s duty had taken it most of that time, Nalgol had to admit the Empire had been doing pretty well while the Grand Admiral was in command. Before he'd been murdered by that Noghri traitor Rukh.

Or had apparently been murdered. That had been a nifty little sleight of hand. How had he pulled it off, anyway?

More to the point, why had he been lying low all these years, letting incompetent megalomaniacal fools like Admiral Daala bleed the Empire of resources without gaining anything to show for it?

And why, now that he *was* back, had he linked up with Moff Disra, of all people?

Nalgol grimaced to himself. He'd never liked Disra. Had never really trusted the man, for one thing—he'd always struck Nalgol as the type who would fight viciously to keep his share of the scraps of the Empire rather than watch it grow to someone else's advantage. If Thrawn had thrown in with him, maybe he wasn't as smart as legend had it.

Of course, Dorja had vouched firmly for the Grand Admiral, both for his character and his military genius. But then, Argona just as firmly vouched for the competence of Disra himself. So what did any of them know?

But at least it *was* Thrawn back there. The genetic analysis he'd done had confirmed that beyond the whisper of a doubt. It was Thrawn, and everyone said he was a genius. He would just have to hope they were right.

A movement to the left caught his attention, and he turned to see one of the scout ships cut across the edge of the cloaking shield, changing course to stay inside it. "Well?" Nalgol demanded.

"We're nearly on top of it, sir," the comm officer reported. "A small course change and we'll be there."

"Feed the course to the helm," Nalgol ordered, though if that hadn't already been done he was going to be angry. "Helm, get us moving. Comm, what about the *Obliterator* and *Ironhand*?"

"Our scouts have made contact with theirs, sir," the fighter control officer said. "They're coordinating our courses to make sure we don't bump into each other."

"They had better," Nalgol warned icily. Skulking around out here blind and deaf was bad enough; it would be the height of professional humiliation if the three Star Destroyers managed to fumble their sightless way into collisions with each other. All the more so if the cloaking shields went down and the spectacle was laid bare right out in the open for all of Bothawui system to see.

But at the moment, of course, they couldn't see. That was the whole point of this exercise. As far as the Bothans' homeworld defense apparatus was concerned, there was nothing out here except the exhausts of a handful of small ships moving apparently aimlessly around.

Small ships . . . and one not-quite-so-small comet.

"We're under way, Captain," the helm announced. "ETA, five minutes."

Nalgol nodded. "Acknowledged."

Slowly, the minutes ticked by. Nalgol watched the blackness outside the viewport, occasionally glimpsing a drive flare as one or another of his scouts ducked back inside the shroud of the cloaking shield to check on the *Tyrannic*'s progress and then ducked back out again. The timer ran down to zero—he sensed the huge ship slowing—

And then, abruptly, there it was, off to starboard: a slice of dirty rock and ice poking through the edge of the shield, sliding rapidly sternward. "There!" he snapped. "We're passing it!"

"We're on it, sir," the helm called back. Sure enough, even as Nalgol watched, the aft motion of the comet's edge came to a stop and then slowly backed up until it was hanging off the starboard side just ahead of the command superstructure. "We're stabilized now, Captain."

"Tether lines?"

"The shuttles are on their way with them now, sir," another officer reported. "They'll be secured in ten minutes."

"Good." The tether lines weren't nearly strong enough to physically hold the Star Destroyer and comet together, of course. Their purpose was merely to give the helm the necessary feedback to make sure the orbiting bodies stayed in the same relative positions as the comet continued its leisurely drift inward toward Bothawui. "Any word from the other two Star Destroyers?"

"The *Ironhand* has successfully tethered," the comm officer reported. "The *Obliterator*'s in position; they should be tethered about the time we are."

Nalgol nodded, taking a deep breath and letting it out quietly. So they'd made it. They were here, presumably unobserved by the Bothans.

And now there was nothing to do but wait. And hope that Grand Admiral Thrawn was really the genius everyone claimed he was.

CHAPTER

8

"Yeah, all right," the greasy-looking man on the comm display said, his eyes narrowed with suspicion. "Let's try it again."

"I've already told you twice," Luke said, putting some grouchy weariness into his voice and expression. "It's not going to change just because you think it ought to."

"So tell me again. Your name is—?"

"Mensio," Luke said tiredly, glancing out the viewport at the hundreds of asteroids drifting past and wondering which one this particular sentry was hiding on. "I work for Wesselman, and I've got a shipment to deliver to you. Which part of that don't you understand?"

"Let's start with the part about you and Wesselman," the man growled. "He never mentioned anyone named Mensio before."

"I'll have him send you a complete crew list when I get back," Luke said sarcastically.

"Watch your mouth," the other snapped. For a long moment he stared hard at Luke's face. Luke gazed back, trying to look as bored and unconcerned as possible. All things considered, the face of Luke Skywalker had to be one of the most recognizable in the galaxy. But with darkened hair and skin, an artificial beard, a Gorezh-style slant added to the outer corners of his eyes, and a pair of scars slicing across one cheek, he should be able to pass completely unrecognized.

"Another thing is that Pinchers usually makes this run," the sentry said at last. "How come he's not here?"

"He came down with something and can't fly," Luke said. Which was true, more or less. Pinchers should still be snoozing in peaceful oblivion back on Wistril under the influence of the Jedi healing trance Luke had put on him.

His associates were not going to be happy with the smuggler for letting Luke get the drop on him that way. On the other hand, when he came out of the trance he ought to be healthier than he'd been in years.

"Look, I haven't got all week to sit out here dishing the dust with you," Luke continued. "You going to let me in, or do I take it back to Wesselman and let him charge you a double delivery fee? I don't care—I get paid either way."

The sentry growled something unintelligible. "All right, keep your blaster tucked. What have you got?"

"A little of everything," Luke told him. "Some Norsam DR-X55 lift mines, a few Praxon emergency survival pods, some GTU power armor suits. Plus one or two little surprises."

"Yeah? The captain hates surprises."

"He'll love these," Luke promised. "Surprise number one is a set of hyperdrive boosters. Surprise number two is an SB-20 security breach droid." He shrugged. "Course, if he doesn't want them, I'll be happy to take them off your hands."

"Yeah, I'll bet you would." The sentry snorted. "Okay, fine, come on in. You know the in-route, or do I gotta draw you a map?"

"I know it," Luke said, mentally crossing his fingers. There were supposedly only two safe paths in through the maze of asteroids to this particular base of the Cavrilhu Pirates: one of which was safe for the inbound trip, the other for the outbound. He'd pulled visuals for the routes from Pinchers's mind while setting up the healing trance, and would feel reasonably confident about tracing out the path in his X-wing.

Doing the same in a lumbering Y60 Thalassian cargo hauler was another matter entirely. Especially when the Y60 no longer had any sublight drive units behind its central group of drive nozzles.

"Sure," the sentry sneered. "Try not to hit anything big."

The display went dead. Luke switched it off from his end, then keyed the makeshift intercom he'd rigged to the hollowed-out area where the central drive units had once been. "We're on our way," he announced. "You doing okay back there?"

There was a twitter of acknowledgment from Artoo, along with a warble that sounded distinctly nervous. "Don't worry, we'll get through just fine," Luke soothed him. "You just make sure the ship's ready to fly."

The droid warbled again, and for a moment Luke thought back to the covert shroud gambit he and New Republic Intelligence had cooked up for his penetration into the Imperial-held world of Poderis during the Thrawn campaign. There, too, he'd had Artoo and his X-wing stashed aboard a larger ship for a quick exit.

But this was a smuggler's freighter they were flying now, not a carefully designed breakaway vehicle. It was going to be a different matter entirely to get the X-wing clear if they needed to get out of here in a hurry.

Well, he'd cross that dune when he reached it. In the meantime, the preferred option would be to keep them from having to make that quick exit at all. And the first step in that was to convince the pirates' sentries that he was indeed a legitimate member of their supply network.

Resting his hands on the freighter's controls, he ran through his Jedi calming exercises. "May the Force be with me," he murmured, and headed in.

It wasn't nearly as bad as he'd expected. With typical smuggler's finesse, Pinchers had modified the Y60's engines and control surfaces to make the freighter faster and more maneuverable than its ungainly appearance would have implied, and even with the central drive section removed there was more than enough power left to do the job. The ship easily handled the sharp turns and backtracks necessary to keep it out of reach of the pirates' defense setup, as well as the more mundane problem of not bumping into any of the asteroids rolling past.

The whole trip rather reminded Luke of one of Leia's war stories, the one about the *Falcon*'s dizzying escape through the asteroid field after the Rebels' evacuation of Hoth. But of course, he wasn't flying full-bore through the floating rock pile the way they had, with TIE fighters and Imperial Star Destroyers breathing down his neck.

On his way out, of course, things might be different.

He reached the center of the maze to find himself approaching a large but otherwise undistinguished asteroid. According to New Republic Intelligence's meager information and supplemented by the snippets he'd pulled from Pinchers's mind, the pirates' base consisted of a series of tunnels and chambers originally burned into the rock by some enterprising but unsuccessful pre–Clone Wars mining operation. The landing bays were camouflaged as valleys in the uneven surface, and as Luke approached the asteroid a ring of lights came on between two sharp-edged ridges to indicate his designated landing site. He eased the freighter into the opening—felt a brief jolt as he passed through an atmosphere barrier—and with a multiple bump of landing legs he was down.

A lone man was waiting for him at the bottom of the landing ramp. "You Mensio?" he demanded gruffly, giving Luke's disguised face a quick once-over. His hand, Luke noticed, was resting with total lack of subtlety on the butt of his holstered blaster.

"You expecting someone else?" Luke countered, resting his hand on his own blaster in response and looking around the landing bay. The room beneath the atmosphere-shield ceiling was more or less circular, roughly carved from the rock of the asteroid, with a half-dozen pressure doors spaced more or less evenly around the perimeter. Austere in the extreme. "Yeah, I'm Mensio. Nice place you got here."

"We like it," the man said. "We just talked to Wesselman."

"No kidding," Luke said, still looking around. The New Republic Intelligence agent on Amorris was supposed to have locked Wesselman away incommunicado for the next few days. If he'd failed—or if the supplier had somehow escaped— "I hope you said hi for me."

"Yeah, we did," the pirate said darkly. "He says he's never heard of you."

"Really," Luke said casually, reaching out to the other with the Force. There was a level of suspicion in the pirate's mind, but no hint of the certainty that would mean such a conversation had actually taken place. This had to be a bluff.

Or rather, a test. "That's funny, you talking to him and all," Luke went on, finishing his inspection and focusing his gaze on the pirate. "Wesselman told *me* he was going to be out of touch for the next few days." He probed the other's mind a little deeper—"Heading out to Morshdine sector, as I recall. Something about picking up a load of unregistered Tibanna gas for you."

The pirate gave him a smile that was half sneer, and as he did so his suspicion faded away. "Yeah, that's where he's going, all right," he conceded. "Hasn't gotten there yet, though. We're still trying to contact him."

Luke shrugged, wishing he knew what Wesselman's exact itinerary was supposed to have been. If the supplier got too far behind schedule, the pirates' suspicions would probably start rising again. Too late to do anything about that now, though. "Well, when you do, say hi for me," he said. "So. Did I pass?"

The pirate sneered again and lifted his left hand. Four of the six pressure doors slid open and four tough-looking thugs stepped through into the landing bay. Holstering their drawn blasters, they headed toward Luke's freighter. "Yeah, you passed," he said. "You got any fancy locks or booby traps on your cargo hold we should know about?"

"Nope, everything's clear," Luke said. "Help yourselves. You got any food around here? That shipboard stuff gets worse every day."

"Sure," the pirate said, pointing to one of the two doors that hadn't had a guard waiting behind it. "Snack area's through there. Don't drink it dry—we'll have you unloaded in a couple of hours, and I don't want you tackling the out-route half-drunk. It'd make a mess, and I'd be the one who'd have to clean it up."

The indicated door led into a room about ten meters long and four wide, with a pair of tables equipped with bench seats arranged down the center. Along the right-hand wall stood various music and vid stations; along the opposite side was a waist-high counter with a gleaming SE-5 service droid waiting behind it.

"Good day, fine sir," the droid said brightly as Luke stepped into the room. "May I be of assistance?"

"You got any tomo-spiced karkan ribenes?" Luke asked, glancing around. There were no exits that he could see that might lead from this room into the rest of the complex. Not surprising, really, considering the sort of visitors the snack area catered to.

"Yes, fine sir, I most certainly do," the droid assured him, shuffling over a few steps and producing a package from beneath the counter. "It will take only a few moments to prepare them."

Luke grunted. "Fine."

It took just under four minutes, in fact, for the droid to heat the slab of ribenes and arrange them artistically on a plate. Luke spent the time wandering around the room, ostensibly looking at the vid stations, actually hunting for hidden spy cams.

He'd spotted three of them by the time his meal was ready. Even in a completely isolated room, the Cavrilhu Pirates weren't taking any chances.

"May I provide you something to drink?" the droid asked as he presented Luke with the plate.

"Don't bother," Luke said. "I've got better stuff on my ship."

"Ah," the droid said. "Will you need a set of utensils?"

Luke gave him a scornful look. "With spiced ribenes? You must be kidding."

"Oh," the droid murmured, looking a little nonplussed. "Well . . . do enjoy, fine sir."

Luke turned away, suppressing the out-of-character reflex to thank the droid. Tearing one of the ribenes off the end of the slab, he munched on it as he headed back out into the landing bay.

The pirates hadn't been idle in his absence. They'd gotten the Y60's wide cargo ramp lowered and were beginning to bring the big transport boxes out on repulsorlift floater carts. "I hope you're watching the corners with those things," Luke warned one of them, jabbing toward the floater cart with his ribene. "I don't want my restraint rings getting all chewed up."

"Tuck your teeth in," the other growled, flipping his head to toss a short braid back over one shoulder. "Nothing's gonna get chewed up. 'Cept maybe your skin if you give us any static."

"Yeah—you and who else?" Luke fired back, heading past him up the ramp. "You don't mind if I check for myself."

"Just don't get in the way."

There were two other pirates in the cargo hold, one just settling his box into place on his floater cart, the other already starting for the ramp with his load. Luke crossed to the side bulkhead, stretching out with the Force as he pretended to examine the restraint rings for damage. In the near distance, somewhere down one of the asteroid's corridors, he could sense two more of the pirates returning for their next load. He estimated the timing . . . yes. He should just be able to make it.

The last of the two pirates was almost to the ramp now. Grunting with apparent satisfaction as to the safety of his equipment, Luke changed direction, crossing the hold toward the access door leading into the freighter's living section. The pirate maneuvered his cart down the ramp and turned around the side of the ship.

And for perhaps the next ten seconds, Luke was alone.

There was no time to waste, but he and Artoo had had plenty of time to practice on the flight here and had gotten the drill down to a science. Whistling softly, Luke stepped to the box the two of them had prepared, at the same time getting a Force grip on his ribene plate and sending it flying smoothly across the hold. Artoo had heard the whistled signal, opening the access door as the meal neared it. Luke took another moment to ease the plate as far into the living section as he could see, then set it down on the deck and pulled open the side panel on the box beside him.

Inside, well packaged against random bumps, was Wesselman's fancy SB-20 security breach droid. It wasn't going to do the pirates any good now, not with most of its insides cut away, but the shell that was left would make an ideal hiding place for a quiet infiltration of their base. Curling himself up, Luke squeezed into the narrow space and pulled the box's side panel closed again.

Just in time. Beneath him, the deck vibrated slightly as the returning pirates climbed up the ramp. Luke stretched out with the Force, sensing as he did so their sudden suspicion. He ran through his sensory enhancement techniques—

"Control, this is Grinner," a murmured voice came to Luke's ears, as clear as if the pirate had been standing right beside him. "You see our smuggler anywhere?"

"Last I saw, he was headed into the hold," the faint voice of the pirate Luke had talked to earlier came in response. "Said he was worried about his restraint rings."

"Yeah, he was there when we left," another voice agreed.

"Fine," Grinner said. "So where is he now?"

"Probably inside," the second voice said. "He was headed that direction when Fulkes and I were leaving, chomping down on a plate of ribenes."

"Probably looking for something to wash down the tomo-spice with," a new voice added. "He told the service droid he had some good drinking stuff aboard."

"Maybe," Grinner grunted, the word almost covered over by the soft hiss of metal on steelhide as he drew his blaster. "Or maybe he's trying something cute, like hiding in one of these boxes. You want to get a scanner crew down here, Control?"

"Steady, Grinner," the unfamiliar voice advised him. "Let me run a check first."

For a long moment the hold was silent. Keeping his
Force hold on the side of the box, Luke unsealed the flap of
his tunic and got a grip on his lightsaber. If they didn't buy
this, he would have to take them out . . .

"You can all decompress," Control's voice said. "He's
gone inside, all right. The plate he took out of the snack
room is about five meters inside that door in front of you.
There's no way he could have stashed it in there and gotten
back out to the hold in the—let's see—in the nine seconds he
was out of sight."

There was a faint snort and the sound of Grinner's
blaster being holstered again. "Yeah, okay," he said.
"There's just something about this guy I don't like."

Luke took his hand off his lightsaber, letting his breath
out slowly in a silent sigh of relief. His original idea, back
when he'd first borrowed this ship, had been to simply take
whatever food he'd scrounged into the box with him. But
that plan had felt wrong, somehow, and he and Artoo had
worked out this variation instead. He was very glad now that
they had.

"So get him unloaded and out of here," Control said.
"You see any sign of that SB-20 droid he said he brought? I
want that one next."

"Uh . . . no. Only droid box I see is an R2 unit."

"That's the one," Control said. "A SB-20 is an R2 shell
with espionage gear and programming tucked away inside."

Luke's box lurched as the pirate got his float cart underneath it. "Never heard of it."

"They're not exactly advertised at droid depots," Control said acidly. "The captain's been after Wesselman for one
for years."

Grinner grunted. "And this one just happens to show
up here today, huh? Convenient."

"Give it a rest, Grinner," the other pirate in the hold
said. "Okay, I've got the droid. Where do you want it?"

"Electronics shop," Control told him. "The captain
wants Pap and K'Cink to check it out."

"Right."

A moment later they were off, angling down the ramp

and across the landing-bay floor. Luke braced himself against the droid shell, listening to the sounds around him and trying to ignore the violent shaking that was really only the small bumps and vibrations of the float cart. He had assumed he would be taken to whatever storage place the rest of the cargo was bound for, which would presumably have given him a certain amount of privacy for his exit from the box. On the other hand, the electronics shop was probably closer to the command areas of the base, which was his ultimate goal. All in all, a fair trade-off.

They passed through one of the pressure doors, and for a few minutes the only sounds were the hum of the float cart's repulsorlifts and the pirate's footsteps and raspy breathing. Then, gradually, more sounds began to filter in: other voices and footsteps, mostly distant but occasionally passing close by. Luke stretched out with the Force, sensing a variety of human and alien minds in the vicinity. There was an odd change of echo as they apparently left the corridor and entered a larger room; another change, this time in reverse, marked where they left the room and passed into a corridor again. The float cart turned around a corner, then another; entered another open space filled with the dull rumble of muted voices—

"Lanius?" Control's voice said.

"Yeah, you got me," the pirate pushing Luke's float cart said.

"Change of plans—Pap's got something torn apart in the shop and doesn't have room for your droid. Go park it in the Level Four storeroom."

"Yeah, okay." The float cart slowed and changed direction. "Too much to ask for them to make up their minds?"

"Very funny," Control growled. "Just hustle it, okay?"

"I'm hustling, I'm hustling," Lanius grumped under his breath.

The cart moved on; but even as it again changed corridors, Luke began to feel an odd sensation tingling at the back of his mind. Somewhere—somehow—something had suddenly gone wrong.

He stretched out with the Force again, trying to track

down the sensation. Ahead, a door hissed open and the cart again entered a large room. It seemed to be taking a long time to get across it . . .

And then, abruptly, the cart stopped. "What the—" the pirate spat.

"Get out of the way, Lanius," the voice of Control boomed over a loudspeaker. "You've got yourself a rider."

The pirate bit out a curse, and there was a scramble of feet as he darted away from the lift cart. "All right, whoever you are," Control continued. "We know you're in there— we got a clear scan from the security corridor. Come on out."

Luke grimaced. So that's what that tingling sensation had been: a premonition of the mess he was now in. A pity he hadn't paid more attention to it, though offhand he couldn't see what he could have done to change anything at that point.

And anyway, berating himself for errors in judgment would gain him nothing. Pulling out his comlink, he thumbed it on. "Artoo?" he said softly.

There was no answer, just a quiet burst of static. "Oh, and we've also jammed your transmissions," Control added. "I'm afraid the only one you're going to be able to talk to is me."

So Luke was on his own. Tucking his lightsaber a little deeper into its hiding place, he sealed the tunic flap loosely across it. "Okay," he shouted. "Hold your fire—I'm coming out."

He released his Force grip on the side panel and let it swing open. Three pirates were visible, standing well back from the box, their blasters steady on him. Five others, he could sense, were spread out around the box outside his field of view.

Five others, plus a Defel skulking somewhere in the shadows as backup. Once again, they weren't taking any chances.

"Well, well," Control's voice said as Luke eased his way out of the disemboweled droid and stood up. "Took a wrong turn, did you, Mensio?"

"No, I think it was Lanius who took the wrong turn," Luke said, keeping his hands away from his blaster as he looked around. They were in a large, high-ceilinged room, with stacked boxes lining two of the walls. His box had been set down in an otherwise unoccupied corner away from the rest of the merchandise; the eight pirates were arrayed in a rough semicircle around him. He didn't spot the Defel, but it was probably somewhere between him and the only door, across the room behind the ring of blasters. "I came to see your captain, not your inventory."

One of the pirates facing Luke growled something unintelligible. "I think you ought to know that Hensing there really despises sarcastic jinks," Control said.

"Really," Luke said, sending another casual glance toward the door area. The glow panel switch was just to the side of the panel: a simple push plate that he could trigger with the Force. Perfect. "Sorry to hear that."

"You could get a lot sorrier," Control warned. "He has a theory that jinks get less sarcastic when they've had a hand or two blown off."

Luke smiled grimly, flexing the fingers of his artificial right hand. "He's right about that," he said. "Take my word for it."

"Just so we understand each other," Control said. "Take out your blaster—I'm sure you know the routine."

"Sure," Luke said, pulling out his blaster with exaggerated care and lowering it to the floor in front of him. "You want the spare power packs, too?" he asked, pointing to the two small flat boxes riding the other side of his gunbelt.

"No, you're welcome to hide behind them if you'd like," Control said. "Just kick the blaster away from you."

Luke complied, using the Force to make sure the weapon skidded to a halt precisely at Hensing's feet. "Happy?"

"Happier than you're going to be," Control said. "I don't think you realize how much trouble you're in here, Mensio."

It was time, Luke decided, to switch tacks. "Fine, no more nonsense," he said, putting an edge into both his voice and his posture. "I'm here to talk to your captain about making a deal."

If Control was impressed by the new Mensio, his voice didn't show it. "Sure you are," he said. "What, you couldn't call for an appointment?"

"I wanted to check out your security," Luke told him. "See if you're the sort of people my employer would be interested in doing business with."

"And what would this business consist of?"

"I was instructed to discuss it with your captain," Luke said loftily. "Not underlings."

Hensing growled again, lifting his blaster. "Then your employer is either stupid or a fool or both," Control said. "You have five seconds to give me something solid. After that, I turn Hensing loose on you."

"If you insist," Luke said, crossing his arms across his chest and looking across the room at the glow panel switch. That warning tingle had returned . . . "We understand that you're using clones to crew some of your ships. We want to discuss hiring some of them from you."

Control tsked. "Sorry—wrong answer. Take him." The pirates lifted their blasters—

And reaching out through the Force, Luke flipped off the glow panels.

There was a snarled curse, almost drowned out by the sputtering of multiple blaster bolts cutting through the air where Luke had been standing. But Luke was no longer there. A Force-strengthened leap had sent him sailing over their heads toward the door, lightsaber ready in his hand. If they'd been overconfident enough not to leave a guard outside the door—

There was a flicker of premonition, and he had the lightsaber in guard position just as he spotted the Defel's pale red eyes gazing down at him from the top of one of the stacks of boxes. He sensed rather than saw the weapon tracking toward him, igniting the lightsaber just as the blaster's flash sparked from between the red eyes.

The green blade blazed into existence, startlingly bright in the darkness, deflecting the Defel's blaster bolt harmlessly away. But even as he hit the floor beside the door, Luke realized the Defel had won this round. His shot had missed, but he had forced Luke to reveal both his location and his true identity.

The other pirates weren't slow in picking up on either. Someone across the room swore—"It's Skywalker!" another shouted—and suddenly a fresh volley of blaster fire was raining through the air toward him.

Luke backed to the door, letting the Force guide his defense. The door had probably been sealed; jumping sideways toward it to temporarily throw off his opponents' aim, he slashed twice with his lightsaber. A flat dive out the opening, and he was free.

The corridor outside was deserted. Rolling back to his feet, lightsaber at the ready, he stretched out with the Force, seeking the ambush that must surely be lurking nearby. But there were no other presences that he could detect. "Giving up already?" he called.

"Hardly," Control's voice came from a speaker set into the ceiling a few meters away. "Rather foolish of you to give away your identity so quickly."

"I prefer to think of it as an overabundance of confidence," Luke countered, stretching out a little harder. Still nothing; and if he'd really caught them off guard, it wouldn't be smart to give them time to regroup. Picking what he hoped was the direction he'd come from, he set off at a fast trot. "You ready to tell me where you're getting your clones from?" he added toward the speaker. "I'd really rather not have to hunt down your captain and ask him personally."

"Hunt all you like," Control said, his voice now coming from a different speaker farther down the corridor. Clearly, they were tracking Luke's movements. "You won't find anyone here who knows. But thank you for confirming that was what you came here to learn."

"You're welcome," Luke said, clenching his teeth as the tingle of danger again tugged at him. Ahead, the corridor curved gently to the right; and somewhere beyond the curve he could finally sense other presences waiting for him.

It was a classic bottle-squeeze setup: pin the enemy in a

curve or angle where he would be trapped in a crossfire without the two ends of the crossfire shooting at each other. He could sense the pirates he'd left behind in the storeroom piling out into the corridor now; a few more heartbeats, and there would be blaster fire coming at his back.

But the pirates' contingency plans were unlikely to have included the possibility of a Jedi running loose in their base. Just this side of the curve, a heavy blast door revealed the presence of a side corridor leading out of the trap to the left. The blaster he'd left back in the storeroom wouldn't have made a dent in it; but he had a far more efficient way of opening doors than the pirates could have anticipated. Skidding to a stop in front of the blast door, he ignited his lightsaber and slashed through the lock mechanism. It began sliding ponderously open—

There was a flicker of warning, and Luke spun around just in time to sweep the lightsaber blade across three incoming blaster bolts. The pirates from the storeroom, seeing their bottle-squeeze about to fail, were charging full speed toward him, firing as they ran. Luke blocked two more bolts—the rest were going wide—and ducked through the still opening blast door into a wide corridor.

The corridor's appearance was a surprise. Unlike the rough-hewn feel of the rest of the base, this area looked like it might have been transplanted straight from inside a capital starship. Smooth metal-lined walls formed a square cross section about four meters wide, the corridor itself stretching twenty meters before ending in a T-junction with another of the more typical rocky corridors.

The only light was the spillover coming from behind Luke and the similar glow from the far end. Even so, there was enough illumination to see that all the surfaces of the corridor—walls, ceiling, and floor—were covered with a decorative pattern of three-centimeter-diameter circles spaced about ten centimeters apart.

The corridor itself was deserted, and Luke could sense no one skulking around the corners ahead. Apparently, he had indeed caught them off guard.

But his danger sense was still tingling. Something about

the corridor? Still, with two groups of enemies behind him, there was nowhere to go but through. Senses alert for a trap, he headed down the corridor.

He'd made it four steps when, without warning, gravity abruptly reversed itself, sending him falling toward the ceiling.

There was no chance for physical or mental preparation. His head and shoulders slammed into the metal, sending a jolt of pain arcing through him, the rest of his body tumbling down with a dull thud and more pain. He gasped for breath—the impact had knocked most of the air out of him—but before he could get more than half a lungful he was falling again, this time sideways toward one of the side walls.

He landed hard on his right side, a fresh stab of pain lancing through head and shoulder and hip as he scrabbled around for a handhold. But there was nothing to grip on the smooth metal. Stretching out to the Force, he sensed the gravitational field starting to change again; and then his new floor suddenly became the ceiling again, and he was falling toward the far wall.

But not toward flat metal this time. Twisting his head around, he saw that what he'd taken to be decorative circles drawn in the wall were in fact the heads of flat-tipped metal rods. They had extruded outward from the wall now, rising like a forest of blunted spears to meet his descent.

Clenching his teeth, Luke reached out to the Force and threw out his hands to meet the oncoming bars. With their tight spacing there was no chance for him to slide between them; but if he could grab two of them and slow his fall, he could at least keep from landing on them at full speed. He caught hold of the two pointed at his face and chest, reaching to the Force for the strength to slow himself. He succeeded, and for a brief moment held himself balanced over them in midair—

And then he was slammed onto them anyway as a corresponding set of bars from the wall behind him jabbed hard into his back and legs, driving him forward. He grunted as the wind was again knocked out of him, trying to twist around against the forest of bars digging into him.

But even as he struggled to work his left arm through the rods pinning it, two more sets of bars slid out from the floor and ceiling, slamming into his shoulders, head, and legs and pinning him even tighter in place. There was another flurry of gravity changes that did little except jam every part of his body in random turn against the various sets of bars—

And then gravity settled back to its original vector, leaving him suspended more or less upright in the room.

"Well, well," Control's mocking voice said into the silence. "Surprised, are we?"

"A little," Luke conceded, fighting past the dizziness left over from the gravity changes and looking around as best he could with his head pinioned rigidly in place. The entire corridor had become a huge three-dimensional crosshatch of rods, filling the whole space between the blast doors that had slid into place at both ends, sealing him inside.

"We set this up about five years ago," Control continued. "Your Yavin academy was seeding the galaxy with cocky little would-be Jedi, and we figured it would be only a matter of time before one of them dropped in on us. So we figured to have a surprise ready for them. Never figured on having the Grand High Moffling himself show up. So, what do you think?"

"It's inventive, I'll give you that," Luke said, testing the strength of the bars with his shoulders and arms. He might have saved himself the effort. "I hope you're not expecting it to hold me for long."

"You might be surprised," Control said. "I take it you haven't noticed where your lightsaber ended up?"

Luke couldn't even remember when during all those gravity switches he'd dropped it. Now, straining out of the corner of his eye, he spotted the weapon fifteen meters away across the room, wedged just like he was within the interlocking sets of bars. "You can see it's a tighter group of bars over at that end," Control pointed out. "Holds the thing pretty solidly in place."

Luke smiled. Clearly, for all his preparation, the pirate

hadn't learned enough about Jedi. Reaching out with the Force, he activated the lightsaber's switch. With a *snap-hiss* the green blade flashed into existence; reaching out again, Luke attempted to twist the handle sideways.

Nothing happened.

"You see the genius of the design," Control said conversationally. "It's held at just the right angle so that the blade sticks out in the gap between bars, without touching any of them. Clever, eh?"

Luke didn't answer. The lightsaber seemed to be solidly wedged in place . . . but if the blade wasn't touching the bars, the handle ought to slide freely either backward or forward. Getting a Force grip on it, he slid it forward.

"Oh, it'll go that direction, all right," Control said as the lightsaber began to move. "Unless it gets hung up by its switch or something. But that won't do you any good. The blade still won't touch any of the bars—"

The tip of the blade had reached the wall now. Luke continued forcing it that direction, pushing the blade straight into the metal plating.

"—and naturally we weren't stupid enough to put any critical equipment behind the walls for you to cut into," Control finished. "A little more impressed now, are we?"

"Maybe a little," Luke said. "Now what?"

"What do you think?" Control retorted, his voice suddenly dark. "We know what you Jedi can do, Skywalker—don't think we don't. I figure that from that little ride through our base alone you've probably already dug out enough dirty silt about our operation to send everyone here to Fodurant or Beauchen for the next twenty years. You think we're going to just sit here and let you do that to us, you're crazy."

Luke grimaced with the irony. Control was right: using his full Jedi strength, he almost certainly could have invaded the pirates' minds that deeply. But with his new reluctance to use his power so casually, he had in fact done nothing of the sort. "So what do you want to do, make a deal?"

"Hardly," Control said. "We want you to die."

"Really," Luke said dryly. The bars here might be too

strong for human muscle, but that was hardly the limiting factor for a Jedi. Bending enough of the bars out of the way for him to get to his lightsaber would be a long and tedious job, but he had more than enough depth in the Force to accomplish it. "From old age, or do you have something more immediate in mind?"

"I'm actually kind of sorry," Control said. "Seems a waste, dusting you like this, especially after what this Jedi trap cost to build. But no one's offering bounties on captured Jedi these days. Even if they were, I don't suppose that cage would hold you long enough for us to collect. So there it is. Good-bye, Skywalker."

There was a click, and the speaker fell dead . . . and in the silence, Luke heard a sound that hadn't been there before.

The quiet hiss of escaping gas.

He took a deep breath, stretching out to the Force. There were Jedi poison-neutralizing techniques that should be able to handle whatever they were pumping in at him. Still, he'd better not dawdle on getting out of here. Closing his eyes, reaching more deeply to the Force, he began bending one of the bars away from his face—

And then, suddenly, his eyes snapped open as the truth belatedly hit him.

The pirates weren't pumping poison in. They were pumping the air *out*.

And not even a Jedi could survive for long without air.

Luke took another deep breath, pushing away his rising fear. *A Jedi must act when he is calm, at peace with the Force.* All right. Artoo and the X-wing might already be in the pirates' hands. Even if they weren't, there was no way for the snubfighter to maneuver its way through the cramped and twisting corridors. He was on his own here, with no resources but the few pieces of equipment he was carrying: a comlink, glow rod, datapad—

And two spare blaster power packs.

Luke reached out with the Force, lifting the small flat boxes off his belt and floating them up to where he could see them. Back during the height of the Rebellion, the mechanical genius General Airen Cracken had found a way to rig blaster power packs to explode. All it took was two or more packs fastened together with their overload sturm dowels removed, and in thirty seconds they would blow with the power of a medium-sized grenade.

The blast should have enough power to shatter or twist any of the bars in its immediate vicinity. Unfortunately, it would do similar damage to Luke himself.

But with a little ingenuity . . .

It was the work of a few seconds to remove the overload dowels from the power packs. Then, holding them pressed together with the Force, he maneuvered them carefully through the maze of bars toward the far blast door. If Control was still monitoring him—and if the pirate knew about this trick—he would probably conclude that Luke was trying to punch a hole in the blast door and let in some air. He would also undoubtedly conclude that the metal was more than strong enough to withstand such an explosion.

Which was fine with Luke. The longer the pirates operated under false assumptions, the slower they would react when they finally figured out what he really had in mind.

His makeshift bomb was nearly to the blast door now, with only about ten seconds left to go. Keeping the bomb moving, he reached out to the Force and slid his lightsaber backward along its single line of free movement until the belt ring was pressing against the wall. The bomb reached the other end of the lightsaber's track and Luke settled it there against one of the bars.

The critical question now, he knew, was whether the explosion and resulting burst of shrapnel might damage the lightsaber. On sudden impulse, he stretched out and ignited the weapon, bringing the green blade snapping out to point directly toward the bomb. The blade should disintegrate whatever shrapnel hit it, providing at least some protection for the handle and the mechanism inside. Now there was nothing to do but wait and fight to keep from passing out in the rapidly thinning atmosphere—

And with a tremendous blast of fire and thunder, three seconds early, the power packs blew up.

Luke bit down hard as a dozen red-hot metal splinters stabbed and slashed into his left arm and side. But the results were all that he could have hoped for. Across the room, visible through the drifting smoke, the neat array of bars had been altered by the explosion. Not much, but maybe enough. Reaching out to the Force, he slid the lightsaber forward to the bomb-mangled bars and twisted the handle.

Not much, but indeed enough. The lightsaber, partially freed from its confinement, could now reach to the side just enough to snick off the end of one of the nearest bars. Luke twisted again, this time sending two more bars clattering to the floor. He twisted again, and again, each sweep going a little wider as he methodically carved out some space around the lightsaber—

And suddenly the weapon was free, spinning like a propeller as it cut through everything in its path.

White spots were beginning to dance in front of Luke's eyes as he sent the weapon through the blast door, cutting a triangular hole that brought a welcome gush of air rushing into the partial vacuum. He took a deep breath; and as his vision cleared he brought the lightsaber back toward him, the spinning blade mowing through the bars like a scythe through a field of tallgrain.

A minute later he was back in the rocky corridors, thumbing on his comlink as he headed for the landing bay and his ship. "Artoo?" he called. "You there?"

The only answer was another burst of jamming static. Picking up his pace, using Jedi techniques to suppress the pain in his side and arm, he prepared himself for the pirates' next move.

But that move didn't come. He emerged from the corridor into a large but deserted chamber and crossed into another corridor without seeing or sensing anyone.

For that matter, he hadn't sensed anyone since his escape from their Jedi trap. Were they all hiding somewhere? Or had they all simply packed up and left?

The rock floor beneath his feet shook slightly, and somewhere in the distance he heard the faint sound of an explosion. He was through the corridor and into another room when he heard and felt a second explosion, this one noticeably closer.

And abruptly his comlink twittered. He thumbed it on—"Artoo?"

"Not quite," a familiar voice answered dryly. "Are you in trouble *again*, Skywalker?"

Luke blinked with surprise, then smiled with the first genuine pleasure he'd felt since arriving at this place. "Of course I am," he told Mara Jade. "Have you ever known me when I wasn't?"

CHAPTER

9

"Offhand, I can't think of a time," Mara had to admit, gazing out the *Starry Ice*'s bridge viewport at the asteroid field stretched out in front of them. "Though I have to say that taking on a whole nest of pirates alone is beyond even your usual audacity level. What are you doing in there, anyway?"

"Attempting to get out," the other answered dryly. "What are you doing here?"

"Karrde asked me to check on you," she said. "Seemed to think you might need a hand."

"That I do," he conceded. "Where are you?"

"At the moment, on the outside looking in," Mara told him, frowning. Had that been an explosion over there on the Cavrilhu's main asteroid? "Are you setting off bombs or something?"

"No, but somebody is—I can hear explosions in the distance. Can you see what's happening?"

Seated at the next console, Captain Shirlee Faughn tapped Mara's arm. "Take a look at the starboard end of the asteroid," she murmured, pointing. "We've got a flotilla heading for deep space. I make it . . . eighteen ships."

"Terrific," Mara muttered. "You've got trouble, Luke—your rats are staging a mass desertion. Faughn's got readings on eighteen ships; probably more on the way. Ten to one those explosions you're hearing are the base's self-destruct system kicking in. You got any transport?"

"I had a Y60 freighter when I came in, with Artoo and a hidden X-wing aboard," Luke said. "But I haven't been able to raise him."

"Well, don't panic yet," Mara advised, giving the displays a quick glance. "They're still jamming your primary comlink frequency—we just happen to have the equipment to sneak in on a harmonic. How far are you from your landing bay?"

"I don't know exactly—"

Faughn snapped her fingers, pointed to one of Mara's displays. "Hold it," Mara cut in. "Their jamming's just gone off. Let me release your comlink back to primary freq."

She looked across the bridge at the comm station. "Corvus?"

"Already cleared," the other reported. "I'll key you back in on primary."

Abruptly the comm speaker burst into a staccato flow of astromech droid machine language. "Slow down, Artoo," Luke's voice cut in through the warbles and squeals. "I can't understand a thing you're saying."

"He says he and the X-wing are okay," Mara told him, watching as the translation scrolled across her computer display. "They were coming for him, so he popped the X-wing out of its hiding place—"

She grimaced. "And chased them away by blasting the landing bay's atmosphere shield generators."

There was a long moment of silence. "Which I presume means the landing bay is now full of hard vacuum?" Luke asked.

"Up to its brim," Mara confirmed. "I suppose it would be too much to hope there might be a vac suit locker near the bay somewhere."

"I don't know, but I wouldn't want to count on it," Luke said.

"Me, neither," Mara agreed. "Faughn, you used to fly Y60s, didn't you?"

"More often than I care to remember," the other

woman said. "You thinking about him trying a cold-shirt crossing?"

"It's the simplest way to get him out of there," Mara said. "Can he do it?"

"I doubt it," Faughn said. "Skywalker, is the freighter's landing ramp up or down?"

"Down, last I knew."

The R2 unit twittered, the droid's confirmation scrolling across the display. "It's still down," Mara said.

"In that case, not a chance," Faughn said, shaking her head. "The Y60's ramp mechanism is a piece of junk. Getting it sealed and repressurizing the ship would take at least fifteen minutes."

"I was afraid of that," Mara said. "A little long for him to hold his breath."

"What about his X-wing?" Faughn suggested. "It can't take very long to pressurize a cockpit that size."

"Except that most fighter canopies are pressure-locked these days," Mara pointed out. "Opening them to vacuum without squeezing the manual override usually pops the ejector seat. It's a safety mechanism—I don't think the R2 can override it."

"You're right, he can't," Luke said. "I'd better hope I can find a vac suit."

"Sure." Mara hissed softly between her teeth, measuring the distance to the asteroid with her eyes. The chances that the pirates would have vac equipment within handy reach of potential escapees were somewhere between slim and none. "In case you can't, we're coming in."

Out of the corner of her eye she saw Faughn turn startled eyes on her. "Jade, we don't know the safe path in," the other woman muttered.

"No, but Skywalker's astromech droid does," Mara reminded her. "Droid, how about feeding us some numbers?"

The R2 warbled acknowledgment, and a course layout appeared on the computer display. "Got it," Mara said. "Let's go."

Faughn turned back to the helm, still obviously less than enthusiastic about risking her ship this way. There was a brief surge of acceleration, and the *Starry Ice* began moving forward. "The path doesn't look too bad," Mara told her, studying the display.

"It didn't," the captain said, tapping her nav display. "There's just one slight problem: the asteroids aren't in the same relative positions anymore."

Mara shifted her attention to her own nav display. Faughn was right. "Blast—they've scrambled it," she said, getting out of her chair and heading for the door. "We'll have to bantha-roll our way in. I'll take Number One; get Elkin and Torve to the others."

She had reached her turbolaser station and was strapping in when Faughn signaled. "We've just tripped an automatic beacon warning us away," the captain reported. "Ought to be hitting the first wave of trouble anytime."

"Understood," Mara said, kicking the turbolaser into emergency warm-up and wishing for about the twentieth time this trip that the *Jade's Fire* wasn't stuck on Duroon getting its nav systems refitted. Karrde had done a good job of arming his freighters, but the *Fire* had as much sheer laser power as the *Starry Ice* and a lot more maneuverability on top of it.

But it wasn't here, and there was nothing she could do about it. Rubbing her palms briefly on her jumpsuit to dry them, she got a firm grip on the controls and stretched out to the Force. She might not be as glorious and powerful a Jedi as the great Luke Skywalker, but she'd be willing to match her finely honed danger sense against his any day.

The problem was that the danger sense wasn't particularly directional. And there were a lot of different directions out there for trouble to come from.

"Here we come, Luke," she called into her headset. "Last chance for you to wave your hand and sweep all the traps away."

The instant the words were out of her mouth she was sorry she'd said them. Luke was too far away for her to fully touch his mind; but even so, she could sense him wincing from her remark. She opened her mouth to apologize—

And suddenly her danger sense flared, an asteroid drifting along nearby catching her full attention. She spotted a circle of unnatural smoothness on its edge—the faint glint of metal—

Her turbolaser flashed, shattering the suspect asteroid into rocks and rubble. From the expanding dust cloud came a single reflexive burst of answering turbolaser fire: too little, too late, and well wide of its target.

"Good shooting, Mara," Elkin's voice came in her ear.

Mara nodded, too preoccupied with her task and her guilt over that snide remark to reply. Her guilt, and a growing annoyance at herself for feeling guilty in the first place. After all, it was Skywalker and his apprentice Jedi, not her, who were playing fast and casual with their power. If having someone point it out bothered him, that was his problem, not hers.

There was another flicker of warning; but before she could identify the source of the danger, multiple shots of red fire lanced out from Torve's turbolaser and a string of small boulders exploded prematurely into clouds of knife-edged shrapnel bursts. Mara winced as a few stray shredders bounced off the *Starry Ice*'s deflector shield in front of her canopy; and then the ship was past that trap and on its way to the next. Resettling her fingers on the controls, Mara again stretched out to the Force.

Among the three of them they had blasted eight more traps by the time the *Starry Ice* reached the main base. "We're here," Faughn's voice announced in Mara's ear. "Skywalker? Where are you?"

"I'm at my landing bay," Luke replied. "Artoo, fire a few blasts at the rim to mark it."

The droid beeped, and a shadow between two rocky ridges flickered with laser fire. "Okay, we've got you," Faughn said. "Coming in."

The laser flashes stopped; and as they did, another of the muted explosions flickered on the asteroid surface, uncomfortably close to the target bay. "There goes another blast," Mara said.

"You've been missing most of the performance out there," Luke said. "I've been hearing one go off every ten seconds or so. They seem to be working their way my direction."

Another explosion flashed, this one even closer to the landing bay. "Too close, if you ask me," Faughn grunted. "You sure you want to risk putting down there, Jade?"

"Not especially," Mara conceded, "but we don't seem to have a lot of choice. You're going to owe us big for this one, Luke."

"I'll put it on your account," Luke promised. "Better hurry—no, wait. Back off!"

"What?" Faughn asked.

"You heard him," Mara snapped as her own danger sense tingled. "Back off!"

The *Starry Ice* lurched back; and as it did so one of the ridges framing the landing bay began crackling with sequential blasts like an Endor Day multistage show rocket. "Jade, this is crazy," Faughn said. "I can't put down there. The whole area could go anytime."

"She's right," Luke said . . . and as Mara stretched out to the Force she felt a subtle grimness touch his emotions. "I guess we've only got one option left."

Wave your hand and sweep all the traps away? "What's that?" she asked aloud.

"I'll have to meet you halfway," he said. "You have a docking bay that'll handle my X-wing?"

"We've got a pair of half-ports with tractor assists," Faughn told him. "They'll put an air seal around the cockpit, anyway."

"Good. Artoo, get out there right now and dock with them—"

"Wait a second," Mara cut him off. There was something in Skywalker's voice and thoughts that told her he was about to try something really stupid. "You're not thinking of cold-shirting it all the way out to us, are you? We can't get in close enough for that."

"I know," Luke said. "I'm going to have to go into a Jedi hibernation trance as soon as I clear the blast door."

She'd called it, all right: something really stupid. "And how are you expecting to accomplish that?" she demanded.

"You'll have to go into the trance right after you've blown the door. That won't leave you any air reserve."

"If I cut open the door properly there should be a burst of air that comes out with me," Luke pointed out. "That ought to give me enough to start the hibernation, as well as nudging me your direction."

"You've got rotten odds."

"Last-ditch options are like that. And if we take too much time discussing it, we won't have any odds at all."

"Sounds like one of Solo's lines," Mara growled. But he was right; and as if to emphasize his words, the other flanking ridge began its own disintegration. "You win. Let's do it."

"Right," Luke said. "Artoo, get going."

The droid gave an unhappy twitter, but the X-wing lifted obediently out of the landing bay and headed toward the *Starry Ice.* "Faughn?" Mara called.

"Tractor assist is ready at the half-port," Faughn said. "The outer door of the starboard airlock is open, with an atmosphere barrier in place, and Krickle's standing by inside with a medpac. We're ready whenever he is."

"You copy that, Luke?"

"Yes," he said. "I'll set up the phrase 'welcome aboard' to snap me out of the trance."

" 'Welcome aboard,' right."

"Okay, here we go. Don't miss me."

Mara smiled tightly. *Don't miss me.* Once, those words would have had a totally different connotation for her. Luke Skywalker in her blaster sights, the Emperor's dying command that she kill the upstart Jedi echoing through her mind . . .

But she'd gone through that crisis ten years ago inside Mount Tantiss, and the Emperor's voice was now only a distant and powerless memory.

Skywalker would have his own crisis to go through one of these days. Maybe he was in the middle of it right now.

She hoped so.

There was a flicker from Luke's emotions. Mara concentrated, visualizing the flash of his lightsaber as the green blade slashed through the thick metal of the blast door—

And then, abruptly, he vanished.

"Faughn?" Mara called, closing her eyes as she stretched out as hard as she could. But Luke's presence was no longer detectable, at least not by her. Either he'd gone into his hibernation trance, or else he was dead.

"Here he comes," Faughn said.

Mara opened her eyes. He was there, all right, looking like a broken puppet as he glided rapidly toward the *Starry Ice*. His limbs flailed limply as his body tumbled slowly end over end, the flickering light from the asteroid's ongoing self-destruction adding a surreal air to the whole scene.

With a jolt that startled her, the *Starry Ice* began moving down toward the surface: Faughn, maneuvering the ship to match Luke's trajectory.

Or rather, trying to match it. Mara frowned at the approaching figure, trying to extrapolate his trajectory and impact speed—

Faughn, with access to the ship's computer, got the answer first. "We've got trouble," she said tightly. "With the speed I'm having to use to catch him, he's either going to bounce off the hull or else hit the back airlock wall hard enough to break his neck."

"You just get him inside," Mara said, hitting the quick-release on her restraints and scrambling to her feet. "I'll make sure he lives through it."

He was almost there by the time Mara reached the airlock, cartwheeling toward them far faster than was healthy. "Computer says we're right on target," Faughn's voice called over the speaker as Mara peered through the atmosphere barrier. "Impact in ten seconds."

Taking a deep breath, Mara braced herself against the airlock bulkhead and stretched out to the Force.

The Emperor had taught her the basics of using the Force to move objects, rudimentary training that Skywalker himself had developed further during their trek through the Wayland forest and later for a brief time at that Yavin academy of his. She'd kept up practice on her own after that, and had thought she'd become pretty proficient with the technique.

But moving small objects like her lightsaber was one thing. Catching Luke as he fell toward her was something else entirely, rather like trying to stop the *Starry Ice* with her teeth. She threw everything she had into the effort, dimly aware that her whole body had gone rigid with the strain, fighting to at least slow him down before he barreled past her through the atmosphere barrier. She could sense him slowing—knew it wouldn't be enough—

And at the last possible second she stepped away from the bulkhead directly into his path.

He slammed into her full tilt, the impact driving both of them back and down. "Welcome aboard," Mara gasped, an instant before the two of them slammed together to the deck.

A landing that was considerably less painful than she had expected it to be. She blinked, trying to shake the lingering stars from her vision—

"Thank you," Luke murmured into her ear.

The stars cleared, and Mara found herself looking up into a strange face—Luke's face, she realized, heavily disguised. He was straddling her, hands and feet on the deck, apparently having come out of his trance just in time to take his share of the impact instead of adding extra dead weight to hers. "You're welcome," she managed. "Nice disguise."

"Thanks," he said. "It worked, too, mostly."

" 'Mostly' doesn't count for much, does it?" she said. "How come you didn't use a Force illusion, like you have before?"

"I've been trying to cut back on my use of the Force except when absolutely necessary," he explained. "It didn't seem necessary in this case."

"Ah," Mara said. That was interesting. Very interesting indeed. "So. You want to get off me, or were you just getting comfortable?"

"Oh—sure," he said awkwardly, some of that old farmboy embarrassment flicking across his face as he scrambled off her. "Sorry."

"No problem," Mara said, getting to her feet and running a critical eye over him. Some nasty-looking shrapnel tears in his clothing, with what were probably some equally nasty injuries underneath them. "Looks like you need a pass through the medical bay."

"No time," he said, shaking his head. "I'm okay for now, and we've got to get out of here. Did my X-wing get docked?"

"I don't know," Mara said, slapping the control pad to close the outer airlock door. "Faughn?"

"It's been secured in B-port," the captain said. "Skywalker, you know a safe route out of this death trap?"

"I used to," Luke said, keying the inner door. "It's probably not any safer than any other path now."

"We'll follow the pirates," Mara decided, waving Krickle away as he hurried up with his medpac and leading Luke down the corridor toward the *Starry Ice*'s half-ports. "They'll probably shoot at us, but you can't have everything."

"Problem: we seem to have run out of pirates to follow," Faughn said. "Nothing's left the asteroid in nearly two minutes."

Mara felt her stomach muscles tighten. "Which means the grand finale of their self-destruct system is probably ticking down right now."

"Probably," Faughn agreed. "What do we do, pick a direction and go?"

"More or less," Mara told her. "Start pulling away from the main base, but not too fast. I want to be on my turbo-laser before we get into anything nasty."

"Give me time to get out there, too," Luke added. "I can run ahead of you and trigger the traps."

"Only if you can see them coming," Mara pointed out, giving him a hard look. "I've got a better danger sense than you do; maybe I should take your ship and break trail."

"I can do it," he said firmly. "Anyway, it's my responsibility—you're here because of me."

He had a point. "If that's how you want it," Mara said, pointing down the corridor. "Take the first left, then break right. Make it fast."

She needn't have worried. By the time she reached her turbolaser station the X-wing was already burning space ahead of them. "I'm ready," she announced as she strapped in again. "Get going, Luke. Good luck."

"May the Force be with you," he said with what she decided was probably mild reproof. "Stay sharp."

The trip in through the asteroids had been nerve-racking. The trip out, to Mara's surprise, was almost casually easy. Time and again the X-wing would shift course slightly and fire, setting off a distant cluster trap or shredder bomb or automatic turbolaser nest, usually before Mara's own danger sense had even triggered. It quickly settled into a pattern: the X-wing would maneuver, fire, and dodge, with the *Starry Ice* following stolidly behind, its own turbolaser crew needing to do only occasional cleanup work. Whether by design or accident, Luke seemed to be running slightly above the freighter, doing his most thorough job of minesweeping within Mara's angle of fire. Most of the cleanup work thus wound up in Elkin's or Torve's sectors, leaving Mara little to do except help watch for any surprises the pirates might have left behind, wait patiently for them to clear the asteroid field, and wonder darkly if Luke was deliberately being overprotective just to annoy her.

It was on one of her visual sweeps of the sky ahead that she spotted the ship.

Her initial thought was that it was a TIE fighter; it was similarly sized and at first glance had something of the same silhouette. But even as she opened her mouth to alert the others the craft made a turn—

"We've got company," she snapped. "Poking near the edge of the asteroid field at about twenty by fifty."

"Got it," Faughn said. "Looks like . . . what *does* it look like?"

"You got me," Mara said. "I thought it was an Imperial, but those aren't TIE solar panels on its sides."

"Whatever they are, it's got two more of them flaring aft at the tail," Elkin pointed out.

"Doesn't necessarily mean it's not an Imperial," Faughn

grunted. "Skywalker? You up on current Imperial starfighter design?"

"Not really," Luke said, his voice showing signs of the strain as he was forced to split his attention between the intruder and the more immediate task at hand. "I've never seen anything like that before, though."

Mara gazed out at the distant spacecraft. Clearly, it was watching them. Did it realize they'd spotted it? "I think one of us ought to try for a closer look," she said.

"Let's not, shall we?" Faughn growled. "We don't need to borrow any more trouble than we've already got."

"Besides, with our luck it'd just be another of those useless Qella things," Corvus added scornfully. "Like the one Lando Calrissian chased all over space."

"I say we take a look," Mara said, putting the firmness in her voice that made it an order. "Luke, you're the faster ship. You want to see if you can catch it?"

"I can try," he said, an odd tone to his voice. Was he feeling the same thing about that ship that she was? "Can you spare me?"

"I think so," Mara said. "We have to be pretty close to the edge of the pirates' defense sphere by now."

"Okay. Artoo, get all the recorders and sensors going. We're going to want a complete record of this."

The droid beeped acknowledgment; and with a suddenness that surprised even Mara the X-wing angled off and shot toward the intruder. It dodged past the drifting asteroids, cutting close beside them for the maximum of cover. Mara kept her turbolaser targeted on the other spacecraft, wondering tautly whether they would choose to fight or run.

But the X-wing was still closing, and so far there was no reaction. Could the intruder somehow be looking the other direction? Ridiculous. So what was it waiting for?

Luke was nearly to close-combat distance now. Behind him, a stray asteroid floated leisurely between the intruder and Mara's line of sight—

Her only warning was a sudden jolt in Luke's emotions. An instant later she caught a single glimpse of the intruder as it flicked at incredible speed across the sky, making for the edge of the asteroid field.

"There he goes!" Torve yelped as Mara tried to swing her turbolaser around to target the distant spacecraft. But too late. Even as she fought to get a lock on it another asteroid cut across between them, again blocking her view. There was the flicker of pseudomotion from the asteroid's edge, and the ship was gone.

Someone on the intercom swore softly. "I give up," Faughn said. "What the blazes *was* that?"

"You got me," Mara said. "Luke? You still there?"

"Right here," Luke replied. "Did you get all that?"

"Only part of it," Mara told him. "He waited until we were blocked by an asteroid before making his move."

"Interesting," Luke said. "The ship gave off a very unusual energy signature as he took off—I recorded what I could of it, but I doubt my sensors were able to pick up more than a fraction of what was really there."

"Maybe that's why he waited until we couldn't see him."

"Probably," Luke agreed. "He'd have guessed a ship your size would have better sensors than mine."

Mara rubbed her lips. "Well, unless you want to follow his hyperspace vector, there's not a lot we can do about him right now. How about feeding us what your sensors got?"

The astromech droid made a rude sound. "It's all right, Artoo," Luke soothed. "We can consider this their rescue fee."

"*Part* of their rescue fee," Mara corrected. "We'll settle on the rest later."

"Understood," Luke agreed. "Here it comes."

"Got it," Faughn said.

"Thanks," Mara said. "You need anything else, Luke?"

"Not at your prices," he said dryly. "Seriously, thanks for everything."

"Glad we could help," Mara said. "Don't forget to have those injuries looked at."

"I won't," he assured her. "Artoo's already pulling up a

list of the nearest New Republic medical facilities. See you later."

"Right. Watch yourself."

The comm clicked, and with a flicker of pseudomotion the X-wing made its jump to lightspeed. Mara gazed after it, a strange mixture of emotions chasing each other through her mind. The glowing reports she'd read of Luke's glorious achievements . . . and yet, they were a far cry from what she'd seen him do just now. Had something happened to him?

Or was he finally coming to his senses?

"Jade?" Faughn asked. "What now?"

Mara exhaled softly, putting Skywalker out of her mind. "We shoot a report off to Karrde," she said, doing a quick time calculation. "See if he wants us to get back on schedule for the Nosken rendezvous or else try to track the pirates' escape route."

"Right," Faughn said. "Incidentally, Jade, in case no one's ever mentioned it before, you and Skywalker make a pretty good team."

Mara gazed out at the drifting asteroids. "Bite your tongue, Faughn," she said softly. "Bite your tongue."

CHAPTER

10

It was a hot day in this part of Dordolum. Hot and sunny, with an oppressively still and heavy atmosphere that seemed to wrap around the silent lunchtime crowd like a wet grov-fur blanket.

The speaker currently shouting at the crowd from his perch atop the Stand of Public Expression was adding to the heat, too. But unlike the weather his heat was a fiery one, a mixture of words and thoughts and stage presence carefully designed to inflame the emotions and stir up the dozens of long-simmering resentments represented out there today. Practically everyone listening to the diatribe harbored at least one such quiet grudge, whether it be Ishori toward Diamala, Barabels toward Rodians, or Aqualish toward humans.

Or almost everyone toward Bothans. Letting his eyes drift across the crowd to the elaborate sign of the Bothan-owned Solferin Shipping Company directly across the plaza to their right, Drend Navett permitted himself a private smile.

It was a good day for a riot.

The speaker had made it to his main topic now, and as he hammered in graphic detail at the horror that had been the destruction of Caamas and the Bothans' cowardly and loathsome role in it, Navett could sense the crowd's anger finally edging toward the mindless fury that he'd been waiting for. Slowly, careful that his movement not break the spell for those around him, he began drifting toward the area closest to the shipping company. Klif might be a genius at demagoguery; but it was he, Navett, who knew how to gauge a crowd's mood and pick the right time for action.

Almost there. Navett was in position now, within easy targeting range of the shipping company. Dipping a hand into the bag hanging unobtrusively at his side, he withdrew his weapon of choice and waited. Another few seconds . . . and . . . *now*.

"Justice for Caamas!" he shouted. "Justice *now*!" Cocking his arm over his shoulder, he spun and hurled at the Bothan building—

And right on target, the overripe blicci fruit hit the door, splashing with a sickening thud and leaving a brilliant red stain behind.

There was a startled gasp from a couple of Duros standing nearby. But neither they nor anyone else in the crowd was going to be given enough time to think about what they were being suckered into here. From a half-dozen other places in the crowd the cry for justice was echoed, and a half-dozen other pieces of fruit splattered the building. "Justice for Caamas!" Navett shouted again, hurling another blicci fruit. "Vengeance for genocide!"

"Vengeance!" someone picked up the call, the cry accompanied by more of the nuisance missiles. "Vengeance for genocide!" Navett threw another blicci fruit, and another—

And then from somewhere an alien voice called hoarsely, echoing the call for vengeance . . . and as if that were somehow a signal, the crowd suddenly and gratifyingly collapsed into a mob. A rain of foodstuffs began to pelt the building, drawn from lunch bags and cartons and propelled by the mindless fury and pent-up rage that Klif had so skillfully stirred up in them.

A rage that Navett had no intention of wasting on a few fruit stains. Reaching past the last blicci fruit in his bag, he pulled out a rough stone. *Violence begets violence*, he silently quoted the old maxim, and let fly.

It hit its target window dead on, shattering the plastic with a crash that could barely be heard above the roar of the mob. "Vengeance for genocide!" Navett shouted, waving his fist at the building and pulling out another stone.

The crowd were fast learners. The rain of fruit and eggs continued, but it began to be joined by some of the edging stones that lined the plaza's walkways and flower beds. Navett threw another stone as four more windows became jagged holes, then took a quick moment to search the skies around them. Even taken by surprise this way, the Dordol authorities wouldn't take forever to respond.

And there was the expected response now, rapidly approaching from the direction of the spaceport: three brightly colored customs airspeeders with an escort of maybe half a dozen speeder bikes. Moving fast, too; they'd be at the plaza in less than two minutes.

Which meant it was time to go. Slipping a hand inside his tunic to his hidden comlink, Navett tapped the call button twice, the signal for the rest of his agitation team to move to the edges of the mob and vanish into the afternoon sunshine. Then, reaching past the last two stones in his pouch, he pulled out his final present to the Bothans.

It was a grenade, of course. But a very special grenade. Navett had personally taken it from the dead hand of a Myomaran resistance fighter ten years ago, during the Empire's brief reoccupation of that world under the meteoric reign of Grand Admiral Thrawn. What made this particular grenade so useful was that that resistance cell had somehow talked a visiting Bith into designing their weaponry for them. When the remains of the grenade were studied—as they most certainly would be—the New Republic would be forced to the conclusion that even the generally pacifist Bith were beginning to join in on the side of the anti-Bothan sentiment.

Perhaps that wouldn't matter. Perhaps none of this really mattered. Perhaps the aliens and alien-lovers had so beaten down the Empire that nothing Navett and his team did could make any difference anymore.

But as far as their duty was concerned, such possibilities didn't really matter either. Navett had seen the glory of the

Empire, as well as its darker days . . . and if that glory couldn't be revived, then it was only fitting that he help bury it beneath the ashes of the New Republic.

Pulling the safety, he flicked the detonator and threw. The grenade dropped neatly through one of the broken windows on the upper floor and vanished inside. He was halfway to the edge of the crowd when it went off, collapsing the roof and sending a spectacular fireball roiling into the sky.

He was out of the plaza and walking unconcernedly down the street with the rest of the noonday strollers when the authorities arrived at the scene of the fire.

The petition scrolled to the end past the long list of signatures. Leia looked up from her datapad, an ache in her stomach. No wonder President Gavrisom had looked so solemn as he ushered her into his private office. "When was this delivered?" she asked.

"Approximately one hour ago," Gavrisom said, the tips of his wings brushing restlessly across the stacks of datacards that awaited his attention. "Under the circumstances, I thought you and Councilor Fey'lya should be given advance notice."

Leia looked at Fey'lya. The Bothan was hunched in his seat, fur pressed completely flat against his skin. "Why me?" she asked.

"Because you were the one who found the Caamas Document in the first place," Gavrisom said, flicking his tail in a Calibop shrug. "Because like the Caamasi you've had a world destroyed from underneath you and can therefore understand their plight better than most. Because as a revered hero of the battle for freedom, you still have a great deal of influence with the members of the Senate."

"I can't match the influence of these signatures," Leia warned, gesturing toward her datapad. "Besides"—she hesitated, looking again at Fey'lya—"I'm not sure I don't agree with them that this is a reasonable compromise."

"A compromise?" Fey'lya asked, his voice dead. "This

is not a compromise, Councilor Organa Solo. This is a sentence of ruin for the Bothan people."

"The three of us are alone in this room, Councilor Fey'lya," Gavrisom reminded him mildly. "There's no need for rhetorical hyperbole."

Fey'lya looked at the Calibop, his eyes as dead as his voice. "I speak neither rhetoric nor hyperbole, President Gavrisom," he said. "Perhaps you do not comprehend how much time and effort would be involved in even merely locating an uninhabited world that would be suitable for the remaining Caamasi." His fur rippled. "But then to further insist that we bear the costs of re-forming that world to Caamas's original specifications? We cannot possibly afford such an undertaking."

"I'm familiar with the likely costs of such a project," Gavrisom countered, his tone still patient. "It was done at least five times during the Old Republic—"

"By peoples arrogant in their power and their wealth," Fey'lya snapped, suddenly seething to life. "The Bothan people have neither such power nor such wealth."

Gavrisom shook his mane. "Come now, Councilor, let us be honest here. The current state of overall Bothan assets is quite adequate to cover such a project. Certainly it would be a serious sacrifice, but not a ruinous one. I would further suggest that it represents your best chance of resolving this matter quickly and peaceably."

Fey'lya's fur rippled stiffly across his body. "You do not understand," he said quietly. "The assets you speak of do not exist."

Leia frowned. "What are you talking about? I've seen the market reports. There are whole pages of listings of Bothan holdings."

Fey'lya looked her in the eye. "They are lies," he said. "It is nothing more than a cleverly contrived datapad illusion."

Leia looked at Gavrisom. The other's restless wings had suddenly stopped moving. "Are you saying," the Calibop asked carefully, "that the leaders of the Combined Bothan Clans are engaged in fraud?"

The Bothan's rippling fur became even stiffer. "It was to be only a temporary deception," he said, his voice dark with pleading. "As our financial troubles themselves are only temporary. A gripful of bad business decisions has drained the Combined Clans of their resources and left us deeply in debt. And then this controversy arrived, causing even more uncertainty. New investors and contacts were needed, and so . . ."

He trailed off. "I see," Gavrisom said. His voice was still calm, but there was an expression on that long face that Leia had never seen there before. "You put me in a most awkward position, Councilor Fey'lya. How exactly do you suggest I proceed?"

Fey'lya's violet eyes met the Calibop's pale blue ones. "We can recover, President Gavrisom," he said. "It will just take a little time. Premature revelation of this information would be devastating, not only for the Bothan people but also for those who have invested with us."

"Who have trusted you," Gavrisom corrected coldly.

Fey'lya's eyes slipped away from that accusing glare. "Yes," he murmured. "Who have trusted us."

For a long minute the room was silent. Then, rustling his mane again, Gavrisom looked at Leia. "You are a Jedi Knight, Councilor Organa Solo," he said. "As such, you have the wisdom of the ages and the guidance of the Force. I would ask your recommendation."

Leia sighed. "I wish I had one to give," she said.

"Have you made any progress in the search for the names of the Bothans involved with Caamas?"

"Not yet," Leia said. "Our Intelligence people are still working on the original datacard, but Crypt Chief Ghent tells me we already have everything we're going to get from it. We're also searching through the old Imperial archives at Kamparas, Boudolayz, and Obroa-skai, but so far we haven't found anything."

"It was probably kept in the Special Files section," Gavrisom said with a whinnying sigh. "The records Imperial forces were ordered to destroy before retreating."

"Probably," Leia said. "We're still hoping a copy somewhere might have survived."

"A small hope, though."

"Yes," Leia had to concede. "Fey'lya, how much time will the Combined Clans need to get back on their feet?"

"The current projection is to have our major debts retired within three months," the Bothan said. "But at that time we will still be far from the financial position we are currently thought to be in."

Gavrisom made a noise deep in his throat. "And how long until you'd be able to take on this kind of project?" Leia asked, tapping her datapad.

Fey'lya closed his eyes. "Perhaps ten years. Perhaps never."

Leia looked back at Gavrisom. "I wish I could offer you advice, President Gavrisom," she said. "But at the moment I can't see a clear path here."

"I understand," Gavrisom said. "May I encourage you to meditate and seek further guidance through the Force?"

"I'll certainly do that," Leia assured him. "The one thing that is clear, though, is that the Bothans aren't going to be able to meet the demands of this petition anytime soon."

"Indeed," Gavrisom said heavily. "I'll have to attempt to buy some time."

"How, by offering it for debate?" Leia asked doubtfully. "That could be risky."

"More than merely risky," Gavrisom agreed. "If someone decided to bring it up as an official bill, the full Senate could end up ratifying it. At that point I would have no maneuvering room at all."

Leia grimaced. No room for Gavrisom, and even less for the Bothans. They would then have to go ahead and create a new homeworld for the Caamasi or face the consequences of defying New Republic law.

"But as you know, the President is not entirely without resources," the Calibop continued. "And there are certain parliamentary tricks that can be applied. I should be able to hold this up for a while."

Leia looked at Fey'lya. "But not for the next ten years."

"No."

There was another brief silence. "Well," Gavrisom said. "There seems to be little we can do right now. Except for one thing: I want the Combined Clans' financial records examined to confirm that the situation is indeed as described. Councilor Organa Solo, would you be willing to travel to Bothawui for such a purpose?"

"Me?" Leia asked, surprised. "I'm not a financial expert."

"Yet you surely must have been taught the basics by your father Bail Organa when you were younger," Gavrisom pointed out.

"The basics, yes," Leia said. "But that's all."

"That will be all you need," Gavrisom assured her. "The trickery will be in the falsified documents, not the true ones." He gestured to Fey'lya with one wing. "She *will* be allowed to see the true ones, will she not?"

"Of course," Fey'lya said, his fur rippling unhappily. "I'll alert the Combined Clan leaders you will be coming."

"You'll do no such thing," Gavrisom said firmly. "They are to have no notice whatsoever."

Fey'lya's eyes flashed. "You insult the integrity of the clan leaders, President Gavrisom."

"You may see it any way you choose," Gavrisom said. "But they are to have no advance warning. And do not forget that Councilor Organa Solo is a Jedi Knight. If your clan leaders are not genuinely surprised by her arrival and request, she will be instantly aware of it."

Leia kept her face expressionless. In point of fact, she'd always found the average Bothan somewhat difficult to read, and wasn't at all sure she'd be able to tell if the clan leaders had been tipped off.

But of course Fey'lya didn't know that. "I understand," he muttered. "When do you wish her to leave?"

"As soon as possible," Gavrisom said. "Councilor Organa Solo?"

"We could probably leave within a couple of hours," Leia said, running quickly through a mental list of the necessary arrangements. Han would want to come along, of course. Come to think of it, it would be a good chance for the two of them to have some quiet time together. "Chewie and the Noghri can watch the children here for us."

"The Noghri," Fey'lya murmured, an edge of bitterness to his voice. "They should have killed that Devaronian on Wayland. Then none of this would have happened."

"The Devaronian did nothing deserving of death," Gavrisom said quietly. "And there has been far too much killing throughout the galaxy already."

"With more yet to come," Fey'lya countered darkly. "Would sacrificing one life to prevent it have been such a bad bargain?"

"That is a question all beings eventually ask themselves," Gavrisom said. "For those who wish to remain civilized, there can be only one answer." He settled his wings back into resting position across his withers and back. "Thank you both for coming, Councilors. I will speak with you again later."

Moff Disra laid down his datapad. "Very satisfactory," he said, looking at the others. "It all seems to be going quite well."

"It all seems to be going quite slowly," Flim countered sourly, leaning back in his seat with his feet hoisted up on a corner of Disra's ivrooy desk. "We have, what, a few pirate raids and maybe a hundred riots to our credit?"

"Patience is a virtue," Tierce reminded him. "Even for soldiers. Especially for soldiers."

"Ah, well, that must be the problem," Flim countered. "I'm a con artist, not a soldier. But I can tell you that in *my* world, you can't afford to string things out too long. You have to hook the target, taut the line, and then boat him— zip, zip, zip. You give him too much time to think, and you'll lose him."

"We're not going to lose them," Tierce soothed. "Trust me. This is a delicate stew we're creating. It merely needs to simmer a bit longer."

"Then maybe you should turn up the heat a little," Flim

said. "This is my greatest role ever; and so far the only people who've seen it have been the two of you and four Star Destroyer captains. When do I get to *really* show it off?"

"Keep it up and you may not get to show it off at all," Disra told him, trying hard to hold on to his temper. Flim was starting to show all the eccentricities and quirks of a self-important stage entertainer, a personality type Disra had always despised.

"Don't worry," Tierce soothed. "You'll get your chance for at least a private performance for the Rebels. But not until we know where it will do the most good. We need to know which alien governments are for heavy sanctions against the Bothans and which are for forgiveness and peaceful conciliation."

"Which means you'll probably be showing off for a Mon Calamari or a Duros," Disra growled, glaring under his eyebrows at Tierce. This particular scheme was one of the Guardsman's latest brain twists, and Disra still wasn't at all sure he approved of it. The whole idea here was to use Flim to quietly inspire their Imperial forces, not scare the New Republic into coming down on their heads.

"Actually, the time is much closer than it looks," Tierce went on, ignoring Disra's comment. "Our spies on Coruscant have heard rumors of some petition that's been filed with the President. If they can get hold of a copy and circulate it publicly, that should speed up the process. A few more days, I think, and we'll be able to move on to the next phase."

"I hope so," Flim said. "Incidentally, I presume it's occurred to you that there's a very simple way the New Republic could resolve this whole crisis and cut the ground out from under us."

"Of course it has," Disra said with strained patience. "All they need to do is find out which specific Bothans were involved with Palpatine's agents on Caamas."

"And you've taken steps to prevent this from happening?"

"What do you take me for, a fool?" Disra snapped. "Of

course I have. The only intact set of records is here on Bastion, and I've already dealt with them."

"Actually, that's not entirely accurate," Tierce said thoughtfully. "The records at the Ubiqtorate base on Yaga Minor may also contain a copy."

Disra frowned at him. "Why haven't you said anything about this before?"

"The subject of enemy information raids hadn't come up before," Tierce said. "I knew you'd been into the Bastion records; I suppose I was assuming you'd taken care of the Yaga Minor copies as well."

"I haven't, but I can," Disra said. "I'll head out for Yaga Minor tonight."

"That might not be a good idea," Tierce said. "You going personally, I mean. The general in charge of the base knows Admiral Pellaeon fairly well; and with the Bastion library right here at hand, you really don't have a good excuse to examine his records."

Disra frowned at him. "So who's going to go there? You?"

"I *am* the logical choice," Tierce pointed out. "General Hestiv doesn't know me by either name or sight, and I can make up a story that won't link me to you. As long as Pellaeon's grand tour of the Empire doesn't drop him there the same time I am, there shouldn't be any problems."

"Except how you're going to get into the Special Files section," Disra said.

Tierce shrugged. "I'll use a copy of your decryption method, of course."

Disra frowned a little harder. "You know, this is the second time you've tried to get that decrypt from me," he pointed out. "One might wonder why you're so anxious to get hold of it."

"Would you rather the Rebels got to the Caamas Document first?" Tierce countered. "What in the Empire are you so afraid of, anyway?"

"I'm not sure," Disra said darkly. "Perhaps that all you really want—that all you've ever wanted from the start—is to get your nose into those files. Maybe I'm thinking that once you've gotten whatever it is you're looking for, you'll vanish and leave us holding the bag."

Tierce smiled tightly. "A minute ago you were upset that I seem to be taking over your grand project," he pointed out. "Now you're worried that I might suddenly desert it? Make up your mind."

"You haven't answered my question," Disra bit out. "What is it you're looking for in those files?"

"I don't know," Tierce said. "The Emperor had many secrets, some of which are bound to be useful to us. But I can't know which ones until I have a chance to look them over, can I?"

"If it's all that simple and aboveboard, why didn't you suggest it in the first place?" Disra demanded. "I could have let you look through the Bastion records."

"Fine," Tierce said. "Consider the request made. However, if I go look at the files at Yaga Minor I can take care of two problems at once, can't I?"

Disra grimaced. Except that if Tierce did his searching at Yaga Minor, he wouldn't be able to look over the Guardsman's shoulder while he did it.

Across the desk, Flim stirred. "We're all in this together, Your Excellency," he reminded Disra. "Whatever secrets Major Tierce digs up, he can't possibly use them by himself as effectively as he can together with the two of us."

"Exactly," Tierce said, nodding. "In fact, I'll go further: one of the files I'm hoping to find will *only* be useful in conjunction with the two of you."

So there *was* something specific he was after. "And that mysterious secret is . . . ?" Disra prompted.

Tierce shook his head. "Sorry. I'll definitely need help from the two of you to utilize it; but it's possible the two of you *won't* need me. No offense, but at this point I'd prefer to remain indispensable."

Disra grimaced; but he could tell that this part of the conversation was now over. He'd pushed Tierce as far as the Guardsman was willing to be pushed, and had learned all he was likely to learn, and that was it.

At least for now. "You're still indispensable as the master tactician of our little group," Disra reminded him, waving a hand in dismissal. "But if this will make you feel a little safer—"

He broke off at a quiet beep from the desk. "What's that?" Flim asked.

"My private comm," Disra said, frowning as he opened a drawer and looked at the access code. What in the Empire—?

"You going to answer it?" Flim prompted.

"Stay out of sight," Disra said curtly, keying for the connection. "Both of you."

He straightened up and faced his desk display, arranging his expression into something hard and regal. The status report that had been on the display cleared and became a face—

"All right, Disra," Captain Zothip snarled. "Let's hear it. What in blazes is going on?"

"It's *Your Excellency*, Captain," Disra corrected him. "And I was about to ask you that same question. You know the rules about contacting me this way."

"Vader take your rules! I want to know—"

"You know the rules," Disra repeated, the sheer iciness of his tone somehow silencing the other. "This channel is never to be used except in case of emergency." He lifted his eyebrows. "Or are you trying to tell me something has happened that the Cavrilhu Pirates can't handle?"

"Oh, it's been handled," Zothip said viciously. "It cost me two men and one of my best bases, but it's been handled. What I want to know from *you* is how and why Luke Skywalker just happened to drop in for a visit."

Disra frowned. "What are you talking about?"

"Don't twist me around, Disra," Zothip warned. "Skywalker was at Kauron, asking about your precious clones. Got out of our Jedi trap, and we wound up having to blast and bust."

"I mourn with you in your loss," Disra said sarcastically. "What does this have to do with me?"

"What *doesn't* it have to do with you?" Zothip shot back. "First you pull out all your clones—no explanation—

and now suddenly Skywalker drops in for a visit." The pirate's eyes hardened. "You know what *I* think? I think you decided you don't need us anymore and pointed Skywalker our direction to try to close us down. What do you say to *that*?"

"I say I'm looking at a pirate chief who's lost his nerve," Disra said bluntly. "What in the Empire would I have to gain by eliminating the Cavrilhu Pirates? Even assuming I could pull off such a feat?"

"You tell me," Zothip grated. "I hear Admiral Pellaeon's people have been sniffing around the boots of our financial associates on Muunilinst and Borgo Prime. Maybe you're trying to burn your skyarches behind you before he connects us together."

Disra snorted. "Let me tell you something. Not only am I not worried about Admiral Pellaeon, neither you nor anyone else in the galaxy has reason to worry about him, either. Not for long, anyway."

"Really," Zothip said, scratching under his shaggy black beard. "I thought good Imperials didn't assassinate each other anymore."

"He's not going to be killed," Disra assured him with a smug smile. "He'll simply stop being a threat, that's all."

At the side of the desk, Tierce muttered something under his breath and snagged Disra's datapad. "Yeah, sure, whatever," Zothip said. "So then what was Skywalker doing here?"

Disra shrugged, watching Tierce out of the corner of his eye. The other seemed to be writing a message at furious speed. "Perhaps he identified you during that botched job at Iphigin," he suggested to Zothip. "You said yourself that the ships that drove you away were a YT-1300 and an X-wing. Solo and Skywalker?"

"Could be, I suppose," the pirate conceded with ill grace. "He still knew I'd been using your clones."

Disra waved a hand in dismissal. "He was hunting shoal darters, Zothip. Trying to make a connection—any connection—between you and the Empire. He doesn't know anything."

"Maybe nothing about *you*," Zothip growled. "But what about *me*? He's a Jedi Master, remember? He could have picked up all sorts of dirt from my men."

"Then you'd better bury yourselves somewhere for a while, hadn't you?" Disra suggested, feeling his patience starting to shred around the edges. He didn't have time for this. "Someplace where big bad Jedi can't find you."

Zothip's face darkened. "Don't try to dismiss me like a child, Disra," he said, his voice rippling with soft menace. "Our partnership's been extremely profitable, for both of us. But you don't want me as your enemy. Trust me on that."

"That works both directions," Disra countered. Tierce had finished whatever he was writing and had stepped around behind the desk, holding the datapad just over the display where Disra could read it. "Trust *me* on that," the Moff continued, leaning casually forward as he tried to talk and read at the same time. "There's no reason to end our relationship over something this trivial."

"Trivial?" Zothip echoed. "You call the loss of a major base *trivial*—?"

"Besides, I have another job to offer you," Disra said, leaning back in his seat again and throwing Tierce a faint smile. Score another one for their master tactician. "If you're interested, that is."

Zothip studied Disra's face suspiciously. "I'm listening."

"In approximately three weeks Admiral Pellaeon and the *Chimaera* will be leaving Imperial space for a secret meeting at Pesitiin," Disra said. "I want you to attack him there."

Zothip laughed, a single ranphyxlike bark. "Right, Disra. Attack an Imperial Star Destroyer with a few Telgorn Pacifiers and maybe a *Kaloth* battlecruiser or two. Sure, no trouble."

"I don't mean attack with any intent of doing serious damage," Disra said patiently. "All that's necessary is for him to come under fire. You can do *that*, can't you?"

"I *can* do it, sure," Zothip said. "Question is, why should I?"

"Because I'll pay you twice your usual fee for harassing New Republic shipping." Disra let his voice drop to a soft purr. "And because if you do, the Cavrilhu Pirates will be first in line to reap the rewards when all of this is over."

"You're expecting there to be enough rewards to be parceled out, are you?"

"More than you can possibly imagine," Disra assured him.

Zothip snorted. "You'd be surprised how much I can imagine," he said. But there was a thoughtful edge to his gaze now. "Okay, I'll run with this a while longer. Pesitiin, you say?"

"Right," Disra said. "One other thing: I want whatever ships you send against the *Chimaera* to be marked with Corellian insignia."

"Do you, now," Zothip said, scratching under his beard again. "Any particular reason?"

"The same reason I don't care whether or not you actually inflict any damage on him," Disra said. "Why don't you see if you can figure it out for yourself?"

"I'll do that," Zothip promised. "In the meantime, you see if you can figure out how to deposit the fee into our account, all right?"

Disra smiled thinly. "A pleasure doing business with you, Captain Zothip."

"As always, Moff Disra," the other countered. "I'll be in touch."

The display blanked. "Through the proper channels next time, if you please," Disra muttered toward the empty screen, allowing himself to slump slightly in his seat. Conversations with Zothip always left him feeling drained. "At any rate, that should keep him off our backs for a while."

"As well as performing a useful service for us," Tierce said, taking the datapad back and blanking it. "There's another military virtue for you, Flim: never throw away allies until you're absolutely sure you won't need them anymore."

"We have similar rules in the fringe," Flim said dryly. "Not so eloquently put, of course. What exactly was that all about?"

"What, Zothip's attack on Pellaeon?" Disra asked.

"The attack itself I understand," Flim said. "You're trying to make Pellaeon think the New Republic has rejected his peace offer and is ambushing him instead."

Disra cocked an eyebrow at the con man. "Very good—you're learning. Though of course vision is always clearer in backsight."

"You're too kind," Flim said, tilting his head slightly in a faintly mocking salute. "What I don't understand is why Corellian insignia instead of New Republic ones."

"Because that would be too obvious," Tierce told him. "It would imply all of Coruscant had flatly rejected the idea of a meeting. Pellaeon knows they wouldn't do that, and would guess it was a setup."

"This way it will look like it's just Bel Iblis, who's a Corellian, who is turning him down," Disra added. "Pretending they're Corellian defense ships should also help explain why there aren't any Star Cruisers or other major capital ships in the attack."

"Right," Tierce said. "Also bear in mind that we don't want Pellaeon giving up entirely on this surrender idea, at least not yet. If Bel Iblis has rejected his advances without official sanction, then Pellaeon's next move would be to seek someone else to make his overtures to. That will take time, which plays into our hands. More importantly, it will also require him to leave Pesitiin prematurely. Even if enough of Major Vermel's message got through before he was captured at Morishim, chances are Pellaeon and Bel Iblis will miss each other."

"It should work quite well," Disra said casually, carefully concealing his own surprise. That last part hadn't even occurred to him until Tierce brought it up, but he had no intention of letting either of the others know that. Tierce was entirely too self-assured as it was, and Flim wasn't nearly respectful enough toward either of his superiors for Disra's taste. "In the meantime, in Major Tierce's words, our stew needs a little more stirring. Are we ready for the Bothawui riot yet?"

"If not, we're very close," Tierce said. "We'll use

Navett's team, I think—they've been the most successful agitators."

"And we definitely want this one to be memorable," Disra agreed. "I'll order them into position."

"We should also start activating the rest of the sleeper groups," Tierce said. "There's no way to precisely plan our timetable, and we don't want them still asleep when we need them."

"Yes." Disra snorted gently. "Especially considering that if the real Thrawn were in charge, he'd probably have had the whole operation timed down to the minute."

"We'll just have to do the best we can," Tierce said. "And trust our enemies to fill in the gaps for us. Meanwhile, I'll get over to Yaga Minor and see what I can dig up."

"Let's hope you find something useful," Flim said, getting to his feet. "One thing that still bothers me. What *was* Skywalker doing nosing around a Cavrilhu Pirate base?"

"As I told Zothip, trying to connect us to them," Disra said. "Don't worry, he won't be able to."

"But—"

"Besides, it's irrelevant," Tierce cut him off. "Very soon now a few clones and a grubby little pirate gang will be the least of the Rebellion's worries."

CHAPTER

11

The door slid open, and Karrde stepped onto the *Wild Karrde*'s bridge. "Good afternoon, gentlemen," he said. "How are we doing?"

"Fine, Chief," Dankin said, half turning around in the helm seat to look at him. "We're almost to the Nosken system—just a few more minutes."

"Good." Karrde took a step toward him, sending a quick look around at the other stations—

And paused, frowning. "What are you doing up here, H'sishi?" he asked the young Togorian female at the sensor station.

She turned to face him. [Dankin asked me to take the station,] she said, her mewling Togorian speech as purringly feline as her appearance. [He said it was time I took some bridge practice.]

Karrde looked at Dankin. The other was gazing studiously at his board again, his face in profile, but even so Karrde could see the secret amusement bubbling there. "Yes, I suppose it is," he said, taking a second look around the bridge at the other stations. Odonnl, in the copilot seat, was wearing the same expression as Dankin. So was Pormfil at the engine monitor, though on his Kerestian face it was a little harder to spot. Even Chin, who tended to be rather grandfatherly toward new recruits these days, was having to try hard not to smile. "Have you done a status check against the baseline recently?" he asked, looking back at H'sishi.

The Togorian's yellow eyes seemed to cloud over a little. [No, Chieftain,] she said. [I will do one now if you request it.]

"Please," Karrde nodded. "The baseline datacard is in the computer room."

[I obey,] H'sishi said, uncoiling her lithe body from her seat. She padded across the bridge, her claws making little clicking sounds against the metal floor as she walked, and exited.

"All right, gentlemen," Karrde said mildly as the door slid shut behind her. "Am I going to have to guess?"

"Oh, it's nothing much, Chief," Dankin said, radiating a thoroughly unconvincing innocence. "It's just that she's never been to Terrik's place before. I thought she'd get the best view if she was up here when we came out of hyperspace."

"Ah," Karrde said. "And you were curious to see how high she'd jump?"

"Well . . . yeah, maybe a little," Dankin admitted.

"We like to think of it as her full initiation into the crew," Odonnl added helpfully.

"I see." Karrde looked around at the others, all of them grinning openly now. "I suppose it hasn't occurred to you that startling a Togorian this way might be just the slightest bit dangerous?"

"Oh, come on, Captain, it's harmless fun," Odonnl said. "Mara lets us do this when *she's* on the bridge."

"Anyway, Cap't, these are a long tradition," Chin said. "Billey's folk surely cooked up something like it when you joined up with them, hee?"

"Billey's people weren't nearly so creative," Karrde said dryly. "As for Mara, her excuse is that she wants to use the Force to examine how new crew members behave under stress."

"Sounds like a good reason to me," Dankin offered. "Better we check them out here than find out what they're made of when we're in the middle of a genuine crisis."

"You're rationalizing, of course," Karrde pointed out.

"Probably," Dankin agreed shamelessly. "Come on, Chief, give us a break. It's been deadly quiet around here lately."

"An enraged Togorian would certainly break up the monotony," Karrde said, shaking his head. Still, horseplay aside, they did have a point. If H'sishi was going to become a permanent member of the *Wild Karrde*'s crew, they really did need to find out how she reacted when startled. "Be it upon your own heads. I'll watch from over there."

He stepped over to the bulkhead beside Chin, where he had a good view of the sensor station; and as he did so, the door slid open and H'sishi padded back in. [I have the datacard, Chieftain Karrde,] she said, holding it up for his inspection.

"Good," Karrde confirmed, giving the label a quick check. H'sishi had a good grasp of spoken Basic, but her Aurebesh reading skills were still a little shaky. "Go ahead and set it up."

[I obey.] She sat down at her console again, clawed hands tapping delicately at the controls.

"Here we go," Dankin said. "Stand by sublight engines."

Gripping the levers, he eased them back. The mottled sky turned to starlines and collapsed to stars—

And there, floating in the darkness directly ahead of them, was an Imperial Star Destroyer.

H'sishi came half out of her seat, hissing something vicious-sounding in her language that Karrde didn't catch. Her mouth was stretched wide open, the fangs glistening whitely in the pale bridge lighting. Her fur stood stiffly out from her body, making her look half again as big as normal, and in her yellow eyes was a crazy fire.

"Star Destroyer directly ahead," Dankin called out, as if someone on the bridge might somehow have missed it. "Range, two kilometers."

"Turbolaser batteries swiveling toward us," Odonnl put in. "Pormfil?"

"Engines at full power," the Kerestian said, his eight cheek nostrils wheezing rhythmically.

"Picking up a transmission, Cap't," Chin announced.

"Acknowledge it," Karrde said, watching H'sishi closely. She hadn't moved, but was still half standing staring at the dark bulk and glittering lights ahead. "Are they activating any tractor beams?"

For about half a second the bridge seemed to hold its collective breath. Then, with a quiet hiss, H'sishi sank back into her seat and began tapping keys on her control board. [No tractor beams have yet been activated,] she mewled. [The turbolaser batteries . . .]

Her stiffened fur seemed to wilt a little as she tapped more keys. [There is no power in them,] she said, sounding confused. [No. There is power in . . .]

She turned to face Karrde, her yellow eyes narrowing. [There are three functional turbolaser batteries,] she said. [No more.]

"Good," Karrde said calmly. "That means we're in the right place. Always good to know that. Chin?"

"The owner awaits, Cap't," Chin said, smiling openly now as he tapped the comm key. "He'd like to speak with you."

"Thank you," Karrde said. "Hello, Booster. How are things?"

"Never better, you old pirate," Booster Terrik's cheerful voice boomed from the bridge speaker. "Welcome to the *Errant Venture*. You shopping today, or just breaking in a new crew member?"

H'sishi hissed softly, her fingers rubbing gently against the control board. But she said nothing. "We're shopping," Karrde said. "For information, mostly."

"Are you really," Booster said in a tone that made Karrde picture him rubbing his hands together. "Well, well. This is definitely my star-shining day. You want to bring the *Wild Karrde* aboard, or should I send you a shuttle?"

"We'll come aboard if you have the space," Karrde said. "I'm not in the market for any hardware myself, but I imagine my people will want to browse."

"Well, come on in, then," Booster said cheerfully. "Traders' Alley is open and ready for business, as are the rest of our little boutiques. Go ahead and take—let's see—Docking Bay Fifteen. I'll have someone there to escort you up to the bridge after you've turned your people loose. Don't forget to remind them that Traders' Alley is a cash-only business."

"Of course," Karrde said. "I'll see you soon."

He motioned to Chin, and the other shut down the comm. "Take us in, Dankin," he said. "You know how to get into the docking bays?"

"No problem," Dankin said, getting busy at his board.

At the sensor station, H'sishi stood up and turned to face Karrde. [Was this then a joke, Chieftain?] she asked. Her tone and expression were rigid, not betraying anything of what she was thinking. [I do not appreciate being made to look foolish.]

"You didn't look foolish," Karrde assured her. "You merely looked startled, after which you returned to your assigned duties."

The Togorian looked briefly around at the others. [Humans enjoy making others look foolish,] she said, an edge of challenge in her voice.

"Humans do enjoy jokes," Karrde acknowledged. "But humor was not the primary purpose of the exercise."

H'sishi's fur had been stiffening again. Now, slowly, it settled back down. [You wished to see if I would run in fear.]

"Or freeze, or panic," Karrde agreed. "If you had done any of those things—"

[I would have been executed?]

Karrde shook his head. "I don't execute my people, H'sishi," he told her. "Not unless a serious crime has been committed against me or the organization. No, you'd simply have been moved to a different position, some post where you'd be less likely to face this kind of stress. An information gatherer, perhaps, or else a shadow business liaison."

H'sishi's ears twitched. [I do not wish such a post.]

"I'm glad to hear that," Karrde said, "because frankly I

think you would be wasted there. You'd be far more useful aboard the *Wild Karrde* or one of my other ships."

The Togorian seemed to think about that. [I would prefer to stay here, if that would be possible.]

"I think there's a good chance of that," Karrde said. "We'll speak more about it later." He gestured to her control board. "You can return the datacard to the computer room—we won't need to run that baseline check until we leave."

H'sishi showed her fangs again. [I obey, Chieftain,] she said. Delicately plucking the datacard from its slot with the tips of her claws, she padded from the bridge.

"Well, gentlemen," Karrde said, stepping over behind H'sishi's vacated chair. "You've had your joke, and we all lived through it. Did she pass?"

"Definitely," Dankin said. "With banners waving, I'd say."

"Agreed," Odonnl nodded. "Took her a second to gather her wits, but then she got right back down to business."

"And she did not forget how to use her console, as some have done," Pormfil added, whistling emphatically through his nostrils. "I do not believe even Elkin did so well when he was thus tested."

"Perhaps," Karrde said. "Though I'd wager H'sishi left something behind that Elkin didn't."

Pormfil sniffed the air. "The aroma of nervous sweat?" he suggested.

"No." Karrde pointed at the group of small indentations in the edge of H'sishi's control board. "Claw marks."

A familiar figure was waiting for Karrde and Odonnl as they headed down the *Wild Karrde*'s ramp. "Ah—Captain Karrde," Nawara Ven said, dipping his head in a formal Twi'lek bow. "It is good to see you again."

"And you, Ven." Karrde nodded back. "I trust life is treating you well?"

"It is all enjoyment aboard the *Errant Venture*," Ven

said, smiling thinly. "Come. Booster's waiting for you on the bridge."

The Twi'lek led the way toward a bank of turbolifts, limping only slightly on his artificial leg. "I notice you've lost some of your turbolasers," Karrde commented. "My people were reading only three active batteries as we came in."

"Fortunes of business, I'm afraid," Ven said, keying the turbolift call. "We had to break two of them down for parts for three others, but then had to sell those three to purchase components for the hyperdrive."

"By my count, that still leaves five from your original ten batteries," Karrde pointed out.

"Yes," Ven said, rearranging his head-tail on his shoulder as the turbolift door slid ponderously open. "The other two are currently under repair."

"Ah."

They stepped into the turbolift. The door closed again, and the car began to move. "Only two of the turbolifts in this section are still working," Ven said. "You'd be amazed at how many things there are to go wrong on a Star Destroyer."

"I can imagine," Karrde said. "Back during the height of the Rebellion I heard a Special Operations man describe a Star Destroyer as 174,000 design flaws waiting to be exploited."

Ven tossed his head. "A low-end estimate. Booster finally gave in and hired a group of two hundred techs— Verpine, actually—to upgrade some of our systems. That was seven months ago, and they're still at it."

"I suppose that's what you get when you try to run a ship this size with less than what's supposed to be the bare-minimum skeleton crew," Karrde suggested, looking around the car. "Entropy will always get ahead of you. I presume Booster isn't thinking of selling?"

Ven favored him with a sly grin. "Why? Are you thinking of buying?"

"I could probably be persuaded," Karrde said. "Certainly if it comes down to the ship falling into someone else's hands. I wouldn't want to face down a Hutt in one of these things."

"Oh, I don't know," the Twi'lek said dryly. "Given the Hutts' past performance, it might be entertaining to watch."

"Not if it was someone like Jabba."

"True," Ven conceded. "At any rate, I'll pass your offer on to Booster."

The turbolift car settled to a slightly clunky stop, and the door slid open to reveal the aft bridge. "Booster asked me to apologize for not welcoming you in person, incidentally," Ven said as he waved them toward the archway that led to the main bridge. "You'll understand in a moment why he couldn't."

"No problem," Karrde said, glancing casually around at the aft bridge consoles. Here and there an indicator light still winked, but for the most part the consoles seemed to either be on standby or to have been shut down completely. He stepped into the archway, turning back around to throw a quick look at the aft bridge's hologram pad—which also seemed to be shut down—

"Talon Karrde!" Booster's voice boomed. "Welcome aboard."

Karrde completed his turn. Booster was striding down the command walkway toward them, arms flung wide open in expansive welcome.

And walking right behind him— "And look who else has come to visit the old man," Booster continued, half turning to gesture just as expansively at them.

"Yes, indeed," Karrde said, motioning Odonnl forward. "Odonnl, I don't believe you've met Booster's family. This is his lovely daughter Mirax, and his son-in-law Commander Corran Horn. Former—I'm sorry; *current* member of General Wedge Antilles's celebrated Rogue Squadron."

"Ah," Odonnl said guardedly. "Pleased to meet you. That's the group Ven here used to be with, isn't it?"

"Nawara and I used to fly together, yes," Corran said, his tone equally guarded. "Booster, I suppose I don't mind that Karrde knows we're here, but—"

"Relax, Corran," Booster soothed, stepping forward to

briefly grip Karrde's hand. "Karrde's top people are just as trustworthy as he is."

Corran shot Karrde a decidedly ambivalent look. "That makes me feel so much better."

"Don't worry," Karrde assured him, offering his hand. "We won't tell Coruscant one of its most revered heroes is associating with riffraff."

Corran took the proffered hand, his face relaxing into a slight smile. "I appreciate that. How's Mara doing these days?"

"Quite well, thank you," Karrde said. "As a matter of fact, she should be along anytime—she's temporarily flying with the *Starry Ice*, which is supposed to be meeting me here." He shifted his gaze to the woman. "Hello, Mirax; it's been a long time. Where's the little one?"

"Valin's right down there," Mirax said, giving Karrde a far more genuine smile than her husband's as she waved toward the starboard crew pit. "And he's six years old—not so little anymore."

"Indeed not," Karrde said, taking a couple of steps to the side and looking down the crew pit. The boy was perched on a couple of extra cushions in one of the chairs, staring at one of the displays, completely oblivious to the visitors or the scattering of Booster's men manning some of the other consoles. "Teaching him to fly the ship?"

"Hardly," Mirax said, coming up beside him and smiling fondly down at her son. "Dad set up one of the tractor beam consoles so he could play games. Do you want to say hello?"

"Don't disturb him," Karrde said. "Perhaps we'll have time later. Is he still keeping up with his music?"

"Like a mynock with his tail on fire," Booster said wryly. "I just bought him a new chordokeylo—he'd already worn out his first one. But seriously, Karrde, I'd appreciate it if you would keep Corran's presence here to yourself. This is supposed to be a quiet meeting—only a handful of New Republic officials know anything about it."

"I understand," Karrde said, eyeing Corran again. "A secret mission, eh? Cloak and blade, skulking around darkened cantinas, whispered conversations with shadowy contacts—that sort of thing?"

"I'm sure you realize we can't discuss it with you," Corran said, his face not quite stony.

"Yes, of course," Karrde said. "Say no more." He nodded toward the crew pit. "Though I can't say I approve of your superiors allowing you to take your family along on such a dangerous mission."

"It's nothing like that," Booster said with a touch of mild exasperation. "All Corran needs is a little information—"

"Booster!" Corran snapped, glaring at his father-in-law. "Seal your word port, will you?"

"Perhaps I can help," Karrde offered. "I do have certain information sources of my own. Some of which, I daresay, are better even than Booster's."

"Thanks for the offer," Corran said. "We'll manage."

"He does have a point, Corran," Booster said, rubbing his cheek thoughtfully. "Maybe you ought to lay the situation out for him."

"No." Corran shook his head. "No offense, Karrde, but this is high-level stuff. You're not authorized to know anything about it."

"Yes, but—" Booster began.

"No, that's all right," Karrde said, holding up a hand. "If his superiors don't even want outsiders knowing he and his family are here, they certainly wouldn't want him discussing his errand."

"Exactly," Corran said. "Thank you for understanding."

"So if I may, I'll just borrow Booster for a few minutes to discuss *my* errand," Karrde continued, reaching into his inside jacket pocket and pulling out a datacard. "But before I forget, Mirax, I brought this for your son."

Mirax frowned as he handed her the datacard. "What is it?"

"An Ettian tonal card for his chordokeylo," Karrde told her blandly. "I understand it's proper etiquette for a guest to bring a small gift for his hosts' children."

Corran leaned over her shoulder to look at the datacard, a slightly sandbagged look on his face. "But how did you know—?" He looked back at Karrde, shifted a rapidly hardening glare to his father-in-law. "Booster?"

"Not guilty," Booster said hastily, holding up both hands. "I didn't tell anyone you were coming. Not even my own people."

"As I said," Karrde said quietly. "My information sources are quite good."

For a minute the bridge was silent. Corran looked at Booster, then at Mirax, got no help from either of them, and finally looked back at Karrde. "What's it going to cost me?" he sighed.

Karrde shrugged. "Whatever it's worth, of course. We can negotiate price later."

Corran looked at Booster. "I've heard *that* before."

"If you'd prefer, we could leave that part up to Councilor Organa Solo," Karrde offered. "In the past she and I have always been able to arrive at a mutually acceptable arrangement."

"I'd hate to think what some of those arrangements might have cost us," Corran growled. "All right, fine. I presume you're aware we've had a lot of demonstrations and riots lately against Bothan businesses and consulates."

"Over the revelations contained in the Caamas Document," Karrde murmured.

"Right. Well, in and among all these protests we're starting to hear the name 'Vengeance' being batted around. Not as a word, but as a group or organization."

Karrde looked at Odonnl. "Have we heard anything about that?"

"I haven't personally," Odonnl said. "But there's a lot of stuff our sources send in that I don't have time to look at."

"We'll do a data search when we get back to the *Wild Karrde*," Karrde said. "What are Coruscant's conclusions?"

"No conclusions yet, just questions," Corran said. "The main ones being who and what this Vengeance is . . . and whether they're home-grown or getting help from outside."

"Let me guess. The Empire?"

Corran's eyes narrowed slightly. "You say that like you don't believe it."

"Not exactly," Karrde corrected. "I say that like someone who rather cynically notices that whenever anything goes wrong in the New Republic, official blaming fingers immediately zero in on the Empire."

"That's a little unfair," Booster said. "Especially considering the Empire's long history of this kind of meddling."

"I'm not saying they're not involved," Karrde said. "I'm simply warning against the automatic assumption that they are."

"But—"

"No, he's right," Corran said reluctantly. "There are a lot of beings who remember the Empire doing exactly the same thing to us: blaming the Rebellion for everything, then using that as an excuse to tighten their grip. That's why my visit here was supposed to be kept secret, in fact—General Bel Iblis didn't want it leaking out that we were even thinking in this direction."

Karrde nodded. He should have guessed Bel Iblis would be the one who'd put this Ratitan whisperfly in Corran's ear. Unlike some of the New Republic's leaders, Bel Iblis knew how to keep his eye on his goal. And, when necessary, to ignore the shortcomings of the people he might have to deal with in order to reach that goal. "Understood," he said. "We'll check our files; if there's nothing there, we'll start some quiet inquiries and see what we can find."

"Sounds good," Booster said. "And as long as we're trading wish lists here, you also had some information you wanted, right?"

"Two simple questions, actually," Karrde said. "First of all: our friend Luke Skywalker is trying to locate the Cavrilhu Pirates. Any idea as to which rock they might have buried themselves under?"

"I know they've got a base on Amorris," Booster said, pulling out a datapad and keying it on. "And—let's see—seems to me their major stronghold is—right; here it is. A hollowed-out asteroid in the Kauron system."

Karrde shook his head. "They've abandoned their Amorris site," he told Booster. "And according to Mara, Skywalker just finished chasing them off their asteroid."

"What did he do that for?" Booster held up a hand. "Never mind; I don't want to know. Well, if those are gone then I can't help you. Second question?"

"Before he went to Kauron, Skywalker helped stop a pirate raid at Iphigin," Karrde said, glancing casually around the bridge. No one else was in earshot. "No idea which group was involved. During the battle, he sensed what he thought was a group of clones aboard one of the pirates' ships."

No one moved, but the atmosphere was suddenly rigid. "I thought the Empire had already run through its supply of Mount Tantiss clones," Mirax said, a shadow of dread in her voice.

"That's what Coruscant says," Booster confirmed, not sounding any happier than his daughter. "At least to us outsiders. Corran?"

"As far as I know, it's the truth," Corran said. "It's been years since we ran across any clone casualties in military action."

"How long has it been since you looked for them?" Odonnl asked.

"Good point," Corran conceded. "I don't know."

"It's hard to believe there could be any of them left," Booster said. "They were some of the best and brightest troops Thrawn had. You'd think Daala or someone else would have spent them long ago."

"Unless Thrawn put some in deep cover where Daala couldn't find them," Karrde said.

"What for?" Booster scoffed. "Saving them? For what?"

"And why would they suddenly be making their appearance now?" Corran added.

"We don't know that they *are* suddenly making their appearance," Odonnl reminded him tartly. "Maybe they've been out there all along and it's just that you hotshot military guys haven't noticed."

Corran took half a step toward him. "Look, Odonnl, when we're busy trying to keep peace around the galaxy—"

"Easy, gentlemen," Karrde said, stepping between them and holding up a hand. "Let's try to remember we're all on the same side here, shall we?"

Odonnl's lips puckered. "Yeah. Sure."

"Why don't you head back to the *Wild Karrde*, Odonnl," Karrde suggested. "Get started on that data search."

"Sure," Odonnl muttered again. "Good idea."

"I'll escort you down," Ven offered, stepping forward. Karrde looked at him in mild surprise—the Twi'lek had been so quiet he'd almost forgotten he was there. "It's easy to get lost on a ship this size."

The expression on Odonnl's face clearly indicated his opinion of that as an excuse, but he merely nodded and headed aft, Ven at his side. "My apologies, Commander Horn," Karrde said quietly as the two of them crossed under the archway and disappeared into the aft bridge. "Odonnl doesn't have the same fond memories of the New Republic military that I do."

"That's all right," Corran said darkly. "I have certain unfond memories of smugglers myself."

"Corran," Mirax said warningly, taking his arm.

The X-wing pilot patted her hand. "Present company excluded, of course," he amended. "Let's get back to business."

"Thank you," Karrde said. "What we know for sure— and *all* we know for sure—is that Skywalker sensed clones aboard those ships. Our first job is to answer one simple question: whether they're Imperial leftovers, or whether someone else has found another cache of cloning cylinders."

"Someone such as the Cavrilhu Pirates?" Mirax asked.

"That thought has crossed my mind," Karrde agreed soberly. "It could very well be that my two questions for your father are in fact interconnected."

He smiled at Booster. "In which case, of course, I'd expect a discount on price."

Booster rolled his eyes exaggeratedly. "Oh, for—"

"Yo, Captain," a voice called from one of the crew pits.

"What is it, Shish?" Booster called back.

"Got a ship incoming—reads out as the *Starry Ice*," Shish reported. "Pilot wants landing instructions. You want me to fix her up?"

"Key the transmission over to me," Booster instructed him, pulling out his comlink. "She'll probably be asking about you anyway," he added to Karrde as he handed him the slender cylinder. "Might as well save ourselves a little time."

"Thank you." Karrde thumbed the comlink on. "Mara, this is Karrde. How are things?"

"Running quite smoothly, thank you," Mara said. If she was surprised to hear his voice, she was hiding it well. Though now that he thought about it, there weren't a lot of things that ever seemed to surprise her. "Afraid we didn't have time to swing by Dronseen for that cargo."

"That's all right," Karrde said. "Faughn can make the pickup after she drops you here. How did the pirate hunt go?"

"Complete washout," she said. "We tracked their vector to Di'wor but then lost it completely. The traffic around there was fierce—Starspeeder 3000s all over the place."

"It's pollination season for the singfruit groves," Booster murmured. "Peace breeds tourists."

Karrde nodded. "Don't worry about it," he told Mara. "I wasn't really expecting them to leave a trail you could follow. Have Faughn bring the *Starry Ice* aboard and we'll—"

"Jade!" Faughn's voice cut in. "Over there—coming in from starboard."

"I see it," Mara said, her tone suddenly crisp. "Terrik, you've got company—coming in one-one-seven by fifteen, your vector."

Booster was already running along the command walkway toward the forward viewport, Corran right behind him. "One-one-seven by fifteen, Bodwae," he snapped. "What do you see?"

"Nothjing," a bewildered Laerdocian voice said from one of the crew pits. "These *shas'mink* sensors—"

"It's hard to see," Mara put in, her voice coming now from the *Errant Venture*'s main bridge speaker system. "Small and dark—looks a little like a severely modified TIE fighter."

"Doesn't show up well on sensors, either," Faughn added.

"Stjill see nothjing," Bodwae insisted.

"Skip it," Booster said tartly. He and Corran were standing together now by the forward viewports, Booster's head turning slowly back and forth as he searched the sky. "Get the deflector shields up, and stand by turbolasers."

"Shjields shortjing out agajin," Bodwae said. "Turbolasers—"

"I'm getting a transmission now," Shish barked. "Strong signal. It's . . . well, stang it all, I don't know *what* it is."

"Mara?" Karrde asked.

"We're picking up the edge of it," Mara confirmed. "Pretty faint out here, though. So far the computer's not making anything of it."

"There it is," Corran snapped, jabbing out a finger. "Coming straight at us."

"Get that bridge deflector up!" Booster snapped. "*Now!*"

"Mara?" Karrde called.

"We're still out of firing range," she said tightly. "Better take cover."

Karrde glanced around, belatedly wondering where Mirax was. He spotted her at once, heading at a dead run back toward the relative safety of the aft bridge, her bewildered-looking son Valin clutched in her arms. For a moment he considered joining her, realized it was already too late, and turned back instead toward the forward viewports. He could see the unknown intruder now, burning space directly toward them. Like no ship he'd ever seen . . .

"Brjidge deflector not comjing up," Bodwae snarled. "Shjip gojing to hjit."

"Hit the ground!" Booster snapped, grabbing Corran's arm and dropping them both flat on the command walkway. Karrde took a long step toward the nearest crew pit, realized he wouldn't have time to jump down into it, and stopped. The intruder was still coming—

And then, at the last second, it made a strange corkscrewing maneuver to one side and shot around and above past the viewport.

It took Karrde a second to find his voice. "Mara?"

"You all right?" she asked anxiously.

"Yes, we're fine," he assured her, breaking his paralysis and starting down the command walkway toward where Booster and Corran were still stretched out on the deck. "Where did it go?"

"Overshot the command superstructure, cut around behind the drive nozzles where we couldn't see it, then jumped to lightspeed," she told him. "Same trick as the one Luke spooked."

Karrde frowned out the viewports. "This was the same type as that one?"

"It looked like it," Mara told him. "Torve's doing a scrub of the sensor data now."

Booster and Corran were back on their feet by the time Karrde reached them. "Did you see that?" Booster demanded, shaking his head as he brushed himself off. "Of all the stupid, cherfer-brained stunts—"

"Captain, this is Torve," the young man's voice cut him off. "It's confirmed: same type of ship as before."

"Where did you see this other ship?" Booster asked.

"In the asteroids near the Cavrilhu's Kauron base," Karrde told him. "Mara, what about that transmission?"

"We're running it now," she said. "It consists of what seems to be a short message, followed by a pause, followed by a repeat of the message. So far we're not coming up with a match to any known language, code, or encrypt."

"Probably something useless like that Qella ship Calrissian chased halfway across the galaxy," Booster said with a scornful sniff.

"That's what we thought at first," Mara said. "I don't think so anymore."

"Why?" Booster asked. "Just because it was transmitting something?"

"Because it was transmitting specifically toward this ship," Karrde said. "And the fact that it paused and then repeated itself implies it was expecting an answer."

Booster scratched his cheek. "Does kind of sound that way, doesn't it? Mara, you're running Imperial codes against it, too, aren't you?"

"First thing we tried," she told him. "Nothing came even close."

"Yet they came in for a close look at an Imperial Star Destroyer," Karrde mused. "And before that they were poking around a pirate base with suspected Imperial ties."

"Sounds like they're either already involved with the Empire or else want to be," Mara said.

"Or maybe it's something else entirely," Faughn put in, her voice suddenly tight. "I've just run a phoneme analysis on that transmission; and I think I've found the name 'Thrawn' in there."

Karrde frowned. "Let's hear it."

There was a brief pause; and then over the comlink came a sputter of alien language. Squarely in the middle of the gibberish—

"I heard it," Booster said. "It was kind of broken up, like he was stuttering or something."

"That's because you were getting his full name there," Mara said, her voice suddenly grim. "Mitth'raw'nuruodo. *Thrawn* was what he called his core name."

Out of the corner of his eye, Karrde saw something flash across Corran's expression. "So you were on a full-name basis with the guy?" Booster asked with forced casualness.

"Hardly," Mara said. "But I did know his full name. And there weren't a lot of people in the Empire who did."

Karrde chewed his lower lip. "You know anything about his history? His early history with the Empire, I mean?"

"Not really," she said. "Some Imperial commander ran into him on a deserted world just inside the Unknown Regions while chasing smugglers. He was impressed by his tactical ability, and brought him back to Coruscant. Rumor was his own people had exiled him there, incidentally."

"Why?" Booster asked.

"I don't know," Mara said. "But it could be that ship was someone who's finally figured out where he went and has come looking for him."

Booster snorted. "They're going to be real disappointed when they find out they're ten years too late."

"Maybe not," Corran muttered. "It could be it's not Thrawn they're looking for."

Karrde studied the other's face. There was something there, all right. "I take it that's not an idle guess," he said mildly. "Would you care to share it with the rest of us?"

Corran's lip twitched. "I wasn't supposed to say anything about this to anyone but Booster," he said reluctantly. "But under the circumstances . . . That Devaronian you got the Caamas Document from, Karrde? He found some other datacards in the same batch. One of them was labeled 'The Hand of Thrawn.' "

Karrde nodded slowly. So that was the secret Leia had been holding out on him at Wayland. And the reason she'd been giving Mara such a strange look.

"The datacard was so badly scrambled that they couldn't get anything from it," Corran continued. "Councilor Organa Solo thought it might be Thrawn's version of an Emperor's Hand. General Bel Iblis wanted me to ask Booster if he'd run across the term before."

"Never," Booster said, shaking his head. "Karrde? Mara?"

"No," Karrde said.

"Me, neither," Mara said. "And personally, I find it hard to picture Thrawn having that kind of shadow agent. He wasn't into the same kind of political manipulation that the Emperor was. Besides, he had the Noghri if he needed something special done."

"Yet there was a datacard with that title in the Emperor's private files," Karrde pointed out. "It must mean *something*."

"How do you know it was from his private files?" Booster asked.

"Because if it was something Bel Iblis could have looked up in the Kamparas archives, he wouldn't have sent Corran to ask you about it," Karrde pointed out.

"Point," Booster rumbled. "So you figure these ships are looking for either Thrawn or this Hand of Thrawn?"

"Or else the person in the ship *is* the Hand of Thrawn," Mara said. "Whichever, it's starting to look more important than ever that we try to track these ships down."

"Agreed," Karrde said. "How do you suggest we start?"

"We've got the vector from their jump a few minutes ago," Mara said. "We also got the vector from the Kauron ship. Faughn's plotting an intercept point."

"Got it," Faughn said. "It's an unexplored system in Gradilis sector, right on the boundary between Wild Space and the Unknown Regions. It's listed as the Nirauan system, so someone must have visited the place, but there's no other data."

"Sounds too easy," Booster rumbled. "They wouldn't really be stupid enough to jump directly to their base like that, would they? Especially not with us watching."

"Depends on how they make their jumps," Karrde pointed out. "They may not have the computing power aboard to handle complicated hyperspace calculations. Or it could be that their return home is preprogrammed to make sure none of their ships go astray."

"They also may not realize we can still pull their vector for a few microseconds after they jump," Mara added. "Both times now they've made sure they were out of our line of sight before kicking in their hyperdrive. They might think that's all they need to do."

"At any rate, it's a place to start," Karrde said, an odd reluctance seeping into him.

A reluctance Mara evidently could hear in his voice.

"Would we rather not go?" she asked. "We could just turn all this over to the New Republic and let them handle it."

"Corran?" Booster prompted.

The X-wing pilot was still staring out the viewport at the stars. "I can take it back to Bel Iblis, no problem," he said, sounding vaguely distracted. "But I doubt he'll be able to do anything about it, at least not now. This whole Caamas thing has everybody in a knot-tie twist."

Karrde nodded, his instinctive reluctance turning still darker. Booster was right: this was too easy. A trap, perhaps, or at the very least a wild tresher hunt and a waste of time.

But if it wasn't . . .

"No, you'd better check it out," he sighed. "Have Faughn transmit her schedule to Chin before you jump; we'll sort her assignments out among the other ships."

"Right," Mara said. "Anyplace in particular you want us to rendezvous when we get back?"

"Just get in touch with the network—they'll find me," Karrde told her. "And be careful."

"Don't worry," Mara assured him grimly. "If they're trying some game, they'll be sorry they tried it on us. See you later."

Karrde thumbed off the comlink. "Good luck," he said softly.

"Don't worry, they'll be fine," Booster said, plucking the comlink from Karrde's hand and replacing it in his own belt. "Mara and Faughn are both pretty sharp, and the *Starry Ice* is a good ship. Better than this one, anyway," he added, glowering as he brushed past Karrde and stomped back down the command walkway. "All right, Bodwae, what the blinking mradhe muck is going on with those shields?"

He squatted down to hear the Laerdocian's excuses; and as he did so, Karrde stepped over to Corran's side. "You were right here when that alien ship went past," he said quietly. "Did you happen to sense anything unusual about it?"

Corran threw him a sideways look. "What do you mean?"

"I mean whatever it is that Skywalker picks up when he

gets near a group of clones," Karrde told him. "Whatever this disturbance is that it creates in the Force."

For a long moment the only sound on the bridge was the argument going on behind them, now become three-way as Shish joined in on Bodwae's side. "I don't know what Luke senses when there are clones nearby," Corran said at last, his voice barely audible. "All I felt here was the presence of something alien."

Karrde nodded. "I see."

Corran turned to face him. "My . . . talent . . . is not exactly public knowledge, Karrde," he said, his tone somewhere between challenge and threat.

"Yes, I know," Karrde replied evenly. "Wise of you to keep it that way."

"I think so," Corran countered. "Problem is, you're in the business of selling information."

"Ah, but I'm also in the business of survival," Karrde said. "And in this big, dangerous galaxy one occasionally needs a helping hand." He cocked an eyebrow. "I always think it's nice when there are cards in that hand which the opposition doesn't know about."

Corran's forehead furrowed slightly. "So that's how it works, huh? You keep quiet, and I owe you one?"

Karrde looked back along the command walkway. From around the corner of the aft bridge Mirax and Valin had reappeared, Mirax looking cautious, the boy tugging impatiently at his mother's hand with the obvious wish to run to Daddy. "Yes, you owe me one," he told Corran. "But be assured that when I collect, it'll be something safe. I owe Mirax that much." He considered. "Either that, or something vital that absolutely has to be done."

Corran snorted gently. "That covers a lot of ground."

Karrde shrugged. "As I said. It's a big, dangerous galaxy."

CHAPTER

12

The west wall of the Resinem Entertainment Complex was dirty and salt-encrusted, discolored with age and pitted by the debris from the explosion fifteen years earlier that had leveled the rival gambling hall down the street. From the far side of the fifty-meter depression that marked the explosion's center the Resinem's west wall was said to be rather attractive, the random bits of damage weaving themselves into intriguing visual patterns, particularly in the shifting glow of a Borcorash sunset.

But sunset was long past, and Shada wasn't on the far side of the pit, anyway. She was three-quarters of the way up the west wall, digging her climbing hooks carefully into the various cracks and cavities; and from this perspective, all she could tell was that the wall was dirty and not much fun. *Join a smuggling group*, she thought darkly for about the fifth time since beginning her climb. *Visit a side of the galaxy the tourists never see.*

It wasn't fun, but it was necessary. Very soon now Mazzic and Griv would be escorted onto the Resinem's ultra-private top floor for a meeting with a smooth-talking Kubaz who represented a shadowy Hutt crime cartel. Griv was carrying a small case full of ryll, the Kubaz would be carrying a similarly sized case full of Sormahil fire gems, and in theory the gathering would break up with a simple and mutually profitable exchange.

In theory.

Somewhere in the distance off to her right an airspeeder swung around in preparation for landing; and as its landing lights sent a brief splash of pale illumination across the wall in front of her, Shada felt a fresh surge of depression sweep through her. She hadn't been home to Emberlene for over twelve years now, not since Mazzic had hired her on as his bodyguard, but the grime and deterioration of this wall had brought all those memories back as if it had been yesterday. Memories of growing up amid the ruins of what had once been great cities. Memories of the death that had struck so often around her: death by disease, by malnutrition, by violence, by hopelessness. Memories of pervasive hunger, of eking out an existence by the vermin she was able to catch and kill, and on her share of the meager foodstuffs that came in from what was left of the countryside's arable land.

And on the outworld supplies that finally began coming in. Supplies not donated by caring offworlders or a generous Republic, but earned by the blood and sweat and lives of the Mistryl shadow guards.

They were the elite of what remained of Emberlene society, commissioned personally in their crusade by the Eleven Elders of the People; and from her earliest childhood Shada had wanted with all her heart to be one of them. The Mistryl roamed the starlanes, a sisterhood of exquisitely trained warrior women, hiring out their services and combat skills to the oppressed and powerless of the galaxy and receiving in exchange the money vital for keeping the remnants of their devastated world alive.

A world whose people no one had ever even noticed, let alone cared about. Unlike, say, Caamas.

With an effort, she choked down the ripple of resentment at all the attention Caamas had been getting the past couple of weeks. The destruction of Emberlene was too far in the past to get emotional about anymore, even for her. No one in the galaxy had cared back when it was attacked; they

certainly couldn't be expected to care now. Yes, it was unfair; but no one had ever claimed the universe was fair.

From just above and to her left came a soft, questioning
burp. Shada paused, looking up into the darkness, and spotted the reflection from a faint pair of close-set eyes looking
down at her from deep shadow. "It's okay," she murmured
toward the eyes, cautiously pulling herself up for a closer
look. On this part of Borcorash it was probably a harmless
blufferavian, but it never hurt to be careful.

The caution turned out to be unnecessary. It was indeed
a blufferavian, resting on a nest built into a particularly deep
niche in the wall. From beneath its wing she caught a
glimpse of a couple of speckled eggs.

"Don't worry, I'm not hungry," she soothed the creature. Once upon a time, she remembered darkly, she'd been
quite good at catching avians that size. They'd tasted much
better than the city's scavenger insects . . .

Shaking away the thoughts, she shifted her weight to
free up one hand and pulled a safety anchor off her climbing
harness. Her Mistryl instructors would probably have criti-
cized her use of a safety line, pointing out that it took time
to fasten the anchors and that a true Mistryl would never slip
in the first place. But her climb training was many years in
her past, and all the speed in the galaxy would gain her nothing if she fell before reaching the rooftop.

On the other hand, if there was anything to Mazzic's
suspicions about this meeting, getting up there too late
would be just as futile as not getting there at all. About two
meters of wall left, she estimated as she glanced upward,
with maybe twice that number of minutes left before Mazzic
and Griv arrived upstairs. Locking the slender, nearly invisible safety line into the anchor, not waiting until the faint hiss
of the molecular welding between anchor and wall had faded
away, she passed the blufferavian's nest and continued her
climb.

She had made it to the top, and was just reaching a hand
up toward the edge, when she heard a faint sound.

She froze, listening, but the sound wasn't repeated. Easing her hand down, she pulled another safety anchor from

her harness and set it against the wall as far to her left as she
could reach. Hoping the hissing sound was too quiet to be
heard by whomever was up there, she locked her safety line
into the anchor and also locked the feed at her harness. Now,
if she was shot at when she poked her head up over the edge,
dropping down would swing her around that point in a tight
arc to pop up a meter and a half to the side. It wasn't much,
but in a gunfight the ability to throw off an opponent's aim
even that much could make all the difference. Easing her
blaster from its holster, she flicked off the safety—

"Hello, Shada," a soft voice said from directly above
her.

She looked up. A cloaked figure was standing at the
edge looking down at her. But even in the gloom Shada
could see enough of the other's face . . . "Karoly?" she
murmured.

"It's been a long time, hasn't it?" Karoly D'ulin said.
"Just put your blaster up here on the roof, would you? Then
come on up."

Shada reached up and set the weapon beside Karoly's
feet. Then, remembering to unlock the line feed from her
harness, she pulled herself the rest of the way.

Straightening up, she took a quick look around. Here at
the edge the roof was flat, but a few meters inward it rose at
a sharp angle another meter or so before flattening out again.
Beyond the rise Shada could see the top of the long skylight
enclosure that crowned the upper room.

The room where Mazzic was about to get down to business.

"You're probably the last person I would have expected
to see up here," she commented, looking back at Karoly.

"I imagine so," Karoly agreed. She'd picked up the
blaster while Shada was finishing her climb, and now tucked
it away somewhere inside her cloak. "You can take off those
climbing hooks, too—we'll be going back down by one of
the interior stairways. Just set them down on the roof, if you
would."

"Of course," Shada said, unstrapping the hooks from
her forearms and setting them down on the roof beside her.

They weren't all that useful as weapons, but Karoly obviously wasn't interested in taking chances. Kneeling down, she undid the foot hooks as well, then straightened up again. "Happy?"

Karoly pursed her lips. "You act as if we're enemies, Shada. We're not."

"I'm glad to hear that," Shada said, studying the younger woman's face. It had indeed been a long time since they'd worked together—almost twenty years, in fact, since Tatooine and that near fiasco with the Imperials' Hammertong project. The memory Shada had brought away from that incident was one of Karoly as young and inexperienced and a bit prone to becoming flustered.

But the memory wasn't the woman who now stood before her. Sometime in those twenty years Karoly had developed grace and poise, and an air of considerable competence. "How did you know I'd be coming up this side?"

"We didn't," Karoly said, shrugging. "The rest of the approaches to the rooftop are also being watched. But I thought I spotted you slipping around the side of the building in that layered blue dress of yours, and I guessed you might try this way." She gestured to Shada's elaborately coiled and plaited hair, then at her tight-fitting combat jumpsuit and climbing harness. "I must say, the dress suited that hairstyle better than the fighting gear. What are those things holding it together?"

"They're lacquered zenji needles," Shada told her. "Mazzic likes me to look decorative."

"Useful camouflage for a bodyguard," Karoly said. "Speaking of camouflage, I'd guess one of the needles must be a disguised signaler or comlink. Just drop it on the roof, all right?"

Shada grimaced. "You don't miss a trick, do you?" she said, pulling the signaler out from its place behind her right ear and adding it to the pile of climbing hooks. "I'm so glad we're not enemies. Who is this 'we' you mentioned?"

"I have a client with me." Karoly nodded toward the higher section of roof. "He's over there."

Crouched beside the skylight with a sniper's blaster rifle? "Doing what?"

"Nothing that concerns you," Karoly said. "As of right now, you've been pulled off the job."

Shada frowned at her. "What are you talking about? I've been with Mazzic for over twelve years now. You can't end that kind of relationship with the snap of a finger."

"We can, and we are," Karoly said. "It's clear now that Mazzic's group isn't going to become the galaxy-spanning organization that the Mistryl hoped when they first planted you on him. And with Talon Karrde's Smugglers' Alliance all but defunct, the Eleven have decided you're just being wasted here. It's time for you to move on."

"Fine," Shada said, taking two steps back away from Karoly along the roof edge and craning her neck as if trying to see if she could catch a glimpse of Karoly's client. "I'll tell Mazzic tonight that I'm resigning as his bodyguard. We can leave in the morning."

Karoly shook her head. "I'm sorry. We leave now."

Shada looked back, leveling a hard stare at Karoly and surreptitiously gauging the distance between them. Three meters; just about right. "Why?" she demanded. "Because your new client wants to murder him?"

Even in the dim light she could see Karoly wince a little. But when the other woman spoke her voice was firm enough. "I suggest you try to remember who we are, Shada," she said. "We're Mistryl. We're given orders and we follow them."

"I'm also Mazzic's bodyguard," Shada said quietly. "And once upon a time the Mistryl were given honor and obeyed duty. Not just orders."

Karoly snorted under her breath. "Honor. You *have* been out of touch, haven't you?"

"Apparently so," Shada countered. "I've always tried to believe that being a Mistryl put me a few steps above the garbage heap of mercenaries and assassins-for-hire. Forgive my naïveté."

Karoly's face darkened. "We do what's necessary to keep our people alive," she bit out. "If some slimy Hutt wants to back-blade some other slimy smuggler, that's none of our concern."

"Correction: it's none of *your* concern," Shada said. "It is mine. I have a job to do, Karoly; and you can get out of my way or you can get hurt." She reached up to her harness and locked her safety line—

Karoly's hand seemed to twitch, and suddenly there was a small blaster in it. "Freeze it," she ordered. "Move your hands away from your body. Empty."

Shada held her arms loosely out from her sides, fingers spread to prove she wasn't holding or palming anything. "You'll have to kill me to stop me," she warned.

"I hope not. Now turn around."

This was it. Arms still held away from her body, Shada rotated ninety degrees to face the skylight—

And taking a step backward, she dropped off the edge of the roof.

She'd half expected Karoly to get a quick blaster shot off before she disappeared over the edge. It didn't happen; Karoly either freezing with surprise or else too self-controlled to fire uselessly. But Shada didn't have time to speculate on which it was. The safety line snapped taut, and suddenly she was caroming off the wall as she swung down and to her right, pivoting about that last anchor she'd set near the rooftop. Another two seconds, she estimated, and she would pass the midpoint of her oscillation and swing up again to the rooftop where Karoly and her blaster waited.

She had just those two seconds to find a way to take down her onetime friend.

The startled blufferavian didn't even have time to squawk as Shada snatched it from its nest. She managed to grab one of the eggs with her other hand; and then she was swinging back up toward the roof.

And her two-second grace period was over. Even as she cocked the bird over her shoulder in throwing position Karoly appeared above her at the edge of the roof, hurrying toward the spot from which Shada had jumped, her eyes and blaster tracking down the side of the building. She caught sight of Shada—floundered off balance for a split second as she tried to halt her forward movement and shift her aim—

And with a grunt of exertion, Shada hurled the blufferavian at her face.

There was no time for Karoly to think, no time for her even to pause and evaluate. There was a sudden confused flurry of wings in front of her as the blufferavian tried to recover its equilibrium; and in the absence of thought, powerfully ingrained Mistryl combat reflexes took over. She jerked back, the movement eroding her precarious balance even further, twisted the muzzle of her blaster toward the incoming missile, and fired.

The blaster bolt caught the blufferavian dead center, and suddenly the flapping wings became a turmoil of flame and sparks and acrid smoke. Karoly ducked away from the fireball, twisting her head to the side—

Just in time to catch Shada's thrown blufferavian egg squarely across the bridge of her nose.

She gasped as the egg splattered into her eyes, throwing her free hand up to try to wipe away the semiliquid mass blinding her as Shada hit her safety-line feed release again and vaulted up on to the rooftop. Circling a couple of meters to her right to get out of the line of fire of the blaster still waving in her general direction, she angled in.

She reached Karoly just as the younger woman got her eyes cleared, kicking the blaster out of her hand as she tried to bring the weapon around toward her. The blaster hit the edge of the roof behind Karoly and bounced off into the darkness below. "*Shassa*," Karoly hissed the old curse, jumping to her right out of Shada's reach and producing a gleaming knife from somewhere. "Shada—"

"I'm obeying my duty," Shada said, sidestepping to her right away from the knife tip. "You've still got the option of getting out of my way."

Karoly hissed something else and lunged forward. Shada sidestepped again toward her right, feinted toward Karoly, took another quick step to the side and then changed direction back toward the skylight.

But Karoly had anticipated the move. Blinking more of

the egg out of her eyes, she took a long step the same direction, her knife waving warningly. Shada countered by stepping perilously close to the roof edge and taking two quick strides along it in an attempt to get around onto Karoly's left side away from her knife hand. Karoly spun around in response, knife held ready. "Don't make me do this, Shada," she snarled.

Snarled. And yet, Shada thought she could hear a buried note of pleading there as well. "All right, Karoly," she said softly. "I won't." Snapping on her climbing harness's feed lock again, she leaped backward one last time along the edge of the roof—

And the safety line that her carefully choreographed sparring maneuvers had threaded neatly around behind Karoly snapped up tautly to catch the younger woman across the tops of her low boots. Flailing her knife uselessly as her feet were yanked out from under her, she fell with a painful sounding thud flat onto her back.

Shada was on her in an instant, one foot coming down on Karoly's knife wrist as she slapped away the other hand and then jabbed stiffened fingertips into the soft spot beneath her rib cage. With an agonized grunt Karoly folded up around the impact and toppled over on her side. Shada jabbed again, this time behind Karoly's ear, and the younger woman relaxed and lay still.

Breathing hard, Shada reached over and snatched the knife from Karoly's limp hand, cutting her safety line before she wound up tangled in it herself. The fight hadn't taken long and had been reasonably quiet, but odds were that Karoly's client had heard the ruckus and would be coming to investigate. If she could arrange to meet him halfway—

A movement at the corner of her eye was her only warning. But it was enough. Even as she threw herself to the side in a flat dive a blaster bolt sizzled through the air where she'd been standing. She rolled back to her knees, eyes sweeping the raised section of rooftop and locating her assailant: a prone figure in a black poncho and hood, the protruding snout of his blaster rifle tracking toward her.

Snapping her hand up, Shada threw Karoly's knife toward him.

The sniper rolled instantly to the side, leaning his head into the relative protection of his arms and rifle, the weapon now spitting its deadly fire on repeater mode as it tracked toward her. But in this case the old bounty hunters' reflex had betrayed him. The knife spun precisely into its intended target: not the dodging sniper himself, but the flicker of blaster fire from his weapon. It cut across right in front of the gun barrel, the bolts catching the blade and blasting it apart in a blaze of molten shards and reflected light.

And for the next pair of heartbeats the sniper would be effectively blind.

Two heartbeats was all Shada needed. She came all the way up off the roof, leaping over the sputtering blaster fire now tracking blindly toward her, fingers darting into her plaited hair for one of the lacquered zenji needles. It came free in a cascade of loosened coils; and as her feet hit the roof again, she threw it.

And with a muffled clatter the blaster fell silent.

She was beside the sniper in an instant, twisting the weapon out of the dead man's hands and running across the roof. If the sniper was merely the backup and not the main attack, she might still have failed. Skidding to a halt beside the skylight, she crouched at its edge and peered down into the high-ceilinged room below.

She hadn't failed. Three meters below her was an ornate decorated table, with Mazzic and Griv on one side and the Kubaz and a rough-looking human on the other. The two sides had already exchanged cases and were in the process of checking their new prizes. The Kubaz shut his case after what seemed to be a cursory examination, standing stiffly behind the table with an obvious air of expectation about him. It took Mazzic another minute to be similarly satisfied with his side of the trade, then he too closed his case. He nodded pleasantly to the Kubaz and took a step back from the table, his mouth moving with what were probably his usual farewell remarks. The Kubaz remained where he was . . . and as Mazzic and Griv took another step back, his air of expectation gave way to one of puzzlement. His long snout twitched in indecision, clearly wanting to look up but just as clearly not wanting to telegraph the surprise ending he was still expecting.

Still, if a surprise was all he wanted, Shada could oblige him. Lining the blaster rifle up on the base of the alien's long snout, she tapped the barrel lightly against the skylight.

All four of them looked up. The Kubaz's expression was impossible to read, but his companion's more than made up for it. His mouth fell open in stunned disbelief, his hand dropping to the blaster belted at his side. Shada shifted her aim to his forehead; slowly, he raised the hand—empty—to his chest. Out of the corner of her eye she saw Mazzic throw her an abbreviated salute, and then he and Griv walked out of her field of view.

Shada kept her weapon trained on the Kubaz and his friend for a count of thirty. Then, throwing them the same salute Mazzic had just given her, she backed away from the skylight.

"It's over?" Karoly's voice asked from behind her.

Shada turned to look. The younger woman was standing beside the dead assassin at the edge of the upper roof, her expression impossible to read. "Yes," Shada told her. "Your client decided not to go back on the deal after all."

Karoly looked down at the body at her feet. "The Eleven aren't going to be happy about this."

"I'm used to people not being happy with me," Shada sighed, lowering the blaster rifle to the rooftop. "I'll get by."

"This is not a joking matter, Shada," Karoly growled. "You've been given a direct order. You stay with Mazzic now and they'll have a squad on you before the week's over."

"I'm not staying with Mazzic," Shada said. "As I told you, I'll resign as his bodyguard tonight."

"And you think that will fix *this* with the Eleven?" Karoly scoffed.

"I suppose that depends on whether any of them still remembers who we are," Shada said, a deep sense of sadness flowing into her. A sadness that felt as if it had been collecting around her heart for a long, long time. "The Mistryl that I joined twenty-two years ago was an honorable clan of warriors fighting to preserve what was left of our people. Honorable warriors don't knowingly deal in murder. I would hope at least some of the Eleven remember that."

"Maybe the Eleven have changed." Karoly looked away across the dark rooftops of the city. "Maybe the Mistryl have changed."

"Maybe they have," Shada said. "But I haven't." She studied her friend. "But then, neither have you."

Karoly looked back at her. "Really. I'd like to know what I said to give you that impression."

"It's not what you said," Shada told her. "It's what you did. After I kicked your blaster away, when you pulled that knife on me."

"Pulling a knife convinced you I was on your side?"

"Yes," Shada said. "You still have my blaster."

Karoly put her hand to her side. "Yes, I suppose I do. I imagine you want it back."

Shada shrugged. "It might be harder to explain what happened here if you still have it when you get back to Emberlene."

"Point," Karoly conceded. She flicked her wrist, and the blaster sailed in a flat arc to drop neatly into Shada's waiting hand. "Speaking of Emberlene, I'd stay away from there if I were you. For that matter, I'd stay away from any other Mistryl, period. For the next ten years, if you can manage it."

"I won't need to hide that long," Shada said, sliding the blaster back into its holster. "Looks like the galaxy is coming to a boil again over this Caamas thing. The Eleven will soon have more important things than me to think about."

Karoly spat something. "Caamas. Caamas, and Alderaan, and even that mudwater Noghri planet Honoghr. It almost makes me laugh sometimes when I think about which worlds get cried over."

"Being bitter about it won't help," Shada said.

"So what will?" Karoly retorted. "At least being bitter proves you're not dead yet."

"Perhaps," Shada said. "If that's what you're willing to settle for."

"I suppose you've found something better?"

"I don't know," Shada said. "There has to be something, though." She pointed to a small rectangular shedlike structure on the far side of the skylight. "That the exit over there?"

"One of them," Karoly said. "If you don't mind taking a chance on running into the Kubaz and his pals on the way down."

Shada smiled tightly. "They'll make room for me."

Almost unwillingly, Karoly smiled back. "I'm sure they will." The smile faded. "But understand this, Shada. Whatever I did here, I did it for—well, the reasons are complicated. But if the Eleven send me after you . . ."

"I understand," Shada nodded. "I'll try not to put you in this position again."

"Never mind me," Karoly said. "You just be careful of *you*." She cocked her head slightly. "You have any idea what you're going to do?"

Shada looked up at the stars. "As a matter of fact," she said quietly, "I do."

"Hold still, please, sir," the Emdee droid said in its deep voice, its mechanical fingers wielding the probe with microscopic precision as he lined it up. "I expect this to be the final pass."

"Good," Luke said, taking a deep breath and cultivating his patience. He'd been sitting here for nearly half an hour now, but it was almost over.

The droid eased the probe into Luke's right ear, with a sensation that oscillated between an itch and a tickle. Luke braced himself; and then, with a loud slurping sound it was over.

"Thank you, sir," the Emdee said, lowering the probe into the reclamation container beside him and discharging a final few drops of bacta into it. "I again apologize for the time and inconvenience this has caused you."

"That's all right," Luke assured him, sliding off the table and rubbing the last vestige of the itch/tickle away with a fingertip. "I know it's easy to say there'll never be another bacta shortage like the one during the war. It's not always so easy to believe it."

"I was with this facility during that time," the Emdee said gravely. "We could not afford to buy the black market bacta, even if it had been available to us. I saw many die who could have been saved."

Luke nodded. And as a result, for the past twelve years the medics in charge here had made it a rigid policy to conserve every single drop of bacta, even to the point of siphoning it out of patients' ears when necessary. "I can't say this last part was very pleasant," he said. "On the other hand, I'd hate to have arrived and found out you didn't have enough bacta to treat me."

"Perhaps it is simply the path of old habit," the droid said. "Still, I am told it is wise to remember the past."

"It is indeed," Luke agreed soberly, nodding to the bacta reclamation container. "And even wiser to learn from it."

Artoo was waiting in their assigned room, plugged into the desk and warbling softly to himself as he conversed with the medical facility's main computer. His dome swiveled as Luke came in, the warbling changing to an excited whistling. "Hi, Artoo," Luke said. "Keeping busy?"

The little droid made an affirmative-sounding twitter, which changed to something questioning. "Oh, I'm fine," Luke assured him, patting his side. "Some of the shrapnel was in pretty deep, but they got it all out. A little dip in a bacta tank, and I'm good as new. The medic said I shouldn't fly for another hour or so, but it'll probably take that long to get the ship rolled out and prepped anyway."

Artoo whistled again, rotating his dome around in a complete circle. "Yes, I see they did a good job with you, too," Luke agreed. "Did you ask them to take a look at the X-wing?"

Another affirmative twitter. "Good," Luke said. "Then I guess the only question left is where we should go next."

Artoo's dome swiveled back again to face him, a distinctly suspicious note to his next warble. "We're not out here on vacation, Artoo," Luke reminded him, pulling up a chair beside the droid where he could keep an eye on the desk's computer display for more complicated translations. "We're here to track down those clones and find out where they're coming from. We're not going to accomplish that by going home to Yavin or Coruscant."

He looked out the window at the hills rising steeply behind his room, their carpet of gold-colored grasses gleaming in the afternoon sunlight. Yes, the mission statement itself was perfectly straightforward. Unfortunately, the necessary procedure for completing it was anything but. He'd tried the surreptitious approach to that Cavrilhu base; all he'd gotten for his trouble had been yet another swim in a bacta tank. And, of course, the chance to see Mara again.

He grimaced. Mara. He'd been expecting to run into her again ever since that pirate raid he and Han had thwarted off Iphigin—in fact, he wouldn't put it past Han to have had something to do with Mara showing up at the Kauron asteroid field that way. He'd expected to run into her, and had secretly dreaded the prospect.

And yet, looking back on it, the encounter hadn't been nearly as tense as he'd feared it would be. She'd been cooperative and polite, or at least as polite as Mara ever got. More significantly, the quiet but strong animosity he'd sensed radiating toward him at their last couple of brief encounters hadn't been present.

Or maybe it had been there and he just hadn't noticed. Maybe his deliberately diminished use of the Force these days had simply prevented him from sensing that deeply into her mind without a deliberate probe.

He scowled out at the hills. There was definitely some kind of cause and effect at work here—that much he was sure of. The question was, which was the cause and which the effect?

Artoo warbled questioningly. "I'm trying to figure it out," Luke told him, glancing at the translation. "Just relax, okay?"

The droid warbled again and fell into an expectant silence. Luke sighed and settled back into his seat, gazing out at the hills. Mara was a puzzle, but she was a puzzle that would have to wait. At the moment, his immediate future was focused on this cloning question.

His future . . .

He glanced back at Artoo, the memory of their time with Yoda drifting to mind. Luke's Jedi training, and that first time he'd gotten a glimpse into the future.

A glimpse that had nearly resulted in disaster. He'd rushed off madly to Cloud City to try to save Han and Leia, and had instead nearly gotten all of them killed.

But he'd learned so much about the Force since then. And he *had* been able to draw other visions of the future without doing anything rash. Lately his efforts in that direction had been strangely unrewarding; but as long as he was supposed to take it easy for an hour or so anyway, it wouldn't hurt to give it a try.

"Artoo, I'm going to meditate for a while," he told the droid, slipping out of the chair and settling himself cross-legged on the floor. "See if I can get some direction. Don't let anyone disturb me, all right?"

The droid buzzed an affirmative. Taking a deep breath, Luke closed his eyes and stretched out to the Force. His thoughts—his emotions—his entire being—slipped into the proper pattern . . .

And suddenly the whole universe exploded in front of him into a brilliant kaleidoscope of color and motion.

He gasped, the vast image wavering momentarily like desert heat-shimmer as he nearly lost control. It was like no vision he'd ever had before. Like nothing he'd ever seen before. A hundred different scenes, a thousand different possibilities—brilliant colors, sharp-edged sounds, joy and contentment and fear and death—all of it swirled together with the fury and randomness of a Tatooine sandstorm. Lines of possibility wove around each other or else crashed together, sometimes merging, sometimes bouncing apart again, always forever changed by the encounter. Familiar faces were there among unfamiliar ones, passing in front of him or else flickering behind other events unfolding at the edges of his sight. He caught a glimpse of Wedge and Rogue Squadron as they swept past in the fury of battle; saw his Jedi students inexplicably fanning out across the New Republic, leaving the Yavin academy all but deserted; saw himself standing on a balcony against the wall of a darkened canyon, gazing down at a sea of thousands of tiny stars; saw Han and Leia facing a huge mob—

Han? Leia? With an effort, he grabbed on to that last line, trying to stay with it long enough to see more. For a moment he succeeded, the image sharpening into focus: Leia standing in a wide hallway, her lightsaber blazing in her hands, as a mass of bodies pushed through a tall door; Han, standing on an outside balcony with drawn blaster, looking down at the crowd. The crowd inside flowed mindlessly forward—a hidden rooftop sniper lined up his blaster rifle—

And then they were gone, vanishing into the swirling mass of sights and sounds. For a moment Luke tried to join the flow himself, the taste of fear mixing with the other sensations of the vision as he tried to catch up and see what was going to happen to them. But they were gone, and with a sense that came from outside himself he knew that he'd seen all of that vision that he was going to. Easing out of the flow, he made his way back to the single fixed point in the storm, the solidness of his own being. He'd learned all he could here, and now it was time to leave. He began to draw back, the vast array of images beginning in turn to recede and darken.

And then, abruptly, one final vision appeared in front of him: Mara, surrounded by craggy rock and floating in water, her eyes closed, her arms and legs limp. As if in death.

Wait! he heard himself shout. But it was too late. Mara's image faded with the rest of the vision—

And with a sudden gasp of air he found himself back in his room, gazing out the window at the hills.

Hills that no longer glowed golden, but were instead outlined by the subtler gloss of starlight.

"Whoa," he muttered, rubbing his eyes. He would have sworn that vision had only lasted a few minutes.

Beside him, Artoo twittered in obvious relief. "Yes, it took longer than I expected, too," Luke agreed. "Sorry."

The droid warbled questioningly. Getting to his feet, wincing at the sudden prickling sensation in muscles left too long in one position, Luke looked at the question scrolling across the computer display. "I don't know," he had to concede. "I saw a lot of things. But I didn't see anything that seemed to have anything to do with our search."

Which might mean, he realized suddenly, that hunting for clones was no longer what he was supposed to be doing.

But then what *was* he supposed to do? Go to wherever Han and Leia were and warn them? Go find Mara and warn *her*?

He took a deep breath, shifting tired muscles. *Always in motion is the future*, Yoda had told him after that first vision on Dagobah. At the time Luke had wondered about that remark; his vision of Han and Leia in Cloud City had seemed so simple and straightforward. But if Yoda had instead seen something more akin to this last vision, with all its tangles and complications, then it all made sense.

Or *had* he seen something like that? Could it be that what Luke had experienced here was something entirely different? A special event reserved for special occasions?

It was an intriguing possibility. But for the moment, it was an issue he could put aside. What mattered was that he'd received the guidance he'd sought, and needed to act on it.

All he had to do was figure out exactly what that guidance was.

Stepping over to the window, he looked up at the stars. *You will know*, Yoda had also told him, *when you are calm, at peace*. Taking a deep breath, Luke set about calming his mind.

Artoo's soft warbling was starting to take on a concerned tone by the time he turned back around. "All right," he told the droid. "I saw a world with a wide, deep canyon that had buildings built into the sides and a lot of lights at the bottom. Check the main computer and see where that might be."

Artoo warbled an acknowledgment and jacked into the

computer outlet. Luke stepped to his side and watched as a planet name and description came up on the display. "No, it wasn't Belsavis," he said. "The surface wasn't covered with glaciers, and there were no domes. It was also a lot more pleasant." He frowned, pulling the image back from his memory. "There were bridges arching all the way across the canyon I saw. There were . . . I saw a group of nine of them, arranged in a diamond pattern: one starting on one level, two more side by side crossing from the next level down, three on the next, then two and then one."

Artoo whistled and searched some more. A half-dozen more systems scrolled across the display—

"Wait a minute," Luke said. "Back up one—Cejansij system. See if there are any pictures in the datafile."

The display backed up, then altered to a succession of orbital, aerial, and ground pictures. Luke watched as they went past . . . and by the time the series came to an end, he knew it was the place. "That's it," he said. "The Canyonade on Cejansij. That's where we're going."

The droid twittered uncertainly, his question scrolling across the bottom of the display. "I don't know why," Luke told him. "I just know I need to go there."

There was another twitter, this one sounding slightly incredulous. "To be honest, I don't understand it myself," Luke conceded. "I saw a lot of things in that vision, things that are happening or maybe are about to happen. I saw my students leaving the academy—why, I don't know. I saw Leia and Han in some kind of trouble—"

The droid warbled anxiously, and another question appeared. "No, I don't know if Threepio was with them," Luke told him. "The point is that there are a lot of places out there we could go where I might be able to affect things. Too many places."

He pointed at the view of the vast canyon. "But the Canyonade is the only place where I actually saw myself. The one part of the vision where I felt peace."

He looked out at the stars again. "So that's where we'll go."

For a moment there was silence. Then Artoo warbled

again. "Point taken," Luke agreed with a smile. "If we're going to go, let's stop dithering and go."

Besides which, he told himself as they headed for the docking bay, *Leia's a Jedi in her own right. She can take care of herself. And Han's got a long history of beating the odds, too.* And Rogue Squadron could manage without him, and wherever his Jedi students had been going they surely had a good reason for doing so. Whatever this trip to Cejansij was all about, all of them could do without him for a while.

Forty minutes later, once again in space, he pulled the hyperdrive lever and sent the X-wing jumping to lightspeed. Trying hard not to think about the vision he'd had of Mara.

CHAPTER

13

Ceok Orou'cya, First Secretary of the Combined Bothan Clans, was urbane, polite, and completely gracious. But beneath the polish, as near as Leia could tell, he also seemed genuinely surprised by her visit.

And beneath the surprise, she suspected, was a great deal of worry.

"You must understand my position here, Councilor Organa Solo," he said for the third time as he ushered Leia, Han, and Threepio past the outer reception station and into the sumptuous three-story lobby/atrium that filled the front third of the Combined Clans Center Building. "Your visit, unannounced this way, is highly irregular. Your request"—his fur twitched despite obvious efforts to control it—"is even more so."

"You have the letter from Gavrisom," Han put in gruffly. "You have the letter from Fey'lya. What more do you want?"

The secretary threw a sideways look at Han, and despite the seriousness of the situation Leia had to fight to keep from smiling. Han was at his absolutely most intimidating: standing stiff and tall, scowling unblinkingly, his hand resting on the blaster holstered at his side. The knuckles of his gunhand were slightly whitened with pressure as he gripped the weapon, a subtlety she'd suggested to him on the trip here from Coruscant and one that clearly wasn't lost on its intended audience.

He would have been even more intimidating with Barkhimkh and Sakhisakh standing there beside him. But Bothans didn't much like Noghri, and Leia had decided this situation was ticklish enough already without that extra strain. The two Noghri were lurking somewhere outside, a quick comlink call away if they were needed.

But she wasn't expecting them to be. Between the official weight she was bringing to bear and the threat of more physical consequences from Han, they had Orou'cya in a tight squeeze already. With luck, that should give them a good chance of getting to the financial records before anyone was able to hide or alter them.

"I personally need nothing more, Captain Solo," the secretary said. "The problem is that only one of the Combined Clan leaders may grant authorization to see the records you are requesting, and none are on this part of Bothawui at present."

Han took another step toward him. "You've got the letter from President Gavrisom—"

"Please." Leia held up a hand. "Secretary Orou'cya, I understand your situation. I believe that there may be another way out of the problem. Do I understand correctly that in his capacity as New Republic representative Councilor Fey'lya would also have access to the financial records we seek?"

The Bothan's eyes darted between the two of them, clearly suspecting a trap. "I believe he does," he answered cautiously. "I would have to check the regulations."

Leia looked at Han, lifted her eyebrows slightly. "Here," Han said, thrusting a datacard at the secretary. "I've marked the place."

Orou'cya started to take the card, hesitated, then dropped his hand back to his side. "I'll accept your word on that," he said. "But I don't see how that point is relevant. Councilor Fey'lya isn't here, and a mere letter cannot extend such privileges to another person."

"True," Leia said with a nod. "However, such privileges

do extend to Councilor Fey'lya's personal possessions, do they not?"

Orou'cya frowned. "What do you mean?"

"I mean possessions such as his personal computers," Leia said. "Or his droids."

The Bothan looked at Threepio, and this time the fur definitely flattened. "His—? But—"

Han nudged his shoulder with the datacard. "That part's marked, too."

"And here's the record of Fey'lya's ownership," Leia added, producing another datacard.

Mechanically, Orou'cya took the two datacards, his eyes on the golden droid standing silent and aloof with quiet hauteur.

At least, that's what Leia hoped he saw. In actual fact, Threepio was being aloof and silent for the simple reason that he was too embarrassed and chagrined for words. It was bad enough, he'd complained over and over on the trip here, that Luke had "given" him to Jabba the Hutt during their rescue of Han on Tatooine. But to be summarily sold to a Bothan diplomat without any notice whatsoever was an utter disgrace.

It didn't matter to him that the sale was only on datafile and not genuine. As far as he was concerned, the deceit involved only made it worse.

But Orou'cya didn't know that. "I see," the Bothan said, his voice rather flat, his eyes still on Threepio. "I . . ." He trailed off.

"Records room's on the third floor, right?" Han demanded into the silence.

"If you'd rather wait down here," Leia added, "I'm sure we can find what we're looking for by ourselves."

Orou'cya's fur seemed to wilt. "No, I must escort you," he murmured. "Follow me, please."

He led them across the atrium to a wide, free-span ceremonial stairway arching gracefully between the first and second floors, apparently the only route from the more or less public departments on the first floor to the private offices and meeting rooms above. At the top of the stairway was a wide overlook balcony, also clearly designed with ceremony in mind.

Ceremonial or not, though, the Bothans hadn't scrimped on security. A pair of armed guards stood at the bottom of the staircase, and Leia could see the camouflaged poles of a static barrier built into the banisters on either side a few steps up.

She also wondered how many of the privacy-glazed office windows peeking through the short trees and bushy borscii and kasvus vines from the top two floors had hidden guards watching the stairway and the atrium. Knowing the Bothans, probably at least one of them.

But no one, hidden guards or otherwise, interfered as Orou'cya led the party to the top of the staircase, then along a corridor to a more standard set of stairs leading to the third floor, and finally to a door marked simply ARCHIVES. There the secretary paused; but if he was having second thoughts, they weren't going to be given time to ripen. Brushing past him, Han opened the door and went in.

Five other Bothans were in the room, seated at various data retrieval stations. All of them were looking at the door as Leia stepped inside behind Han with expressions and postures that could have been either surprise or guilt. "That one will do," Leia said, pointing to an unoccupied retrieval station near the door. "Go ahead and get started, Threepio."

Silently, Threepio shuffled off toward the station. "Thank you, Secretary Orou'cya," Leia added to their escort. "We'll call you if we need any further assistance."

"I will be available for whatever you require," Orou'cya said. Turning, he left the room, closing the door behind him.

Beside Leia, Han made a rude-sounding noise. "You'd think Fey'lya would have mentioned in his letter that we're on their side here," he muttered.

"I'm sure he did," Leia agreed. "But these are Bothans. They see hidden blades everywhere."

Han grimaced. "Especially coming from other Bothans."

"It's how their internal politics work," Leia reminded him, squeezing his arm. "Come on, let's get this over with."

•   •   •

The order had specified a large crowd, and Navett had assured Major Tierce that his team could deliver. But now, looking at the edges of the crowd that he could see from his rooftop vantage point—a crowd that had already overflowed all available standing space in the Merchant's Square—even he was impressed. This time Klif had definitely outdone himself.

"Navett?" Pensin's voice came from the tiny speaker in Navett's left ear. "Looks like they're ready to move."

"Right," Navett said, moving the attached microphone a little closer to his lips. It was a military-style comlink, scavenged from a stormtrooper helmet, and would probably be trouble if he was caught with it. But the hands-free design was more private and convenient than standard civilian cylinder types, with a better real-time encryption. Anyway, he wasn't planning to get caught. "You'd better get in position. What's the makeup like?"

"It's a real mix this time," Pensin said. "Got a bunch of spacers of all types from the port area, but there are a lot of shoppers and merchants, too. Everything from human to Ishori and Rodian. Got a bunch of Froffli, too—I can see those stupid hair spurs poking up above the rest of the crowd."

"Good." Aside from the general hotheadedness of the species itself, the Froffli government was one of the few that had already come out publicly for sanctions against the Bothans. A species grounded on vindictiveness; and the fact that the Bothans had spent the past fifteen years systematically grinding the Froffli light-machinery industry to dust certainly hadn't helped matters. "Make sure you're out of their way when they start their charge."

"Don't worry," Pensin said dryly. "Oops—okay, there they go. Next stop, the Combined Clans Building. You all set?"

"All set," Navett said, stroking the stock of the Nightstinger sniper's blaster rifle lying on the roof beside him. "Let's do it."

• • •

"Shh," Han said, frowning with concentration. "You hear that?"

Leia looked up from the retrieval station. "I didn't hear anything."

"It sounded like thunder," Han said, straining his ears. "Or a crowd or—there it is again."

"It's a crowd," Leia said, that Jedi look on her face. "And they're getting louder."

Han looked at the other Bothans in the room. None of them seemed to have noticed the noise. "Must be pretty good-sized if we can hear them all the way in here."

The Jedi look was getting more intense. "I don't like this, Han," she said. "There's something not right here."

"Maybe it's one of those demonstrations that have been cropping up lately," Han said, moving toward the door. "Stay here—I'll go check it out."

The Bothans in the archive room might not have figured out what was happening, but the rest of the building was already on it. The corridor outside was alive with hurrying Bothans, some carrying boxes of datacards or other equipment, others just hurrying. Crossing past an overview that looked down on the atrium, he saw what seemed to be the entire first-floor staff hustling up the big ceremonial stairway, most of them carrying boxes and equipment, too.

A handful of Bothans were bucking the trend, heading down the stairs. All of that group were carrying blasters.

The atrium, Han decided, didn't look like a particularly good place to be at the moment. Fortunately, he wasn't going to have to go down there. Both the second and third floors had observation balconies facing the front of the building where he'd be able to assess the situation. Threading his way through the hurrying Bothans, he headed that direction. A bit of trial and error to find which office the balcony was connected to, and he pushed open the sliding privacy-glass door and looked outside.

It was worse than he'd feared. The crowd was *huge*, filling the entire street as humans and aliens continued to stream toward the building. He stepped out onto the balcony for a better look; and as he did so, a figure near the front of the crowd shouted and waved wildly as he pointed up. Automatically, Han's hand dropped to his blaster—

"Citizens of the New Republic," a deep Bothan voice called from somewhere nearby. "I respectfully appeal to you for calm."

The crowd responded with even more noise, none of it sounding especially calm or respectful. Stepping to the edge of his balcony, Han craned his neck and looked down at the second-floor balcony beneath him. There he was: a distinguished-looking elderly male Bothan wearing the elaborate sigil and signet of a clan leader. "No clan leaders on this part of Bothawui, huh?" Han muttered, straightening up again. He was no expert, but it sure didn't look like the sort of mob that a little Bothan sugar-talk would do much for.

Which suggested the smart thing would be for him to get back inside and back to Leia. Just in case. Giving the crowd one last look, he started to turn away.

The front of the crowd had reached the Combined Clans Building now, the people behind them pushing and jostling past and filling in around the sides. Resting the stock of his blaster rifle against his shoulder, Navett squinted experimentally through the macrobinocular sight running along the barrel. Almost time . . .

And then, just as he'd known they would, the Bothans sent a representative onto the lower balcony to talk to the mob. The figure lifted his hands for silence—without any noticeable effect, of course—and Navett was just beginning to line up his crosshairs when another figure appeared, this one on the upper balcony.

A human? Frowning, Navett shifted his aim upward and tightened his focus . . .

And felt his eyes widen in disbelief. Han Solo—it was *Han Solo*. Hero of the Rebellion, New Republic shipping liaison, and general all-around troublemaker. And there he was, standing on a balcony right in front of him.

Navett had always considered himself to be leading a charmed life; but sometimes even he couldn't believe his own luck.

"Navett?" Pensin's voice came excitedly in his ear. "Up on the top balcony—"

"I see him," Navett said, striving to sound cool and professional. Han Solo himself. This was just too good to be true.

"So which one do we do?"

Navett smiled tightly. "Both, of course. You've got a spare, don't you?"

"Well, yes—"

"So we do both," Navett told him. "And we start with Solo. Give me a count."

"Right," Pensin said. "Five seconds, four, three—"

Han had been gone only a few seconds when the door suddenly bounced open again. "Councilor Organa Solo," Secretary Orou'cya said, breathing heavily. "We desperately need your assistance. There is a mob moving on this building."

"Yes, I know," Leia said. "What is it you want me to do?"

"Defend us, of course," the Bothan snapped, jabbing a hand at the lightsaber hanging unobtrusively beneath her loose overjacket. "Are you not a Jedi?"

Leia suppressed a sigh. There were still so many people out there who refused to see Jedi in any role except that of armed defender or combatant. "Perhaps I could try talking to them," she suggested gently.

"Askar Clan Leader Rayl'skar has already gone to do that," Orou'cya said, fur rippling with nervous impatience. "Please—they may break in at any time."

"All right," Leia said, standing up. So much for there being no clan leaders on this part of Bothawui; but this wasn't the time to bring that up. "Threepio, you'd better come, too."

"Me?" the droid gasped, cringing back as only Threepio could do. "But—Mistress Leia—"

"I might need you to translate," Leia cut him off. "Let's go."

They had to buck the general flow of Bothans streaming upward as they descended the main stairway. "Mistress Leia—there seems to be some considerable concern among the residents here," Threepio called over the hurrying feet and the rumble of the crowd outside. "Might I suggest we reconsider our strategy?"

"There won't be any trouble," Leia assured him, grabbing hold of one of his arms to keep them from getting separated. "Most of the time the worst these demonstrators have done is to throw spoiled fruit and stones. If I can persuade them that their concerns are being considered, maybe I can get them to disperse without even doing that much."

They reached the bottom of the stairway, easing through the three-deep cordon of Bothan guards blocking off the lower end, and hurried toward the front doors. "I merely thought we might wish to reevaluate," Threepio continued, his rapidity of speech increasing with his nervousness, which was increasing with roughly every other step. "There are two balconies we could speak from, after all, and even spoiled produce properly placed can be hazardous to the inner workings of a droid—"

"Quiet," Leia cut him off, braking to a halt a few meters from the door. Suddenly something felt different out there; a hint of evil purpose flickering at the edges of the simmering anger and resentment of the crowd. She stretched out with the Force, trying to pin it down—

And then, to her horror, an all-too-familiar sound split through the rumble like a crack of lightning through distant thunder.

The sound of a blaster shot.

There was no warning. None whatsoever. One minute Han was looking out over the crowd, wondering if he should call Leia and suggest she come out here and talk to them; and then the next minute there it was, making a sound like a boot in wet mud as it came out of nowhere to hit the wall by his left shoulder. He half turned to look at it, got just a glimpse of a mass of a soft-looking gray clay with a small tube connected to a multifaceted crystal embedded in the middle—

And suddenly it seemed to explode in a brilliant flash of blaster fire.

He wrenched back, twisting his face away from the flash as a needle-jab of pain stabbed into his left shoulder. From somewhere below him came a scream of pain, and even as he dropped behind the minimal protection of the balcony's guardrail he heard the sound and caught the flicker of reflected light from a second shot. Yanking his blaster from its holster, blinking around the hazy purple blob floating in front of his eyes, he tried to see where the attack was coming from.

Wherever the gunman was, he didn't seem in a hurry to give away his position by shooting again. But his first two shots had already done enough damage. Below and ten meters ahead, the crowd had opened a circle around a Mishtak writhing in agony on the ground. A few meters behind him, in the middle of another circle, a Leresai lay still.

With the two shots the crowd had gone deathly quiet. A motion caught the corner of Han's eye: someone moving on a rooftop a block away. He half stood up, lifting his blaster—

"There he is!" someone shouted.

Han looked down again. Someone in the crowd was pointing up; but he was pointing at *Han*. "Wait a minute—" Han began.

"There he is!" the man shouted again. "There's the murderer!"

And as if on signal the crowd suddenly came to life again. Roaring like a hundred berserk rancors, they surged forward beneath the balcony.

And with a slam that shook the whole building, they threw open the doors.

•   •   •

"Han!" Leia blurted as the second blaster shot rang out.
If he'd been the target—

No, she realized with a flood of relief. She could still feel
his presence, alert and tense. But *somebody* out there had
been hit; she could sense the waves of pain. Stretching out
with the Force, she tried to locate it.

And then, suddenly, there was a horrendous roar from
the crowd outside—

And in front of her the doors slammed open and a solid
wall of beings poured into the atrium.

"Oh, my!" Threepio gasped. "Mistress Leia—"

"Get behind me!" Leia snapped, taking a long step to
the side and grabbing for her lightsaber as she threw a quick
glance at the ceremonial stairway at the other end of the
atrium. With some serious effort, she should be able to reach
it ahead of the crowd.

But Threepio didn't have that kind of speed. And if she
abandoned him to the mob . . .

"Get behind me," she ordered the droid again, igniting
the lightsaber. She had come here to talk, and she had better
get started. The nearest of the crowd shied away as the lightsaber blade blazed into existence, many of them probably
only noticing her for the first time. "Citizens of the New
Republic," she shouted, holding the lightsaber high. "I'm
New Republic Councilor and Jedi Knight Leia Organa Solo.
I call on you to *stop*."

The people nearest Leia faltered in their charge, many of
them coming to an almost reluctant halt. Or rather, trying to
do so. The rest of the crowd behind them, unaware of Leia's
presence, were still pushing forward. Jostling those in front
or forcing their way around and past them, they continued
to flow into the building.

But at least the momentum of the crowd had been
slowed, and Leia had the beginnings of an attentive audience.
Now if she could project her voice to enough of them—and
could find the right words to say with that voice . . .

She took a deep breath, running through her Jedi strength enhancement techniques, and opened her mouth—

And at that moment there was a shout from the Bothan guards grouped at the foot of the stairway, and a half-dozen blaster bolts flashed into the crowd.

And the whole thing went straight to chaotic hell.

Leia had thought the crowd had been at the peak of its noise level. She'd been wrong. The screams from the injured were all but lost in a roar of fury and terror so loud it hurt her ears. The front rank of the crowd fell apart, many of the beings trying to hide behind the short trees and bushes or else scurrying madly for cover toward the offices lining the atrium's edges. Others simply froze where they were, unwilling to turn tail and run but equally unwilling to walk into massed blaster fire.

The Bothans fired again, sparking more screams; but this time the shots were answered. From a dozen places in the crowd blasters opened up, and six of the guards toppled to the floor.

"That's it!" a voice from the mob shouted over the roar. "Everyone—get them!"

"Wait!" Leia shouted. "Stop!"

But it was too late. The crowd, mindless with rage, was rolling forward now like a flash tide, blasters firing freely as the atrium suddenly became a war zone. Even those whose advance had been slowed by the sight of Leia's lightsaber were no longer listening, and in fact most had already deserted her or been dragged away by the mob. Twice she had to lift her lightsaber high over her head as the buffeting and shoving nearly sent someone into the blade. Dimly over the noise she heard Threepio wail something, but by the time she was able to turn around he had vanished. A Khil bounced toward her, whistling excitedly through his hullepi and waving a blaster toward the stairway, completely oblivious to the lightsaber blade he was drifting toward—

And with a dark recognition of defeat, Leia shut down the weapon, using the Force to keep the Khil from slamming into her. There was nothing more she could do here. Those who were still firing were halfway across the crowd, impossible for her to reach, and none of the beings nearest her had done anything to deserve the death or dismemberment that was the only punishment her lightsaber could mete out. Too many minds here for her to quiet—too many flailing bodies for her to move aside with the Force—and all that was left was for her to try to keep from getting trampled.

And then, through all the chaos that surrounded her, she caught a faint hint of something different. Someone not far away; someone quietly terrified for her safety.

Han.

She strained to see, but without the blazing lightsaber blade to keep them at bay the crowd had closed in and was now pressing too close for her to be able to see anywhere but up. For a moment she searched the silent windows facing down into the atrium as she fought to keep her balance, but if Han was up there she couldn't spot him.

But there was something there, almost directly above her head now: a thick tendril of borscii vine jutting out from the atrium wall. Pushing through the crowd in that direction, using the Force to ease people aside when necessary, she maneuvered herself beneath it. Then, stretching out again to the Force, she bent her knees and jumped.

The tendril was no more than two meters above her, an easy jump for a Jedi. She made it with half a meter to spare, grabbing on to the tendril and using it to pull herself to the main body of the borscii vine where it clung its meandering way up the wall. From her new vantage point she was able to see Han now: crouched beside the railing on the ceremonial balcony, his blaster pointed down the stairway, his eyes searching anxiously through the mob for signs of his wife. Flanking him on either side, looking ready to dive off the balcony into the crowd if and when it became necessary, were Barkhimkh and Sakhisakh.

How and when the two Noghri had managed to sneak into the building Leia didn't know. But at the moment it didn't matter. The Bothan guards at the foot of the stairway were down, shot or trampled, and the entire weight of the mob seemed to be pressed against the static barrier a few steps up.

But it wouldn't hold them back for long. Even at this distance she could see the faint sparking that meant the barrier was about to go down . . . and when it did, it would be a disaster for everyone. If Han and any hidden Bothan guards opened fire as the crowd stormed up the stairway, the result would be the slaughter of dozens or even hundreds of people.

But if they *didn't* open fire, there would be an equally callous slaughter of the Bothans who had escaped to the upper two floors. One way or another, a large number of people were about to die.

Unless . . .

One of the Noghri had spotted her now, pointing the others' attention her direction. Han half rose from his crouch, his mouth working with shouted words she couldn't hear. *I'm all right*, she thought desperately toward him, risking her grip to try to wave him back. If he or the Noghri headed down into that chaos, they'd probably get torn apart.

But no—he understood. Sinking back into his crouch, he waved the Noghri back, his eyes locked on hers across the atrium. *All right*, that expression seemed to say, *if you don't want us to come get you, what* do *you want?*

Here, she thought toward him, risking her grip again and unhooking her lightsaber. For a moment she fought against the bushy tendrils trying to entangle it; then she got it free and held it up. Cocking her arm over her shoulder, she threw it across the atrium, catching it midway in a Force grip and guiding it the rest of the way to drop into Han's hand. For a few heartbeats he fingered the weapon, frowning across the distance at her. She gestured and sent her thoughts toward him . . .

And abruptly he got it. Nodding his understanding, he ignited the weapon and turned the blade to point down.

And began cutting the stairway free from the balcony.

The action hadn't gone unnoticed. Someone in the crowd roared, and a pair of blaster bolts lanced out, missing Han by bare centimeters as he ducked away. The Noghri at Han's side—the second Noghri, Leia noticed with mild surprise, had somehow pulled a vanishing act—fired back, and the other blaster went silent.

Something brushed the back of Leia's head. She twisted around, her mind flashing back to the deadly vine snakes of Wayland—

But it wasn't a vine snake, or for that matter any other kind of creature. It was a length of synthrope, dangling from one of the windows directly above her.

With Barkhimkh's anxious face looking down at her from behind it.

Grabbing the rope, she started to climb. She was nearly to the window when, behind her, the stairway crashed to the floor.

"Admiral Pellaeon?"

With a jolt, Pellaeon snapped awake, the disturbing dream vanishing into the darkness of his quarters. "Yes?" he called.

"Major Tschel, sir," the bridge officer's voice came from the intercom. "There's a transmission coming in for you, marked with your personal encrypt."

"Understood," Pellaeon said, heaving himself wearily from his bed and padding over to the computer station. "Transfer it down here, Major," he ordered, dropping into the chair.

"Yes, sir."

The comm light went on, confirming the connection, and Pellaeon began keying in the proper decrypt code. Traveling around the Empire trying to beg, argue, or cajole acceptance of his peace initiative was tiring enough; but having to then endure these nightmares on top of it was only making the situation worse. Tonight's edition had featured Grand Admiral Thrawn, reproving him in a calm but bitter voice for allowing what he'd created to slip away . . .

The computer beeped acceptance of the decrypt, and a quarter-sized image appeared on the hologram pad. "Admiral Pellaeon, this is Commander Dreyf," the figure identified himself. "I have a preliminary report for you on my back-track of Lord Graemon and his finances."

"Very good," Pellaeon said, suddenly fully awake. "Continue."

"To be blunt, sir, the man's a snake," Dreyf said, not even bothering to hide his contempt. "He looks to have a finger in every stewpot from Muunilinst to Coruscant and back again. We've already uncovered fifteen separate lines to New Republic financial and commodities interests, and we haven't even scratched the surface yet."

Pellaeon nodded grimly. Yes, that fit the expected pattern. For Moff Disra to operate this way they had to have equally shady counterparts to Graemon on the New Republic side of the political borders. "What about connections to known pirate gangs?"

"Nothing specific with Graemon yet," Dreyf said. "But we have a pretty solid connection between General Kyte and someone who is definitely linked to the Cavrilhu Pirates. Kyte sent a transmission to the contact right after your meeting with the Muunilinst defense hierarchy eleven days ago. We're following it up."

"I see." So Kyte was indeed a part of this. Despite all the indicators, Pellaeon had hoped he was wrong. To have Fleet officers involved in treasonous activity was doubly painful. "Have you been able to backtrack Graemon's contacts the other direction?"

"Not yet," Dreyf said. "He's not the top of the stack, though—that much I'm sure of."

"No, he's not," Pellaeon agreed. Still, whatever the connection was between him and Disra, it would be well hidden. Too well hidden, perhaps, for Dreyf and his limited resources to dig out. "Keep at it," he continued. "I want the facts, and I want the evidence."

"Yes, sir," Dreyf said. "If I may make a suggestion, Admiral, all these business connections to the New Republic ought to be enough to bring down Lord Graemon, if that's what you want."

"I have no particular interest in bringing any specific person down," Pellaeon said, not entirely truthfully. "Trade

with the New Republic may be technically illegal, but you
know as well as I do that we need the resources too badly for
anyone to actually bother enforcing the laws."

Besides which, he added silently to himself, if and when
his peace initiative succeeded all that official isolationism
would have to be changed anyway. But of course Dreyf had
no idea any of that was in the works. "What I want—and *all*
that I want—is to find out who's been manipulating Imperial
personnel and funds this way and have them stopped," he
added aloud. "Clear?"

"Perfectly, Admiral," Dreyf said. "Don't worry, sir; no
matter how deep they've buried themselves, we'll dig them
out."

"I'm sure you will, Commander," Pellaeon assured him.
"Was there anything else?"

"Actually, sir, yes," Dreyf said, consulting a datapad. "I
just got word from one of my people on Bothawui who was
tracking down one of Lord Graemon's connections there.
He says there's been a bad riot over at the Combined Clans
Building in Drev'starn, apparently over this Caamas Document thing."

Pellaeon frowned. "Any other details?"

"Only that there were definitely casualties," Dreyf said.
"No idea of the number yet. Apparently it's just happened—
the news hasn't even hit the various services yet. It'll probably take them a while to sort things out, but I thought you'd
like to know."

"Yes, thank you," Pellaeon said. "Anything else?"

"No, sir, not right now."

"Very good," Pellaeon said, nodding. "Keep me informed, Commander. Out."

For a few minutes he remained seated at the computer
station, gazing at the empty display as he turned that last bit
of information over in his head. *The New Republic is unstable; ultimately, it has no choice but to self-destruct.* How
many times, he wondered, had that thought been hurled at
him in the three weeks since he'd begun this campaign to
persuade the leaders of the Empire that it was time to concede defeat? A hundred times, it seemed, maybe more; and

each time he'd stood against it, repeating his same list of arguments over and over again to the point where their precise and polished phrasing now came automatically to his mind and lips.

And yet . . .

He'd read the reports of the riots that had been springing up over this Caamas revelation and controversy; had skimmed the Intelligence summaries of the increasingly heated debates taking place in the New Republic Senate and various sector assemblies; had read the threat analyses of the growing belligerence between ancient rivals all across the galaxy.

Was he wrong and all the rest of them right? *Was* the New Republic on the verge of destroying itself?

And if it was, what in the Empire was he doing trying to make peace with them?

With a sigh, he levered himself out of his chair and crossed back to his bed. No, it didn't seem reasonable right now; but then, nothing ever seemed reasonable in the lonely stillness of the deep night. He'd had good and proper reasons to start on this path, he knew, and he could only assume that those reasons would still seem valid when he examined them again in the light of day. And if this controversy over the Caamas Document got in the way of the process—

Pellaeon frowned in the darkness, the memory of a comment Thrawn had once made flickering to mind. *Examine all obstacles carefully*, the Grand Admiral had admonished him. *With a little ingenuity, they can often be turned into levers*.

If the Caamas Document was tearing the New Republic apart . . . what might they offer in exchange for the Empire's help in putting that controversy to rest?

Reaching across the bed, he snagged his datapad and keyed for his list of upcoming meetings. Returning to Bastion was out; aside from the disruption it would cause in his schedule, any attempt to pull a copy of the Caamas Document out of the Imperial Library there would undoubtedly be relayed directly to Disra, and he had no interest in giving the Moff any advance warning of his intentions.

But there was also a complete set of Imperial records at the Ubiqtorate base at Yaga Minor. And four meetings from now, that was where the *Chimaera* was going to be.

Keying off the datapad, Pellaeon set it back on the nightstand and lay down again. Yes, that was what he would do. Try to find a copy of the complete Caamas Document and offer it to the New Republic in exchange for political concessions.

Assuming, of course, that that meeting did indeed take place.

For a moment he considered checking with the bridge to see whether there were any messages waiting from Major Vermel. But the comm officers already had explicit instructions to alert him immediately if any such messages came through. Reminding them of those instructions twice a day would only make them wonder what was going on.

Besides, it had only been eleven days since Vermel's ship could have reached Morishim. With the political situation on Coruscant the way it was, General Bel Iblis might well have needed this much time simply to get the New Republic hierarchy to accept the idea of a meeting.

No, Vermel would call eventually. And in the meantime, Pellaeon had four more meetings with most likely hostile senior Fleet officers to get through before he could head to Yaga Minor.

The first of which would be in barely six hours. Rolling over, closing his eyes, he cleared his mind and tried to get back to sleep.

Han shook his head. "No," he said, wincing slightly as Leia carefully dabbed salve onto his left shoulder. "I did *not* fire. Not into the crowd; not anywhere."

"Those we spoke to claim you did," Orou'cya insisted. "They say a blaster shot came from your balcony."

"Did Clan Leader Rayl'skar also fire?" Sakhisakh demanded. "The survivors say that as well."

"They are mistaken about that," Orou'cya said, his

huffy voice in odd contrast to the wariness with which he eyed the Noghri. "Clan Leader Rayl'skar had no blaster."

"Well, I didn't fire mine," Han insisted.

The Bothan's fur rippled. "If that is your word, I must accept it," he sighed. "It does not really matter."

Han grimaced. No, probably it didn't. With twenty-seven of the rioters dead and maybe forty more injured—and with the first floor of the Combined Clans Building a total loss—it hardly mattered anymore who had started it.

Except to the news reporters, of course. Most of whom were blaming him.

The door opened and a pair of Bothan guards stepped in, carrying a few bent pieces of gold metal. "Here is the rest, First Secretary," one of them said, offering their prizes to Orou'cya. "We have completed our search, and there is no more to be found."

Han scowled at the fragments. They'd been sweeping up pieces of Threepio for nearly an hour now, from nooks and crannies all over the first floor. It was like Cloud City all over again, only worse.

"He'll be all right," Leia murmured to him. "It didn't look like any of his major components had been seriously damaged while they were being kicked around. Most of it is cosmetic."

"We can repair him, if you'd like," Orou'cya offered.

"No, thanks," Han said, wishing Chewie were here instead of back on Coruscant minding the kids.

Or maybe not. The last time the Wookiee had had to put Threepio back together, the droid hadn't exactly bubbled over with gratitude. "We've got people on Coruscant who can do it."

"Of course." Orou'cya hesitated. "Speaking of Coruscant, Councilor Organa Solo, Clan Leader Rayl'skar has been in contact with the New Republic government. President Gavrisom would like to speak with you at your earliest convenience."

Han looked up at Leia. "You want me to need some extra looking after?" he murmured, just loud enough for her to hear.

Leia made a face, but shook her head. "No, I'd better not put it off," she said, handing him a bandage. "The sooner we get our side of the story to him, the better. May I use your communications room, Secretary Orou'cya?"

"Of course, Councilor Organa Solo," the Bothan said gravely, gesturing to the door. "Follow me, please."

They went out, the other two Bothans following, Sakhisakh rather conspicuously inviting himself along. Scowling again, Han took advantage of his new solitude to relieve himself of a few choice words; and he'd just gotten the bandage in place on his shoulder when the door opened and Barkhimkh came in. "Leia's gone to the comm room," he told the Noghri.

"I know," Barkhimkh said, stepping over to him and holding out his hand. "But I wished you to see this first."

Frowning, Han picked up the charred and twisted device from the Noghri's hand. "What is it?"

"The remains of an Imperial delusion," Barkhimkh bit out, his voice harsh with contempt. "A redirection crystal and blast tube filled with Tibanna gas are mounted in a wad of adhesion material and placed near one who is to be accused of a murder. A sharpshooter then fires a shot into the crystal, which redirects the energy into the tube."

"Which then fires just like a regular blaster." Han nodded grimly. Suddenly this whole thing was coming clear. "A random shot into the crowd, and I get blamed for it."

"Yes," Barkhimkh said blackly. "Once again, you have been blamed for something that was not your fault."

"Yeah, but this time they've done a real good job of it," Han said. "Wait a second, though. How come no one saw the sharpshooter's blast?"

"He was most likely using a Xerrol Nightstinger sniper weapon," Barkhimkh said. "It fires an invisible bolt."

Han frowned. "You're kidding. I've never heard of a blaster that could do that."

"The Empire did not advertise its existence," the Noghri said. "And aside from that single advantage it was a decidedly inferior weapon. The blaster gas required cost well over a thousand per canister, could only be used in specially designed blasters, and only permitted three to five shots per canister before replacement. Hardly a weapon for common usage."

"Yeah," Han said. "On the other hand, not exactly a weapon someone would just happen to be carrying around, either."

"True," Barkhimkh agreed. "Whatever it was that began this confrontation, there is no doubt it was Imperial agents who turned it into a riot."

"The problem being how to prove that," Han said, hefting what was left of the gadget in the palm of his hand. "I don't suppose this would be enough on its own."

The Noghri shook his head. "The device is a single-shot weapon, designed to disintegrate upon use. I know what it was solely from your description of what occurred."

And because Noghri assassination teams had used the gadgets themselves on occasion? Probably, but there wasn't any point in bringing that up. Even now, ten years after learning the truth and switching sides, the Noghri were still touchy about their long service to the Empire. "Well, at least *we* know about it," he said. "Who's in charge of the Imperial Fleet right now, anyway? I've kind of lost track."

"The Supreme Commander is Admiral Pellaeon," Barkhimkh said. "He commands the Imperial Star Destroyer *Chimaera*."

Han felt his lip twist. "One of Thrawn's people, right?"

"Pellaeon served directly under the Grand Admiral," the Noghri confirmed. "Many considered him Thrawn's primary protégé during those months."

"He sure seems to have picked up the tricks of the trade pretty well," Han growled. "We'll have to find a way to make him pay for that."

He handed the device back. "Here—try to keep what's left of it in one piece until we can get it back to the ship. And don't mention it to the Bothans, either."

"I obey, Han clan Solo," the Noghri said, bowing his head briefly as he slipped the device into a side pouch. "Will you be able to use this information?"

"Oh, we'll use it all right," Han assured him, brushing

the soot from his hands. Nearly sixty humans and aliens dead or injured; the New Republic in general and he in particular being blamed for it; and Supreme Commander Pellaeon and Imperial agents at the bottom of it. "Trust me, we'll use it."

The dark Noghri eyes gazed at his face. "How?"

Han shook his head. "I have no idea."

CHAPTER

14

The starlines faded into stars, and they were there.

Wherever in space "there" was.

"Reading three planets in the inner system," Faughn said, the last syllable half swallowed as she stifled a yawn. The normal crew rotation had put her off-duty when they were due to reach the Nirauan system, but she'd insisted on being awakened for the end of their trip.

Gazing out at the dim red star, Mara wondered whether it had been worth it.

"Second planet looks habitable," Torve reported. "It's got atmosphere—temperature seems okay—"

"We've got movement," Elkin snapped. "Bearing fifty-three by seventeen."

Mara threw a quick look at the instruments. As per her orders, the *Starry Ice* had come out of hyperspace in full sensor-stealth mode, and there was no indication of the kind of serious high-focus probe that should be necessary to penetrate that protection. Still, given they were dealing with alien technology, that might not mean anything. "Where's he headed?" she asked Elkin.

"Second planet for sure," Elkin said, keying his board. "Hang on—let's see if I can bracket his endpoint."

"Is it the same kind of ship that buzzed Terrik's Star Destroyer?" Faughn asked.

"The profile looks right," Torve said. "Can't tell for sure without doing a sensor focus."

"Endpoint coming up now," Elkin reported. "It's a spot in the northern hemisphere, lower latitudes."

"Anything around it?" Faughn asked.

"Nothing obvious," Torve said. "At least, nothing putting out a readable energy spectrum."

"This whole place makes me nervous," Elkin growled, drumming his fingertips restlessly on the edge of his control panel. "Why isn't there anything on either the planet or system in the datafiles? It's got a name—*someone* must have been here once."

"Oh, someone was here, all right," Faughn agreed. "But probably not for very long. For a while back in the Old Republic you could basically just come into an unknown system, do a quick life-forms scan, and file for development rights—the 'name it, claim it' law, they called it. You had systems all over the Outer Rim put on maps and asset lists without anyone having the slightest idea what was actually there."

"I remember reading about that," Mara said. "The Corporate Sector was especially bad about abusing the privilege, and we're not all that far from there."

"Right," Faughn said. "Still, all that having been said, I have to agree with Elkin's guts on this one. If this is somebody's military base, where are the defenses? Where's the base itself, for that matter?"

"No one said it *was* military," Mara reminded her. "They're using an alien technology—that's all we know."

She looked out the viewport. "And it's all we're going to know as long as we stay out here."

"I don't know," Faughn said. "We've confirmed this is the system. Maybe we should head back and get some backup."

"Unfortunately, we *don't* know this is really the system," Mara pointed out. "It could be just this month's rendezvous point. If we leave now, they may all be gone by the time we get back."

"I suppose," Faughn said reluctantly. "Well . . . looks

like that target zone is rotating away from us. We could give them a few hours to get around the horizon, then ease the ship in."

"That assumes they don't have a network of warning sensors scattered around the planet," Torve put in. "If they do, it won't matter whether the main base is line-of-sight to us or not."

Faughn shrugged. "It's a calculated risk."

"But not one the whole ship has to take," Mara said, mentally sifting through the possibilities. Along with its escape pods, the *Starry Ice* carried three shuttle-sized ships: two cargo-movers and a highly illegal New Republic Defender in system starfighter Karrde had appropriated from somewhere. "What's the sensor-stealthing like on that Defender?" she asked.

"Minimal," Faughn said. "On the other hand, it's got a pretty small sensor cross section to begin with, and of course no hyperdrive emissions at all. If their equipment isn't too good and you take it easy, you ought to have a fair chance of sneaking in."

"All right," Mara said, stretching out to the Force. There was no particular tingling from her danger sense. At least, not yet. "We'll go with your idea of letting the target zone rotate away from us for a few hours. Maybe upgrade the Defender's stealthing a little while we wait. After that . . . I go in and take a look."

From a distance the planet had looked dark and grim and desolate. Up close, Mara decided, it didn't look a whole lot better.

There was vegetation, certainly, everything from squat trees with wide, fan-shaped leaves to ground-hugging plants impossible to see clearly at the speed she was making. But the usual variety of color that was the norm on most of the worlds she'd visited seemed to have skipped Nirauan somehow. Everything here seemed to be done in shades of brown or gray, with only occasional splashes of dark red or deep violet to break up the monotony. Possibly it was a natural adaptation to the dim red light of the planet's sun; perhaps in the infrared part of the spectrum the plants were actually quite colorful. Somehow, she doubted it.

"Starting to get into some hills now," she said to the recorder fastened to one end of the Defender's control panel. "They look pretty craggy, actually—whatever dirt was on them seems to have eroded away." She glanced down at her displays. "Still no indication of sensor probes."

She looked back up from her board, frowning at the landscape ahead. Up there, between two of the craggier hills . . . ? "Looks like a sort of gully up ahead," she said. "No—make that a full-fledged ravine. In fact . . ."

She brushed the Defender's control stick gently, risking a little more altitude to get a better look. Her first impression had indeed been correct: the deep canyon ahead was pointing right toward the target zone.

And in fact, unless the terrain was somehow deceiving her, it looked like it would take her all the way in.

"I think I've found my route," she said, tapping a key to download the navigational information onto the recorder's data track. "Looks like a straight run right to their door."

Unless the unknown aliens had the ravine sensor-rigged, of course, in which case it would be a straight run into an ambush. She would just have to trust her danger sense to give her enough warning.

The ravine was indeed just as it had looked from a distance: fairly straight, its width varying from fifty to a hundred meters, its depth averaging around a hundred meters but dipping as deep as three hundred in places. Most similar ravines Mara had seen had been cut by rapid rivers, but the bottom of this one was dry. The walls were composed of craggy gray rock, with small bushes and tenacious vines clinging to the sides. "Still no sign of sensor activity," she told the recorder as she settled into the task of flying down the narrow passage. Standard military logic, she knew, would be for her opponents to launch their attack somewhere along these first few kilometers, while her maneuverability was limited but before she got unnecessarily close to their base. Stretching out to the Force, keeping a wary eye on the pale blue-green sky above her, she kept going.

But no attack came. The ravine widened, narrowed, then widened again, at one point changing from a canyon into the open side of a cliff where the left wall had crumbled down into a wide, forested valley beyond. The breath of open air was only a brief one; a moment later the wall rose again on her left and she was again flying through a ravine. As if inspired by its view of the forest, the vegetation was now becoming thicker and more varied, with the bushes and vines often completely covering the rocky walls.

And there was something else new, as well. "I'm seeing holes in the sides of the ravine now," she reported, trying to look into some of them as she passed. But she was going too fast to see more than that they were too deep for the sunlight to penetrate all the way to their backs. "Offhand, I'd say they don't look particularly natural," she continued. "It could be a colony of avians or vine-crawlers, or it could be part of a sensor array. Suggest the next person in bring a better sensor package to—wait a second."

She eased off on the throttle, frowning ahead. The ravine was widening again; and up there to her right— "I think I may have found the front door," she told the recorder tightly. "Looks like a cave entrance up ahead on the right, just this side of a slight right-handed angling. Good-sized opening—a little maneuvering and the ships we saw could make it inside." She pursed her lips. "And I've now got a decision to make: take the Defender, or head in on foot."

The Defender was slowing to a halt now, and she shifted to full repulsorlifts as she tried to think. The obvious decision, of course, would be to take the Defender in. But in this case, obvious didn't necessarily mean smart. So far there'd been no response from their quarry, which meant they either hadn't noticed her yet or else didn't consider her a threat.

And either way, a lone person on foot would probably get farther before sparking a reaction than a New Republic starfighter roaring in with laser cannons charged and ready. "I'm going in on foot," she told the recorder, easing the Defender down to the ground beside a clump of bushes and keying for a bioscan of the air outside. "There've been no hostile acts toward me yet, and it would be nice if I could keep it that way."

Reaching down to the small weapons locker beside her right knee, she opened the panel. "But just in case I can't, I'm taking my BlasTech, sleeve gun, and lightsaber," she added. "That should give me a head start on whatever happens."

She slid the BlasTech blaster into the holster on her hip and secured the smaller weapon in the forearm holster hidden beneath her left sleeve. She picked up the lightsaber . . .

And paused, gazing at the weapon, feeling the cool metal against her skin. It had been Luke Skywalker's lightsaber once, made by his father and passed down to him on Tatooine by Obi-Wan Kenobi. Luke had given it in turn to her after the Empire's massive counteroffensive under Grand Admiral Thrawn had finally been stopped.

Then, she and Luke had been allies. Now . . .

With a grimace, she hooked the lightsaber onto her belt. Now, she wasn't sure what they were.

Or rather, she wasn't sure what he was.

The bioscan beeped: the air was breathable, with no toxins or dangerous microorganisms that should be able to get through her broad-scale immunization. "Looks okay out there," she said, dragging her thoughts away from Skywalker and back to the immediate business at hand. Shutting down the repulsorlifts, she shifted the Defender's systems to standby and double-checked that the recorder was set to pulse-transmit back to the *Starry Ice*. "I'll take my comlink, keyed to the recorder."

She clipped her comlink to a hands-free position on her collar, then popped the canopy. Nirauan's air rushed in, cool and crisp, with the subtle yet exotic odors of a new world. Unstrapping, she stood up, pulling the Defender's survival pack from its storage locker and hooking its straps over one shoulder as she climbed down the side to the ground. Settling the pack securely onto her shoulders, taking one last look around, she closed and locked the canopy and set off toward the cave.

The grasslike vegetation underfoot was short and broad-bladed, with a tendency to cling to her boots, but otherwise it didn't impede her movements. She listened as she walked, but there was only the rustling of the vegetation and the quiet whisper of the breezes through the ravine. No animal or avian sounds at all.

But they were there, she knew, glancing up at the small holes that dotted the ravine's sides. The animals were there. In the holes, or nesting in the bushes, or lurking under the rock-climbing vines. She could feel their presence.

And at least some of them were watching her. . . .

"I could have been wrong about this," she said into the comlink, drawing her blaster. "That could just be a cave up there. I guess I'll find out soon enough."

Cautiously, she worked her way to the cave. Just as cautiously, she eased an eye around the edge.

It was a cave, all right. A dirty, musty, rough-walled cave, stretching back blackly into the distance, with a thick matting of dead leaves on the ground at the entrance, cobwebs of some sort wafting randomly in the breeze, and a lingering hint of dankness from distant standing water.

She lowered her blaster, feeling both anticlimactic and a little bit foolish. "I'm here," she said to her comlink. "And if this is a disguised landing bay, they've done a terrific job of it."

She stepped back from the cave's mouth, shading her eyes as she peered up the side of the cliff. Nothing but cliff that she could see. Just beyond the cave, as she'd already noted, the ravine veered slightly to the right. More from curiosity than any expectation of seeing anything interesting, she walked to the far side of the cave and looked around the bend.

And caught her breath. Straight ahead, perhaps ten kilometers farther along, the ravine came to an abrupt end at the base of a massive bluff. And sitting atop the bluff, black against the pale sky, was a building.

No, not just a building. A fortress.

Mara took a deep breath. "I've found them," she said, fighting to keep her voice steady as she pulled a set of macrobinoculars from their pouch in the side of her survival pack. There was something about the sight of that structure that was sending an unpleasant tingle through her. "There's some kind of fortress sitting on a bluff at the far end of the ravine."

She activated the macrobinoculars and focused on the fortress. "Seems to be built of black stone," she reported, zooming in the view. "Reminds me of that old abandoned fortress on Hijarna we sometimes used as a rendezvous point. I can see—looks like two, maybe three towers from this angle, plus something that might have been one more broken off near the base. In fact . . ."

She lowered her view down the bluff to where the ravine began, the tingling sensation growing even more unpleasant. "In fact, if you set up the angles right," she said slowly, "you could make a case that whatever the shot was that took out that tower was the same blast that gouged out this ravine."

And if so, that would have been one impressive blast. The Death Star could have done it, but not much else in either the Imperial or New Republic arsenals. "Regardless, I guess that's my next stop," she decided, sliding the macrobinoculars back into their pouch. Taking one last look at the fortress, she turned and headed back toward the Defender. She glanced inside the cave, crossed to the other side—

And froze, pressing her shoulder against the cool rock beside the cave opening. Something had suddenly set off her danger sense . . . and as she waited, she heard it again.

The soft, distant whine of an air vehicle.

"I think I'm about to have some company," she muttered into her comlink, giving the sky a quick scan. Nothing was visible yet, but the sound was definitely coming closer. Carefully, still watching the sky, she took a few steps back into the shadows of the cave.

Abruptly her danger sense flared; but even as she spun around she knew it was too late. From deep in the cave to her right something dark shot past, flapping a puff of dank air into her face as it swooped past her head and darted back into the darkness. She dropped into a crouch, blaster tracking toward the flying shadow, but it was already out of sight. She fired once into the ceiling, the blast of light giving her a brief glimpse of rough walls and hanging spikes of rock. She spotted the flying shadow, shifted her aim warningly toward it—

She had only a glimpse of the second shadow as it dropped from somewhere above her and deftly snatched the blaster from her hand. Stifling a curse, she yanked her light-saber off her belt with her left hand, igniting it and in the same motion tossing it to her right hand.

And suddenly the whole cave seemed to come to a screeching halt.

It was, Mara realized, a bizarre characterization of what had just happened. But the impression nevertheless remained. Whatever the flapping creatures were, they were suddenly watching with new eyes.

And speaking with a new voice.

A new voice? Mara frowned, listening hard. No mistake: there were indeed new sounds murmuring through the cave.

Through the cave . . . or through her mind.

Backing into a slight depression in the wall, she stretched out as hard as she could with the Force. The almost-voices seemed to sharpen, but they remained right on the tantalizing edge of comprehension. "Terrific," she muttered to herself. An alien and possibly hostile aircraft on its way, and here she was, pinned down by equally alien creatures who were smart enough to grab her blaster away. Creatures she could almost, but not quite, communicate with. "Where are Skywalker and his bag of tricks when you need them?"

It was as if an emotional seismic shock had rippled through the cave. Suddenly the almost-voices were clamoring even louder at the edge of her mind. "Skywalker?" Mara demanded. "You know him?"

Again the almost-voices clamored, this time with a coloring of frustration in their tone. "Yeah, I'm frustrated, too," Mara snapped back. "Come on, speak up. Or whatever it is you're doing. What does Skywalker have to do with you?"

If they gave an answer, she never heard it. From the mouth of the cave to her left came a whisper of movement. She spun around, swinging her lightsaber to defense position—

And felt her mouth drop open in astonishment. Moving awkwardly into the mouth of the cave was a huge cloud of dark, vaguely mynocklike creatures, their wings flapping madly.

And in the center of that cloud, supported on the backs of those beneath it as it was hauled by the half-hidden claws of the ones above, was her ship.

"What in blazes?" she snapped, jumping forward.

Too quickly. Her foot caught on a pile of dead leaves, throwing her off balance. She twisted around, trying to recover, and instead swerved the opposite direction. Out of the corner of her eye she saw a sharp-edged stone jutting out from the cave wall rushing at her—

She woke gradually, painfully, with a matting of what felt like dried blood on the side of her head and eyes that didn't seem to want to open.

It was perhaps half a groggy minute more before she was conscious enough to realize that her eyes *were* in fact open. It was simply a matter of its being too dark to see anything.

"Uh-oh," she muttered, her voice echoing oddly. Had she been unconscious long enough for it to become night? Or had she been dragged or carried farther back into the cave?

The survival pack was still strapped to her back. Pulling the glow rod from its pocket, she flicked it on.

She had indeed been moved deeper into the cave. And, for good measure, it had also become night outside.

"Nice to know I can still call 'em," she muttered in disgust, glaring at her chrono. She'd been unconscious for nearly three hours, far longer than she would have expected. Either she'd hit the wall harder than she realized, or else her kidnappers had dropped her a few times on the way here.

Wherever "here" was.

For a moment she played the beam from the glow rod around the walls and high ceiling of the cavern around her, comparing it with her memory of the brief glimpse the illumination from her earlier blaster shot had given her. But nothing matched. That put her at least thirty meters inside, she estimated, probably more. Not an unreasonable hike, assuming she didn't get lost in a maze of side passages. And assuming her Defender was waiting somewhere along the way for her to find.

And assuming that if assumptions one and two worked out there would be some place for her to go.

She looked at her chrono again. Three hours. The recorder had been set up to dump a pulse-transmission back to the *Starry Ice* if she either shut off the comlink or else stopped talking for fifteen minutes. Which meant Faughn had had the record of her trip for over two and a half hours now, including that last startled yelp before she'd knocked herself out. The question was, what had she decided to do with it?

Unfortunately, there was only one likely answer. Faughn had no other fighters aboard; had no way to come to Mara's aid except to bring the *Starry Ice* itself in. She knew better than to risk her ship that way, particularly when she was the only one who had the information Mara had sent.

Which meant the *Starry Ice* was long gone. And with no hyperdrive on the Defender, that meant Mara was stuck here.

"I suppose I could walk to the fortress and see if they've got a room to rent," she muttered. But that really didn't sound like a smart idea; and even as she said it, she could hear a strong note of disapproval enter the almost-voices tickling at the edge of her mind. "Don't worry, I'm not going anywhere," she growled. It was their fault she was marooned here, after all.

On the other hand, depending on who or what had been in the aircraft she'd heard, it was possible they'd also saved her life. Under the circumstances, she supposed, it was a fair trade-off.

And it wasn't like this was permanent exile, either. A few days—two weeks at the most—and Karrde would have a force here to get her out.

In the meantime, she had survival to worry about. Balancing the glow rod on an outcropping where it could give her some working light, she unstrapped her pack and began setting up camp.

CHAPTER

15

Lando looked up from his datapad at the grizzled man sitting across the tapcafe table from him, face half-hidden behind his mug. "You must be joking," he said, waving at the datapad. "Fifty thousand? A *month*?"

The other shrugged. "Take it or not, Calrissian—makes no difference to me. But if you want to hire the best, you gotta expect it to cost you."

"Oh, come on," Lando growled. "This is *me* you're talking to, Reggi. We both know the Soskin Guard is hardly the best."

"Maybe not," Reggi allowed, taking another swig from his mug. "But they're the best you're gonna have any shot at hiring."

"Look, I'm talking about running ore freighter security here," Lando said, fighting against the sinking feeling he'd had so many times in the past ten days. "Not invading Alion or boarding a Star Destroyer or something."

"Too bad," Reggi said, wiping his mouth with the back of his sleeve. "Those sound like more fun—the Soskins might give you a discount on one of them."

"My point is that we're not talking the kind of job that's worth fifty thousand," Lando pushed ahead doggedly. "We're talking one shipment of ore per month out of Varn, plus a few shiploads of casino customers coming in and out. That can't be worth more than, say, five thousand a month."

Reggi sighed. "Look, Calrissian—" He paused, glanced around the tapcafe. "Look over there," he continued, pointing across at a group of aliens hunched together around a table, their horny heads almost touching. "See those Clatear? They've got a six-hundred-year-old feud going with the Nhoras that five separate generations of Jedi tried to stop and couldn't. Ever heard of it?"

Lando nodded. "Yes."

"Good," Reggi said. "Well, with this new hands-off policy that's come out of Coruscant, they figure no one outside their sector is going to care anymore what they do to each other. Ergo, it's time to start fighting again.

"Now, the Clatear, they've got a pretty good military— they were under Imperial guns a lot for a while—so they're in pretty good shape. The Nhoras were luckier—or maybe not, depending how you look at it. They got ignored by the Empire, so they've got nothing much to fight with."

Lando sighed. He could see where this was going. "So they're hiring mercenaries."

"You got it, old friend," Reggi said approvingly. "They've got the Dhashaan Shield in to guard their systems—even talked old Dharus himself out of retirement to handle logistics and strategy for them. And they're ladling out thirty thousand for them. That's per *day*."

He shook his head in disbelief. "It's definitely a seller's market out there for anyone with soldiers and ships, Calrissian. Everyone's figuring on settling old grudges. And who out there hasn't got a grudge or two against someone?"

"But the Nhoras are hiring for a full-scale war," Lando said, trying one last time. "All I want is someone to help keep pirates off my shipments."

Reggi shrugged. "Some of those pirate gangs are worse than taking on a whole system defense force. Course, that depends on the system."

Lando grimaced. "Reggi, look—"

"And if you're going to bring up Taanab again, don't," the other interrupted him. "You've been squeezing that bit of history for favors for, oh, must be fifteen years now. Not going to do you any good this time."

"It's always nice to see gratitude," Lando said frostily, getting to his feet. "See you around, Reggi. Have fun with whichever war you settle on."

The afternoon Cilparian sunlight seemed especially harsh after the cool dimness of the tapcafe. For a minute Lando stood beside the entrance, studying the business flags that flew all up and down Spacer's Street and wondering if it would be worth the effort to try checking out their current clientele.

No. Reggi was right: any mercenary group worth hiring these days was looking for bigger game than freighter escort duty. And a higher pay scale than Lando could afford.

After nearly two decades of agonizing struggle, the galaxy had finally found peace . . . and all they wanted to do with it was get back to the petty little wars the Emperor's New Order had so thoughtlessly interrupted.

With a tired shake of his head, he turned back toward the spaceport.

The noise of the crowd reached him long before he came into sight of them. It was a good-sized mob, as these things seemed to be going: probably three hundred humans and aliens, milling noisily around the entrance to Docking Bay 66. This group was better organized than most, though, with signs as well as the usual shouted demands for justice for Caamas.

The mood he was in, he would have welcomed the opportunity to shove his way through them, maybe get a chance to burn a little of the simmering resentment out of his system. But the universe wasn't going to cooperate even that far with him today; the *Lady Luck* was two bays down in 68. Muttering under his breath about people who had nothing better to do than protest something that had happened before most of them were even born, he stomped past the crowd and headed toward his bay. As far as he was concerned, the sooner he got off Cilpar, the better.

He was a good ten meters past the edge of the crowd when a stray fact managed to penetrate his blanket of grouchy

self-pity. These protests invariably targeted Bothans: Bothan
merchants or diplomats or businesses. But there were no
Bothans at Mos Tommro Spaceport—they used a different facility entirely.

So what were the protesters doing here?

Keeping a wary eye on the crowd, he backed into an
alley out of their sight and pulled out his comlink. He keyed
it to run through the *Lady Luck*'s comm system and
punched for the spaceport control center. "This is Lando
Calrissian in Bay 68," he identified himself to the bored
voice that answered. "I'd like a listing of the ships in Bay
66."

"There will be no need for that," a calm voice said from
the alley behind him.

Lando spun around, his hand twitching aside the edge of
his cloak with practiced ease and landing on the butt of his
holstered blaster. Standing a few meters away, decked out in
full diplomatic regalia, were a pair of white-maned, leathery-
faced Diamala. "Yes?" he asked cautiously. "Can I help
you?"

"Yes, I believe you can," the taller of the two aliens said.
"Allow me to introduce myself. I am Porolo Miatamia, Senator to the New Republic. May I confirm that my ears did
not deceive me and that you are General Lando Calrissian?"

"Former general, yes," Lando nodded, releasing his grip
on his blaster and shutting off his comlink. The crowd of
protesters at Bay 66 was starting to make sense now. "May I
confirm in turn that this is not a chance meeting?"

Miatamia smiled thinly, the only way Lando had ever
seen a Diamal smile. "You are correct," the Senator assured
him. "My aide spotted you five streets away as you were
approaching." One fan-shaped ear dipped to point at the
Diamal beside him. "We have paralleled you to this point,
seeking a way to confirm your identity."

"You've confirmed it," Lando said. One of the more
irritating Diamalan social characteristics—annoying to him,
anyway—was this tendency of theirs to trample the ground
flat around an issue before actually getting to it. "Is there
some service I can perform for you?"

Miatamia's ear flicked in the direction of the crowd. "My ship is in Docking Bay 66," he said. "There are . . . persons . . . who disapprove of my government's stance on the Bothan issue."

"Yes, I've heard," Lando said. So it was now the Bothan issue, not the Caamas issue. Interesting. "Your government wants to forgive and forget, or some such thing."

The Senator eyed him closely. "Would you then prefer to inflict mindless vengeance against innocents?"

Lando spread his hands. "Hey, this is politics. I'm just a simple businessman trying to turn a little profit."

Miatamia eyed him a moment longer. Then one of his ears twitched. "As that may be," he said cryptically. "At any rate, the protesters have made their point. I have therefore appealed to the spaceport authorities to remove them so that I may return to my ship."

Lando nodded. After that lethal riot on Bothawui a week ago, he could understand the Senator's reluctance to try to push his way through the crowd. "Let me guess. They refused to lift a finger."

"There is no need to guess: I can positively state that that was their response," Miatamia said. "We were departing from their offices when we noticed you and made our tentative identification."

"I understand," Lando said. "What service may I perform for you?"

Miatamia's other ear twitched. "I wished to ask you to use your position and influence with the New Republic to intercede on my behalf."

His influence with the New Republic. Right. "I wish I could help you," he said. "Unfortunately, I'm afraid my influence these days is limited to a select number of friends and associates. None of whom is currently on Cilpar."

"I see." Miatamia was silent a moment. "In that event, perhaps you would be willing to speak to the crowd. As a hero of the Rebellion, you would have a calming influence."

Lando snorted under his breath. "I very much doubt my past activities would get me very far with them, Senator.

There's a bad tendency these days for people to forget what happened back then."

"Then you refuse to help me?"

"It's not a refusal," Lando said, trying hard to be patient. It was a language thing, of course; for all their calmly logical veneer, Diamala had a tendency to use words in nonstandard ways. One reason why a lot of people didn't like dealing with them. "I'm simply pointing out that there's nothing I can do to help you."

And then a sudden thought occurred to him. "At least, nothing I can do to get you to your ship," he continued before Miatamia could respond. "If all you need right now is to get to Coruscant or back home, that's another matter."

Both ears twitched this time. "Explain."

"My ship is docked in Bay 68," he said. "I would be honored to take you wherever in the New Republic you wished to go."

"Others of the crew are still outside," the aide pointed out. "Trapped away from the ship by the crowd. Do you offer them transport as well?"

"I was thinking mainly of you and Senator Miatamia," Lando said, looking at him. "My ship has rather limited living space."

He shifted his eyes back to Miatamia. "But it seems to me that the crowd isn't interested in your crew, just in the attention of the Senator. Once you're not here to give them that attention, there won't be much point in them hanging around."

"You speak reason," Miatamia said. "Now speak cost."

"No cost, Senator," Lando assured him, waving a hand in invitation back toward his docking bay. "I would be honored to have such a distinguished personage aboard my ship."

The other didn't move. "Speak of the cost, please. There is always a cost."

So much for finding a subtle way to bring up the topic aboard the *Lady Luck*. "There is no cost," Lando repeated. "However, my underwater mining operation is having problems with pirate attacks. I thought perhaps I might be able to make an arrangement with the Diamalan military to provide extra security for my shipments."

"The primary task of the Diamalan military is to protect Diamalan interests," Miatamia said. "However, there may be room for discussion."

"Thank you, Senator," Lando said. "Honest discussion is all I ask. Shall we go?"

The short trip across the street to the docking-bay door was just a shade worse than Lando had expected it would be. The two Diamala refused to run or even to hurry—a matter of dignity, apparently—and they were no more than halfway to the door when the crowd waiting two bays down spotted them. Fortunately, having no compunctions of his own against a little judicious haste, Lando had already reached the other side and was keying the door open by the time the mob started its belated surge toward them. The Diamala made it inside in plenty of time, with only a few minor fruit juice stains from glancing impacts as souvenirs.

"They are barbarians," the aide said, his voice icy cold, as Lando sealed the door behind them. "No being should have the right to attempt such dishonoring of another."

"Peace," Miatamia said in the same tone as he flicked a few drops of juice from his sleeve with his fingertips. "Few other beings have the wisdom or capacity for proper expression that characterize the Diamala. Rather than considering them as barbarians to be shunned, or even as wrongdoers to be punished, you must see them as children who merely need instruction in civilized behavior."

He looked at Lando. "Do you not agree?"

"I think any such discussions should be postponed, Senator," Lando said, not about to let himself get dragged into that kind of conversation. "At least until we're safely off Cilpar."

"You speak wisdom," Miatamia said, his ears twitching again. "Please; lead the way."

•   •   •

Tierce looked up from the display . . . and from his expression alone Disra knew he'd hit solid ore. "You have a target?" he asked.

"I do indeed," Tierce said. "Senator Porolo Miatamia, Diamalan representative to the New Republic." He swiveled the display around to face the other. "And you'll never guess who he's hitched a ride with."

Disra scanned the report, feeling his own eyes widen a little. "They must be joking. *Lando* Calrissian?"

"No joke," Tierce assured him. "And no error, either. The reporting agent back-checked against the Mos Tommro Spaceport lift records. Calrissian, the Senator, and the Senator's aide all took off together in Calrissian's yacht."

"Did they indeed," Disra murmured. No wonder Tierce was looking so self-satisfied. The Diamala were even louder advocates of the forgive-and-forget attitude than either the Mon Calamari or the Duros. An ideal choice for the little drama Tierce had in mind.

And to have a close friend of Han Solo's along for the ride made it even more perfect. "What's their destination—oh, here it is. Coruscant."

"Yes." Tierce had called up a star chart and was laying rate-of-passage tracklines across it. "Assuming Calrissian heads straight for Coruscant, we should have no trouble intercepting them wherever we want along the way. The only question is whether Flim and I can rendezvous with the *Relentless* before they grab the yacht."

"It won't look good if they have to wait for you to show up," Disra warned. "This is supposed to look like one of Thrawn's casual-omniscience tricks."

"Kindly do not lecture me on the subtleties of my own plans," Tierce said coldly, manipulating the tracklines across the starfield. "It'll be a bit tight, but I think we can manage it."

"Yes," Disra said as he looked over the numbers himself. "I'm still not wild about this plan, Tierce. We have no idea how the New Republic will react."

"Of course we know," Tierce said patiently. "I've already explained all of that to you."

"You've given me your guesses," Disra corrected. "But that's all they are. Guesses."

"If you're not willing to take some risks, you shouldn't have started this scheme in the first place," Tierce said, his voice chilling a few degrees. "It's still not too late for you to back out if you've lost your nerve."

Disra glared at him. "It's not a question of my nerve, Major," he growled. "It's a question of not taking unnecessary risks to achieve our objective."

Tierce met his gaze evenly. "This one is necessary, Your Excellency," he said. "Trust me. Now, we'll need an Interdictor Cruiser, too." He lifted his eyebrows slightly. "And we're on something of a tight schedule here."

With an effort, Disra swallowed back the rest of his argument. Tierce hadn't sprung this new scheme on him until after his return from Yaga Minor, and he still wasn't sure how the Guardsman had talked him into it. But if they were going to do it, they had blazing well better do it right. "Fine," he growled. "Get out of my chair and I'll issue the orders."

CHAPTER

16

"Well, General," Admiral Pellaeon said, leaning back in his seat as he accepted a small glass of Kareas brandy from the other, "how are things at Yaga Minor?"

"About the same as always, Admiral," High General Hestiv said, waving at the distant planet centered in his office viewport as he poured a little of the brandy into his own glass and sat down again behind his datacard-strewn desk. "Very quiet."

"I understand there's been some recent unrest among segments of the Yagai population," Pellaeon said.

"Completely negligible," Hestiv said, waving a hand in dismissal. "Actually, since the overwhelming majority of the populace is completely loyal, they mostly take care of the handful of dissenters themselves. The only time we normally have to lift a finger is to protect the dissidents from overzealous loyalists."

"Allowing you to take the moral high ground."

"Exactly," Hestiv said. "It makes for a refreshing change from our usual image among aliens."

"Yes," Pellaeon murmured, sipping his drink. "A pity the Emperor didn't work harder at that kind of public relations himself twenty years ago."

"A pity someone who wasn't so insanely blind with power didn't overthrow him while there was still time,"

Hestiv countered, an edge of bitterness in his voice. "There must have been hundreds of competent administrators or Fleet officers who could have kept the Empire alive."

Pellaeon felt a catch in his throat. "There was one, at least," he said quietly.

Hestiv's lip twitched. "Yes—Grand Admiral Thrawn. I've always regretted the fact that I never had the chance to meet him."

For a moment the two men sat in silence. Then Hestiv cleared his throat. "But I don't suppose it gains us anything to count the might-have-beens," he said. "That was the past, this is the present; and I presume, Admiral, that you're here to discuss the future."

Pellaeon took another sip of his drink. "Yes," he said, watching the other closely. "To put it bluntly, the war against the New Republic is over, and we've lost. In my professional military opinion, it's time to talk peace."

The muscles around Hestiv's eyes tightened. "You mean surrender."

"I'll be negotiating for terms," Pellaeon said. "If I do a proper job, I think we should be able to keep most of what we have."

Hestiv snorted. "Such as it is."

"We still control over a thousand inhabited systems," Pellaeon reminded him mildly. "Would you prefer we allow the New Republic to whittle that number down further before we accept the inevitable?"

"The New Republic's in no shape to do much whittling at the moment," Hestiv said. "It looks to me like they're poised to go for each other's throats, not ours."

"Certainly they have problems," Pellaeon said. "But if you're expecting them to collapse into a full-fledged civil war over Caamas or anything else, I think you're being unrealistic."

"Begging the Admiral's pardon, but I respectfully disagree," Hestiv said. "Particularly if we engaged in a little judicious pushing of our own."

Pellaeon stifled a sigh. Yet another argument he'd heard over and over again on this trip. "So you'd have us encourage them in their self-destruction," he said. "Emptying your shipyards if necessary; draining all the manpower and resources from your Ubiqtorate base. Leaving this system totally defenseless."

"If it's necessary to go that far, yes," Hestiv said. "This is a military base, Admiral. That's how its resources are supposed to be used."

"Granted," Pellaeon said with a nod. "And what do you suppose will happen when they find out we've been goading them?"

"There's no reason they need to find out," Hestiv argued. "We don't have to use our Star Destroyers or TIE fighters or anything else obviously Imperial."

"No." Pellaeon shook his head. "We can keep up such a charade for a while, maybe even a long while. But in the end, they'll find out. And then they'll unite again, at least long enough to destroy us."

Hestiv looked out the window at the blue-green sphere in the distance. "At least that way we'd go down fighting," he said with obvious difficulty. "Your way . . . there's no honor in surrender, Admiral."

"There's no honor in wasting lives for nothing, either," Pellaeon countered.

Hestiv smiled wryly. "I know. But at least if you're dead you don't have to live with the shame of it."

"There are some in the Fleet who would call that a noble warrior attitude," Pellaeon said. "Personally, I'd call it stupid. If we're destroyed—if we all die—the concepts and ideals of the New Order die with us. But if we surrender, we can keep those ideals alive. Then, if and when the New Republic self-destructs, we'll be positioned to rise again. Maybe then the galaxy will finally be ready to accept us."

Hestiv grimaced. "Perhaps."

"There's no disgrace in backing out of a no-win situation, General," Pellaeon said quietly. "I saw Grand Admiral Thrawn do it more than once, forthrightly and without embarrassment, rather than waste his men and ships. That's no more or less what I'm proposing we do now."

Hestiv swirled his drink restlessly in his glass. "I presume you've already consulted with the Moffs about this."

"I have," Pellaeon said. "In the end, they agreed."

"Reluctantly, I suppose."

"None of us is exactly enthusiastic about it," Pellaeon said. "We simply recognize that it has to be done."

Hestiv took a deep breath, exhaled it. "I suppose you're right. I wish you weren't." He lifted his glass, drained it in a single swallow. "Very well, Admiral. You have my support, which I presume was the real reason you came to Yaga Minor. Is there anything else I can do for you?"

"As a matter of fact, there is," Pellaeon said, pulling out a datacard and handing it across the desk. "First of all, I'd like you to run this list of names through the Ubiqtorate base's computer system."

"Certainly," Hestiv said, sliding the datacard into its slot and keying his terminal. "Anything in particular you're looking for?"

"Unaltered information," Pellaeon told him. "These are people I suspect of having shady financial ties to Moff Disra, but we haven't been able to track the connections."

"And Disra wouldn't let you look through the Bastion records?" Hestiv suggested with a wry smile.

"I'm sure he would have," Pellaeon said. "I just don't happen to think I'd be able to trust what those records said."

"Well, you can trust these," Hestiv assured him, keying his board. "No one gets into my records without proper and double-confirmed authorization. That major from the *Obliterator*—Tierce—certainly found that out when he tried to—"

"Major Tierce?" Pellaeon interrupted him. "Major *Grodin* Tierce?"

"Yes, that's the one," Hestiv said, frowning. "He was here on behalf of Captain Trazzen, only we couldn't make contact with the *Obliterator* to confirm the authorization so we wouldn't let him into the system. Why, is something wrong?"

"Yes," Pellaeon gritted. "Major Tierce isn't attached to the *Obliterator*. He's Moff Disra's aide."

Hestiv's expression turned to stone. "Is he, now."

Pellaeon gestured toward the terminal. "Is there any way to tell which records he might have tapped into?"

"I just told you he didn't get in."

"Oh, he got in, all right," Pellaeon said darkly. "Through a terminal no one was watching, or perhaps he brought one of his own and tapped in at a junction point. But he most certainly didn't leave without whatever it was he came here to do."

Hestiv was keying his board. "You're right, of course. I'll order a check; and while we're at it, let's have them run his ID again."

The examination took just under an hour; and in the end, they found what Pellaeon had begun to suspect they would find.

Nothing.

"This doesn't make any sense," Hestiv growled, glaring at his display. "We know he was here, and presumably not just for his health. But there isn't a single sign of access or tampering. So what in blazes did he *do*?"

"Did you check all the records?" Pellaeon asked, swiveling the display around and running an eye down the listing.

"Of course we did," Hestiv said, his tone a little huffy. "Everything from the basic maintenance files on up to—"

"No," Pellaeon said, staring at the display as a sudden chilling thought hit him. "You didn't check everything. You couldn't have."

"Begging the Admiral's pardon—"

"Because there are records you don't have access to," Pellaeon cut him off, scrolling down the listing. "Specifically, the Special Files section."

Hestiv's eyebrows lifted. "You can't be serious," he said. "Are you suggesting a lowly major could access the Emperor's own sealed records?"

"I agree it sounds unbelievable," Pellaeon said. "But we're running out of options."

"But a *major*?"

"He's an aide to a very slippery Moff," Pellaeon reminded him. "I wouldn't put it past Disra to have found a way into the Special Files. In fact, considering his ambition and lack of discernible ethics, I'd probably find it more surprising if he hadn't."

"I still don't believe it," Hestiv said heavily. "But as you say, we're running out of options." He cocked an eyebrow. "I don't suppose *you* can get us into those records to check this out?"

Pellaeon shook his head. "The codes and procedures were lost long before I rose to the position where I would have been instructed in their use."

"Pity," Hestiv said. "If we can't get in, we aren't going to be able to figure out what he was doing in there."

"That *is* the big question, isn't it?" Pellaeon agreed, rubbing his chin thoughtfully. "He couldn't have been looking up something—the records at Bastion are duplicates of the ones here. Which implies his purpose was to add, delete, or alter."

Hestiv muttered something under his breath. "Which implies those names you're investigating may have more of a history with the Empire than you thought."

"Perhaps," Pellaeon agreed soberly as another unpleasant thought struck him. "But there's one other possibility. If I wanted details on the attack that destroyed Caamas, where would I look?"

Hestiv shrugged slightly. "There should be copies of all the media and official reports in the regular files, both current-time and follow-up."

"And if Palpatine was personally involved, as the rumors suggested?"

Hestiv exhaled noisily. "Anything like that would be in the Special Files section, wouldn't it? You think that's what Tierce was really after?"

"Or he was after that plus Disra's ally list," Pellaeon said. "As long as he was in the files anyway, why not do both?"

"Why not, indeed?" Hestiv said, drumming his fingers thoughtfully on the desktop. "The question is, what would Disra want with the Caamas files?"

"Whatever it is, I doubt very much that it has anything other than Disra's personal aggrandizement at the core," Pellaeon said sourly. "And for that reason alone, I want to know what it is. I think, General, that the two of us ought to begin a quiet search for someone who might be able to access those records for us."

"I'll begin making inquiries immediately," Hestiv promised. "Where can I contact you if I'm successful?"

"I'll be out of contact for a while," Pellaeon said, standing up. "I'll communicate with you when I get back. Thank you for your assistance."

"Anytime, Admiral," Hestiv said. "And best of luck with . . . with everything."

And it was finally time, Pellaeon knew as he headed down the corridor from Hestiv's office toward the docking bay where his shuttle was berthed. The Yaga Minor shipyards were the last stop on his tour of the Empire's meager defensive facilities, and he had gleaned as much support from the senior military as he was going to get.

It was time now for the lonely journey to Pesitiin.

He grimaced. It had been three weeks now. Three weeks since Major Vermel would have arrived at Morishim to try to contact General Bel Iblis. Three weeks since he and his Corellian Corvette had vanished without a single trace. The increasingly unavoidable conclusion was that he'd been intercepted somewhere along the way, either by random pirates, overeager New Republic forces, or dissident Imperials.

He'd been a good officer, even a friend, and Pellaeon would mourn his loss and miss his service. But at the moment the critical question was whether he'd been able to deliver his message before that interception occurred.

There was no way for Pellaeon to know. He would simply have to show up at Pesitiin and see if Bel Iblis did likewise.

And if the other did not . . . well, he would deal with that when and if it became necessary.

CHAPTER

17

Its official name was the Grand Rim Promenade; and even on a world that prided itself on engineering achievements as much as Cejansij clearly did, it was a remarkable achievement indeed. Thirty meters wide at its greatest expanse, attached to the eastern wall of the Canyonade about two-thirds of the way from floor to rim, it stretched the entire length—over ten kilometers—of the canyon. Small trade and vending booths were set up all along the canyon wall, the commercial areas interspersed with conversation circles or tiny contoured meditation gardens or sculpture clusters. At other spots the wall had been left completely open to allow unobstructed observation of interesting natural vegetation clumps or the small waterfalls that dribbled softly down toward the canyon floor below.

The far more interesting view, though, was on the other side of the Promenade. Beyond the chest-high, elaborately tooled metal-mesh guardwall one could look down into the Canyonade itself, to the city that had been created across the floor and sides. At regular intervals the guardwall opened up into the skyarches that curved gracefully across the canyon to the lesser and more utilitarian walkways on the far side. The skyarches were arranged in diamond-patterned groups of nine: three connecting with the Promenade, two each connecting with the walkways above and below it, one each from the walkways above and below those.

An impressive achievement, made all the more so by the fact that the entire three-hundred-year-old structure was held solidly in place without any repulsorlift support whatsoever. Walking along the Promenade, gazing across through the gathering darkness at the scattering of lights across the canyon and down below, Luke wondered if anyone in these modern days would have both the skill and the self-confidence to undertake anything of this magnitude.

Rolling along at Luke's side, Artoo twittered uneasily. "Don't worry, Artoo, I'm not going to get too close to the edge," Luke soothed the little droid, shifting his shoulders beneath his hooded cloak. "Anyway, it's not dangerous—the brochure said there are emergency tractor beams set up to catch anyone who falls."

Artoo warbled a not entirely convinced acknowledgment. Then, rotating his dome for a surreptitious look behind them, he beeped a question. "Yes," Luke told him soberly. "He's still following us."

Had been following them, in fact, since shortly after their arrival on the Promenade: a large bulky alien, slipping in and out of the other pedestrians with unlikely grace. Luke wasn't sure exactly when he and Artoo had been spotted and identified; possibly during the turbolift ride down from the spaceport, possibly not until they'd arrived on the Promenade itself.

For that matter, it was entirely possible they hadn't been identified at all. Their tail could simply be a local thief hoping to relieve a helpless stranger of his astromech droid.

If so, he was going to be in for a surprise.

Artoo twittered again. "Patience," Luke told him, looking around. They had come to the end of one of the groups of wall-hugging businesses now and were starting into a wide area that featured only a waterfall and two currently unoccupied conversation areas. Quiet, peaceful, and as private as Luke had yet seen up here. An ideal place for holding an impromptu conversation.

Or for springing an ambush.

"Let's pause here a moment," he said to Artoo, crossing over toward the outer edge of the Promenade. They were roughly in the middle of the quiet area now, with the waterfall rippling softly behind them. Picking a section of guardwall, Luke stopped walking and leaned his elbows on the top rail, stretching out to the Force as he did so. There was a subtle change in the emotions of their pursuer now: a change that felt to Luke like the other had made a decision. "He's coming," Luke muttered to Artoo. "I think he's alone, but there could still be trouble. Keep back out of the way, all right?"

The droid acknowledged with a nervous twitter, rolling a meter back in response. Resettling his elbows on the guardwall, Luke gazed out into the Canyonade, a gentle shiver running up his back as he listened to the quiet footsteps approaching from the side. As near as he could tell, this was the exact spot where he'd seen himself in that vision . . .

The footsteps stopped. "Pardon me," a gentle voice asked. "Are you the Jedi Master Luke Skywalker?"

Luke turned, getting his first clear look at the being who'd been following them. He was of an unfamiliar species: tall and broad, with dark shell plates half-hidden beneath a fur-trimmed cloak. His head was large, with alert black eyes and small spikes where the mouth would be on a human. "I'm Skywalker, yes," Luke confirmed. "And you?"

"I am Moshene Tre," the alien said. "*Un'Yala* of the Cas'ta tribe of the Rellarin people of Rellnas Minor."

He reached a Wookiee-sized hand to the collar of his cloak and turned the edge back. Fastened on the underside was a distinctive gold-filigree pin. "I am also a New Republic Observer. I am honored to meet you, sir."

"And I you," Luke said, nodding in greeting as his last vestiges of tension faded away. The Observers were an experimental, quasi-official part of the New Republic, created in this latest round of governmental policy reorganization. Moving freely about their assigned sectors, their job was to report directly to the High Council and Senate whatever they saw or heard, with a particular eye toward improper governmental activities that the local or sector authorities might prefer to keep out of sight.

There had been some early fears that the Observers might evolve into the kind of secret security forces that the Empire had used with such devastating effect during its reign of terror. So far, though, that didn't seem to be happening. The various governments that had undertaken to sponsor Observers had chosen their candidates carefully, with an eye toward hiring only strongly ethical beings and then strictly defining the limits of their mandate. The fact that the Observers were assigned to sectors far away from their homes and any local or species rivalries undoubtedly helped encourage their sponsors to pick candidates who were as incorruptible and impartial as possible.

A similar system had been used in the Old Republic, Luke knew, with the Jedi Knights acting in the Observers' role. Perhaps someday his academy graduates would be numerous enough—and trusted enough—to once again take on that duty. "What may I do to help you?" he asked.

"Please forgive my impertinence in walking within your shadow," Tre continued. "But I felt a burden to speak with you, and needed to be certain of your identity before I approached."

"I understand," Luke said. "No harm done. How may I help you?"

The Rellarin stepped up to the guardwall beside Luke and waved a massive hand downward. "I wished you to see what is happening in the Canyonade tonight. To see, and to understand."

Luke turned back to the guardwall and looked down. All he could see were the normal street and vehicle lights of a modern city. "Where am I supposed to be looking?" he asked.

"There," Tre said, pointing toward a large diamond-shaped area near the center of the Canyonade directly across from where the two of them stood. Though bordered by normal street illumination, the area itself was almost completely dark, with only a handful of tiny lights showing near the center.

"It looks like a park," Luke hazarded, mentally calling up the map of the Canyonade he'd looked at on the way into the spaceport. "Tranquillity Common, perhaps?"

"That is correct," Tre said. "Do you see the lights in the center?"

"Yes," Luke said. "They're . . ."

He paused, frowning. In the past few seconds, as he and Tre had been speaking, the number of lights had seemingly doubled. Still grouped closely together . . . and then, even as he watched, a new circle of lights was added to the group.

"They are lights of peace," Tre said. "Tonight, the peoples of Cejansij gather together in support of justice."

"Yes," Luke said. He could see all too well where this one was going. "Justice."

"I perceive from your tone of voice that you do not yet understand," Tre said, his own tone one of mild reproof. "The High Council and Senate dismiss all such demonstrations as riots by the violent or ignorant, or else as plots by the Empire. But such is not always the case."

"I don't think the Senate sees things quite that simplistically," Luke said. Still, he had to admit that Tre had a point. "So what third category would the demonstration down there fall into?"

"As I said: the support of justice," the Rellarin said. "The white lights you see are in remembrance of the peoples of Caamas. Soon now—yes; there. Do you see?"

Luke nodded. Around the group of white lights, a thin circle of blue lights had appeared. As he watched, more were added, creating an ever-growing ring of blue around the white. "I see them."

"They signify remembrance for the victims of the Vrassh Slaughter," Tre told him. "The land the perpetrators gained by that act has yielded great wealth to them; yet neither the Pas'sic government nor the New Republic has insisted that any of that wealth be given to the survivors' families, as both the custom and ancient law of that world demand."

"One of my Jedi students was of the Vrassh," Luke said, his heart stirring at the memory. "He had a great deal of anger to work through before his training could properly begin."

"Their rage is understandable," Tre said. "Yet there is no such anger in those gathered below." He gestured again toward the growing circle of lights. "Not in the way humans define anger. They are quiet and peaceful, threatening no one. But they will not forget those who were wronged, nor will they allow those in power to forget."

"Yes," Luke murmured. "There are indeed some things that must never be forgotten."

For a few minutes they stood in silence and watched. The circle of blue lights continued to grow; and then, as the white center had given way to blue, the blue gave way to yellow. The yellow was joined and encircled in turn by red, then by pale green, then violet, and finally an outer ring of white. "They are all gathered," Tre said when the series of concentric rings was complete. "Those are the ones who have tonight donated their time in remembrance. Others will donate their time other nights; and as all look down upon the lights they too will remember. And all of Cejansij will strengthen in their resolve to petition the seats of power until all such wrongs are righted."

Luke shook his head. "Except that none of these wrongs *can* be righted, *un'Yala* Tre," he said. "Not Caamas, not any of them."

"The Cejansiji understand that," the Rellarin said. "They know the dead cannot be brought back to life, nor devastated worlds be made whole again. They merely seek such justice as is within the power of mortal beings to grant."

"And what justice would they seek for Caamas?" Luke persisted. "The punishment of the entire Bothan race for the crimes of a few?"

"Many would say that such would not be true justice," Tre agreed. "But others would not share that opinion, and their voices too must be heard." He pointed to the circles of lights. "But now see. They demonstrate that justice cannot be limited to any one people or event. Justice must exist for all."

Luke frowned. The neat circles were breaking up, the different colors starting to mix together at the edges. His first thought was that the demonstration had ended and the participants were starting to leave. But the overall group of lights didn't seem to be getting any larger. The colors continued to bleed together, the rings giving way to a more homogeneous mix of color—

And suddenly he understood. The participants were leaving their own circles of remembrance and interweaving with the people in the other circles. It was a quiet yet deeply moving demonstration of unity.

"Some of those now in the Common do indeed believe that the entire Bothan species should be held accountable for the crime of Caamas," Tre said quietly. "At least in regard to reparations to the surviving Caamasi. Other Cejansiji reject that argument, yet agree that in suppressing knowledge of their part in the crime the Bothan leadership has forfeited any right to claims of innocence. There will also be visiting offworlders in the Common, holding lights alongside them, whose opinions will be equally varied."

"Sounds like it's about the same here as everywhere else in the galaxy," Luke said.

"True," Tre said. "The point I wished to make, Master Skywalker, is that these differences are not the result of enemy plots or even posturings among political rivals. They are the genuine and honest differences of opinion among the many beings who make up the New Republic. To dismiss any of them as unimportant or unthinking is to insult the honor and integrity of those beings and their cultures."

"I know," Luke said. "I'm sure the Senate does, too. The problem is how to reconcile all those differences. Not just over Caamas, but also in a thousand other matters."

"I do not know how you will succeed," Tre said. "I only know that it must be done, and that it must be done quickly. Already I have heard the stirrings of genuine anger at the Senate's inaction on this matter. There are other even more disturbing stirrings: whispered suggestions that the New Republic no longer cares what any world does against its neighbors or adversaries. Even now some are preparing to settle old grievances, while others seek new alliances for protection."

Luke sighed. "I've lost track of how many times the New Republic government has been accused of being too heavy-handed in one crisis or another over the past few years. Now they're trying to let the sectors and systems do more of their own governing; so of course they're being accused of doing nothing."

"Does this surprise you?" Tre asked. "The one truism in all politics is that loud voices will be raised against any decision that is made."

"Yes," Luke said, looking down at the flickering lights below.

"Many of those now demonstrating will be gathering later tonight at the ThoughtsAreFreedom tapcafe," Tre said. "It is on the far side of the Common, at the western corner of the diamond. If you choose to meet with them, they will be pleased to speak their thoughts to you."

"I'm sure they will," Luke said, carefully hiding a grimace. "Thank you for taking the time to show me this."

"It is my sworn duty to provide information to the leaders of the New Republic," the Rellarin said gravely. "It is a swearing I take most seriously."

He placed his fingertips together and inclined his head. "I thank you in turn for your time and attention, Master Skywalker, and I urge you to visit the ThoughtsAreFreedom this night. You will gain much knowledge there." Inclining his head again, he turned and headed back along the Promenade.

Behind Luke, Artoo whistled softly, and he turned to see the little droid standing up on mechanical tiptoe as he gazed at the lights of the Canyonade below. "It's impressive, all right," Luke agreed soberly. "That's what makes this so hard to deal with. So much of it really *is* honest differences of opinion."

Artoo warbled again, his dome swiveling pointedly in the direction of the skyarch to their left: the direction they would go to get across the Canyonade and down to the tapcafe Tre had mentioned. "I suppose we ought to go take a look," Luke said reluctantly. "Though I doubt we'll get any new information there. It'll just be more opinions."

He pushed away from the guardwall and started walking toward the entrance to the skyarch. "If you want real information you have to go to someone like Talon Karrde," he continued as Artoo rolled alongside like a well-trained pet. "In fact, I've been thinking that maybe we ought to try to get in touch with him."

Artoo made a rude-sounding noise. "I hope that's for the current attitude toward him on Coruscant," Luke warned, "and not for Karrde himself. He's done a lot for the New Republic."

The droid gave an ambiguous twitter, followed by a remarkably good impression of a pile of coins clinking together. "Yes, I know he's been paid for his help," Luke acknowledged. "You might remember that money was the reason Han first got involved with the Rebellion, too, and he's turned out pretty good."

They reached the entrance to the skyarch and stepped onto the umbrella-roofed, guardwalled bridge. Like the Rim Promenade itself, the Canyonade's skyarches were remarkable examples of engineering skill, curving gently and gracefully across the half-kilometer gorge without the benefit of extra supports or suspension cables. The right side of the walkway was finished in a simple nonslip surface, clearly designed for casual strollers or those who wanted to pause and linger over the view of the Canyonade below. The left side, in contrast, was equipped with a pair of slideways for the serious traveler who merely wished to go from one side to the other.

It would have been a pleasant walk, Luke thought with a quiet pang of regret, but he didn't seem to have the time lately for such simple pleasures. "The important point is that Karrde has always come to us first with information that we need," he added to Artoo, ushering the droid onto the slideway and stepping on behind him. "Whether he admits it or not, he really is on our side."

Artoo swiveled his dome around to face Luke, made an I-suppose-so sort of grunt, then rotated back to face forward

again. The slideway was speeding up, Luke noted with interest, accelerating steadily as they approached the center of the
arch. Presumably the entire strip wasn't speeding up, which
would create quite a challenge for anyone trying to get onto
the strip behind him. Composed of some kind of pseudo-
fluid material, he guessed, using a variant of laminar flow to
create variable speeds along its length. One more engineering
marvel to add to the list.

They reached the top of the arch, and he was just thinking of asking Artoo to analyze the slideway for him, when
he felt a flicker in the Force. It wasn't much; little more than
a twinge in the near distance. But it was enough.

Somewhere very near at hand, someone was preparing
for murder.

He stepped off the slideway, fighting for a moment with
the abrupt change in speed before he regained his balance.
Artoo, suddenly missing him, squawked in surprise—then
squawked again as Luke stretched out with the Force and
lifted him bodily into the air. "Quiet," Luke admonished as
he set the droid down on the stationary section of the walkway. Looking around, he stretched out again with the Force.

The murderous intent was still there, somewhere close
by. But though there were a handful of other pedestrians in
sight, there was nothing he could see that appeared to fit the
sensation.

At least, not on this particular skyarch.

He turned around, peering upward beneath the edge of
his skyarch's roof and through the guardwall mesh of the
skyarch running parallel one level above him. And there they
were, perhaps ten meters farther along from where he stood:
two cloaked and hooded figures standing with their backs
pressed against the guardwall, the smaller child-sized figure
clinging to the taller one. Beyond them, Luke could just
make out the shadowy forms of three assailants moving
slowly and confidently in on them. In the hand of one of
them, he caught the glint of a blade.

There was no time to waste, and exactly one route that
had any chance of getting Luke to them in time. It would
take a hefty jump, but nothing that a Jedi drawing on the

Force couldn't easily handle. The only imponderable was whether the Canyonade's safety tractor beams would react fast enough to snatch him in midair and whisk him helplessly away.

There was only one way to find out. "Wait here, Artoo," he murmured. Stretching out to the Force, he hopped over the slideway to the top of his skyarch's guardwall. For a pair of heartbeats he crouched there, steadying his balance as he did one final visual measurement of the distance up and across to the other skyarch. Then, taking a deep breath, he again drew on the Force and leaped.

The emergency tractor beams were obviously not as hair-trigger as he'd feared, and he reached the other side without so much as a nudge from them. Catching the top of the other skyarch's guardwall, he swung his legs through the opening between guardwall and roof to land in a slight crouch on the nonmoving section of the walkway.

He took in the tableau laid out before him in a glance. The two prospective victims, as he'd already seen, were standing ahead and to his right, their backs pressed against the guardwall. The hood on the taller of them had slipped back, revealing the lined face and white hair of an old woman. The face of the child clinging to her side—most likely a grandchild or even great-grandchild, considering the woman's age—was still completely in shadow. But Luke didn't need to see an expression; the way the child clutched the old woman's side was all the evidence anyone needed to recognize the silent terror there.

A terror that was well founded. From the lower skyarch Luke had seen three knife-wielding men closing in on them. Now, from his new vantage point, he could see that those three were merely the inner circle of a much larger group. Nine other men were standing a few paces farther back, forming a semicircle around their intended prey. All nine of them had the hardened faces of men whose lives had been shaped by violence and cruelty; all nine had blasters out and ready.

And at the moment, all nine of those faces—and five of those blasters—were pointed at Luke.

"That's far enough," Luke called, straightening up from his landing crouch. "Put down your weapons."

"I've got a better idea," one of the men snarled, his voice as nasty as his appearance. "Why don't you turn around and walk away. While you still can."

"I don't think so," Luke said, trying to sound more confident than he felt. With five—six, now—blasters trained on him, it was going to be a race to see whether he could get his lightsaber out fast enough to deflect the shots that would be coming his direction the instant he made a move toward the weapon.

But there was the slideway two steps to his left. One section going each direction; both moving at reasonably high speed . . .

"We're wasting time," one of the other men spat. "Burn him and let's—"

And in that instant, in the middle of the sentence, the child moved.

It was so quiet and so smooth that at first Luke didn't realize what was happening. The child rotated out of his panicked death grip on the old woman toward the nearest of the knife-wielding assailants, one arm swinging across the man like a stylized slap across his chest that fell short of its intended mark. The arm movement seemed to deflect the child like a ricocheted stone toward the second assailant; the slapping movement again, and he was now swinging toward the third man—

And with a gurgling gasp, the first man collapsed into a heap on the ground.

Someone swore with startled viciousness, the blasters pointed at Luke wavering as sudden confusion intruded on what had two seconds earlier been a solidly secure situation. Heads turned back toward the child and his grandmother—

And then the second man crumpled, and the third man started to do the same, his knife now inexplicably in the child's hand. But only briefly; an instant later, with an abbreviated flick of the wrist, the knife flashed across the short distance to bury itself in the chest of one of the other assailants.

And as it did so, the hood fell back far enough to finally expose the child's face.

It wasn't a child beneath that cloak. It was a Noghri.

That single glance was the last clear view any of them had of the alien. For some, it was the last clear view of anything they would ever have. Even as Luke grabbed for his lightsaber the Noghri became a blur of motion: diving, rolling, slashing with blades now in both hands, evading the frantic sputtering of blaster shots with casual ease. A grenade clattered to the walkway at the old woman's feet, vanished as Luke reached out through the Force to maneuver it through the gap between guardwall and roof and send it hurling straight up.

By the time it exploded harmlessly far above them, the battle was over.

"Master Skywalker," the Noghri said, nodding gravely from the center of the carnage as he slid his two assassin's knives back into concealment. "I am honored by your presence, and grateful for your assistance."

"Such as it was," Luke said, shaking his head in astonishment. He'd seen Noghri in training and practice combat and had thought he knew the limits of their fighting skills. He hadn't even been close. "Somehow, I think you would have managed quite well without me."

"Your pardon, but that is not true," the Noghri demurred, stepping over the bodies and coming over to him. "Your distraction was most timely, allowing me nearly four extra seconds I would otherwise not have had."

"Not to mention the grenade," the old woman added. She had crouched down beside one of the dead and was going through his pockets with practiced fingers. "If not for your quick action, we could all have been killed. Thank you."

"You're welcome," Luke said, eyeing her with growing doubts as she finished her search and moved on to the next body. A Noghri warrior and a woman with the expertise of a professional pickpocket were not exactly what he'd had in mind when he'd come leaping to the rescue. "May I ask who you are?"

"Not who you're probably afraid I am," the woman said, pausing in her search to flash him a smile. "It's really quite honest and mostly respectable. My name is Moranda Savich; Plakhmirakh here is currently attached to me as my bodyguard. We work for an old acquaintance of yours: Talon Karrde."

"Really," Luke said. "Oddly enough, I was just thinking about trying to make contact with Karrde."

"Well, you've come to the right place," Moranda said, straightening up. "He's just arrived on Cejansij."

"You're joking," Luke said, frowning. "What's he doing here?"

"Who ever knows what Karrde's doing anywhere?" Moranda countered philosophically. "Why don't you come along and ask him yourself?"

Luke looked down through the guardwall at the city lights below. Once again, he'd managed to be in the right place at the right time. The Force was indeed with him. "Thank you," he said to Moranda. "I believe I will."

"Chief?"

Karrde looked up from his desk to find Dankin's head poking around the open office doorway. "Yes, what is it?"

"Savich and her Noghri guard are here," Dankin said. "She's got the data drop you wanted."

"Good," Karrde said, frowning slightly. Back when the *Wild Karrde*'s bridge crew had been preparing to spring Booster Terrik's *Errant Venture* on the unsuspecting H'sishi, Dankin had been wearing a half-concealed grin. He was wearing the same grin now. "And?" Karrde prompted.

The grin came fully out of concealment. "And they also brought you a surprise."

"Really," Karrde said, letting the temperature of his voice cool a couple of degrees. "I hope you remember how much I like surprises."

"You'll like this one, Chief," Dankin assured him, stepping aside and gesturing. Plakhmirakh and Moranda Savich emerged around the doorway and stepped into the office, the latter holding a data drop cylinder in her hand. And coming in behind them—

"Well, I'll be Kesseled," Karrde said, getting to his feet. "A pleasant surprise indeed. Hello, Skywalker."

"Karrde." Skywalker nodded in greeting. "I'm surprised to find you here."

"The feeling is mutual," Karrde agreed. "Are you alone?"

"Artoo's with me," Skywalker said, nodding back over his shoulder. "He spotted a G2-9T repair droid working off your cargo bay and stopped for a chat."

"I hope he enjoys it," Karrde said, taking the cylinder from Moranda and glancing at its markings. "That's the last G2 I'm ever going to buy. Any trouble, Moranda?"

"We were jumped on the way back," she told him. "Twelve men, very professional, no indications as to who they were working for."

"Probably one of the Hutts," Karrde said, turning the cylinder over in his hand. "They weren't exactly thrilled about losing this."

"Could be," Moranda said. "Whoever they were, Plakhmirakh took care of them."

"With assistance from Master Skywalker," the Noghri added in his gravelly voice. "He arrived at exactly the proper moment."

"Jedi Masters have that knack," Karrde said dryly, handing the cylinder back to Moranda. "Good. Take it to Odonnl, then you can go and relax in the crew lounge while he checks it out and issues your payment. Would you be interested in taking on another assignment?"

"Only if it's more fun than courier work," Moranda said. "Apart from the attack, it was all rather boring." She waved a hand each toward Luke and Plakhmirakh. "And with these two around, even that part wasn't very exciting."

"I'll try to do better the next time," Karrde promised. "As a matter of fact, I have one job in particular where your talents might prove useful. Check back here after you've been paid and we'll talk, all right?"

"Fine," Moranda said, nodding. Plakhmirakh gave an abbreviated Noghri bow, and together they left the office.

Karrde cocked an eyebrow at Skywalker. "Thank you for your help. I believe it's now my turn to owe you one."

"Hardly," the other said. "Plakhmirakh vastly overrates my assistance back there."

"Yes, they don't generally need much help, do they?" Karrde agreed. "I've been very pleased with their service. Aside from running interference against Hutt hirelings, what brings you to Cejansij?"

Skywalker shrugged. "The Force, actually," he said. "I was trying for a vision of the future, and I saw myself here. So here I am."

"Ah," Karrde said. "Not a scheduling technique I'd be comfortable with, personally."

"I'm not exactly used to it myself," Skywalker said. "On the other hand, I was just thinking about trying to get in touch with you, and here you are, so it seems to have worked. What are you doing here, anyway, if I may ask?"

"It's not a secret," Karrde assured him. "At least, not from you. I've been looking into the possibility that outside agitators might be involved in some of the protests that have been cropping up around the New Republic. Since Cejansij has a long history of peaceful demonstrations, I thought it would be an obvious target for subversion."

"Makes sense," Skywalker mused. "Though maybe it's *too* obvious."

"Depends on how subtle our unknown agitators decide to be," Karrde said. "I thought it still worth checking out. You said you'd wanted to talk to me?"

"Yes," Skywalker said. "I've been wondering if you'd made any progress on our clone hunt."

"None whatsoever," Karrde conceded. "None of my information sources have heard even a whisper of clone activity. If they're out there, whoever's using them is keeping it very quiet."

"Mm," Skywalker murmured. "How about the Cavrilhu Pirates?"

Karrde shook his head. "They seem to have gone to

ground." He cocked an eyebrow. "Not that I really blame them. Being chased out of your most secure base by a Jedi Master must be a rather disconcerting experience."

"You were chased off Myrkr by Grand Admiral Thrawn, and *you* didn't panic," Skywalker reminded him.

Karrde forced a smile. The memories of that time still provoked unpleasant twinges. "Perhaps I'm made of stronger stuff. Or perhaps I just don't panic quite so noticeably."

On his desk, the intercom twittered, and he leaned over to touch the switch. "Yes?"

It was Dankin, his expression suddenly and uncharacteristically grim. "Priority message coming through from the *Starry Ice*," he said tartly. "Faughn says Mara's been captured."

Karrde felt his stomach tighten as he dropped back into his desk chair. "Is Faughn still on?"

"Mostly," Dankin said. "The signal's a little funny—too many relays in the mix—but it's mostly clear. Comm 5."

Karrde keyed to the channel, dimly aware that Skywalker had circled the desk and come up beside him. "This is Karrde. Faughn?"

"Yes, sir," Faughn's voice came, wavering slightly with the distortion of multiple hyperspace relays. "We reached the Nirauan system and observed an unidentified spacecraft land on the second planet. Jade took our Defender and went in. We got a pulse transmission from her recorder that indicated she was in trouble. Captured, maybe worse."

Karrde could hear his heart thudding in his ears. "Dankin, do we have a copy of the recording?"

"Right here," Dankin's voice said.

"Play it."

He listened as it played through: the flight and landing, Mara's discovery of the cave and fortress, her startled exclamation and that final sickening thud. "Get H'sishi started on a scrub right away," Karrde ordered. That thud had sounded far too much like the sound of a body hitting the ground. . . . "I want everything you can get off that recording."

"We're already on it."

"We did some scrubbing of our own on the way here," Faughn said. "There's definitely breathing and a human-tempo heartbeat after she goes silent, so at least at that point she was still alive. There are fifty or more flying creatures in the cave—we can sort out at least that many sets of wings flapping—though that may not have been who she was talking to. Oh, and from the different speeds of the sound through air and bone, it looks like that thud was something hitting the front or side of her head."

Karrde grimaced. "An attack."

"Or an accident," Faughn said. "We know she was moving just before it happened, and that she was inside a cave. She could have run into a wall or something."

"We can try an echo analysis," Dankin suggested. "Try to figure out how close she was to the wall when she was hit."

"Yes." Karrde looked up at Skywalker, standing in dark silence beside him, troubled eyes seemingly focused on empty space. "You know anything about this?" he asked the Jedi. "Either the planet or whoever she was talking to?"

Skywalker shook his head slowly, his eyes looking even more troubled. "No. But I did see a vision of Mara, the same time I saw myself here. And where she was . . . it might have been a cave."

"I hated to leave her there," Faughn said. "But I also didn't want to risk all of us disappearing without letting someone know what had happened. Especially given those ships and that fortress."

"No, you did the right thing," Karrde assured her. "The question now is how we get her out." He looked up at Skywalker. "Or rather, who we send to do the job."

Skywalker must have heard the challenge in his voice. His eyes came back from whatever they were staring at to look down at Karrde. "You're suggesting *I* go?"

"Someone there seems to know you," Karrde pointed out. "At least, Mara thought so. You may be the only one he—or it, or they—will be willing to talk to."

"I can't leave," Skywalker said, the words coming out

almost mechanically, his attention clearly elsewhere. "I have duties here."

"You have a duty to Mara, too," Karrde countered. "For that matter, you have a duty to the rest of the New Republic. You saw one of those ships—you know we're dealing with an unknown culture here. If that fortress she saw is made of the same material as the one on Hijarna, they'll be able to sit in there and shrug off any attack we could throw at them. *And*—"

"All right," Skywalker said. "I'll go."

Karrde blinked, taken slightly aback by the suddenness of the decision. He'd expected to have to argue at least a few more minutes and probably throw in something concrete before the other agreed.

But he also knew better than to question a decision he was already pushing for. "Good," he said. "Tell me what you need in the way of equipment or supplies, and we'll get it for you. You'll want a bigger ship, of course—Dankin, what do we have available?"

"No time for that," Skywalker said before Dankin could answer. "My X-wing's over in Docking Rectangle 16. If you can download a copy of the nav data to Artoo, we'll get it refueled and be on our way."

"You can't carry a passenger in an X-wing," Faughn objected. "If she's hurt—"

"Then we take her ship and leave the X-wing behind," Skywalker cut her off. "We're wasting time."

"You won't get very far in a Defender," Karrde reminded him, keying his board on a hunch. Yes, the timing and distances would work. "Let me suggest a compromise: you leave here in your X-wing and I'll have the *Dawn Beat* bring the *Jade's Fire* to meet you off Duroon. Her droid won't be activated, but you and your R2 should be able to fly it without any trouble."

Skywalker shook his head. "I don't want to try to sneak onto Nirauan with a ship that big."

"Then leave the *Fire* hidden somewhere in the outer system and ride your starfighter in," Faughn suggested. "The

docking port should handle an X-wing without any problems."

Skywalker hesitated a heartbeat, then nodded. "All
right."

"Good," Karrde said. "Dankin, get onto spaceport control and have a fuel order cut for his X-wing. Number one
on the priority list, and you can bribe or threaten whoever
you have to to get it there. Then put together the most com-
prehensive survival kit you can that will fit an X-wing's
cargo hold. Two cubic meters and 110 kilograms, as I recall."

"Got it," Dankin said. "What kind of backup are we
going to send in behind him?"

"As much as we can throw together," Karrde told him,
keying for a list of available resources. His organization's
fleet was impressively large; but scattered around the entire
New Republic the way it was, it would take precious time to
collect any kind of attack force together . . .

"I don't want any backup," Skywalker cut into his mus-
ings. "Bringing in the *Jade's Fire* is risky enough; the more
ships in the system, the better the chances one of them will
be spotted. It'll be better for me to try to slip in by myself."

"But you can't get her out alone," Faughn said.

"I can," Skywalker said softly. "I have to."

"You can't," Faughn insisted. "Karrde? Tell him."

For a long moment Karrde studied the younger man, his
mind flicking back to that first meeting between the two of
them aboard the *Wild Karrde* so long ago. Even back then
Skywalker had never been what he would have called brash;
but looking at him now Karrde was struck by the quiet ma-
turity ten years had added to his face. "It's his call, Faughn,"
he said. "If he says he can do it, then he can."

Skywalker nodded. "Thank you," he said.

"I think the thanks are all on the other side," Karrde
pointed out, trying to force a smile. "All right: fuel and supplies, and the *Jade's Fire* at Duroon. What else do you need
us to do?"

"Just what you're already doing," Skywalker said.
"Keep looking into these riots, and if you find anything get
the information to Leia."

"Done," Karrde said. "Anything else?"

"Yes," Skywalker said, a shadow crossing his face. "Could you get word to Leia on Coruscant and tell her where I've gone?"

"I'll go myself," Karrde promised, getting to his feet again. "We'll leave as soon as you're gone."

"Thank you," Skywalker said. He turned and headed for the office door—

"You said you saw Mara in a vision," Karrde called after him. "What was she doing?"

Skywalker paused in the doorway. "She was in a rocky place, floating in water," he said, not turning around. "And she looked dead."

Karrde nodded slowly. "I see."

He was still standing there, gazing at the open door, long after Skywalker had gone.

CHAPTER

18

Quite unfairly, the battle alarm sounded right in the middle of dessert.

For a split second Wedge considered shoveling the last three bites of his citros snow cake into his mouth at once, decided running to the landing bays with a full mouth lacked the proper dignity, and regretfully left the cake orphaned on the mess-room table.

"Starfighter wings, check in," the *Peregrine*'s fighter co-ordinator was calling as Wedge slid on his flight helmet and dropped into the cockpit of his X-wing. "Rogue Squadron, where are you?"

"Right here, Perris," Wedge said, glancing around to confirm that the rest of the squadron were indeed present in the bay. "What's going on?"

"Don't know for sure," Perris growled. "All I know is that we just got a panic call from the Sif'kric system. General Bel Iblis talked to them for maybe five minutes, and suddenly we're getting ready to fly. Okay, you show green—launch when ready."

"Copy. Okay, Rogues, let's go."

Twenty seconds later they were in space, driving forward along the *Peregrine*'s flank toward vanguard position. "I don't suppose this might be a drill," Rogue Six suggested on their private frequency.

"Well, if it is, the general owes me another dessert," Rogue Twelve put in. "Anyone been following local politics in this sector?"

"I have, a little," Rogue Nine said grimly. "My father-in-law's got some interests here. Ten to one it's the Frezhlix; they've been feuding with the Sif'kries ever since we chased the Empire out of the area."

"Maybe they've finally decided to finish it," Rogue Two suggested.

"With General Bel Iblis and a New Republic task force right next door?" Rogue Six put in incredulously. "What are they using for brains, groat cheese?"

"All ships, this is General Bei Iblis," the general's voice came on the command frequency, cutting off the conversation. "We've just been informed that a strong Frezhlix force is moving on the Sif'krie homeworld of Sif'kric. As that system is only a few minutes away, we've been asked to go take a look."

Terrific, Wedge thought sourly as he glanced back over the New Republic task force. One *Katana*-fleet Dreadnaught, two Nebulon-B escort frigates, and three starfighter squadrons; and they were supposed to take on a force big enough to attack a whole planet?

Bel Iblis might have been reading his mind. "Obviously, we're not planning to go head-to-head with them," he continued. "In fact, we're going to have to be very careful we don't overstep our legal bounds here. That's all I can say until we get there and assess the situation. Commander Perris?"

"All ships, check in," Perris ordered. "Prepare to jump to lightspeed on my mark."

"What does he mean, legal bounds?" Rogue Six asked as the fleet began its check-in.

"My guess is that whoever called Bel Iblis wasn't someone who could officially ask for New Republic assistance," Wedge told him. "Some minor bureaucrat, maybe just a rattled space-traffic controller. If we don't have an official request—"

"Rogue Squadron: go," Perris ordered.

"Copy," Wedge said. He pulled back on the hyperdrive lever, squinted as the starlines flared, and they were off.

It was a twelve-minute flight to the Sif'kric system. Alone in the solitude of hyperspace, he spent those minutes running a final check on the X-wing's systems and armaments, and wondering how the legendary General Garm Bel Iblis was going to pull this one off.

The timer clicked down toward zero. Settling himself, Wedge pushed the lever back. The starlines flared again—

He blinked. What in space—?

On the Rogues' private channel, somebody snorted. "You must be joking," Rogue Two said. "*That* is an invasion fleet?"

Wedge looked at his tactical readout, shaking his head in silent agreement. Two forty-year-old Kruk battle-wagons, five *Lancer*-class frigates probably half that age, and maybe thirty modern Jompers customs pursuit ships.

"So much for the big bad threat," Rogue Eight commented contemptuously. "We could probably chase them out of here all by ourselves."

"I don't know," Rogue Eleven said. "*Someone* seems plenty worried about them. Take a look at the far planetary rim—must be twenty freighters scurrying for cover."

"And another hundred who aren't going to make it," Rogue Seven pointed out. "There to portside—the Frezhlix force has got them cut off."

"I get it," Rogue Nine said. "Those clever little scumrots. That must be the annual pommwomm plant shipment."

"Frezhlix attack force, this is General Bel Iblis of the New Republic," Bel Iblis's voice announced. "Please state your intentions."

"I am Plarx," a thickly accented voice shot back. "I speak for the Frezhlix. Our intentions do not concern the New Republic. This is a private matter between ourselves and the Sif'kries."

"I'm afraid I cannot accept that," Bel Iblis said. "Any aggression against a New Republic member is our concern."

"This is not aggression, General Bel Iblis," the Frezh

countered. "We are a delegation come to discuss the Sif'krie vote on the Drashtine Initiative."

There was a pause, Bel Iblis no doubt having someone look up what exactly the Drashtine Initiative was. "Corran, what are these pommwomm plants you mentioned?" Wedge asked.

"They're a type of hot-world shrub that grows on the system's inner planet," Rogue Nine said. "You can get about eight different exotic medicines and twice that number of food flavorings out of them. Problem is, they have to be processed within thirty hours of picking or they're useless."

"So that's what the Frezhlix are doing," Rogue Seven growled. "They don't have to invade anyone or set up a long-term blockade ring. All they have to do is keep those freighters back for a few hours, and the Sif'kries are out a bunch of money."

"Try about twenty percent of their annual gross product," Rogue Nine put in. "We're talking serious economic warfare here. No wonder they sounded panicked when they called."

The main channel crackled to life again. "Speaker Plarx, this is General Bel Iblis. I've reviewed the Drashtine Initiative, and I see no justification for this kind of confrontation."

"Then you did not review it closely," the Frezh snarled. "The Sif'krie government cast the deciding vote that prevented our sector's Senator from adding his voice to the growing condemnation of the Bothan government and people."

"The vote was legally taken—"

"The vote was wrong!" Plarx snapped. "To allow the Bothans to escape proper punishment will merely encourage further atrocities like Caamas in the future. The Sif'krie government must be made aware of that and given the opportunity to change its vote."

"A convenient enough excuse," Rogue Two muttered.

"He's got a point, though," Rogue Five said. "Heavily wrapped in local politics and blackmail, but a point."

"I understand your feelings on this matter," Bel Iblis

said. "But at the same time we cannot stand by and allow you to interfere with interstellar commerce this way."

"Untrue," the Frezh said. "I encourage you to review New Republic regulations on such matters, General Bel Iblis."

There was another pause. "He's right," Rogue Twelve said grimly. "This is intrasystem, not interstellar. We can't move in unless and until we get an official invitation to do so."

"Which means it's all in the government's shockball court now," Rogue Five muttered. "What do you think, Corran? Can they move fast enough to save the plants?"

"I don't know," Rogue Nine said. "But I'd be willing to lay odds the Frezhlix picked a time to pull this stunt when some key Sif'krie official is off-planet or otherwise out of touch."

There was a click on the private channel. "Rogue Squadron, this is Bel Iblis. Commander Horn?"

"Yes, sir?" Rogue Nine said.

"I was given to understand that Booster Terrik has some interests in this sector. Is that true?"

There was just the briefest of pauses. "Yes, General, he does."

"Would those interests occasionally include legitimate shipping? Say, when the need and fees are high enough, such as during the annual pommwomm shipment?"

There was a longer pause this time. "I really don't know, sir," Rogue Nine said, sounding puzzled.

"I think it reasonable that they would," Bel Iblis continued. "Given that assumption, do you suppose one of those stalled freighters out there might belong to him?"

And suddenly, Wedge understood. The legendary General Bel Iblis was going to pull this one off, all right. Maybe. "Do we have IDs on the ships, General?" he asked.

"I'm sending the data across now," Bel Iblis said. "Commander Horn, take a look, please."

"Understood, sir," Rogue Nine said, his voice no longer puzzled. So he'd caught on, too. "Yes. That freighter listed as the *Sycophant Jolly*—over at the far side of the pack? I believe that could actually be the *Hoopster's Prank*, one of Booster's ships."

"I see," Bel Iblis said, his voice suddenly heavy with official weight. "I recognize your familial relationship with Captain Terrik, Commander, and I realize that this is going to be personally painful for you. But you're an officer of the New Republic Fleet; and we cannot and will not bend the rules against smuggling for anyone."

"We understand, sir," Wedge said, pitching his tone to the same seriousness level. "Request permission to check out this suspect ship."

"Permission granted, Rogue Squadron," Bel Iblis said. "Be careful not to accidentally engage the Frezhlix forces."

"Understood, sir," Wedge said. "Rogue Squadron, form up around me."

Kicking power to the drive, he swung the X-wing away from the *Peregrine*. "Looks like the most direct route to the *Sycophant Jolly* is right through the middle of the Frezhlix blockade force," Rogue Eight commented.

"And we certainly don't want to give them time to dump any contraband while we fly around," Rogue Nine agreed.

"I guess we'll have to go through the blockade, then," Rogue Two concluded. "Just everyone be careful not to accidentally engage."

"Very careful," Wedge said. "Let's do it."

They were halfway to the Frezhlix forces before the alien commander suddenly seemed to notice what was happening. "General Bel Iblis, what are your starfighters doing?" he demanded. "You have no legal justification for an attack on my ships."

"Your ships are not under attack, Speaker Plarx," Bel Iblis assured him. "We've identified one of the freighters waiting beyond your delegation as a smuggler flying under a false ID. By New Republic law, we have both the right and the duty to board any such ship and impound its cargo."

It was forever afterward unclear to Wedge just what exactly the Frezhlix commander thought was going to happen next. Whether he thought Bel Iblis was planning to transfer the perishable cargo from all hundred-odd freighters to the *Peregrine*, or just declare all the freighters suspect and insist they be escorted down to the planet for a proper search. But whichever it was, he leaped to the wrong conclusion—and the bait—with both hands. "No!" Plarx shouted. "They are not to approach. Do you hear? They will not approach."

"You can't stop us," Wedge put in. "Move out of the way; we're coming through."

"*No!*" the Frezh shouted. There was a jabber of a hissing, guttural language, and then the comm abruptly shut off. Wedge took a deep breath, preparing himself—

And suddenly the Frezhlix battle-wagons opened fire.

"Evasive!" Wedge snapped, twisting his X-wing hard to starboard as the laser blasts blazed past, one of the shots nearly taking off his upper portside engines. There was another snarl of hissing gutturals, and another salvo of laser fire shot by. "Rogues, re-form," he called. "Return to fleet." Turning his nose farther around, ducking under one final blast of enemy laser fire, he headed back toward the *Peregrine*.

But the Dreadnaught was no longer there. It and the rest of the New Republic fleet, reconfiguring into the general's favorite combat formation, were moving decisively toward the Frezhlix blockade force.

Something that sounded like a wheezing squawk came over the comm. "New Republic force!" the Frezhlix commander snarled. "What are you doing? You have no right to move against me."

"On the contrary, Speaker Plarx," Bel Iblis said, his voice suddenly blade-sharp. "I have every right. You have just opened fire on New Republic spacecraft. Surrender immediately, or prepare to be destroyed."

"I protest!" Plarx gasped. "Your ships provoked us into defending ourselves."

"Last chance, Speaker," Bel Iblis said. "Surrender or face the consequences."

There was a snarl of gutturals; and as the Rogues reached the *Peregrine* and curved around again into their positions in the battle formation Wedge saw that the Frezhlix ships had abandoned their blockade and were turning their guns to face the oncoming New Republic force. Fleetingly, Wedge wondered if Bel Iblis would be gracious enough to simply hold position in the standoff now that he'd broken the blockade, or if he'd insist on making the Frezhlix pay for their aggression.

Plarx took the decision on himself. In an awesome blaze of laser fire the two Kruk battle-wagons opened fire as the Jompers pursuit ships leaped forward to meet the incoming X-wings. "New Republic forces," Bel Iblis said coldly. "Engage at will."

"The Frezhlix government has delivered a sharp protest to me over your actions a few hours ago," Admiral Ackbar's gruff voice came over the *Peregrine*'s comm speaker. "They claim you launched an unprovoked attack on a peaceful delegation."

Standing a respectful distance from the general's chair, Wedge caught Corran Horn's attention and rolled his eyes in a silent gesture of disgust. The other grimaced in agreement. "On the contrary," Bel Iblis told Ackbar. "They were engaged in a clear violation of free economic movement. Besides which, they attacked first."

"That's not the way the Frezhlix tell it," Ackbar rumbled. "They say you clearly overstepped New Republic authority."

"I'm sure they do," Bel Iblis said. "Do you wish me to stand for an inquiry?"

"Don't be absurd, General," Ackbar said; and for the first time since the conversation had started the Mon Cal's voice seemed to Wedge to have relaxed a little. "We need all the good commanders we can get. And I don't doubt the Frezhlix deserved whatever you delivered to them. You said there was a smuggling ship in among the other freighters?"

Bel Iblis glanced up at Corran, who nodded. "Yes, sir, without question," the general confirmed. "One of Booster Terrik's. The Sif'krie authorities have impounded the ship and are checking for contraband."

"I can imagine the conversation that will take place on the *Errant Venture* sometime in the near future," Ackbar said, his voice going a little odd. Mon Cals had a long hatred for smuggling and smugglers, and the admiral was undoubtedly finding a certain poetic humor in what had happened. "Though the justification of your position will be dulled if there was indeed no contraband aboard."

"The regulations don't care whether the search comes up dry or not," Bel Iblis reminded him. "Or are you suggesting that President Gavrisom might not choose to see it that way?"

"The President is bound by certain diplomatic and political necessities," Ackbar said. "However, I'm certain that he will read your report on this incident before rendering any judgment. Still, I suggest you cut your patrol circuit short and return to—"

Abruptly the signal squealed and vanished. "Comm station, what's going on?" Bel Iblis demanded.

"The problem's not at our end, General," a new voice reported. "Looks like the HoloNet carrier's been cut off."

Bel Iblis threw a look at Wedge and Corran. "Trouble on Coruscant?" he asked the comm officer.

"I don't know, sir. I'm checking the other relays . . . no, sir, it's not Coruscant. Looks like the relay at Mengjini has gone down."

"Sir, we're picking up a general alert on the secondary net," a new voice put in. "The relay at Mengjini has allegedly come under attack from a small group of, quote, 'dissident elements,' unquote."

"Acknowledged," Bel Iblis said. "Navigation, plot us a fast course for Mengjini. Comm, relay the alert to all New Republic forces and bases in the area. Tell them we're going in and request backup reinforcements."

He got acknowledgments and turned again to Wedge and Corran. "It looks as if your reports will have to wait," he said. "Get back to your squadron, and get ready to fly."

"Not good," Corran puffed as he and Wedge jogged down the *Peregrine*'s ventral corridor toward their docking bays. "When they start messing with long-range communications, you know they're getting serious."

"We don't have any proof it's this Vengeance group," Wedge pointed out, dodging around a Dresselian crouched over an open access panel.

"Maybe not," the other countered. "But *I* never mentioned Vengeance. You thought of them on your own."

Wedge grimaced. "Yeah," he agreed. "I did, didn't I?"

"Yes, you did," Corran said. "And you're also thinking that between killing riots, overt interplanetary attacks, and now long-range comm-kicking, this has gone way beyond a few zealots protesting Bothan involvement in Caamas."

"Yeah," Wedge agreed soberly. "I can hardly wait to see what happens next."

CHAPTER

19

"Read and cry," Lando said, laying his sabacc cards down on the table. "Twenty-three—a Pure Sabacc run."

"Interesting," Senator Miatamia murmured, his leathery Diamalan face unreadable as he studied his own cards. "I presume the reference to crying is not a literal part of the game as you play it. A Pure Sabacc run, you say?"

"Yes," Lando confirmed, an uncomfortable sensation tickling at the back of his neck. The Senator had made this same dramatic pause on the sabacc pot hand in exactly five out of the eight complete games they'd played since the *Lady Luck*'s hurried scramble off Cilpar. Five games that the Senator had also happened to win.

"Unfortunate," Miatamia said, laying his cards almost daintily on the table. "I have an Idiot's Array. I believe that wins?"

"Yes, it wins," Lando said, shaking his head in disgust. Make that six out of nine. "I can't believe you haven't played this game professionally," he grumbled, starting to gather up the cards.

The Diamal flicked his fingers in the air. "You don't truly believe the Diamala have created our vast financial and business empire from mere common sense and hard work, do you?"

Lando paused, half the cards still on the table, eyeing the Senator suspiciously. Was he actually implying—?

No, of course not. Ridiculous. "That was a joke. Right?"

"Of course," Miatamia said, flicking his fingers again. "Common sense and hard work are all any being or species require to succeed. Luck is merely an illusion, trusted by the ignorant and chased by the foolish."

With an effort, Lando fought down a flicker of annoyance. His professional gambling days were long in the distant past, but the Diamal's obvious contempt still rankled a little. "So in other words, if you're smart enough, nothing ever happens you can't anticipate?"

"Of course the unanticipated may happen," Miatamia said. "But those who are prepared can always find their way through."

"All by themselves?" Lando persisted. "They never need any help?"

"They may," the Diamal said, unruffled. "But anticipating the need for assistance is merely one more part of common sense."

"Ah," Lando said, nodding. "So, in other words, the fact that I recognize my need for extra security for my ore shipments means that I have good common sense."

"It may," Miatamia agreed. "It could also mean—"

And suddenly, with a loud crack of released energy coming from the direction of the *Lady Luck*'s hyperdrive, the mottled sky above them abruptly flowed into starlines.

Lando was at the top of the circular staircase by the time the starlines finished shrinking back into stars. "What is it?" Miatamia demanded from behind him.

"Hyperdrive failure," Lando shouted over his shoulder as he all but threw himself down the stairs. If one of the couplings had failed, he needed to get the power rerouted before it started into surge instability and took out everything else on the circuit. With visions of a major repair job out here in the middle of nowhere looming before him—a repair job that would not exactly endear him to his Diamalan guest—he sprinted across the dining area, past the cabins, and skidded to a halt in front of the engineering control panel.

And frowned. There were none of the glowing red lights that would have indicated major systems failures, or even the blinking red status lines pointing to minor systems failure. In fact, according to the displays, the hyperspace drop-out was simply the normal automatic response of close planetary approach. There was a duly logged note that course comparison with the nav computer indicated that no planets should be in range at the moment . . .

"Oh, no," Lando breathed, leaping up the short stairway and jabbing at the bridge-door release. The door slid open, and he stepped through.

And there it was, floating silently in the darkness directly in front of him: the all-too-familiar shape of an Imperial Star Destroyer.

Biting back a curse, he dived for the helm, slapping the row of emergency power-boost switches on his way. He dropped into the chair, threw full power to the drive, and twisted the yacht's nose hard to starboard.

Or rather tried to twist it. Even with full emergency power, the *Lady Luck* wasn't moving.

Or rather she wasn't moving where Lando wanted her to go.

"We are in a tractor beam," the Senator's cool voice said from behind him.

"I noticed," Lando said shortly, shifting into a sharp up-down wiggling motion. If the tractor beam operator thought his target was trying to go vertical, he might overcorrect and allow the yacht to slip the lock.

But no such luck. "Strap down," Lando ordered Miatamia, letting the tractor damp out the yacht's residual wiggling and taking a quick look around. The Imperials had to have an Interdictor Cruiser around here somewhere . . . yes, there it was, off in the distance to portside, its nose pointed in the *Lady Luck*'s direction.

But not all that precisely pointed. In fact, the projected cone of hyperdrive-dampening gravity waves was not even close to being centered on the tug-and-back contest taking place out here. If Lando could break free of the tractor beam, there was an even chance he could get to the edge of the cone and escape before the Star Destroyer could reestablish the lock.

If. "Call your aide on the intercom and have him strap down," he told the Senator. The *Lady Luck* had one last trick up her sleeve, a little something that one of Luke's exploits a few years back had inspired Lando to install. Powering up the backup proton torpedo launcher, he keyed for a Stage Three torpedo and fired.

The torpedo flashed out from under the yacht's bow, accelerating suddenly as the tractor beam yanked at it. There was a flicker from Lando's board as one of the Star Destroyer's turbolaser batteries began to track it—

And then, no more than twenty meters in front of the *Lady Luck*, the torpedo exploded.

Not into a devastating blast, but into a brilliant cloud of trac-reflective particles. Particles that should, in theory, confuse the lock, tie up the entire tractor beam, and let him slip free.

And it was working. The yacht shuddered for a moment and then jerked hard as the invisible grip was abruptly broken. "Hang on!" Lando shouted, turning the ship's nose hard over. If Luke's experience with the covert-shroud gambit was anything to go by, he would have bare seconds to get to the edge of the Interdictor Cruiser's mass-shadow cone before the Imperials woke up and started shooting.

But even as the *Lady Luck* started to turn, there was a burst of light from behind the particle cloud between him and the Star Destroyer. He had just enough time to see the glittering trac-reflective particles turn a dull, nonreflective black—

And with another jolt the yacht was once again trapped in the tractor beam.

"What now?" Miatamia asked.

"Only one thing we can do," Lando told him, his stomach tight as he shut down the *Lady Luck*'s sublight engines. "We surrender."

•　•　•

Six stormtroopers led the way, clumping along in perfect unison in three ranks of two each. Behind them, their softer footsteps not even trying to stay in step, strode Miatamia and his aide. Lando walked behind the two Diamala, obscurely glad to be in the less noticeable position in the back.

Not that that spot really gained him anything. There were six more stormtroopers behind him bringing up the rear.

Apart from a brief "come with us" from the stormtrooper commander, there had been no communication between captors and prisoners. But Lando had been aboard more than one Star Destroyer in his time, and he didn't need either an invitation or a map to know that they were being herded into senior-officer country. Possibly to the Intelligence officer's nerve center; possibly even to the captain's office complex itself.

He'd been unable to read the ship's ID before the *Lady Luck* had been drawn into the gaping hangar bay, and had been hoping against hope that this was some monstrous practical joke being played on him with one of the New Republic's captured Star Destroyers. With each passing step, with each Imperial officer or crewer who stepped respectfully aside to give the stormtroopers room, the hope faded a little further.

It seemed to take forever, but finally they came to a halt at a door marked simply SECONDARY COMMAND ROOM. "You are expected," the commander said from behind Lando as the leading stormtroopers formed a guard semicircle around the door. "Enter."

"Thank you," Miatamia said, his voice impossibly calm. The door slid open and, without hesitation, the two Diamala strode inside. Reluctantly, Lando followed—

And nearly ran into Miatamia's back as both aliens suddenly jerked to a halt. Lando caught his balance, peering between them to try to see what had startled them so much.

The room was sparsely decorated, with little more than

some tactical wall monitors and a double ring of repeater displays encircling a command chair in the middle of the room. Standing beside the chair was a hard-faced man wearing major's insignia.

And rising calmly from the chair itself—

Lando felt his heart seize up in his chest. No. No, it couldn't be.

But it was.

"Good day, gentlemen," Grand Admiral Thrawn said, gesturing to them. "My apologies as to the rather informal method by which you were brought here. Please, come inside."

The horrified moment seemed to stretch itself toward eternity as Lando gazed in stunned horror at that face. It couldn't be. Grand Admiral Thrawn was dead. He was *dead*. He had to be.

And yet here he was. Very much alive.

No one had yet moved. "Please, come inside," the Grand Admiral repeated, this time with an edge of command in his voice.

Miatamia stirred and continued forward, his movement seemingly breaking his aide's own paralysis. Numbly, Lando followed, sensing as he did so their stormtrooper rearguard filing in behind them.

"That's far enough," the major said harshly as Miatamia came within three meters of the outer display ring. "They've been disarmed?"

"None of them were carrying any weapons," the stormtrooper commander reported. Three of them, Lando noted, had moved up to form a flanking column along their right; a glance over his shoulder confirmed that the commander and the other two had spread out along the wall behind them. A simple yet effective positioning that provided close guard while at the same time keeping the stormtroopers out of each other's crossfire.

"Yes, they *are* keeping a close eye on you, Captain Calrissian," Thrawn confirmed. "After that unpleasantness at Bilbringi, I've agreed to extra precautions. Not that I'm expecting trouble from any of you, of course."

"Of course," Lando said, turning back to look at him. It was a trick, of course. It had to be. Thrawn was dead. The Imperial Command itself had said so.

And yet . . .

"You look remarkably well, Admiral," Miatamia said. "I must confess to my surprise at seeing you here."

Thrawn smiled faintly. "My reappearance has surprised many others, Senator Miatamia. And will surprise a great many more in the days to come. However, I didn't ask you aboard merely to toast my continued health. The actual reason—"

"How did you survive the Bilbringi shipyards?" Lando blurted. "The Imperial reports said you were dead."

"You will not interrupt the Grand Admiral," the major snapped, taking a step toward him.

"Peace, Major," Thrawn said quietly, halting the other's advance with an almost languid gesture. "Under the circumstances, a certain degree of shock is entirely forgivable."

"Yet you do not answer his question," Miatamia said.

It seemed to Lando that a faint flicker of distant pain touched the Grand Admiral's face for a moment. "My survival was due to a unique combination of several factors," he said. "You'll forgive me if I withhold the details."

"But your own Imperial reports?" Lando repeated.

"The Imperial reports said what I allowed them to say," Thrawn said, his eyes starting to flash with annoyance. "It was necessary while I recovered that—"

He broke off. "Perhaps I've misjudged you, Captain," he said, his voice calm again. "And you, Senator. I assumed that when you encountered a being returned from the dead you'd be more interested in what he had to say than the details of the journey. My mistake." His eyes flicked over Lando's shoulder. "Commander, you may escort them back to their ship. Major, have Intelligence confirm the current location of Ishori Senator Dx'ono."

"Our apologies, Grand Admiral," Miatamia said quickly as the stormtroopers started forward. "As you said, we were momentarily shocked. But we listen now."

Thrawn lifted a hand, and the advancing stormtroopers

stopped. "Very well," he said. "My message is quite simple, Senator. You've recently become aware that a group of Bothans were involved in the attempted genocide on Caamas. I've come to offer my aid in bringing those guilty to justice."

Miatamia inclined his head to the side, as if listening to a faint and distant sound. "Excuse me?"

"No, you heard correctly," Thrawn assured him, that faint smile once again touching his lips. "I want to help."

Miatamia twisted his head around to throw a glance back at Lando, turned back again. "How?"

"By identifying the guilty parties, of course," the Grand Admiral said. "If President Gavrisom truly wishes this crisis resolved, he need only ask for my assistance. A visit to Bothawui, a few minutes' conversation with each of the Bothan clan leaders, and I'll know the truth."

Miatamia inclined his head to the side again. "The Bothan leaders claim they do not know which of their people were involved in the crime."

"Oh, come now, Senator," Thrawn said, his tone dark and cold. "Do you really expect they would say anything else?"

Miatamia seemed to digest that. "And you believe you could learn the truth merely by speaking with them?"

The glowing red eyes glittered. "Yes."

There was a brief silence. "Would it not be simpler for you to merely locate the proper Imperial records and give them to us?"

"Of course it would," Thrawn said. "And such a search is already under way. But the Imperial records library on Bastion is quite extensive, and the process could take weeks or even months to complete." He cocked a blue-black eyebrow. "I don't believe you have that much time to spare."

"You seem convinced that the New Republic is facing a serious crisis," Miatamia said. "We have weathered other such crises in the past."

"Your confidence is admirable," Thrawn said, leaning back slightly in his seat. "But I'd advise that you relay my offer to the Rebellion leadership before rashly and unilaterally rejecting it."

"I never stated that I rejected your offer, Grand Admiral," Miatamia said.

Thrawn smiled. "No, of course you didn't," he said, his tone far more knowing than Lando found comfortable. "I would like nothing more than to continue this discussion, Senator—it's been a long time since I've had the pleasure of debating a trained Diamalan mind. But I have other matters to attend to, and you have a message to deliver. Commander, escort them back to their ship. Good-bye, Senator, Captain."

"A question, Admiral, if I may," Lando said quickly as the stormtroopers came up behind him. His mind was finally starting to unfreeze; and if this *was* a trick, this might be the only chance they'd have to unmask it. "I saw you once, from a distance, while you were in the company of the smuggler Talon Karrde. Can you tell me where that was and why you were there?"

Thrawn's face hardened. "If this is a test, Captain, you've chosen your topic unwisely. I've spent a great deal of time during my recovery considering the proper payment to be exacted from Talon Karrde for his many betrayals. I do not like to be reminded of him, except to consider how short his remaining life is going to be. That message *you* may deliver."

"I see," Lando murmured, closing his mouth firmly. His reckless and odds-playing youth was far behind him, and the expression on Thrawn's face was definitely the kind that discouraged further questions.

Once again, though, Miatamia was not so easily put off. "Yet you do not answer his question," he pointed out.

The glowing red eyes shifted to the Diamal, and for a single awful moment Lando thought the Admiral was going to have the three of them gunned down right there and then. But to his relief, Thrawn merely smiled. "The Diamalan mind," he said, his voice utterly calm again. "My apologies, Senator."

He looked back at Lando. "You're referring to my

meeting with Karrde at his base on the planet Myrkr when I was searching for Luke Skywalker. You and someone else—General Solo, I assume—watched our landing from within the forest."

Lando felt a cold chill run up his back. "You knew we were there?"

"I knew someone was there," Thrawn said. "As I'm sure you know, select stormtroopers have extra sensor equipment built into their helmets. One of them caught a reflective glint from the macrobinoculars you were using."

"Yet you did nothing?" Miatamia asked.

Thrawn shrugged slightly. "At the time I assumed it was merely some of Karrde's people, set there to make sure my stormtroopers didn't become, shall we say, overzealous. Given the density of foliage, even a heavy blaster would have been harmless against us from that position, so I ordered that the observers be left alone."

His mouth hardened, just a bit. "Subsequent events, of course, showed the situation to have been otherwise. Does that satisfy your curiosity, Captain?"

Lando managed a nod. "Yes, Admiral. It does."

"Good," Thrawn said coolly. "Thank you for your time, gentlemen, and again my apologies for the unscheduled stop. Commander, see them to their ship."

Thirty minutes later, seated at the *Lady Luck*'s helm, Lando watched as the Interdictor Cruiser and Star Destroyer made their synchronized jump to lightspeed. "As you said, Senator," he murmured. "Sometimes the unanticipated will happen. I'm glad that those who are prepared will always find their way through."

Miatamia said nothing. Perhaps, for once, he had nothing to say.

Grimacing, Lando keyed the board and swung the *Lady Luck*'s nose back on course for Coruscant. President Gavrisom wasn't going to like this. Not one bit.

Neither would anyone else.

•   •   •

There hadn't been any communications planned for this point in the plan. And yet, there was Major Tierce's quarter-sized holographic image, flickering slightly above Moff Disra's private hologram pod. "The transmission's been secured," Disra said, a cold blade-edge of dread grinding into his stomach as he watched the encryption display. If something had gone wrong . . . "What is it?"

"No problems, if that's what you're wondering," Tierce said. "The whole operation went textdoc smooth."

"I'm delighted to hear it," Disra growled. "So why are you risking an open communication this way?"

"I knew you'd be worried," Tierce said blandly. "I wanted to help set your mind at ease."

Disra smiled sardonically, knowing the expression was probably wasted with a holo this size. "Thank you so much, Major—I do so appreciate your concern. So our puppet performed adequately?"

"I'd even go further and say he performed superbly," Tierce said. "He had them in the palm of his hand from the moment they came in to the moment they left."

"No surprises, then?"

"Not really. Calrissian tried to trap him with a question about the time Thrawn visited Talon Karrde on Myrkr. Fortunately for us, he'd actually read the detailed report I'd written up on my time with Thrawn and knew the answer."

"Fortunately for *him*, you mean," Disra said, putting an edge of threat into his voice. "How soon will you be back?"

"That's the other reason I called," Tierce said. "Now that we're here, I think we're going to stay in Rebellion-occupied space for a while."

Disra frowned, the cold blade-edge starting its grinding again. "What for?"

"I'd like to nose around a bit," the other said with a casual wave of his hand. "Send activation signals to some of the sleeper groups we haven't contacted yet—there are still a few we weren't able to send transmissions to because of distance or positioning. Mostly, I want to see what Coruscant's reaction will be to Thrawn's reappearance."

"Probably to send fifty Star Cruisers charging in at

you," Disra snapped. "This is crazy, Tierce. It's also not part of the plan."

"Military plans are always subject to change, Your Excellency," Tierce said calmly.

"This is not what I had in mind for Flim," Disra snarled. "You know that."

"And *you* know that when I joined I said we could do better than what you had in mind," Tierce countered.

Disra ground his teeth savagely. "You're going to ruin everything. And get yourselves killed in the bargain."

"On the contrary," Tierce said, and even on the quarter-sized image Disra could see his self-satisfied smile. "I'm going to start the Empire back on its road to glory."

"Tierce—"

"I have to go, Your Excellency," Tierce said. "We shouldn't stay on transmission too long, even with good encryption. Don't worry, I'm not planning to take the *Relentless* to Coruscant or anything so foolish. I just want to spend a little more time here. Call it a hunch."

"In my experience, relying on hunches is a fast trip to the short end of the odds," Disra growled. But Tierce had him, and they both knew it. Short of sending what was left of the Braxant Sector Fleet to chase him down, there was precious little Disra could do at this point to countermand him. "How long are you planning to stay?"

Tierce shrugged. "A couple of weeks. Maybe more. It depends."

"On what?"

"On whether I get the reaction I'm looking for. I'll be sure to let you know if and when it happens."

"Good," Disra said sourly. "If and when the New Republic fleet appears over Bastion, I'll be sure to let *you* know."

Tierce smiled. "Thank you, Your Excellency. I knew you'd understand. Good-bye."

The image flickered and vanished. Disra leaned back in his chair, glaring at the hologram pod. This was getting out of hand. It was getting *way* out of hand. He'd let Tierce run off restrainer bolt long enough; it was time to reel the Guardsman in a little.

And remind him who was master and who was servant.

At the moment, Disra wasn't exactly sure how to do that. But he would think of something.

CHAPTER

20

The Diamalan Senator finished his report and sat down again on the witness bench beside Lando . . . and for Leia, the Grand Convocation Chamber had suddenly become very cold.

The impossible had happened. Grand Admiral Thrawn had returned.

"I do not see the problem," the Likashan Senator called out, her high-pitched voice making the chamber's sound system squeal. "We are many; the Empire are few. Let us gather together and move against it. And this time, let us not stop until we have utterly destroyed it."

"If you think that's even an option anymore, then you're a fool," the Sronk Senator countered. "I saw full-left-handed what this Grand Admiral Thrawn did to my world's defenses ten standardcycles ago, and with nothing more than seven *Katana*-fleet Dreadnaughts as his weapons. He wouldn't have announced his return if he weren't already prepared to receive the full slamming brunt of our closed right hand."

"They have no more than a thousand worlds remaining," a Senator who Leia couldn't identify put in scornfully. "With no more than a hundred Star Destroyers and a few thousand lesser ships. Do you suggest that such a pitiful force could withstand the full thunder of our trampling hooves?"

"You do not know this Thrawn—"

"Please," President Gavrisom cut in. "All of you. We of the Council certainly understand your concerns and your fears. However, at this point I would urge you to ponder this news without jumping to either hasty conclusions or premature actions."

"A preemptive strike would *not* be a premature action," a huffy voice insisted. "I agree with the Likashan Senator that we must move immediately against the remnants of the Empire."

"Yes," the Likash squealed. "Grand Admiral Thrawn nearly defeated us once; we cannot allow him the time he needs to attack us again."

"He's already *had* all the time he needs," the Sronk shot back. "Weren't you listening to what I said? He wouldn't have revealed himself if he wasn't ready for us."

"But the situation isn't the same as it was ten years ago," Leia reminded them, striving to keep her own voice steady and to keep the growing sense of dread in the chamber from feeding into her own fears. "Back then Thrawn still had nearly a quarter of the old Empire to work with. As has already been pointed out, his resources are almost nonexistent now."

"So let us take the rest away from him," a voice shouted. "Let us destroy him now!"

"We cannot destroy him," Gavrisom said. "Even if we wanted to, which I'm not yet convinced is the proper response to his offer."

"Why not?" the Likash demanded. "The New Republic has far more warships than the Empire."

The Maerdocian Senator roared something in his own language. "Do you imply you would seriously consider allowing him to interrogate New Republic officials?" the translation whispered in Leia's ear. "That way lies madness."

"He doesn't want all of us," the Kian'thar Senator pointed out. "He wants only the Bothans."

There was another roar. "Do you genuinely believe it

would end with the Bothans?" the translation demanded. "If so, your path is toward madness."

Gavrisom tapped a key on his board, shutting down the chamber sound system. The shouting died reluctantly away, and he turned the system back on. "Please," he said mildly. "Let us keep our focus clear in this debate. Certainly we have no intention of permitting an Imperial official to interrogate the leaders of any New Republic member world. However, it is equally unreasonable at this point to suggest a concerted attack against the Empire. While it is true that a state of war technically exists between us, recent hostilities have been few and mostly accidental. More to the point, even though our forces outnumber theirs, those forces are at the moment widely dispersed across the galaxy."

He shook his mane in a gesture of mild reproof. "Attempting, as you are all aware, to bring some measure of stability to the New Republic against the stirrings of hundreds of threatening internal wars."

"How ver' conven'ent," the Garoosh Senator half-whistled sarcastically. "For the Empire, a' least."

"They're probably the ones inciting all the wars," someone suggested with obvious contempt. "That would be just like Thrawn's style. Fanning the fires of stupid hatred and primitive genocidal nonsense—"

"Do not call our long struggle stupid," the Forshul Senator rumbled. "And as for genocide, I find it highly significant that our oppressors the Prosslee stand ready to excuse the Bothans' own actions against the Caamasi. It is the duty of all right-thinking beings to recognize such an attitude as a danger, not only to my people but also to all of Yminis sector—"

Gavrisom touched the cutoff switch again, and the Forshul's voice dropped into a distant and indistinct voice booming from her section of the chamber. "I thank the Senator from Yminis sector for her comments," the President said. "I would also remind her that this is not the time for such speeches."

"President Gavrisom, I would speak," a familiar voice

simmering with familiar anger rolled across the chamber, filling the space even with the sound system turned off.

Leia looked that direction. Ghic Dx'ono, the Ishori Senator, was on his feet, his whole body trembling with the physical rage that in his species always accompanied deep thought. "You may speak," Gavrisom told him, turning the sound system on again. "I would caution you that as this chamber does not wish to hear a tirade against the Prosslee, we also do not wish to hear one against the Diamala."

"I intend no tirade," Dx'ono barked. "I wish merely to remind the chamber that we have only the Diamalan Senator's word that he did indeed face this Thrawn. I would also remind the Senators that he ended his testimony moments ago with an urging that we put the Bothan matter behind us—without punishing the guilty—in order that we might face this supposed new threat."

"The reappearance of Grand Admiral Thrawn is hardly a 'supposed' threat, Senator Dx'ono," Miatamia countered with typical Diamalan calm. "Merely because he was stopped the last time before reaching any Ishori worlds does not guarantee your safety should he be allowed the freedom to advance again."

"Do not accuse me of thinking only of my own worlds," Dx'ono shot back. "The Ishori seek the safety of all peoples in the New Republic. But at the same time we also demand justice for those peoples."

"The Diamala people support all forms of justice," Miatamia said. "We merely do not consider blind revenge to be justice."

"Only a blind observer would consider our demands to be revenge," Dx'ono snarled. "But that is not the issue here," he added quickly as the tip of Gavrisom's wing moved toward the cutoff switch. "The issue is that you have made a statement to this chamber which conveniently adds weight and thrust to your political side, but which is unsupported by any independent sources."

"Do you not consider former General Lando Calrissian to be an independent source?" Miatamia asked.

"By your own testimony he came to you asking for

Diamalan military assistance," Dx'ono barked. "Given that, do you really expect us to consider his words unbiased?"

"On behalf of Captain Calrissian, I resent the implications of that statement, Senator," Leia said, finding herself on her feet. "He's been a stalwart friend and ally, both of the New Republic and the Rebel Alliance before that. If Lando says he saw Thrawn, then he did."

"Once he was a friend and ally," Dx'ono retorted. "Once he was also a smuggler and gambler, experienced at cheating and lying to obtain what he wanted. Now he is a businessman, running a suboceanic mining operation whose profits depend on his obtaining Diamalan assistance. So tell us, Councilor Organa Solo: which of his two backgrounds is he drawing on?"

Leia looked over at Lando, sitting grim-faced and silent behind Gavrisom. "I've known Lando for sixteen years," she said quietly. "I will vouch personally for his character."

"Fine," Dx'ono said with a snort. "You may vouch for him all you like, Councilor. Suppose then, for sake of argument, that he saw a person on that Star Destroyer. But was it Thrawn, or was it something else?"

Leia frowned, trying to read his thoughts across the chamber. But all she could get was the outward anger, masking everything beneath it. "Are you suggesting that the Empire faked the meeting?"

"It could well have been a fake," the Ishori said, glaring at Miatamia. "But I do not necessarily put the blame on the Empire. We all know that there are numerous Imperial Star Destroyers within New Republic territory—some even in private hands, if rumors are to be believed. And as I have already pointed out, the message that was supposedly delivered by this supposed Thrawn conveniently supports the Diamalan stance on the Bothan issue. Coincidence? Or careful manipulation?"

"The ability to manipulate his enemies was one of Thrawn's greatest talents," Fey'lya put in.

"A talent not unique to him," Dx'ono snapped. "The Bothans, for one example, are also masters of the art. So are the Diamala."

"The man in the Grand Admiral's uniform knew about my visit to Myrkr ten years ago," Lando said. "The only people who were there at that time were Thrawn and his stormtrooper escort."

"Not true," Dx'ono shot back. "By your own statement, former General Solo was also there."

Leia felt a sudden stirring of anger. "Are you suggesting—?"

"As was also," Dx'ono continued, cutting Leia off with a dark look, "the smuggler Talon Karrde."

Leia threw a glance at Lando. "Karrde wouldn't be a part of anything like this," she insisted.

"Wouldn't he?" Dx'ono demanded. "Unlike Captain Calrissian, this Karrde has never even claimed any loyalty to the New Republic. He's a smuggler and seller of information, a man whose only concern and loyalty are to profit and gain."

The Ishori drew himself up a little taller, a finger stabbing out accusingly toward Leia. "And a man, furthermore, whose chief links to Coruscant have been to such people as Captain Calrissian and you yourself, Councilor Organa Solo. So now tell us: where exactly do *you* stand on the Bothan issue?"

The question took Leia completely by surprise. "What do you mean?" she asked, trying to stall for time.

"You know what I mean," Dx'ono snarled. "Tell us where you stand, Councilor Organa Solo. Do you believe that full reparations and justice should be demanded of the Bothans? Or do you, like the Diamalan Senator, prefer to allow their horrific crime to go unpunished? Perhaps even enough to create a situation that would force this chamber to that decision?"

"We know where she stands," another angry voice called out. "Did not her bondedmate Han Solo fire on a peaceable protest at the Clans Building on Bothawui?"

"That has not been proved, Senator Shibatthi," Gavrisom broke in sternly, coming to Leia's rescue. "And your accusations are likewise uncalled for, Senator Dx'ono.

As I've already said, this is not the time nor the place for yet another debate on the Caamas issue. Both of you be seated, please."

But the damage had already been done, Leia realized as she sat down again. In a single masterful stroke, Dx'ono had not only cast serious doubt on Miatamia's story but also managed to undermine her own credibility as well. From now on, any attempt she made to defend either Lando or the Diamalan Senator would merely feed into the suspicions he had just planted.

Infighting, suspicions, divisiveness. Yes, it was indeed Thrawn's style.

"This seems a good time to move on to the Admiralty's report on the overall military situation in the New Republic," Gavrisom continued. "Admiral Drayson?"

The admiral stepped to the podium beside Gavrisom; and as he did, a discreet flicker of light caught Leia's eye. The small green comm indicator on her chair arm was flashing.

She frowned, throwing a surreptitious glance around the chamber. No one but her family and closest aides were supposed to have this comm frequency, and they all had strict instructions that it was to be used only in an emergency. But in that case they were also supposed to key the indicator to a three-flash pattern, and at the moment it was merely blinking steadily.

Stifling a flash of annoyance, she activated her chair's privacy field. Drayson's voice dropped to a tenth of its normal volume as she swiveled the comm display up from its storage position along the side of her armrest. If this was Anakin asking if he could open a new package of cookies, she promised herself darkly as she touched the switch, he was going to be grounded for a week. "Leia Organa Solo."

But it wasn't Anakin. "Hello, Leia," Talon Karrde said, nodding politely. "I hope I'm not calling at too inconvenient a moment."

Reflexively, Leia pulled the display as close to her as she could. Of all the awkward times for him to call— "As a matter of fact, it is inconvenient," she told him shortly. "I'm in the middle of a Senate meeting."

"Then I'll make it short," he said, his eyes narrowing slightly. He was too smart, and knew her too well, not to know there was more to it than just that. "I have a personal message to deliver to you, one which I'd rather not put on even an encrypted channel. Unfortunately, one of the line directors at Coruscant Space Control feels that I shouldn't be permitted to land."

Leia frowned, Dx'ono's accusations echoing through her mind. But how could word have gotten out so fast? "Do you have his name?"

"Just his bureaucratic operating number: KTR-44875," Karrde said. "He wouldn't even give me that, incidentally; I had to pull it off his ID plate. He's an Ishori, if that helps any."

Leia grimaced. That explained how the word had gotten out so fast. "It does," she told Karrde. "The Ishori Senator has just finished accusing you and Lando of conspiring with the Diamala to get the Bothans off the hook on the Caamas matter. He tried to rope me in on it, too, just for good measure."

"I see," Karrde said, pursing his lips. "And so of course here I am, calling on you for help. My apologies for the bad timing."

"It's not your fault," Leia said, glaring over the top of the display at the chamber and its hundreds of human and alien faces staring down in her direction. She was *not* going to let them dictate who her friends and associates could be. "You tell this Ishori line director that *I'm* giving you permission to land—I'll transmit the order as soon as you're off the comm. You're in the *Wild Karrde*?"

"Yes," Karrde said. "But I could come down in a shuttle if you think that would be more politic."

Leia snorted. "Ruffled feelings are the least of my worries at the moment. Do you know where the West Championne landing field is? It's about two hundred kilometers south of the Imperial Palace, near the Manarai Mountains."

"I have it on the map," Karrde confirmed, eyeing her

closely. "Is this something new, or has the Caamas debate simply taken a more vicious turn?"

"I don't know yet," Leia said. "It could be either, depending on who you listen to. We have a place on the thirtieth floor of Orowood Tower, about twenty kilometers east of the landing field. I'll call the Noghri caretakers and have them let you in; we'll be out there as soon as I can get away tonight."

"Sounds cozy," he said, still gazing thoughtfully at her. "Not to mention secluded."

"It is," Leia agreed, wincing slightly. It wasn't hard to guess his thoughts: that despite her protestations to the contrary, she didn't want to risk being seen with him anywhere near the Imperial Palace. "You'll understand why I want to meet there when I tell you what's happened."

"Of course," he said equably. "Would it be all right if I used the comm and data retrieval equipment at your retreat until you arrive? Just to keep myself amused, of course?"

Leia smiled. "And to see what you can dig out of the government archives?"

He shrugged. "I might learn something new. You never know."

"I'm sure it's harder for you to learn something you didn't already know than it is for most of us," Leia said dryly. "All right, I'll clear it with the Noghri when I call them."

"Thank you. I'll see you later. Good-bye."

"Good-bye."

With a sigh, she keyed off the comm. Infighting, suspicions, divisiveness. Yes, it was Thrawn's style, all right. She could only wonder what he had planned for them next.

Switching the comm back on again, she keyed for Coruscant Space Control.

All in all, Carib Devist thought as he gazed across the colorful fields of tallgrain rippling across Dorchess Valley, it had been a good day.

It really had. The oppressive summer sun that blazed so

steadily down onto Pakrik Minor during the growing season
had been hiding coyly behind clouds for most of the day,
giving relief from the usual heat. The clouds hadn't burned
off until late afternoon, just in time for the sun to disappear
for an hour and a half behind Pakrik Minor's far more
densely populated sister world of Pakrik Major. By the time
it had reemerged the extra heat was actually almost welcome.

There were still some problems in the fields themselves,
of course, but that was all part of a farmer's life. Carib and
his brothers had had to drive out yet another colony of
worms that had tried to make their home among the inter-
locked tallgrain roots, and had had to deal with a spot of
white-blight that could have wiped out the entire crop
within days if it hadn't been caught. But it had been caught,
and the worms had been rooted out, and none of the droids
had broken down or even gone cranky, and the crops were
actually ahead of growing schedule for a change.

No, it had been a good day; and as Carib propped his
feet up to point toward the magnificent sunset and sipped at
a well-earned glass of R'alla mineral water he decided that it
was indeed good to be alive.

A motion to his right caught his eye: his brother Sabmin
coming toward the house in that battered old landspeeder of
his. Lacy had probably invited Sabmin and his family over to
dinner—she was always forgetting to tell him things like
that.

But no. Sabmin was alone in the vehicle . . . and as the
landspeeder came closer Carib could make out the expression on his brother's face . . .

He was waiting at the foot of the path by the time
Sabmin brought the landspeeder to a dusty halt. "What's
wrong?" he asked without preamble.

"It's happened," Sabmin said, his voice a husky whisper.
"I was up at the cave and—well, it's happened."

Carib glanced back up the path at the house. Lacy was
visible in the kitchen window, carefully pulling the dinner
roast out of the focus cooker. "Walk with me," he said.

He led the way down the path toward the edge of the fields. "You confirmed the message was legitimate?" he asked.

"First thing," Sabmin said soberly. "It carried all the proper Imperial codes."

Carib winced. It had been a long time since the word "Imperial" had been used in this part of Pakrik Minor. "Then I guess it's time," he said, a strange sensation in the pit of his stomach. After ten years of quiet waiting, they were once again being called to service. "Have you said anything to the others yet?"

"No, I came straight here," Sabmin said. "But there's more." He glanced around, as if afraid someone might be listening from among the neat rows of tallgrain. "The activation order came in over the name of Grand Admiral Thrawn."

Carib felt his jaw drop. "That's impossible," he hissed. "Thrawn is dead."

"That's what everyone said," Sabmin agreed soberly. "All I know is that his name is on the order."

They had reached the first row of stalks now. "It could be a lie," Carib said, turning sideways to ease between the rows, sniffing the familiar sour-musky aroma rising around him as his tanned leatheris vest brushed across the leaves. "Or else a trick."

"Hardly a trick they could keep up," Sabmin pointed out. "Even using old holo-recordings of him in transmissions wouldn't fool anyone for long."

"True," Carib said, stopping beside a nearly ripe stalk and touching a finger to the tallgrain string peeking coyly from a gap in its sheath. Grand Admiral Thrawn, who had turned around five years of steady decline and brought the Empire to within sight of total victory. "You realize, of course, that this could change everything."

"I don't see how," Sabmin said. "The fact still remains that we were planted here for the express purpose of being ready to cause havoc if and when we were called to do so." He stroked the tallgrain string. "Well, the planting took root, the crop has ripened . . . and now they're calling for the harvest."

"Yes," Carib said, dropping his hand back to his side. A harvest of terror and sudden death and destruction, almost certainly directed at the ripe fruit that was Pakrik Major hanging overhead. Pakrik Major, and the annual sector-wide conference that had just gotten under way in the capital. A long-delayed strike against the traitors of the Rebellion, courtesy of the Empire. "But that's not my point," he told Sabmin. "My point is that if Thrawn is really back in command, then whatever we're ordered to do won't be simply a grand but meaningless gesture of suicidal defiance. If Thrawn is back, then the Empire might just win."

Sabmin whistled softly. "You're right," he murmured. "I hadn't even thought about it that way."

"Well, you'd better start thinking about it that way," Carib warned. "And we'd better make sure the others do, too. Any idea when the last maintenance check was done on the TIEs?"

"Not more than a month ago," Sabmin said. "I think it was Dobrow who ran it. You want to talk with him tonight?"

"I want to talk with everyone tonight," Carib said, sidling out of the tallgrain rows and starting back up toward the house. "My place, in two hours."

"We can try," Sabmin said, falling into a probably unconscious military step beside him. "Tabric and Hovarb may not be able to make it, though—three of their gornts went into labor this afternoon."

"The gornts can have their litters by themselves," Carib said shortly. "This is important."

Sabmin threw him a frown. "Oh, come on, Carib, aren't you overreacting just a little? It's an activation order, not a full-blown attack plan."

"If Thrawn is in charge, there won't be a lot of time between the two," Carib growled. "Whatever he's up to, he'll have his timetable shaved down to the half second."

They walked the rest of the way to Sabmin's vehicle in

silence. "All right, I'll tell them," Sabmin said as he climbed in. "They'll be here."

Carib sighed. "Let's make it your place instead," he suggested. "It's only three minutes by landspeeder from there to their barn. They can get back in plenty of time if anything goes wrong with the labor."

Sabmin smiled tightly. "Thanks, Carib. We'll see you there."

CHAPTER

21

"There's Lando," Leia said, pointing out the canopy as Han set their Incom T-81 down on the Orowood Tower's third-level airspeeder pad. "Over there, by the entryway, behind that red cloud car."

"Yeah, I see him," Han grunted, shutting down the repulsorlifts. "I still think this is a bad idea, Leia."

"I know you do," Leia said, taking a moment to look past the lighted landing area at the darkened shrubbery perimeter beyond it. There was no one visible, either to her eyes or her Jedi senses. "And I can't say I completely disagree with you. But he insisted on coming."

"You'd just better hope Dx'ono didn't get wind of it and have someone follow him here," Han growled, popping the canopy. "You get someone yelling 'secret meeting' and we'll all have had it."

"I know," Leia said, climbing out of the airspeeder and looking around. There were some airspeeder running lights visible in the sky around them, and the various roads crisscrossing the area around the Tower were carrying their usual quota of landspeeders. None of the vehicles seemed to be particularly heading their direction.

But there were the darkened windows of one of the Tower's five tapcafes gazing down on them from the fourth floor, not to mention all the windows of the apartments stretching up into the night sky. If one of those windows concealed someone with a set of macrobinoculars . . .

Han clearly had already had the same thought. "We'd better get inside," he muttered, taking her arm. "Come on, Threepio, move it."

"Yes, sir," the golden-skinned droid said hastily, levering himself awkwardly out of the back of the airspeeder and shuffling quickly behind them. That was the first time Threepio had said anything, Leia realized suddenly, since they'd left the Imperial Palace. Had he picked up on Han's mood, and was trying to make himself inconspicuous? Or had he been brooding on his own memories of Thrawn's last bid for power?

Lando emerged from his half concealment as they approached. "Han; Leia," he nodded to them. His usual smile of greeting, Leia noted, was conspicuously absent. "Where's Karrde?"

"He's already here," Leia told him as Han keyed the entryway lock. "The Noghri let him in."

"Good." Hunching his shoulders beneath his cloak, Lando threw one last look back into the darkness as he followed Leia in.

Thirty-eight stories tall, the Orowood Tower had originally been planned to be the nucleus of an elaborate and extensive colony of Alderaanians who had been off-planet when the first Death Star destroyed their world. But though the architects had painstakingly crafted every facet of the Tower to fit the Alderaanian style, Coruscant's crowds and near-total land development were simply too alien to their life view for most of the refugees to feel comfortable living there.

Though the rest of the project had been abandoned, there had been hopes that enough Alderaanians would remain on Coruscant to keep the Tower itself occupied, particularly given its spectacular view of the Manarai Mountains. But that final dream had been dealt its death blow by Grand Admiral Thrawn's short-lived but terrifying siege of the planet. When the siege was finally lifted, virtually all the Alderaanians left Coruscant, going to New Alderaan or scattering out among the stars. As one of them had explained to Leia, they had been lucky enough to escape the destruction of one world, and had no desire to settle on an even more tempting target.

And so the grand experiment had settled into vague obscurity, joining the host of other residential centers clustered beneath the mountains, most of which provided secondary or vacation homes to rich industrialists and government officials. Offworlders and aliens, most of whom had never even heard of the fabled oro woods of Alderaan, let alone ever walked among them.

Over the years, the ache of that irony had mostly faded from Leia's heart. Mostly.

The turbolift operated with the typical quiet efficiency of Alderaanian construction, depositing them into the lush garden scene that comprised the thirtieth-floor lobby. No one was visible among the fronds and rock-pile water trickles; but then, no one was supposed to be. "Barkhimkh?" Leia called softly.

"I am here, Lady Vader," Barkhimkh's voice mewed from across the lobby. There was a rustle from the fronds, and the Noghri warrior stepped into view beside the archway that opened into the corridor leading to their apartment. "All is quiet."

"Thank you," Leia said.

"Make sure you keep it that way," Han added as they crossed the lobby.

Barkhimkh bowed his head. "I obey, Han clan Solo."

Karrde was lounging in a Plash self-molding contour chair in the apartment's conversation circle, a datapad in one hand and a glass of amber liquid in the other, as Han keyed the door open. "Ah—there you are," the smuggler said, closing the datapad and levering himself out of the chair as they filed inside. "I was just thinking of asking Sakhisakh to try contacting you."

"We got a later start than I'd expected," Leia explained. "I'm sorry."

"No need to apologize," Karrde assured them. "The children aren't with you?"

"They just left this morning with Chewie to go visit his family on Kashyyyk," Leia told him. "With all that's been happening lately, I thought it would be better for them to be there."

"Between their Noghri guard and a planetful of Wookiees it's hard to imagine anyplace safer," Karrde agreed. "Hello, Calrissian. Nice to see you again."

"Yes," Lando said. "Though you may not think so when we tell you why you're here."

Karrde's expression didn't change, but Leia could feel a tightening of his emotions. "Really," he said easily. "Let's dispense with the formalities, then. Sit down and tell me all about it."

"I'm sorry," the screening system at the other end of the comm said in its maddeningly pleasant mechanical voice. "Communication with the residence you request is restricted. I cannot connect you without a proper authorization code."

"Tell Councilor Organa Solo that it's an emergency," Shada said, putting the most intimidating official tone into her voice that she could as she gazed out the tapcafe window at the Solos' Incom T-81, sitting there on the Orowood Tower's third-floor landing pad. "I'm calling under the authorization of Admiral Drayson of New Republic Intelligence."

The screening system remained unfazed. "I'm sorry, but I cannot connect you without a proper authorization code," it repeated.

Grimacing, Shada keyed the comm off. That had been the last verbal gambit in her repertoire, and it had done nothing but get her the same runaround. The same thing every time she tried, and she was beginning to get very tired of it.

She'd tried the polite, official way first: calling Councilor Organa Solo's office at the Imperial Palace and—when the screeners there wouldn't let her through, either—trying to get into the massive governmental building itself. But with

no official status or business or connections to call on, she'd
hit meter-thick transparisteel walls at every turn. She'd tried
calling the Solos' main home outside the palace next, with
the same results. And now she'd tried to get through to them
at their Manarai Mountain retreat, again with no luck.

And with each rebuff, her obviously idealized vision of
the New Republic had crumbled a little bit more. She'd
hoped they would have more to offer her than the life with
the Mistryl that she'd just turned her back on. It was starting
to look more and more like she'd been mistaken.

But there was nothing to do now but continue what
she'd started. If for no other reason than that there was nowhere left for her to go.

So all right. She'd tried it the polite way and gotten
nowhere. Now she would try it the Mistryl way.

The Tower's second-floor shopping complex was quite
extensive, and it took her no more than five minutes to collect the three items she needed. One minute after that, armed
with a length of brocaded white ribbon, a cheap datapad, and
a bottle of equally cheap but awesomely strong dodbri whiskey, she was in the turbolift heading up.

It would be a short ride, she knew, but she already had
the details mapped out in her mind and set to work with no
wasted motions. Popping the cap off the whiskey, she
splashed a little of the potent concoction onto the collar of
her slightly bedraggled ankle-length dress and then sipped a
little into her mouth. Wincing at the tingle, she swished it
around while she poured the rest of the bottle into the decorative flower boxes that ran around the upper part of the car.
She spat her mouthful back into the bottle, glad to be rid of
it, then turned her attention to the ribbon. The traditional
Coruscant wedding hairbow was tricky to tie, but she knew
a variant that was quick and simple and looked enough like
the real thing to fool anyone but an experienced observer.

By the time the doors opened onto the Tower's rooftop
observation deck, she was ready for her performance. Bottle
clutched in one hand, datapad in the other, she stepped out
of the car and threw a casual and calculatedly unsteady look
around. No one was visible among the deserted tables and

chairs and decorative shrubbery. But then, the group of personal guards that surrounded Councilor Organa Solo seldom were. Getting a fresh grip on her bottle, she set off in a staggering walk for the edge of the roof.

The guard she knew had to be there hadn't made his appearance by the time she reached the chin-high latticework guardrail set into a solid knee-high base. "So fine, Ravis," she muttered to herself in a slurred and despondent voice as she dropped the bottle and datapad onto the roof beside the guardrail. "You don' wanna, huh? Fine. I can get outta your lif', if tha's what you wan'. I can get all the way out—"

She broke off with a single underplayed sob. Digging her fingers into the holes of the lattice, she pressed herself against the barrier and twisted her head sideways to peer over and down at the ground below, her senses alert. There was a single whisper of sound from behind her, and then nothing.

So they were going to need more from her before they made any move. Fine; she could oblige them. Extracting her fingers from the guardrail, continuing to sob softly under her breath, she retrieved the datapad and set it down on a nearby chair, propping it up to be clearly visible. With slightly fumbling fingers she pulled the wedding bow out of her hair, kissed it theatrically, and placed it down in front of the datapad. She took another moment to carefully arrange the two items together; then, squaring her shoulders, she took a deep breath and stepped back to the roof edge. Gripping the lattice again, she climbed up onto the base and swung one leg over the top of the guardrail.

Or rather, tried to. Even as she swung the leg up she heard another whisper of sound, and a hand suddenly grabbed her waist sash, tugging her backward and forcing her to bring her leg back down to maintain her balance. "Do not do this," a gravelly catlike voice mewed softly from behind her.

"Le' me go," Shada moaned, letting go of the lattice with her left hand and slapping ineffectually at his arm. "Le'

me go. He doesn' care 'bout me—he sai' so. He doesn' wan'
me anymore. Le' me *go*."

"This is not the way," the Noghri said, pulling her
gently but firmly. "Come inside and we will speak."

"Done wi' talking," Shada muttered, half turning to
look down at him and making sure he could smell the whiskey on her breath as she threw a quick glance over the rooftop. No one else was visible. "Please—le' me go," she
pleaded, grabbing the lattice again with her left hand and
pulling upward against his grip. "Please."

"No," the Noghri repeated, pulling back with more
ˈrength than she would have thought a creature that small
could manage. Her fingers strained against the pull—

And without warning she let go, spinning halfway
around as she fell straight at him.

The Noghri was fast, all right. By the time she'd rotated
far enough around to see him he'd already moved a step to
the side to get out of her way. His free arm came up, ready
to catch her shoulders and break her fall—

And as she fell into that wiry grip, her hand jabbed hard
into the side of his throat. Without a sound, his legs buckled
beneath him and they collapsed together onto the rooftop.

For a few seconds she lay there, still sobbing drunkenly,
her eyes darting around the rooftop for signs of a backup.
But the Noghri was apparently up here alone.

Which wasn't to say he hadn't checked in before rushing
off to save the despondent drunk bent on self-destruction. If
he had, she didn't have much time. If he hadn't, she wouldn't
have much more.

Stripping off the dress that had concealed her combat
jumpsuit, keeping one eye on the turbolift door, she set to
work.

Karrde turned his glass around in his hand, his eyes on
the remains of his drink as it swirled partway up the side in
response to the movement. "You're sure about all this," he
said.

"I'm sure," Lando said positively. "I searched through

what we've got of the old Imperial archives and found every recording they had of Thrawn. There wasn't much, but it definitely looked and sounded like the man I saw."

"Which doesn't mean it couldn't be a trick," Han put in, throwing a surreptitious look at Leia. If Karrde's attitude was all an act—if he was secretly behind this Thrawn sighting of Lando's—then she ought to have pulled the proof of that from his mind by now.

But her face had the same grim expression that had been there when Lando first started his story; and even as he watched, her eyes shifted to his and she shook her head microscopically in response to his unspoken question.

Han had thought they were being subtle enough. Apparently not. "I take it I'm under some suspicion here," Karrde continued, still studying his glass. "And not just from the Ishori and their allies. Have I passed the test?"

Han looked at Leia again in time to see her lip twitch. "I'm sorry," she said. "For whatever it's worth, I had no doubts myself."

"Thank you." Karrde smiled slightly at Han and Lando. "I won't embarrass either of you by asking if you shared the Councilor's confidence."

"I don't like taking anything for granted," Han told him. "It's not like you've ever sworn allegiance to the New Republic or anything."

Karrde inclined his head. "You're right, of course. My apologies."

He shifted his gaze to Lando. "All right, then. Let's begin with the assumption we're all hoping is true: namely, that you were the victim of a clever trick. First question: how was it done?"

"Shouldn't be all that hard," Han said. "Some facial surgery to make this guy look like Thrawn, then just add in some skin, hair, and eye coloring."

"Facial surgery usually leaves distinctive marks," Lando pointed out. "I know what to look for, and they weren't there. Besides, what about the voice?"

"What about the voice?" Han asked. "Voices can be

faked, too, you know. We did it ourselves with Threepio once, remember?"

"If the voice was really that accurate, it could have been a human replica droid," Karrde suggested. "Like the one Prince Xizor of Black Sun used to have."

Lando shook his head. "It wasn't just the voice, Karrde. Or the face, or anything else you could look at. It was—I don't know. There was a *presence* there, a hidden power and confidence I don't think any droid could fake. It was him. It had to be."

"Could it have been a clone, then?" Karrde persisted. "Thrawn could easily have taken one or more of the cloning tanks out of Mount Tantiss before it was destroyed."

"I've been wondering about that, too," Leia said. "It could also explain where the clones Luke sensed at Iphigin came from."

"A clone of Thrawn would be dangerous enough," Lando agreed tightly. "But turn it around a minute. Couldn't it just as easily have been a clone sitting on the *Chimaera*'s bridge at Bilbringi? What if Thrawn had anticipated everything that was going to happen—everything— and made the necessary arrangements?"

Karrde swished his drink around a little more in his glass. "Then why did he sit back and let the Empire collapse when his leadership could very likely have saved it?" he asked. "No. If he really was alive, he must have been incapacitated by his wound and gone off somewhere to heal."

"That's pretty much what he implied to Miatamia and me," Lando agreed. "He implied he'd been off recovering."

"Unless that's just what he wanted you to think," Leia warned. "Maybe he was simply off doing something else instead."

"Instead of protecting the Empire?" Han objected. "That doesn't make sense."

Abruptly Karrde set his glass down on the low table beside his chair. "All right, then," he said. "Let's assume the worst case: that that really was Thrawn you saw, and that he's back and out for blood. Why suddenly make an appearance now? And why just to you and Senator Miatamia instead of all of Coruscant?"

"Probably to create exactly the situation we're now in," Leia said. "The tension level in the Senate has jumped straight to the ceiling, with a tremendous amount of animosity and suspicion being focused on the Diamala. And, by extension, to everyone on that side of the Caamas issue."

"With a hint that Gavrisom might not want to resolve the crisis thrown in just to stir things up a little more," Lando added. "I hear some of the Senators are already complaining that he's been dragging his hooves on the whole question of reparations for the Caamasi."

Han grimaced. The Bothans' financial crisis . . . "He's doing the best he can," he told Lando.

"Maybe," Lando said darkly. "But it strikes me that there are a lot of other ways Thrawn could have stirred up the government *if* that was all he wanted."

"What else could he want?" Karrde asked. "He surely wouldn't be foolish enough to take on the entire New Republic. Not with only eight sectors' worth of resources at his disposal."

"Maybe he's found a new superweapon the Emperor had stashed away somewhere," Lando suggested ominously. "Another Death Star—a completed one this time—or maybe another Sun Crusher. Or something even more dangerous."

Karrde shook his head. "Farfetched. If there was something like that out there, we surely would have heard of it by now."

"There's another point that needs to be made here," Leia said. "You talked about him taking on the entire New Republic; but that's only if we could get the entire New Republic together to fight him. With the Caamas issue dividing us so strongly—and with the Empire so weak that most people don't even think of it as a threat—that's not a given anymore."

"If it ever was," Han said sourly. "There was never more than a small fraction of the galaxy actually fighting against the Empire."

"And never more than a small fraction of the Empire

fighting against us," Lando pointed out, his eyes on Karrde. "I don't think we realized back then just how much of their energy was going to keeping all these little planetary vendettas and rivalries from blowing up in their faces. Now we're in that same situation; and in my opinion, we simply don't have the resources available to take on whatever Thrawn has planned."

"That of course depends on what he has planned," Karrde said. He was eyeing Lando closely, Han noticed suddenly. As closely as Lando was eyeing him. "So what do you suggest as your next move?"

"*Our* next move," Lando said, leaning on the word, "is to get this blasted Caamas issue out of the way so we can focus on Thrawn. And that means finding out exactly who the guilty Bothans were."

"That could be a problem," Karrde said, his voice studiously calm. "As far as I know, the Imperials have only two complete sets of records left: one at the Ubiqtorate base at Yaga Minor, the other at the current Imperial capital on Bastion."

"I don't suppose you'd happen to know where Bastion is," Leia said.

"I'm afraid not," Karrde said, glancing at her and then returning his attention to Lando. "Bastion's proper name is one secret the Imperials have managed to keep."

"I wasn't necessarily talking about the Imperials," Lando said. "I was thinking someone else might have the records we're looking for."

Han blinked at Lando. Suddenly the other's insistence that he join them here tonight for their talk with Karrde was taking on a whole new dimension. "You mean that Karrde—?"

"I don't have the records, Calrissian," Karrde said. "If I did, I'd have offered them to you long before now."

"I know that," Lando said, his voice heavy with significance. "I was referring to a different source entirely."

"Who also probably doesn't have them," Karrde said coldly.

Lando's expression didn't change. "But who might."

For a pair of heartbeats the two men continued to gaze at each other. Han threw a frown at Leia, saw his same puzzlement mirrored in her own face. "Is there something here we need to know about?" he asked carefully.

"No," Lando said. "Or maybe I should say not yet."

"Leia, Calrissian and I need to have a short talk," Karrde said, getting abruptly to his feet. "Is there a place where we can have some privacy?"

"You can use the boys' bedroom," Leia said, pointing down the hallway. "Last door on the left."

"Thank you." Karrde gestured Lando to the hallway. "After you, Calrissian."

Shada had added an extra anchor to her safety line about two meters above her, on the assumption that if and when the Noghri got reinforcements up to the rooftop they might simply cut the line without bothering to haul her up first for the formality of questioning. Now, dangling a hundred meters above the ground, she eased her low-light eyepiece around the edge of the darkened window beside her and peered inside.

It was a child's bedroom—a children's bedroom, she corrected herself, spotting the second bed pushed against the far wall. Currently unoccupied; and since none of the three Solo children had followed their parents out of the airspeeder, it was reasonable to assume the room would stay that way.

Replacing the eyepiece into its jumpsuit pocket, she pulled out one of her three Zana M6W-9 molecular stilettos and extended its invisibly slender blade. Like a lightsaber, a molecular stiletto could cut through nearly anything. Unlike a lightsaber, though, the Zana's blade was incredibly delicate. A quick thrust against an assailant nearly always resulted in a broken blade—along with a dead assailant, of course—and even the most painstakingly careful cutting job was as likely as not to end up ruining the tool.

Fortunately, the task facing her wasn't going to be large enough to push the odds. With most buildings on Coruscant

she would have had to cut away an entire window to get
inside, but the Orowood's designers had incorporated traditional Alderaanian swing-out panels to allow for free air
flow. All she had to do was maneuver the stiletto blade between the panels and slice through the catch, and she would
be in.

After, of course, finding and disabling whatever alarms
the Noghri had installed.

That task turned out to be easier than she'd expected.
The window carried only a single alarm, ranged to watch for
incoming airspeeders. Apparently, it hadn't occurred to the
Noghri that someone might be crazy enough to rappel down
from the rooftop the way she had. Though of course, to be
fair, they *had* put a guard up there.

Two minutes later she was inside the darkened room,
pulling the window closed behind her and listening hard.
There were the usual soft mechanical noises of any modern
dwelling, along with the muffled sounds of conversation
coming from elsewhere in the apartment. The words were
impossible to decipher through the closed door, but she
could hear at least four distinct voices.

She stood just inside the door, frowning with sudden
indecision. She'd seen Solo and Organa Solo and their droid
arrive in their T-81, and had spotted Calrissian waiting for
them; but who was the fourth voice? Some random friend
who'd happened to drop in? Hardly. A business associate of
Calrissian's? Maybe, except that he'd been skulking alone in
the shadows before the Solos arrived.

One thing was sure: given how furtive all three of them
had been behaving outside, this was clearly a meeting they'd
taken great pains to keep secret. A meeting she doubted any
of them would appreciate being crashed by a total stranger.

Abruptly she tensed. The conversation had paused, and
in its place was a new sound.

Footsteps. Heading her direction.

She was across the room in four quick strides, kneeling
beside the bed by the far wall. It was a spaceship-style bed,
with storage compartments filling the space beneath the mat-

tress itself. But she hadn't planned on hiding under it anyway. Getting a grip on the storage handles, she pulled.

There must have been a lot of junk in those drawers: even with Mistryl-honed muscles behind the tug the bed moved barely twenty-five centimeters away from the wall. But it would be enough; and at any rate, with the footsteps already paused outside her door, it would have to do. Lunging up from her kneeling position, she half dived, half rolled across the bed and slid silently down on her side into the narrow gap.

She just made it. Even as her shoulder and hip settled against the cool floor the bedroom door slid open and two sets of footsteps came inside. The glow panel blazed on, and the door closed again.

"We had an agreement, Calrissian," an unidentified male voice said. Unidentified, yet definitely familiar. Shada searched her memory—

"Which I haven't broken," Calrissian said, his voice sounding a little defensive.

"Really?" the other voice asked coldly. "You've as good as told them there's a secret here. Do you think either of them needs more than that to gather their little shovels together and start digging?"

—and then abruptly the memory clicked. It was the smuggler chief, Talon Karrde.

"Frankly, Karrde, I think they've both got more important things to worry about right now," Calrissian said tartly. "And to be honest, I never understood why you were so obsessed about secrecy on this thing in the first place. So Jorj Car'das was once a competitor of yours—"

"Keep your voice down," Karrde growled. "I don't want the others hearing that name. And Car'das wasn't a competitor. He was something else entirely."

"Fine," Calrissian said. "Whatever. The point is that we can't afford the luxury of silly games anymore. Not with—"

"Silly games?" Karrde cut him off. "Calrissian, you have no idea what you're talking about."

"I know exactly what I'm talking about," Calrissian retorted. "I'm talking about the genius who came *this close* to taking down the whole New Republic ten years ago. What-ever Thrawn's got planned, he has to be counting on the Caamas issue to keep us divided."

Shada felt her breath catch in her throat. Whatever *Thrawn* had planned? But Thrawn was dead.

Wasn't he?

"Thank you for the historical review," Karrde said. "I *was* there, if you'll remember. Let's not act like the whole New Republic's on the edge of desperation and collapse, though, all right?"

"Are you sure we're not?" Calrissian countered. "After all this time, do you really think Thrawn would have shown himself if he wasn't ready to pounce?"

"*If* he intends to pounce," Karrde argued. "There are many other things he could be planning besides an overt attack."

"Oh, *that's* comforting," Calrissian growled. "And all the more reason to get the Caamas issue resolved as quickly as possible. If there's even half a chance Car'das can help, someone has to go see him."

"And you're suggesting I should be that someone?"

"You're the one who knew him," Calrissian pointed out.

"That may not be an asset," Karrde said. "In fact, it could be quite the opposite."

There was the soft sound of a slightly exasperated sigh. "Look, Karrde, I don't know what went on between you and Car'das. What I *do* know is that we're facing Grand Admiral Thrawn here. And not just us—you're facing him, too. Don't forget he specifically said he'd be coming after you."

"Scare words," Karrde murmured.

"I don't remember Thrawn ever relying on scare words the last time," Calrissian said. "Everything he said was backed up with action. But since you've brought up the sub-ject of scare words, what are you so afraid of, anyway?"

There was the sound of footsteps moving toward the window. "You never met Car'das, Lando," Karrde said quietly. "If you had, you'd understand. In his own way he was more ruthless even than Jabba the Hutt."

"Yet you asked Mara and me to go hunt him down."

"I didn't ask *you* to do anything at all," Karrde said. "If you'll recall, I tried to get you to sell me that beckon call outright."

"You also tried to tell me it was just some useless curiosity from pre–Clone Wars days," Calrissian reminded him dryly. "You knew perfectly well I wouldn't fall for a story like that. Anyway, that's beside the point. We tracked him down, and made it back just fine."

"You only tracked him as far as a likely system," Karrde said. "You're asking me to walk into whatever fortress he's set up there and go face-to-face with him."

"If Thrawn isn't stopped, he'll be the one who eventually comes knocking at Car'das's retirement home," Calrissian said. "If Car'das has any brains, he'll thank you for the warning."

"Car'das never thanked anyone for anything in his life," Karrde said bluntly. "And he most certainly hasn't retired, either. He'll be scheming or plotting something—that's the nature of the man. And he will *not* want to be found. Particularly not by me."

Calrissian hissed between his teeth. "Fine," he bit out. "You want to go bury yourself in a hole and wait for Thrawn to come dig you out, you go right ahead. Give me a copy of Mara's route to the Exocron system and I'll go find him myself."

"Don't be absurd," Karrde said. "You and the *Lady Luck* wouldn't last two days alone in the Kathol Outback."

"Who says I'll be going alone?" Calrissian countered. "I thought I'd ask General Bel Iblis and the *Peregrine* along."

"That would be the absolute worst thing you could do," Karrde said, an edge of exasperation starting to color his tone. "You bring a capital warship into the Exocron system and Car'das will either go completely underground or blow it out of the sky. You don't know him the way I do."

"No," Calrissian agreed quietly. "I don't."

There was a long silence. A long, waiting silence. "You should never have given up on your con man origins, Calrissian," Karrde said at last. "You're far too good at it. All right. I'll go."

"Thanks," Calrissian said. "You won't regret this."

"Don't make promises you can't keep," Karrde warned, his usual easy humor back in his voice. "I suppose we should go break the news to the others."

The door whispered open and the glow panels shut off; and as the room went dark again, Shada heaved herself up out of her hiding place. Rolling back across the bed and onto her feet, she crossed the room and slipped out just before the door closed again.

The two men, Calrissian in the lead, were heading down the hallway toward the edge of what looked like an Alderaanian-style conversation circle, both of them completely oblivious to her presence behind them. Moving up, she fell into silent step behind Karrde.

"Okay, I give up," Han said, a puzzled look on his face. "What was *that* all about?"

Leia shook her head. "I don't know," she admitted, replaying the last exchange between Lando and Karrde in her mind as she gazed at the hallway where the two of them had disappeared toward the boys' bedroom. "Some kind of secret they don't want us to know about."

"Yeah, I figured that much," Han said. "What I meant was what's the secret?"

Leia threw him one of her vast repertoire of patient looks, an inventory created by a lifetime of diplomatic service and honed to a fine art by ten years of dealing with three boisterous children. "You know I can't just go in and dig things out of their minds," she reminded him. "It's not even ethical with enemies, let alone friends."

"You Jedi are no fun sometimes," Han said. His tone was bantering, but she could tell from his eyes and mood that he was still uneasy about the situation.

"We're not in the business to have fun," she pointed out.

"You couldn't just sort of, oh, stretch out and get a feel for what they're talking about in there?"

Leia smiled wryly. "I wish you wouldn't do that," she admonished him.

He pulled out one of his own repertoire of innocent looks. "Do what?"

"Suggest that I do something unethical right when I'm trying to persuade myself that it wouldn't hurt anyone," she told him. "That's very disconcerting."

" 'Specially coming from a guy who isn't supposed to have near as good a conscience as you do?" he suggested blandly.

Leia rolled her eyes. "I swear, Han, I think you can read my mind better without Jedi senses than I can read yours with them."

He waved a hand. "Professional secret. One of the things you learn as a scoundrel."

"Of course," Leia said, looking in the direction of the hallway again. "I wonder how unethical it would be to send Threepio in to take notes for them—"

"Lady Vader," a gravelly voice cut in.

Leia jumped; as usual, she hadn't heard or sensed the Noghri's approach. "What is it, Gharakh?"

"Perhaps trouble," Gharakh growled. "The sentry on the rooftop is not responding to his comlink."

Out of the corner of her eye, Leia saw Han roll slightly in his chair to loosen his blaster in its holster. "You've sent a team to check on him?"

"They are on the way," the Noghri said. "But until we know otherwise, we must assume an intruder is attempting to break in. Where are the others?"

"Down the hall," Leia said. Even as she pointed, she felt the subtle change in air pressure as the distant bedroom door slid open. "That should be them now," she added as the sound of approaching footsteps confirmed it.

"I would ask that you stay in this room for the present," Gharakh said. As he spoke, Lando appeared around the corner, followed by Karrde— "If there is an intruder, we will need to seek him out."

—followed by a tall, slender woman dressed in a dark gray combat jumpsuit.

"Don't bother," the woman said quietly. "I'm here."

CHAPTER

22

Their reactions, as reactions went, were quick and efficient. At the same time, Shada had to admit, they were oddly comic to watch.

The shock of the unexpected voice behind him sent Calrissian jumping half a meter into the air, his gunhand getting momentarily tangled in his cloak before he could haul his blaster free. The Noghri's blaster, unsurprisingly, was already out and trained on her, with Solo's not very far behind. Karrde didn't jump nearly as far as Calrissian had; but instead of going for a weapon himself, he merely took a long step to the side to give Solo and the Noghri a clear field of fire. A smart move, but no more than Shada would have expected from someone of his reputation.

Councilor Organa Solo, in contrast to the others, didn't move at all.

Shada didn't move, either. She stood where she was, hands hanging empty at her sides, wondering distantly if the vaunted and probably overrated Noghri combat reflexes would make it more or less likely the guard would overreact to her unexpected appearance by gunning her down.

She almost hoped he would. In many ways, it would be the simplest way to end things.

But the Noghri didn't fire. Neither did Solo nor Calrissian; and with a vague sort of half regret Shada knew she wasn't going to get to go out the easy way.

It was Organa Solo who broke the brittle silence. "Who are you?" she asked, her voice as serene as her face.

"My name is Shada D'ukal," Shada said. "I'm not here to hurt any of you."

Organa Solo nodded. "I know."

Solo threw her a quick sideways glance. "You do?"

"My danger sense would have reacted otherwise," Organa Solo told him. "Long before she arrived in this room."

"What did you do to the guard on the roof?" the Noghri snarled.

"I taught him not to be carelessly compassionate," Shada said. "He's not hurt, except possibly his pride."

There was a quiet mewing of alien language from a comlink attached to the Noghri's collar. "Gharakh?" Organa Solo murmured.

"He is unhurt," the Noghri said. His blaster was still aimed at Shada, but his eyes seemed fractionally less baleful. "They are freeing him from his restraints."

There was a whisper of movement from the corridor behind Shada. She started to turn her head—

"Stand where you are," a Noghri voice ordered from behind her. "Lift your arms."

Shada did as instructed, holding her arms out to the sides as alien hands flitted across her body, wondering where this other group had been hiding. To have sneaked up behind her in what had seemed to be a dead-end corridor—

She smiled to herself. Of course: they'd come from the roof, following her route down the safety line and in through the bedroom window.

And they'd done so with a speed and efficiency that rivaled the best the Mistryl could have offered. Perhaps the Noghri weren't as overrated as she'd thought.

A minute later the probing hands were gone, taking her hip pack and climbing harness with them. "Sit down," the Noghri standing next to Organa Solo ordered, gesturing toward one of the chairs in the conversation circle. "Keep your hands where they can be seen."

"Don't you trust your searchers?" Shada asked, sitting down in the indicated chair. "Or your mistress, for that matter? Councilor Organa Solo already told you I wasn't here to hurt anyone."

The Noghri's eyes seemed to blaze— "Why *are* you here?" Organa Solo asked calmly before the alien could speak.

"I wanted to talk to you," Shada told her, settling her forearms along the chair's armrests. "This was the only way I could do it."

She'd expected an outraged denial, or at the very least a snort of derision. But the other woman merely lifted her eyebrows slightly.

Solo was less of a disappointment. "What's *that* supposed to mean?" he demanded. His blaster, Shada noted, was in his lap, no longer pointed directly at her. But he still had a grip on it.

"It means that unless you're someone with power or money, the corridors of the high and mighty are closed to you," Shada told him, not particularly caring whether she sounded bitter or not. "I've been trying to call for the past three days, and no one would put me through. So much for the great and wonderful New Republic, friend of all the common people."

"So what, you never heard of leaving a message?" Solo growled.

"A message that said what?" Shada countered. "That a nobody with no credentials or status wanted to talk to a great and glorious High Councilor? It would have been tossed out with the next clearing wipe."

"You're talking with me now," Organa Solo said mildly. "What is it you want to say?"

Shada focused on her, the carefully rehearsed words seeming to stick in her throat. Words that would slice through her last ties to the Mistryl, and her people, and her life. "I want to join you," she said, her voice sounding hollow and distant in her ears. "I want to join the New Republic."

For a painfully long moment the only sound in the room was the thudding of her own heart in her throat. It was, predictably, Solo who broke the silence. "You *what*?" he asked.

"I want to join the New Republic," Shada repeated. The second time wasn't any easier than the first. "I have a number of abilities you'll find useful: combat and surveillance, escort and security—"

"Why are you asking us about this?" Solo interrupted, sounding bewildered. "The New Republic has recruitment centers all over Coruscant."

"I don't think you fully appreciate the situation here, Solo," Karrde spoke up before Shada could reply. "Shada hasn't just walked in off the street—or rather, dangled in off the roof. She's chief bodyguard for our smuggler friend Mazzic."

A ripple of surprise ran across the others' faces. "Former bodyguard," Shada corrected. "I resigned three weeks ago."

Karrde cocked an eyebrow. "Your idea?"

Shada felt her throat tighten. "Not entirely."

"I don't see what difference it makes where she came from," Solo persisted. "We're still none of us in the business of hiring."

"Han's right, Shada," Organa Solo said, her eyes studying Shada's face with an uncomfortable intensity. Had those Jedi techniques pulled the secret Mistryl connection from her mind? "There's really nothing we can do for you."

"I'm not asking for charity," Shada bit out. "Frankly, you need me more than I need you. Especially with Thrawn on the loose again—"

"What do you know about Thrawn?" Solo asked sharply.

"I was in the back room just now," Shada said. She glanced over at Karrde, caught the sudden tightening of his expression. "Calrissian implied he was back."

She looked back at Organa Solo. "I also know about the Caamas Document," she told the other woman. "And I know that the only way you're going to get out of the mess you're in is to get hold of an intact copy of it."

Out of the corner of her eye she saw Calrissian throw a significant look at Karrde, a look the smuggler chief carefully ignored. "It would certainly help," Organa Solo acknowledged. "What does this have to do with you?"

"You're going to need help," Shada told her. "I can supply it."

"All by yourself?" Karrde murmured.

"Yes, all by myself," Shada bit out. "You've seen me in action. You know what I can do."

She looked back at Solo. "So do your people, though you might not know it," she said. "Nineteen years ago on Tatooine I helped get you the technical readout for a prototype component of the second Death Star's superlaser."

Another ripple of surprise ran through the room. A ripple that, to Shada's own mild surprise, didn't seem to touch Solo himself. "Really," he said. "Tell us how."

"A friend and I stole the component from an Imperial research base," she said, trying to read his face. Suddenly the one who'd been pushing her the most seemed almost to be on her side. "It was code-named the Hammertong. We flew the ship it was mounted aboard to Tatooine—"

"What kind of ship?" Solo interrupted.

"Loronar Strike Cruiser," Shada said. "Heavily modified—the interior had been gutted so the thing would fit inside. We half buried the ship in a dune and went to the Mos Eisley cantina to find a freighter pilot with a ship who could transport a segment of it for us."

She gestured to Solo. "My partner and I saw you gun down Greedo in there," she said. "We were going to try to hire you, but were picked up by the Imperials before we could get over to you."

"Why?" Solo asked. "I mean, why did they grab you?"

"Karoly and I had disguised ourselves as Brea and Senni Tonnika. Our cam—we'd heard we looked a lot like them," she corrected as smoothly as she could. Now was not the time to mention the Mistryl camouflage prematch files. "We didn't know some Moff had put a detain order on them. Anyway, a Rebel sympathizer sprung us from our police cell and got us a freighter. We flew out a segment of the superlaser component and gave him a droid with the technical readout loaded in."

"What was this sympathizer's name?" Solo asked.

Shada had to search her memory. "Winward," she said. "Riij Winward."

Solo nodded slowly. "So that was you, huh?"

Organa Solo blinked at him. "You knew about this?"

"I read Winward's report," Solo told her. "It was in the briefing textdoc Madine gave us before we headed out for Endor."

His wife shook her head. "I must have missed it."

"Well, there were a couple of small differences," Solo said dryly. "According to Winward, they'd promised him his own segment of the superlaser in return for springing them."

"There was a sandstorm coming," Shada protested. "There was no time to cut another segment and get it loaded."

"And they didn't exactly *give* him the technical readout," Solo added. "He had to sort of borrow their droid to get it."

Shada felt her face warm. "Yes, you're right," she admitted. "I'd forgotten that."

"Charming," Calrissian murmured under his breath.

Shada threw him a glare. "For whatever it's worth, my partners thought we should have killed him rather than let anyone know what we'd done," she bit out. "I stopped them from doing that."

There was another silence. A hard, tense, discomfiting silence. Shada kept her eyes on Organa Solo, trying to read her face. As the ranking political power of the group, it would be up to her to make the final decision . . .

"I've got an idea," Calrissian spoke up. "She said Karrde knows what she can do. So why don't we send her with him?"

Shada looked at Karrde, her impulsive refusal freezing in her throat. She'd just wasted twelve years with one smuggling group, and she hadn't come to Coruscant just to hook up with another one.

But there was something in Karrde's expression . . .

"And just where is it Karrde's going?" Solo asked, cocking his head toward the smuggler chief.

"A special mission," Karrde said. His eyes were still on Shada, that expression still on his face. "Something Calrissian asked me to do."

"Do we get a hint?" Organa Solo asked, a small smile playing around her lips.

Karrde didn't smile back. "It's possible there's a copy of the complete Caamas Document out there that's not in Imperial hands," he told her. "I'm going to see if I can get hold of it."

Solo and Organa Solo exchanged startled glances. "Why didn't you tell us this before?" Organa Solo demanded, the patient amusement gone from her face.

"Because up till now none of this has been any of my business," Karrde said coolly. "Political arguments have nothing to do with me, except insofar as planetary snits and sulkings tend to benefit information dealers."

He looked at Calrissian. "But now a new factor has been stirred into the mix. One which I've been persuaded can no longer be ignored."

Organa Solo hunched her shoulders as if a sudden cold draft had blown across her back. "Thrawn."

Karrde nodded soberly. "Thrawn." He looked at Shada. "And yes, I would be greatly pleased to have Shada's assistance. If she's willing, of course."

Shada grimaced, the irony a bitter taste in her mouth. Nineteen years late, she'd finally made the wrenching decision to shift her allegiance from her own people to the New Republic . . . only to find that the New Republic didn't want her. And the only one who did was as much an outcast from their great and wonderful new society as she was. "Sure," she told Karrde. "Why not?"

"Trust me, Shada, Karrde gets all his best people this way," Calrissian said dryly. "When you get aboard the *Wild Karrde*, ask Mara Jade how *she* got hired."

Something flickered across Karrde's face. "Mara won't be with us," he said. "That's one of the reasons I wanted to talk to you tonight, Leia. Mara's come to some kind of . . . accident."

Calrissian's sly smile vanished, and the others sat up straighter. "What kind of accident?" Organa Solo asked.

"A confusing one," Karrde said with a grimace. "She and the *Starry Ice* tracked one of the unidentified ships your brother saw in the Kauron system—"

"Wait a minute," Solo interrupted. "What's this about unidentified ships?"

"He and Mara saw it skulking around the Cavrilhu Pirates' base," Karrde said. "Didn't he send you a report?"

"Yes, but only a very sketchy one," Organa Solo said. "He just said he hadn't learned anything from the pirates and that he would give us all the details when he got back to Coruscant. There was nothing about any unidentified ship."

"He must not have wanted to say anything on an open channel," Karrde said. "I've got a copy of his and Mara's records of that sighting, plus the data we took when another of the ships buzzed the *Errant Venture*. I'll get copies to you before I leave."

"Forget the ships a minute," Calrissian put in impatiently. "What happened to Mara?"

"The *Starry Ice* tracked it to a small world in Gradilis sector," Karrde said. "Mara went in for a closer look and spotted a fortress, entered a cave for a one-sided conversation with unknown beings, mentioned Skywalker's name in response to something they said or did, and then abruptly went silent."

Calrissian's face had gone rigid. "You mean she was—?"

"No, she wasn't killed," Karrde hastened to assure him. "At least not then—you can hear her breathing on the recording that was pulse-transmitted back to the *Starry Ice*."

"And these beings knew Luke?" Organa Solo asked, her forehead furrowed. With thought or dread, Shada couldn't tell which.

"Knew him, or knew of him," Karrde told her. "There wasn't enough context for us to tell which."

"We need to get hold of him right away," Solo said to his wife. "See if he can tell us anything."

Karrde cleared his throat self-consciously. "Actually, I've already spoken to him. He couldn't shed any light on it, either."

Organa Solo regarded him suspiciously. "And?" she prompted.

"That was the other thing I wanted to tell you," Karrde said, his urbane air cracking just a bit. "He's gone off to find her."

Organa Solo's expression didn't change, but suddenly the temperature in that part of the room seemed to drop a few degrees. "He's *what*?" she asked, her tone ominous.

"She's in danger, Leia," Karrde said. "Luke was the only one who could get there fast enough to make a difference. The only one who had a reasonable chance of dealing with whatever the creatures were Mara ran into. *And* whoever or whatever is up in that fortress. This doesn't just concern Mara; it concerns the entire New Republic."

"And what, you think this Bothan mess doesn't?" Solo growled. He was on his feet now, glaring across the conversation circle at Karrde. "We've got a hundred little wars simmering out there, half of them using Caamas as an excuse to go in and settle old grudges. We've already emptied the New Republic diplomatic corps and Jedi academy trying to find enough mediators to go around, and we still don't have enough. We *need* Luke here."

"I didn't force him to go after her," Karrde countered, not quite glaring back. "He weighed all the factors and made his own decision."

"Except that he didn't know Thrawn was back," Solo countered. "Did he?"

"Let it go, Han," Organa Solo said quietly, reaching up

to touch her husband's arm. "What's done is done. Karrde's right: it was Luke's decision to make. He's made it, and we'll just have to manage without him until he returns."

"If it helps, you can consider my service to be in exchange for his," Karrde said, his mouth still tight. "I'm sorry to have brought such bad news. I really thought you'd be more understanding."

Solo took a deep breath, exhaled it raggedly. "Yeah," he said. "Well . . . when are you heading out?"

"Immediately," Karrde said, crossing to Shada and offering her a hand. "Assuming my new assistant has no errands she has to attend to first."

"I'm ready whenever you are," Shada told him, ignoring the proffered hand and getting to her feet without assistance. "Assuming Councilor Organa Solo's bodyguards are finished sifting through my pack and climbing gear."

"They are waiting for you by the door," the Noghri beside Organa Solo said gravely.

"Fine," Karrde said, nodding to Organa Solo as he moved toward the entrance. "Thank you for your hospitality, Leia. I'll contact you if and when I find anything."

"Two other things, Karrde, before you go," Organa Solo said. "Three, actually. First: will you need a translator droid for your trip?"

"That's a good point," Karrde conceded. "The organization has several, of course, but none are aboard the *Wild Karrde* at the moment. It won't be too hard to pick one up along the way, though."

"That'll take extra time," Organa Solo said. "If you'd prefer, we could lend you Threepio."

Solo made a noise in the back of his throat. "Over his stripped gears, of course."

"That's a very generous offer." Karrde cocked an eyebrow. "It wouldn't have anything to do with the thought that you might be able to get an unbiased report of the trip out of him when we get back, would it?"

"Of course not," Organa Solo said, arching her own eyebrows slightly. "I'm hurt you'd even suggest such a thing."

"Forgive me," Karrde said. "In that case, I accept, with thanks."

"As Han suggests, we'll want a few minutes to talk with him first," Organa Solo said. "We can bring him over to the spaceport when we pick up those spaceship records from you. Second: I wasn't able to tell you this before, but under the circumstances it's something you may need to know. One of the other datacards that Devaronian found at Mount Tantiss was labeled 'The Hand of Thrawn.' "

Karrde nodded. "Yes, I'd heard."

Organa Solo's eyebrows lifted. "How did you—? Never mind; I don't want to know."

"My source and I thank you for your discretion," Karrde said. "There's something else *you* need to know, though. Before Mara went chasing after that unknown ship, we picked up a transmission from it, clearly directed at the *Errant Venture*. We haven't yet been able to decipher the message, but it definitely contained Thrawn's name. His *full* name, not just the core name 'Thrawn.' "

Solo frowned. "I didn't even know he had more name."

"Most people don't," Karrde agreed. "But Mara did. So did whoever was aboard that ship."

"What do you think it means?" Organa Solo asked.

"I don't know," Karrde said. "Maybe we'll have some answers when Skywalker and Mara get back. At any rate, I'll add a copy of that recording in with the others. You said there were three things?"

Organa Solo smiled. A smile that was shaded with tension, but a smile nonetheless. "May the Force be with you," she said quietly.

Almost involuntarily, Shada thought, Karrde smiled back. "And with you," he said. His eyes flicked to Solo and Calrissian. "With all of you," he added. "Good-bye."

"Nice speech you made back there," Shada commented as Karrde lifted the airspeeder off the Orowood Tower's pad and turned its nose toward the West Championne field where the *Wild Karrde* was waiting. "A little over-rehearsed, maybe, but not bad for all that."

"You're too kind," Karrde said, looking at her out of the corner of his eye. She was staring straight ahead at the nighttime Coruscant landscape, her face faintly illuminated by the glow from the instrument board. With better light, he decided, her expression would probably still have been impossible to read. "May I ask which part of the discourse sounded like a speech to you?"

"That bit about why it had to be Skywalker who went charging off to rescue Mara Jade," she said. "You weren't really expecting them to greet that news with shouts of joy, were you?"

Karrde shrugged. "I didn't expect them to be quite so upset about it, either," he said. "Of course, to be fair, I didn't know about Thrawn until this evening."

Shada shook her head. "It's hard to believe he survived."

"Agreed," Karrde said. "On the other hand, it's equally hard to believe the Empire would pull a dangerous stunt like this purely as a bluff. Either Thrawn's really back, or somebody somewhere has a Pure 23 hidden in his vest."

Shada seemed to ponder that. "Suppose this Thrawn is actually just a clone," she said. "Would it be as skilled as the original?"

"I suppose it would depend on how much of his tactical ability was innate and how much was learned." Karrde considered. "And whether or not they used a flash-teaching imprint taken from Thrawn's own mind, and how good the pattern was. I just don't know."

"Because if they have one clone of Thrawn, why not fifty?" Shada went on. "And if they have fifty clones of Thrawn, why not a hundred clones of that crazy Dark Jedi Joruus C'baoth, too?"

Karrde winced. That last possibility hadn't even occurred to him. "Why not, indeed?"

Shada didn't pick up on his rhetorical question, and a dark silence descended on the airspeeder. Karrde flew mechanically, not really seeing Coruscant's magnificent horizon-to-horizon lights.

Or rather, seeing the total destruction of those lights superimposed on his view. Thrawn had threatened such destruction the last time he attacked the planet. This time, he might actually do it.

They were descending toward the reassuring bulk of the *Wild Karrde* when Shada spoke again. "So who's this Jorj Car'das we're looking for?"

With an effort, Karrde shook off the vision of a circle of Star Destroyers closing in on him. "He's someone who used to be in the same business I am," he told her. "Probably still is, actually."

"But not a competitor?" she prompted.

"You were certainly paying attention in there," he complimented her. "Incidentally, just out of curiosity, where in the bedroom were you hiding? I didn't notice any place where anyone bigger than a Noghri could have been tucked away."

"I was on the floor, between the back bed and the wall," she said. "A gap like that always looks smaller than it really is. If Car'das wasn't a competitor, what was he?"

Karrde threw her a smile. "Persistent, too. I like that in my people."

"Delighted to hear it," she said. "If he wasn't a competitor, what was he?"

Ahead, the *Wild Karrde*'s hangar door was sliding open to receive them. "Ask me on the way into the Exocron system," he told her. "Assuming we make it that far."

Shada snorted under her breath. "So, what, you're asking me to risk my life on nothing but your word?"

"You don't have to come," Karrde said mildly. "If you want to leave right now, you're free to do so."

She looked away from him. "Thanks for the permission. I'll stay."

The airspeeder settled with a muffled *clunk* into its slot in the *Wild Karrde*'s hangar. "As you choose," Karrde said as he shut down the engines. "Out of curiosity, why exactly did you leave Mazzic?"

She twisted her shoulders out of the restraints. "Ask me on the way *out* of the Exocron system," she said sardonically. "Assuming we make it that far."

Without waiting for a response she popped her door and dropped feetfirst onto the deck. "I'm sure some of us will," Karrde murmured, watching as she threaded her way between the other vehicles toward the exit.

The only question was which ones.

CHAPTER

23

This time, the alarm didn't come in the middle of dessert. It came instead in the middle of the night.

Wedge jerked awake, hand flailing for a cutoff switch that wasn't where it was supposed to be. His knee twitched to the side, coming up short against something solid; and as the brief stab of pain jolted him fully awake, he remembered where he was. As per orders—and one of General Bel Iblis's hunches—he and the rest of Rogue Squadron were sleeping in their X-wings.

From the sound of the alarm still blaring away, the general's hunch had apparently paid off.

He slapped at the alarm switch, hitting it this time, and keyed the comm. "Antilles," he snapped.

"Full scramble," Commander Perris's voice snapped back. "We've got a panic call in from Bothawui."

"Terrific," Wedge muttered, hitting his engine prestart. Trust the Bothans to ruin a good night's sleep. "Okay, Rogues, you all heard the man. Let's get 'em in the air."

There was a chorus of acknowledgments, and the whine of engine prestarts began to fill their corner of the Di'tai'ni Diplomatic Landing Circle. Someone wearing a maintenance coverall—a Trintic, probably, though it was hard to tell in the dim light—was lumbering across the field toward the X-wings, gesturing frantically at this no doubt unauthorized noise. Wedge gestured him back and keyed in his repulsor-lifts. "What is it, another Clan Building riot?"

"Get a good grip on your helmet," Perris said grimly. "According to the Bothans, a Leresen attack force is on the way."

Wedge blinked. "A *Leresen* attack force?"

"That's what they say," the fighter coordinator confirmed. "A full-class war fleet, and don't ask me what their problem is."

"Pick one," Rogue Three grumbled. "There are so many reasons nowadays to hate the Bothans."

"Let's not sink to the lowest divisory here," Wedge admonished. The X-wings were all in the air now, forming up around Wedge as they pulled for space. "Perris, where's the general?"

"He's on his way up," Perris said. "C'taunmar and her A-wings are flying escort for his shuttle, just in case. We're going to be a few minutes behind you, though, and he said for you to go on ahead."

"And do what?" Rogue Five asked. "Bluff the Leresai until you get there?"

"Sure," Perris said dryly. "Unless, of course, the dazzling Rogue Squadron reputation routs them completely."

"Oh, yeah, right," Rogue Five came back, just as dryly. "Isn't it lucky for the Bothans that we and our dazzling reputation just happen to be only two systems away from them?"

Wedge frowned. It *was* lucky, now that he thought about it. Suspiciously lucky, in fact. "Perris, can you pull the original order that brought us here?" he asked.

"Already pulled," Perris said. "According to Coruscant, the Di'tai'ni government specifically asked for General Bel Iblis to mediate this dispute with their resident non-Tai'ni workers."

"Any idea whether the Di'tai'ni government owes favors or large amounts of money to the Bothan government?" Rogue Nine asked.

"That's a good question," Perris said thoughtfully. "A *very* good question, in fact."

"It's my old CorSec training," Rogue Nine said. "They taught us to always follow the money."

"Well, at the moment the money's irrelevant," Wedge said. They had reached the deeper darkness of space now, almost far enough out to make the jump to lightspeed. "We've been called in to defend a New Republic member from aggression, and that's what we're going to do."

"Good luck," Perris said. "We'll be there as soon as we can."

The panel beeped: the course was set. "Okay, Rogues," Wedge said. "Let's go."

The flight to Bothawui took a little longer than that panic-call run they'd taken a week ago to bail out the Sif'kries and their pommwomm-plant shipment. Somehow, though, it felt a lot shorter. Wedge found his mind bouncing back and forth between questions of imminent Leresen aggression, possible Bothan duplicity, general galactic tension, and what in blazes his squadron was doing in the middle of all of it.

And all too soon, they were there.

"Form up," he ordered as the rest of the X-wings came out of hyperspace around him. "Pick up your long-range scanners."

"I don't think," Rogue Two said tightly, "that that'll be necessary."

Wedge grimaced. "No," he agreed. "I guess not."

It was a Leresen attack force, all right. And for once it looked as if the Bothans hadn't been exaggerating. Spread out across the sky directly ahead of the incoming X-wings were six capital ships, all of alien design and manufacture but each nearly the size of a New Republic Assault Frigate. Another twenty smaller ships filled the gaps between them, with at least five squadrons of *starfighter*-class ships forming a defense perimeter around the whole group.

"Our reputation had better be *really* dazzling today," Rogue Twelve muttered.

"Cut the chatter," Wedge told him, studying the group. They were well outside Bothawui's planetary shield, beyond the range of any ground-based weapons the defenders were likely to have. He couldn't remember whether or not the Bothans had any orbital battle platforms circling their homeworld, but if they did none of them were on this side of the planet at the moment.

Which pretty much left Rogue Squadron all by itself out here. Twelve X-wings and a reputation.

He cleared his throat and keyed the comm for a broadband common frequency. "This is General Wedge Antilles and the New Republic unit Rogue Squadron calling the Leresen task force," he announced. "You're encroaching without permission on Bothan space. Please state your intentions."

"This matter is none of your concern, Rogue Squadron," a startlingly melodious voice responded. "It is a private dispute between the Leresen and Bothan governments."

Wedge glanced at his scanners. No sign yet of Bel Iblis and the *Peregrine*. "May I ask the nature of this dispute?"

"Death and resolution," the melodious voice said. "The death of two Leresai at the hands of the Bothans, and the Bothan refusal to resolve them."

Wedge grimaced, keying to the Rogues' private frequency. Clearly, there was a terminology problem here, some Leresen concept or phrase that wasn't translating properly to Basic. But even so, there was something else he wasn't getting here. "Any idea what he's talking about?" he asked.

"Hang on—I'm checking the records," Rogue Eleven said. "I've got a hunch . . . yep, here it is. There were two Leresai killed in that riot at the Combined Clans Building. Both shot, one of them before the mob broke into the building."

"Thanks," Wedge said, switching back. "Leresen commander, I understand your anger over your loss. What is it you want the Bothans to do in restitution?"

"Leresen law is very precise," the alien said. "Claw for claw, horn for horn, life for life. One guilty for himself, or ten innocent of his tribe."

A cold chill ran down Wedge's back. "What do you mean, ten innocent?" he asked carefully.

"The Bothans have refused to turn over to us members of the clans who killed two unarmed Leresai," the voice said evenly. "Two lives will thus be paid by twenty."

So mathematically precise, Wedge thought. But how exactly they thought they were going to pull off such a trick with all the Bothans huddling safe behind their planetary shield . . .

"Uh-oh," Rogue Four said quietly. "Vector three-six by four-one."

Wedge looked. Just coming into view around the planetary horizon behind and beneath them was a small space station.

"It's a low-orbit, zero-gee-crystal manufacturing plant," Rogue Four continued grimly. "Mon Cal design. If I recall correctly, the normal worker complement is fifteen to twenty-two."

Wedge bit back a curse, keying for private frequency. "Intercept course," he ordered. "I want us between the station and the Leresai."

He switched the comm back as he threw power to the drive. "I understand your anger and frustration with the Bothan government," he told the alien commander. "But you must understand that we can't simply stand by and permit you to kill innocent people. General Garm Bel Iblis will be here soon; perhaps he can mediate—"

"There can be no mediation," the Leresai said with a note of finality in his voice. "The law is the law, and its demands must be fulfilled. Neither you nor any others will stop us."

There was a click, and the conversation was over. "Maybe not," Wedge muttered under his breath as he keyed back to the Rogues' frequency. "But we can sure give it a good try. All right, Rogues, time to get serious. Lock S-foils into attack position." He reached for the control—

"No!" Rogue Nine snapped suddenly. "Don't lock S-foils."

Wedge paused, his hand hovering over the switch. "Why not?"

"I don't know," Rogue Nine said, his voice tight with

strain. "There's something wrong. I can't quite . . . but there's definitely something wrong."

"Rogue Leader?" Rogue Eight asked.

"Stand by," Wedge said, switching his comm to Rogue Nine's personal frequency. "Corran? What's up?"

"Like I said, I don't know," Rogue Nine repeated. "All I know is that I sensed danger when you ordered the S-foil lock. I'm running a diagnostic now, but so far I haven't found anything."

"Is this one of your—?" Wedge hesitated, not wanting to ask about the other's Jedi skills even on a secure channel.

"I think so, yes," Rogue Nine answered the question anyway.

Wedge glanced over at the Leresen task force. They hadn't moved from their position. Waiting patiently for their target to orbit over to them.

And clearly not expecting any trouble at all from Rogue Squadron . . .

He keyed back to the main Rogue frequency. "Everyone hold course," he ordered, turning his X-wing toward Rogue Nine. "You especially, Rogue Nine. I'm coming in close."

A minute later they were flying in tight parade-flight formation, the twin lasers on Wedge's starboard wingtips nearly brushing the underside of Rogue Nine's fuselage. "All right," he said, easing in another couple of centimeters. "You've got my starboard flank; I've got your portside. Give it a fast look and see if you can spot anything that shouldn't be there. If you don't, we'll switch sides."

"No need," Rogue Nine said, his voice taut. "There it is: a thin cylinder running vertically between the S-foils, just forward of the laser power line."

"You've got one, too," Wedge growled. Now that he knew where to look, the add-on was obvious. "Ten to one the whole squadron's been booby-trapped."

"All right, so we don't lock S-foils," Rogue Two said. "We can still fire, can't we?"

"I don't think we should try it," Wedge warned, frowning hard at the innocent-looking cylinder. "In fact—Corran, roll starboard a couple of degrees, will you?"

Rogue Nine's fuselage rolled away slowly from him. "I was right," Wedge bit out, thoroughly disgusted now. "The top of the cylinder's got two branches. One runs into the wing's servo line, the other looks like it feeds right into the laser power line. My guess is that either locking or firing will knock out the lasers. Or worse."

Rogue Twelve cursed feelingly. "Has to have been those two Leresai in the Di'tai'ni maintenance crew who were always hanging around," he said. "So what do we do, try to bluff them?"

Wedge looked out at the Leresen ships. They were on the move now, starting to form up around the manufacturing station speeding helplessly toward them. "No point," he said quietly. "They already know we're out of it."

And so they watched helplessly as the Leresai set about quickly, efficiently, and systematically demolishing the station. Taking their toll of twenty innocent lives in payment for the guilty.

By the time the rest of the *Peregrine* task force arrived, it was all over.

Or, perhaps more accurately, it had just begun.

"It's finally started," Leia announced bleakly as she locked the apartment door behind her and sank down onto the couch next to Han. "The shooting has finally started."

"Yeah, I heard," Han said grimly, radiating concern as he slipped his arm around her. "What's the Senate doing about it?"

"Mostly trying to figure out what they *can* do," Leia told him.

"What's to figure?" Han asked. "The Leresai slaughtered twenty-one Bothans, not to mention shredding a perfectly good space station. Can't Gavrisom just order the Leresen government brought up on charges?"

"I wish it were that easy," Leia said. "Unfortunately, it's not. Three of the High Councilors have already stated they'll vote against any such resolution, on the grounds that we haven't made similar reparation demands on the Bothan government over the destruction of Caamas."

"But they're not the same thing," Han insisted. "In fact, they're exactly opposite. The Leresai killed innocent people; the Caamas thing is about *not* punishing innocent people."

"We didn't demand that the Bothans punish the surviving guards who fired on the rioters, either," Leia reminded him.

She sensed his flash of gruff embarrassment. "Yeah," he growled. "Because of me."

Leia squeezed his knee reassuringly. "Not just because of you, dear," she said. "The Council's position is that the guards' action qualified as self-defense. Unfortunately, not everyone sees it that way."

Han sniffed. "Clan thinking."

"Yes, I know," Leia said. "It doesn't make sense to me, either, to hold a relative or clansman responsible for someone else's actions. But the reality is that family or clan accountability is a central tenet of a lot of cultures out there."

"Maybe," Han conceded. "But you still have to slap down the Leresai. If you don't, it'll just encourage everyone else who has a grudge against the Bothans."

"It already has," Leia said, a shiver running through her. "A dozen other governments have filed notice with the Senate that they're going to be presenting their own lists of demands against the Bothans."

"Or else?"

Leia shrugged. "That's the implied threat."

Han made a rude noise in the back of his throat. "You know what high esteem I hold the Bothans in, hon, but this is getting ridiculous. I suppose Fey'lya's screaming to Gavrisom for protection?"

"He doesn't have to," Leia told him. "The Diamala and Mon Calamari have announced they're sending ships to defend Bothawui against any further aggression."

Han whistled under his breath. "You're kidding. What kind of ships?"

"Big ones," Leia said. "Star Cruisers from the Mon

Cals, some *Nebula*- and *Endurance*-class warships from the Diamala. They say they're protecting the rights of the innocent. Others are saying they're just the latest victims of Bothan manipulation."

"That would be *my* vote," Han said. "Has Bel Iblis proved yet the Bothans were behind that phony Di'tai'ni mediation request?"

"No actual proof, but he personally has no doubts the whole thing was a ruse to keep him and the task force within easy striking distance of Bothawui," Leia said, grimacing. "Between that and the Leresai sabotage of Rogue Squadron's lasers—"

"What, they've admitted it?"

"Not only admitted it, they were proud of it," Leia said. "They consider it the height of honor to keep outsiders from getting hurt in one of their quarrels."

Han snorted. "I'll bet Wedge was real pleased about that."

"He and Garm are about ready to spit blaster bolts," Leia said. "Garm told Gavrisom flat-out that the New Republic is not going to play the lowest piece in anyone else's political games."

"That sounds like a direct quote," Han said. "Here, turn around a little." Pulling his arm from behind her neck, he started massaging her shoulders.

"It was," Leia said, feeling her taut muscles softening reluctantly under the pressure of Han's fingertips. "That feels good."

"Good—it's supposed to," Han said with a touch of forced humor. "You know, messing with someone like Bel Iblis wasn't a smart thing for the Bothans to do."

"I'm sure they know that," Leia agreed. "It shows how desperate they're getting."

She sensed the sideways movement as Han shook his head. "This is crazy, Leia. Don't any of them even care that Thrawn's back?"

"Of course not," Leia said. "Half of them don't believe a word of it—they think the Diamala cooked the whole thing up to scare everyone into letting the Bothans off the hook. The other half concede it may be true, but don't see any way the Empire could possibly be a threat to them anymore."

"Then they're all fools," Han growled. "Thrawn's got something up his sleeve. I'll bet the *Falcon* he does."

"I agree," Leia said with a sigh. "On the other hand, at this point he almost doesn't have to do anything at all. The New Republic's rapidly degenerating into a hundred different armed camps, all polarized around the Caamas issue."

"Can't the Caamasi do anything to stop it?" Han asked. "They can't want this."

"Of course they don't," Leia said. "But you have to understand that Caamas has become more an excuse than it is a genuine issue. Everyone says they have the interests of Caamas and justice at heart, but a lot of them are just using that as a battle cry while they settle old scores."

"Yeah," Han said sourly. "So what do we do?"

"Only one thing we can do," Leia said. "We have to take the excuse away from them; and that means getting the names of the actual Bothans that were involved and putting them on trial."

There was a subtle change in Han's emotions. "Yeah," he said. "Well . . . Karrde's trying."

Leia frowned. "Did you speak to him today? I thought he'd already left Coruscant."

"Far as I know he has," Han said. "No, I just put out the word with a few smuggling people I know that I want to talk to Mazzic."

"What about?"

"I just wanted to find out whether this Shada D'ukal really worked for him," Han told her. "And why exactly she left."

Leia smiled. "You wouldn't be worried about Karrde, would you?"

"No," Han protested. "Course not. He can take care of himself."

"It's all right, dear," she soothed him, patting his leg again. "I like him, too."

"I don't exactly *like* him," Han said, still protesting. "I mean, he can be a real pain in the neck sometimes."

"So could you, dear," Leia reminded him. "Still can, for that matter. You know, I sometimes think Karrde is sort of what you would have been if you hadn't joined the Rebellion."

"Maybe," Han said. "Except for the beard."

"Thank the Force for small favors," Leia said dryly. "Anyway, that's how I spent my day. Aside from chatting with smugglers, how did you spend yours?"

"Thinking, mostly," he said. "I was thinking it was about time we got away for a while."

"And a lovely thought that is," Leia murmured. "But Gavrisom would have a fit if I tried to leave right now."

"That might make it worthwhile all by itself," Han said. "I don't think I've ever seen Puffers throw a fit."

Leia smiled. "I appreciate the offer, Han, I really do. But you know we can't."

"You give up too easily," he reproved her casually. "I'll bet you I could arrange something."

Leia pulled away from the massage, turning to frown at him. There'd been another change in his emotions just then . . . "And assuming I took that bet," she asked suspiciously, "what else would you tell me you did today?"

He favored her with one of his innocent looks. "Me? Oh, nothing much. You taking the bet or not?"

"Out with it, Han," she said, putting some intimidation into her frown. "Where did you book us a flight to?"

As always, the intimidation bounced off without noticeable effect. "Nowhere important," he said, a smile now lurking beneath all the innocence. "I just thought we could take a little jaunt out to Kanchen sector. Pakrik Major, to be exact."

Leia searched her memory. She'd heard of Kanchen sector, and vaguely remembered Pakrik Major being the sector capital. But that was about it. "What's out there that we're interested in?" she asked.

"Absolutely nothing," Han assured her. "Well, I mean except for an annual sector conference that a New Republic official really ought to attend. You know—diplomatic courtesy and all that."

She sighed. "And what crisis are they going through that they need me to mediate?"

"That's the beauty of it," he said, grinning openly now. "There isn't one. Everything out there's real peaceful. We'd sit through a few boring meetings, then head off into the silence and relax."

"You assume there's silence somewhere nearby that we can get to."

"There is," Han said. "Pakrik Major's got a twin planet, Pakrik Minor, where they've got nothing but farms, a few resorts, and lots of undeveloped countryside."

This was sounding better and better. "Farms, you say?"

"Fruit and tallgrain, mostly," Han said with a nod. "And forests and mountains and all the silence you want. And no one here even has to know we're going."

Leia sighed. "Except Gavrisom," she said, feeling a twinge of regret. "And he'll never approve."

Han's grin turned smug. "Sure he will. Fact is, I called him this afternoon and set it all up. He loves the idea."

She blinked. "He *loves* the idea?"

"Well, maybe he doesn't *love* it, exactly," Han backpedaled. "But he's letting us go, and that's what's important. Right?"

"Right," Leia said, eyeing him. "You going to drop the other glove, or not?"

Han shrugged. "He didn't exactly say it outright," he admitted reluctantly, "but I got the feeling he wouldn't mind if the two of us sort of disappeared for a while."

"Even with Thrawn on the loose?"

Han made a face. "Especially with Thrawn on the loose."

Leia sighed, wrapping her arms around his neck. She should have guessed that there would be something like that behind it. Between the Bothan shooting controversy still clinging to Han and her own support of Lando's unsubstantiated claim about seeing Thrawn, the two of them had become political embarrassments. No wonder Gavrisom was jumping at the chance to get them out of the public eye for a while. "I'm sorry, Han," she apologized. "I always ask that one question too many, don't I?"

"It's okay, hon," he said, squeezing her tightly. "We don't have to let them take the shine off this, you know. It was *our* idea to take a vacation, no matter what they think it is."

Leia smiled tightly. " 'You can't throw me out; I quit,' " she quoted the old joke.

"Something like that," he said. "Anyway, I talked to Chewie, and there's no problem with keeping the kids on Kashyyyk a little longer. It'll be some time just for the two of us."

Leia smiled tightly into his neck. "You know, that's almost exactly what I told myself when Gavrisom sent us to Bothawui," she said. "You saw how well *that* turned out."

"Well, this time it's going to work," Han said positively. "No Bothans, no riots, no one shooting at us. Guaranteed."

"I'll hold you to that," she warned, pulling out of the hug for a quick kiss. "When do we leave?"

"As soon as you're packed," he said, squeezing her arm. "And hurry up—*I've* been packed for hours."

"Yes, sir," Leia said, mock-seriously, as she stood up and headed for their bedroom. Some quiet, peaceful time away from trouble and controversy. Yes, it was exactly what she needed.

The tallgrain farms of Pakrik Minor. She could hardly wait.

CHAPTER

24

The scouts had spent the past twenty-eight hours sweeping the system; and when they returned they brought the report Admiral Pellaeon had been expecting. Except for the *Chimaera* itself, the Pesitiin system was about as deserted as a region of space could be.

"Offhand, sir, I'd say he turned down your offer," Captain Ardiff said, coming up beside Pellaeon on the Star Destroyer's command walkway.

"Perhaps," Pellaeon said, gazing out the viewport at the stars. "It's also possible that my suggested timetable was a little optimistic. General Bel Iblis may be having difficulty convincing the New Republic hierarchy that it would be to their benefit to talk to me."

"Or else he's having trouble putting together a big enough combat force to take on an Imperial Star Destroyer," Ardiff said ominously. "It strikes me that this could be a giant rachnid's web we're comfortably settling ourselves into the middle of."

"Relax, Captain," Pellaeon soothed the younger man. For all his budding military capability, Ardiff had a tendency to ramble over his own tongue when he was feeling nervous. "Bel Iblis is a man of honor. He wouldn't betray my invitation that way."

"I seem to recall that he was also once a man of extreme

ambition," Ardiff countered. "And at the moment he looks to be getting lost among the swarm of other generals and admirals infesting the New Republic military. It could easily occur to an ambitious man that capturing you would dramatically increase his visibility."

Pellaeon smiled. "I'd like to believe that after all these years I could still be such a valuable prize," he said. "But I hardly think that to be the case."

"You can be as modest as you want, Admiral," Ardiff said, gazing uneasily out at the starlit sky. "But right now you're about the only thing that's holding the Empire together."

Pellaeon gazed out at the stars. "Or the only chance we have of survival," he added quietly.

"However you want to think about it, sir," Ardiff said, a note of asperity creeping into his voice. "The point remains that Colonel Vermel went out to deliver your message and never returned. Why?"

"I don't know," Pellaeon had to concede. "I take it you have a theory?"

"Yes, sir, the same theory I've had since before we left Yaga Minor," Ardiff said. "I think Vermel learned something, either from Bel Iblis directly or else he overheard something someone else said. That whatever he heard made it necessary for Bel Iblis to lock him up where he couldn't communicate with you. That at best we're wasting our time, and that at worst we're walking into a trap."

"It's still a worthwhile gamble, Captain," Pellaeon said quietly. "We'll give Bel Iblis a few days to show up. After that—"

"Admiral Pellaeon?" the sensor officer called from the starboard crew pit. "Incoming ships, sir. Looks like eight of them, coming in on vector one-six-four by fifty-three."

Pellaeon felt his throat tighten. "Identification?" he asked, trying to keep his voice calm.

"Four are Corellian gunships," another voice called. "The big one's a *Kaloth* battlecruiser—looks like it's been heavily modified. Three are Telgorn *Pacifier*-class assault boats. IDs . . . inconclusive."

"What do you mean, inconclusive?" Ardiff demanded.

"Their IDs don't match anything in the registry," the officer said. "I'm running an overlay check to see if I can unravel them."

"Disguised ships," Ardiff said darkly.

"Smugglers use ID overlays, too," Pellaeon reminded him. "So do pirates and some mercenary groups."

"I know that, sir," Ardiff said. "I also know that there's precious little in this system any of those groups could possibly want."

"A point," Pellaeon admitted. "Communications officer, transmit our identification and ask for theirs."

"Identification transmitted," the other said. "No response."

"Incoming ships have changed course," the sensor officer called. "Now on intercept vector with the *Chimaera*."

Ardiff hissed tensely between his teeth. "Steady, Captain," Pellaeon advised him. "Lieutenant, get me a full sensor scan of the incoming ships. Weapons capabilities and hull markings in particular."

"Acknowledged, sir—"

"Admiral!" another voice cut him off. "Incoming ships have reconfigured into attack formation."

"I think, Admiral," Ardiff said, his voice hard, "that we have Bel Iblis's answer."

Pellaeon closed his left hand into a fist at his side. "Any hull markings, Lieutenant?" he called.

"It's coming up now, sir . . . yes, sir, there are. The gunships are carrying Corellian Defense Force insignia. The others . . . the same, sir."

"Thank you," Pellaeon murmured. He could feel Ardiff's eyes on him, and the heat of the other's anger and bitter vindication. "Captain, you'd best prepare the *Chimaera* for combat."

"Yes, sir." Ardiff half turned toward the portside crew pit. "All pilots to their fighters," he ordered. "Ready to launch on my command. Deflector screens powered up; all turbolasers energized and ready."

"And tractor beams," Pellaeon added quietly.

Ardiff threw him a puzzled glance. "Sir?"

"We may want to bring in one or more of the ships," Pellaeon explained. "Or some of the battle debris."

Ardiff's lip twitched. "Yes, sir. All tractor beams, activate."

Pellaeon took a few steps closer to the forward viewport, moving away from the heightened buzz of activity from the crew pits and aft bridge. Could that really be Bel Iblis out there, blazing toward the *Chimaera* in full battle formation?

No. Ridiculous. He'd never met Bel Iblis in person, but everything he'd ever read about the man indicated a strong sense of honor and dignity. A man like that wouldn't pull what was essentially a cowardly sneak attack, not in response to an honest request for parley. Even in Bel Iblis's losing battles against Grand Admiral Thrawn he'd maintained that same dignity.

His battles against Thrawn . . .

Pellaeon smiled tightly. Yes, there it was. A way, perhaps, to find out whether or not that was really Bel Iblis leading that motley attack force out there.

There was a movement of air at his side. "It's possible he's just being cautious," Ardiff said, the words coming out with obvious reluctance. "The shield overlap that comes from an attack formation like that makes it useful for defense, as well. And he may simply not want to transmit his identity until he's closer."

Pellaeon eyed the young captain with mild surprise. "You impress me, Captain," he said. "One of the most important attributes of a good commander is the ability to think beyond his own expectations."

"I want to be fair, sir," Ardiff said stiffly. "But not at the risk of your ship. Do you want me to launch TIEs or Preybirds?"

"Not yet," Pellaeon said, looking back out the viewport. The incoming ships were visible now, tiny specks rapidly growing larger. "Whatever happens here, I want it clear that we did nothing to provoke hostilities."

For a long minute they stood together in silence and waited. The incoming ships grew steadily larger . . .

And suddenly they were speeding low across the *Chimaera*, raking the Star Destroyer's upper surface with a blaze of turbolaser fire. They pulled up, heading directly for the bridge—someone in one of the crew pits behind Pellaeon yelped with surprise or fear—

And then they were gone, branching to either side around the command superstructure and pulling for the safety of distance.

Ardiff let out a hissing breath. "I think that proves their intentions, Admiral," he said, his earlier nervousness vanished into an icy professionalism. "Request permission to attack."

"Permission granted," Pellaeon said. "But with turbolasers only."

Ardiff gave him a sharp look. "No fighters?"

"Not yet," Pellaeon told him, searching the sky for the attackers. Probably still making their way around after that mad plunge aft. "I have something else planned for the Preybirds."

Ardiff threw a quick glance around them. "Admiral, I respectfully urge you to reconsider," he said, his voice barely loud enough for Pellaeon to hear. "That battlecruiser is packing some serious weaponry. It went by too fast this time to do any major damage, but that kind of skittishness isn't likely to last. If we don't use the fighters to keep them at arm's length we'll just be begging for trouble."

"I understand your concerns, Captain," Pellaeon told him. The attackers had come around into sight now, distant specks swinging around almost leisurely for their second pass. "But I have my reasons. Order turbolaser batteries to stand ready."

He could see Ardiff's throat working, but the captain merely gave him a curt nod. "Turbolaser crews: stand ready," he called harshly.

"Trust me, Captain," Pellaeon murmured, trying hard not to smile as his mind suddenly flashed back ten years. Then, he'd been the earnest captain standing on this same deck, trying in the most diplomatic way possible to make his superior see sense in the middle of a tense combat situation. He'd had much more experience than Ardiff, of course, but that had merely made his frustrations run that much deeper as he stood by helplessly and watched as the *Chimaera* drove hard into certain disaster.

And yet Thrawn had never reprimanded him for his impertinence or lack of understanding. He had merely continued calmly with his plans, allowing the results to speak for themselves.

Pellaeon could only hope that the results of this plan would be even half so eloquent.

The attackers had completed their circling and turned toward the *Chimaera*. "Here they come," the sensor officer called. "Looks like they're going to do a crossways run this time."

"They're worried about running into the command superstructure," Pellaeon commented. "That must mean one or more of their ships almost couldn't pull out in time on that last run."

"Or else they're simply going for variety," Ardiff growled, frustration bubbling beneath the words.

Again the memories flickered, and again Pellaeon carefully suppressed his smile. Right now, in the heat of combat, a smile would definitely not be something Ardiff would understand. "Stand by turbolasers," he said. "Fire at will."

The attackers swept toward them, weapons blazing. The *Chimaera*'s turbolasers answered, and for a few seconds the sky outside the bridge became a dazzling display of green and red fire.

And then the attackers were gone, clawing again for distance, and the Star Destroyer's awesome weaponry fell silent. "Damage?" Pellaeon called.

"Minor damage only," the report came from the starboard crew pit. "Three turbolaser tracking systems in Quadrant One have been knocked out, and there are some minimal hull breaches along the forward ridgeline. They've been sealed off."

"They're trying to knock out all the turbolasers in

Quadrant One," Ardiff muttered. "Once they do that, that battlecruiser can just sit off the bow and blast away at the hull."

"That does seem to be their intention," Pellaeon agreed. "Damage to the enemy?"

"Unknown, but probably minimal," the sensor officer reported. "That overlapping shield configuration of theirs is pretty strong—not easy to punch through."

"But it's primarily ray-shielding?" Pellaeon asked.

"Yes, sir, at least on the battlecruiser," the officer confirmed. "The gunships also have some minimal particle shielding."

"We're not going to have much chance of hitting them with proton torpedoes, if that's what you're thinking," Ardiff warned. "In close, their angular speed is too high for the torpedoes to track; and at any real distance, they'll have all the time they need to target and destroy them."

"I understand the tactics involved," Pellaeon said mildly. "Let's see if we can rewrite the script a bit. Colonel Bas, order one Preybird squadron to launch on my command. Their attack vector . . ."

He paused, following the attackers with his eyes. They had reached the farthest point of their curve now, and were starting to swing back around for another pass. "Attack vector two-three by seven," he decided. "They're to stay on that vector in tight parade-flight formation until otherwise ordered."

He could feel Ardiff's eyes on him. "Parade-flight formation, sir?" the captain echoed, clearly not believing his ears.

"The shield overlap will help protect them from enemy fire," Pellaeon explained.

"Not well enough," Ardiff countered. "Not against a *Kaloth* battlecruiser at close-in range."

"With any luck, they won't need to get that close," Pellaeon said. Just as with their last two runs, he saw, the attackers were coming straight in. Perfect. "Colonel: launch fighter squadron."

"Acknowledged," Colonel Bas said. "Fighters launched."

Pellaeon turned back to the viewport. A few seconds later the Preybirds appeared around the edge of the hull, a clump of close-formation drive trails arrowing straight out toward the incoming attackers. "Stand by Number Eight proton torpedo cluster," he called. "All fifteen torpedoes to fire in three-by-five sequence along vector two-three by seven."

The background hum in the bridge suddenly seemed to falter. "Sir?" the fire-control officer asked hesitantly. "That's the same vector—"

"As the Preybirds," Pellaeon finished for him. "Yes, I know, Lieutenant. You have your orders."

"Yes, sir."

"Fire torpedoes on my command only," Pellaeon continued, watching the Preybirds streaking toward the incoming attackers. Almost there . . . "Colonel Bas, order the Preybirds to perform a full-speed saggery-blossom maneuver on my command. Lieutenant: fire proton torpedoes."

"Torpedoes fired," the other confirmed; and from beneath the *Chimaera*'s bow a tight column of torpedo trails appeared, five groups of three torpedoes each, driving hard directly toward the now-distant drive trails of the Preybirds.

Abruptly Ardiff gave a small snort of understanding. "Ah. Of course."

"Indeed," Pellaeon agreed, watching the departing torpedoes closely, painfully aware of the sliced-second timing that was required. Almost there . . . "Colonel Bas . . . *now*."

For a single agonizing heartbeat nothing happened. Then, with parade-flight precision, the Preybirds broke out of their clustered formation. Turning sharply out and away from their original vector, they formed a brief stylized saggery flower shape as they curved back around toward the *Chimaera*. The enemy turbolaser fire that had been pounding away at their overlapped shields split in response, swinging outward to track each of the individual fighters—

And with a flash of brilliant light the first three proton

torpedoes roared through the undefended center area, blazed their way directly between the two gunships in the lead, and impacted squarely against the bow of the battlecruiser.

Even from the *Chimaera*'s distance the consternation among the attacking ships was instantly apparent. Instantly apparent, and utterly useless. Even as the bunched ships clawed desperately to get some distance between them, the second torpedo group hit, blowing out an impressive cloud of shattered hullmetal and transparisteel. The third group must have run into a piece of the debris from that second blast; all three torpedoes blew prematurely, sending one of the dodging gunships corkscrewing violently into the night with a ruptured hull.

By the time the last three torpedoes had spent their fury, the battle was over. The battlecruiser had been reduced to rubble, and the other ships were running for their lives.

"Brilliantly done, Admiral," Ardiff said, admiration and embarrassment mixing in his voice. "I'm, ah, sorry if I sounded—"

"Understood, Captain," Pellaeon assured him. "Believe it or not, I've been in your place myself."

"Thank you, sir." Ardiff gestured toward the glowing cloud of burning wreckage. "Shall I send a team to retrieve some of the debris? It might be able to tell us who that was."

"Go ahead and send a team," Pellaeon said. "But I can tell you right now that it wasn't General Bel Iblis."

"Really," Ardiff said, his eyes on Pellaeon as he gestured his order to the crew pit. Not questioning, this time, but honestly curious. "How can you be that sure?"

"First things first," Pellaeon said. "While the team is retrieving the debris, I want you to run the record of the battle through the Predictor. It's still on-line, isn't it?"

"Yes, sir," Ardiff said, smiling tightly with understanding. "That's why you let them do that second run against us, isn't it? So that there would be enough data for the Predictor to analyze."

"Exactly," Pellaeon said. "It didn't work very well at figuring out the tactics of a given enemy; let's see if it can work in reverse to figure out the enemy from the given tactics. If we're lucky, it may be able to give us at least a hint of who out there might favor this particular combat style."

"And you're sure it wasn't Bel Iblis?"

Pellaeon looked out at the glowing cloud. "Have you ever heard of an A-wing slash, Captain?"

"I don't think so, sir."

"It's a New Republic battle technique," Pellaeon said, turning back to face him. "It requires highly precise timing, which is why it's hardly ever used. A group of starfighters, X-wings usually, heads directly toward the defense line guarding a capital ship. At the last second the X-wings disengage, veering around and away."

"Rather like what our Preybirds just did."

"Exactly as our Preybirds just did," Pellaeon nodded. "The defenders' natural reaction, of course, is to assume the attackers are attempting a flanking maneuver and veer to follow and engage. But what they don't realize until it's too late is that a group of A-wings has been flying directly behind the X-wings, hidden by the X-wings themselves and their drive glow. By the time they spot that second wave, they're too far out of line to block them, and the A-wings have a clear run through to the now undefended ship."

"Clever enough," Ardiff said. "I can see why you wouldn't want to use it very often, though it certainly worked well enough with proton torpedoes playing the A-wings' role. What does this have to do with Bel Iblis?"

Pellaeon smiled tightly. "I was at the battle where he invented it."

Ardiff blinked in surprise; and then he too smiled. "In other words, it's not a tactic he'd be fooled by?"

"Not a chance in the galaxy," Pellaeon agreed. "But with those Corellian markings, I'd say someone worked very hard to make us think it was him."

Ardiff sobered. "Someone from the Empire?"

"Or someone from the New Republic," Pellaeon said. "We know there are factions on our side who don't want peace. I imagine they have their counterparts on the other."

"Probably," Ardiff said. "So what do we do now?"

"Whoever ordered that attack wanted us to think Bel

Iblis was behind it," Pellaeon said. "The small size of the force, plus the quick and unashamed disengagement, implies he didn't really care whether or not he actually inflicted any damage. His purpose, therefore, must have been to drive us away from here before Bel Iblis could arrive."

"And so we stay?"

"So we stay," Pellaeon agreed. "At least awhile."

"Yes, sir." Ardiff pursed his lips. "You realize, of course, that our unknown opponent may not give up this easily. He may attack again."

Pellaeon turned again to look out at the fiery debris. "Let him try."

To Be Concluded

TIMOTHY ZAHN is one of science fiction's most popular voices, known for his ability to tell very human stories against a well-researched background of future science and technology. He won the Hugo Award for his novella *Cascade Point* and is the author of sixteen science fiction novels, including the bestselling *Star Wars* trilogy: *Heir to the Empire, Dark Force Rising,* and *The Last Command;* the novels *Conqueror's Pride, Conqueror's Heritage,* and *Conqueror's Legacy;* and three collections of short fiction. Timothy Zahn lives in Oregon.

The World of
STAR WARS Novels

In May 1991, *Star Wars* caused a sensation in the publishing industry with the Bantam Spectra release of Timothy Zahn's novel *Heir to the Empire*. For the first time, Lucasfilm Ltd. had authorized new novels that *continued* the famous story told in George Lucas's three blockbuster motion pictures: *Star Wars*, *The Empire Strikes Back*, and *Return of the Jedi*. Reader reaction was immediate and tumultuous: *Heir* reached #1 on the *New York Times* bestseller list and demonstrated that *Star Wars* lovers were eager for exciting new stories set in this universe, written by leading science fiction authors who shared their passion. Since then, each Bantam *Star Wars* novel has been an instant national bestseller.

Lucasfilm and Bantam decided that future novels in the series would be interconnected: that is, events in one novel would have consequences in the others. You might say that each Bantam *Star Wars* novel, enjoyable on its own, is also part of a much larger tale.

Here is a special look at Bantam's *Star Wars* books, along with excerpts from the more recent novels. Each one is available now wherever Bantam Books are sold.

The Han Solo Trilogy:
THE PARADISE SNARE
THE HUTT GAMBIT
REBEL DAWN
by A. C. Crispin
Setting: Before *Star Wars: A New Hope*

What was Han Solo like before we met him in the first STAR WARS movie? This trilogy answers that tantalizing question, filling in lots of historical lore about our favorite swashbuckling hero and thrilling us with adventures of the brash young pilot that we never knew he'd experienced. As the trilogy begins, the young Han makes a life-changing decision: to escape from the clutches of Garris Shrike, head of the trading "clan" who has brutalized Han while taking advantage of his piloting abilities. Here's a tense early scene from The Paradise Snare *featuring Han, Shrike, and Dewlanna, a Wookiee who is Han's only friend in this horrible situation:*

"I've had it with you, Solo. I've been lenient with you so far, because you're a blasted good swoop pilot and all that prize money came in handy, but my patience is ended." Shrike ceremoniously pushed up the sleeves of his bedizened uniform, then balled his hands into fists. The galley's artificial lighting made the blood-jewel ring glitter dull silver. "Let's see what a few days of fighting off Devaronian blood-poisoning does for your attitude—along with maybe a few broken bones. I'm doing this for your own good, boy. Someday you'll thank me."

Han gulped with terror as Shrike started toward him. He'd lashed out at the trader captain once before, two years ago, when he'd been feeling cocky after winning the gladiatorial Free-For-All on Jubilar—and had been instantly sorry. The speed and strength of Garris's returning blow had snapped his head back and split both lips so thoroughly that Dewlanna had had to feed him mush for a week until they healed.

With a snarl, Dewlanna stepped forward. Shrike's hand dropped to his blaster. "You stay out of this, old Wookiee," he snapped in a voice nearly as harsh as Dewlanna's. "Your cooking isn't *that* good."

Han had already grabbed his friend's furry arm and was forcibly holding her back. "Dewlanna, no!"

She shook off his hold as easily as she would have waved off an annoying insect and roared at Shrike. The captain drew his blaster, and chaos erupted.

"Noooo!" Han screamed, and leaped forward, his foot lashing out in an old street-fighting technique. His instep impacted solidly with Shrike's breastbone. The captain's breath went out in a great *houf!* and he went over backward. Han hit the deck and rolled. A tingler bolt sizzled past his ear.

"Larrad!" wheezed the captain as Dewlanna started toward him.

Shrike's brother drew his blaster and pointed it at the Wookiee. "Stop, Dewlanna!"

His words had no more effect than Han's. Dewlanna's

blood was up— she was in full Wookiee battle rage. With a roar that deafened the combatants, she grabbed Larrad's wrist and yanked, spinning him around and snapping him in a terrible parody of a child's "snap the whip" game. Han heard a *crunch,* mixed with several *pops* as tendons and ligaments gave way. Larrad Shrike shrieked, a high, shrill noise that carried such pain that the Corellian youth's arm ached in sympathy.

Grabbing the blaster from his belt, Han snapped off a shot at the Elomin who was leaping forward, tingler ready and aimed at Dewlanna's midsection. Brafid howled, dropping his weapon. Han was amazed that he'd managed to hit him, but he didn't have long to wonder about the accuracy of his aim.

Shrike was staggering to his feet, blaster in hand, aimed squarely at Han's head. "Larrad?" he yelled at the writhing heap of agony that was his brother. Larrad did not reply.

Shrike cocked the blaster and stepped even closer to Han. "Stop it, Dewlanna!" the captain snarled at the Wookiee. "Or your buddy Solo dies!"

Han dropped his blaster and put his hands up in a gesture of surrender.

Dewlanna stopped in her tracks, growling softly.

Shrike leveled the blaster, and his finger tightened on the trigger. Pure malevolent hatred was etched upon his features, and then he smiled, pale blue eyes glittering with ruthless joy. "For insubordination and striking your captain," he announced, "I sentence you to death, Solo. May you rot in all the hells there ever were."

SHADOWS OF THE EMPIRE
by Steve Perry
Setting: Between *The Empire Strikes Back* and *Return of the Jedi*

Here is a very special STAR WARS story dealing with Black Sun, a galaxy-spanning criminal organization that is masterminded by one of the most interesting villains in the STAR WARS universe: Xizor, dark prince of the Falleen. Xizor's chief rival for the favor of Emperor Palpatine is none other than Darth Vader himself—alive and well, and a major character in this story, since it is set during the events of the STAR WARS *film trilogy.*

In the opening prologue, we revisit a familiar scene from The Empire Strikes Back, *and are introduced to our marvelous new bad guy:*

He looks like a walking corpse, Xizor thought. *Like a mummified body dead a thousand years. Amazing he is still alive, much less the most powerful man in the galaxy. He isn't even that old; it is more as if something is slowly eating him.*

Xizor stood four meters away from the Emperor, watching as the man who had long ago been Senator Palpatine moved to stand in the holocam field. He imagined he could smell the decay in the Emperor's worn body. Likely that was just some trick of the recycled air, run through dozens of filters to ensure that there was no chance of any poison gas being introduced into it. Filtered the life out of it, perhaps, giving it that dead smell.

The viewer on the other end of the holo-link would see a close-up of the Emperor's head and shoulders, of an age-ravaged face shrouded in the cowl of his dark zeyd-cloth robe. The man on the other end of the transmission, light-years away, would not see Xizor, though Xizor would be able to see him. It was a measure of the Emperor's trust that Xizor was allowed to be here while the conversation took place.

The man on the other end of the transmission—if he could still be called that—

The air swirled inside the Imperial chamber in front of the Emperor, coalesced, and blossomed into the image of a figure down on one knee. A caped humanoid biped dressed in jet black, face hidden under a full helmet and breathing mask:

Darth Vader.

Vader spoke: "What is thy bidding, my master?"

If Xizor could have hurled a power bolt through time and space to strike Vader dead, he would have done it without blinking. Wishful thinking: Vader was too powerful to attack directly.

"There is a great disturbance in the Force," the Emperor said.

"I have felt it," Vader said.

"We have a new enemy. Luke Skywalker."

Skywalker? That had been Vader's name, a long time ago. Who was this person with the same name, someone so powerful as to be worth a conversation between the Emperor and his most loathsome creation? More importantly, why had Xizor's agents not uncovered this before now? Xizor's ire was instant—but cold. No sign of his surprise or anger would show on his imperturbable features. The Falleen did not allow their emotions to burst forth as did many of the inferior species; no, the Falleen ancestry was not fur but scales, not mammalian but reptilian. Not wild but coolly calculating. Such was much better. Much safer.

"Yes, my master," Vader continued.

"He could destroy us," the Emperor said.

Xizor's attention was riveted upon the Emperor and the holographic image of Vader kneeling on the deck of a ship far away. Here was interesting news indeed. Something the Emperor perceived as a danger to himself? Something the Emperor feared?

"He's just a boy," Vader said. "Obi-Wan can no longer help him."

Obi-Wan. That name Xizor knew. He was among the last of the Jedi Knights, a general. But he'd been dead for decades, hadn't he?

Apparently Xizor's information was wrong if Obi-Wan had been helping someone who was still a boy. His agents were going to be sorry.

The Bounty Hunter Wars
Book 1: THe MANDALORIAN ARMOR
by K. W. Jeter
Setting: During *Return of the Jedi*

The most cunning and dangerous bounty hunter in the universe, Boba Fett, struggles to fight Prince Xizor and defeat his evil plan to smash the power of the bounty hunters' guild.

In the excerpt that follows, he is saved by Dengar Manaroo.

"What happened?"

He could almost have laughed, if any twitch of his raw muscles hadn't hurt so much, pushing him toward unconscious oblivion. Shouldn't hallucinations know these things?

"Sarlacc . . . swallowed me." The words seemed to come of their own volition. "I killed it . . . blew it up. . . ."

He heard another voice, a female's. "He's dying."

The man's voice spoke again, in hushed tones. "Manaroo—do you know who this is?"

"I don't care. Help me get him inside." The female's shadow fell across him.

Suddenly he felt himself rising, dirt and grit falling from his mangled form. The next sensation was that of being thrown across someone's broad shoulder, an arm encircling his waist to steady him. A sense of shame filled the dying man. There had been so many times when he had faced his own extinction—painful or otherwise—the contemplation of his death, and the dismissal of it as being of no concern, had given him strength. And now some weak part of him had summoned up this pitiful fantasy of rescue. *Better to die,* he thought, *than to fear dying.*

"Hang on," came the hallucinated voice. "I'll get you someplace safe."

The man called Boba Fett felt the jostle of the other's footsteps, the motion of being carried across the stony ground. For a moment his vision cleared, the blindness dissipating enough that he could see his own hand flopping limp and disjointed, leaving a trail of splattered blood on the sand. . . .

That was when he knew that what he saw and felt was real. And that he was still alive.

THE TRUCE AT BAKURA
by Kathy Tyers
Setting: Immediately after *Return of the Jedi*

The day after his climactic battle with Emperor Palpatine and the sacrifice of his father, Darth Vader, who died saving his life, Luke Skywalker helps recover an Imperial drone ship bearing a startling message in-

tended for the Emperor. It is a distress signal from the far-off Imperial outpost of Bakura, which is under attack by an alien invasion force, the Ssi-ruuk. Leia sees a rescue mission as an opportunity to achieve a diplomatic victory for the Rebel Alliance, even if it means fighting alongside former Imperials. But Luke receives a vision from Obi-Wan Kenobi revealing that the stakes are even higher: the invasion at Bakura threatens everything the Rebels have won at such great cost.

STAR WARS: X-WING
by Michael A. Stackpole
ROGUE SQUADRON
WEDGE'S GAMBLE
THE KRYTOS TRAP
THE BACTA WAR

WRAITH SQUADRON
by Aaron Allston
Setting: Three years after *Return of the Jedi*

Inspired by X-wing, the bestselling computer game from LucasArts Entertainment Co., this exciting series chronicles the further adventures of the most feared and fearless fighting force in the galaxy. A new generation of X-wing pilots, led by Commander Wedge Antilles, is combating the remnunts of the Empire still left after the events of the STAR WARS movies. Here are novels full of explosive space action, nonstop adventure, and the special brand of wonder known as STAR WARS.

In this scene from the opening of Wraith Squadron, Wedge Antilles must enter into a devil's bargain in order to create a controversial new unit:

"You'll remember when I reorganized Rogue Squadron a few years back, I took the best pilots I could transfer or steal . . . but when it came down to choosing between pilots of equal skill, I always chose the one who had useful ground-based skills as well."

"Yes. You wanted pilots who could also be commandos."

"I got them. And they got quite a workout as commandos, especially in the liberation of Coruscant from the Empire and then of Thyferra from Ysanne Isard."

Ackbar managed to smile again. "You have certainly justified our faith in your experiment. Rogue Squadron performed magnificently."

"Thank you. Speaking for my men and women, I have to agree. But I'd originally thought that Rogue Squadron would be used opportunistically: a strike mission would reveal a ground-based weakness, and we'd have the training and supplies to go down and perform the necessary ground mission. The way it turned out, we keep landing full-fledged commando missions. So I think we need another commando X-wing squadron, one where we choose pilots so as to have a full range of intrusion and subversion skills. Rogue Squadron was designed as a fighter unit first, commando unit second; this time, I want to go the other way around."

Admiral Ackbar's expression, so far as Wedge could read it, was dubious. "Historically, we've had few problems coordinating the efforts of commandos on the ground and fighter pilots for aerial support."

"I don't agree. Commandos can communicate strike locations to the pilots, but the pilots still won't have the familiarity with these locations that the intrusion team will. Commandos who've had their extraction plans busted might want to seize enemy spacecraft to escape; the way things stand, they can't count on having enough pilots to make that escape, while commando-trained pilots could. Normal pilots follow orders and conform themselves to standard tactics—and should! But a commando X-wing unit might develop new tactics. New ways of mounting even ordinary raids and pursuits. New ways of anticipating assaults and ambushes."

Ackbar abruptly leaned back from him, his eyes half closing; it looked to Wedge like a frown of concentration. "What made you say that?"

"Thinking about the subject of the long flight home, and during the time we were garrisoned on Thyferra before that," Wedge said. "Even though the garrison assignment was cut short from the two months originally planned, it still gave me plenty of time to think."

"You haven't heard any news?"

"No, sir. About what?"

Ackbar shook his head. "Please go on."

"Well, that's actually about it. I can dress it up in a formal report for you. But one thing I think is important—I can give you a unit like this for free."

Ackbar snorted, the sound emerging as a series of rubbery pops. "Can you now?"

"Yes, sir. First, the replacement Rogue Squadron is being disbanded, its pilots and X-wings being returned to their original units. Correct?"

"Correct."

"So you'll be issuing a dozen new X-wings to us, won't you? To the original Rogue Squadron."

"Why would we? Your X-wings are in functional shape, are they not?"

"Well, yes, but they're not New Republic property any longer. They were sold to my second-in-command, Tycho Celchu, at the start of our operation against Thyferra. They're his personal property, held in trust for all of us, until and unless he decides to vest ownership in their pilots."

"How uncharitable of you. You could donate their use to the New Republic. I believe one of your pilots has been using his personal X-wing all along."

"Yes, sir. Lieutenant Horn. And Tycho would be glad to loan his snubfighters to the New Republic, for the use of Rogue Squadron, if . . ."

"If the next dozen X-wings out of the factories are assigned to your new commando squadron."

"Yes, sir."

"That's blackmail. It's unbecoming."

"Most unconventional tactics are unbecoming until they succeed, Admiral. I direct your attention to the planet Thyferra . . ."

"Be quiet. There's still the matter of pilots. Fresh out of the Academy, their training costing hundreds of thousands of credits apiece. That is not 'free.' "

"No, sir. I don't want new pilots. I want experienced ones."

"Which is an even more significant expense."

"No, sir, not with these pilots. I want pilots no one else wants. Washouts. Pilots staring court-martial in the face. Troublemakers and screwups."

Ackbar stared back as if he couldn't believe his tympanic membranes. "In the name of the Force, Commander, *why*?"

"Well, some of them, of course, will be irredeemable. I'll wash them out, too. Some of them will be good men and women who've screwed up one time too many, who know their careers are dead but would give anything for one more chance . . ."

"You're more likely to get a proton torpedo up your engines than you are to get a functional squadron out of such pilots. The torpedo might be launched accidentally . . . but that's no comfort to a widow."

Wedge spread his hands, palms up, and smiled. "Problem solved. I'm not married."

"I know you're not. You know what I mean."

"Yes, sir."

"What would become of Rogue Squadron?"

"I'd be happy to remain in charge officially, but for all squadron activities, Captain Celchu is more than qualified to lead . . . and now that he's been cleared of the formal charge of being a brainwashed double agent, there shouldn't be any responsible objection to his full return to duties. I'd return Lieutenant Hobbie Klivan to Rogue Squadron as second-in-command and take Lieutenant Wes Janson as my own second-in-command. Once the new squadron is established, of course, I'd hope to return to direct command of Rogue Squadron."

"You're committed to this idea, aren't you?"

"Yes, sir." Wedge considered what he was about to say. "Since the battle at Endor, the military's public relations groups have represented Rogue Squadron as if we were the lightsaber of the New Republic. A bright, shiny weapon to cut down any dark Imperial holdovers who still stand against us. But, sir, not all battles call for lightsabers. Some of them are fought with vibroblades in back alleys. The New Republic needs those vibroblades too, and doesn't have them."

"I understand." Ackbar nodded agreeably. "Request refused."

Wedge couldn't speak; suddenly all the air seemed to leave his chest. He'd thought he was so close, thought he had convinced the admiral.

"Unless . . ."

Wedge found his voice again. "Unless?"

"I'll make a bet with you, Commander. You get your

chance at forming this squadron. If, three months after it goes operational, it has proven its worth—in *my sole estimation*—you can do as you please. Continue with the new squadron, go back to command Rogue Squadron, whichever you choose.''

''And if I lose?''

''You accept promotion to the rank of general and join my advisory staff.''

Wedge kept the dismay from his face. ''I would seem to win either way, sir.''

''Stop it. You're not fooling anyone. If you had your way, you'd continue flying snubfighters and commanding fighter squadrons until you were a century old. How many promotions have you turned down? Two? Three?''

''Two.''

''Well, if you lose your bet, you accept this one.''

Wedge sighed and thought it over. He needed to keep flying; he wouldn't be happy in any other way of life. But the New Republic military needed this new tactic, needed many new ways of doing things, before they became as tactically fossilized as the Empire had been. ''I accept, sir.''

THE COURTSHIP OF PRINCESS LEIA
by Dave Wolverton
Setting: Four years after *Return of the Jedi*

One of the most interesting developments in Bantam's STAR WARS novels is that in their storyline, Han Solo and Princess Leia start a family. This tale reveals how the couple originally got together. Wishing to strengthen the fledgling New Republic by bringing in powerful allies, Leia opens talks with the Hapes consortium of more than sixty worlds. But the consortium is ruled by the Queen Mother, who, to Han's dismay, wants Leia to marry her son, Prince Isolder. Before this action-packed story is over, Luke will join forces with Isolder against a group of Force-trained ''witches'' and face a deadly foe.

HEIR TO THE EMPIRE
DARK FORCE RISING
THE LAST COMMAND
by Timothy Zahn
Setting: Five years after _Return of the Jedi_

This #1 bestselling trilogy introduces two legendary forces of evil into the STAR WARS literary pantheon. Grand Admiral Thrawn has taken control of the Imperial fleet in the years since the destruction of the Death Star, and the mysterious Joruus C'baoth is a fearsome Jedi Master who has been seduced by the dark side. Han and Leia have now been married for about a year, and as the story begins, she is pregnant with twins. Thrawn's plan is to crush the Rebellion and resurrect the Empire's New Order with C'baoth's help—and in return, the Dark Master will get Han and Leia's Jedi children to mold as he wishes. For as readers of this magnificent trilogy will see, Luke Skywalker is not the last of the old Jedi. He is the first of the new.

The Jedi Academy Trilogy:
JEDI SEARCH
DARK APPRENTICE
CHAMPIONS OF THE FORCE
by Kevin J. Anderson
Setting: Seven years after _Return of the Jedi_

In order to assure the continuation of the Jedi Knights, Luke Skywalker has decided to start a training facility: a Jedi Academy. He will gather Force-sensitive students who show potential as prospective Jedi and serve as their mentor, as Jedi Masters Obi-Wan Kenobi and Yoda did for him. Han and Leia's twins are now toddlers, and there is a third Jedi child: the infant Anakin, named after Luke and Leia's father. In this trilogy, we discover the existence of a powerful Imperial doomsday weapon, the horrifying Sun Crusher—which will soon become the centerpiece of a titanic struggle between Luke Skywalker and his most brilliant Jedi Academy student, who is delving dangerously into the dark side.

CHILDREN OF THE JEDI
by Barbara Hambly
Setting: Eight years after *Return of the Jedi*

The STAR WARS characters face a menace from the glory days of the Empire when a thirty-year-old automated Imperial Dreadnaught comes to life and begins its grim mission: to gather forces and annihilate a long-forgotten stronghold of Jedi children. When Luke is whisked onboard, he begins to communicate with the brave Jedi Knight who paralyzed the ship decades ago, and gave her life in the process. Now she is part of the vessel, existing in its artificial intelligence core, and guiding Luke through one of the most unusual adventures he has ever had.

DARKSABER by Kevin J. Anderson
Setting: Immediately thereafter

Not long after Children of the Jedi, *Luke and Han learn that evil Hutts are building a reconstruction of the original Death Star—and that the Empire is still alive, in the form of Daala, who has joined forces with Pellaeon, former second-in-command to the feared Grand Admiral Thrawn.*

PLANET OF TWILIGHT
by Barbara Hambly
Setting: Nine years after *Return of the Jedi*

Concluding the epic tale begun in her own novel Children of the Jedi *and continued by Kevin Anderson in* Darksaber, *Barbara Hambly tells the story of a ruthless enemy of the New Republic operating out of a backwater world with vast mineral deposits. The first step in his campaign is to kidnap Princess Leia. Meanwhile, as Luke Skywalker searches the planet for his long-lost love Callista, the planet begins to reveal its unspeakable secret—a secret that threatens the New Republic, the Empire, and the entire galaxy.*

The first to die was a midshipman named Koth Barak. One of his fellow crewmembers on the New Republic escort cruiser *Adamantine* found him slumped across the table in the deck-nine break room where he'd repaired half an hour previously for a cup of coffeine. Twenty minutes after Barak should have been back to post, Gunnery Sergeant Gallie Wover went looking for him.

When she entered the deck-nine break room, Sergeant Wover's first sight was of the palely flickering blue on blue of the infolog screen. "Blast it, Koth, I told you . . ."

Then she saw the young man stretched unmoving on the far side of the screen, head on the break table, eyes shut. Even at a distance of three meters Wover didn't like the way he was breathing.

"Koth!" She rounded the table in two strides, sending the other chairs clattering into a corner. She thought his eyelids moved a little when she yelled his name. "Koth!"

Wover hit the emergency call almost without conscious decision. In the few minutes before the med droids arrived she sniffed the coffeine in the gray plastene cup a few centimeters from his limp fingers. It wasn't even cold.

Behind her the break room door *swoshed* open. She glanced over her shoulder to see a couple of Two-Onebees enter with a table, which was already unfurling scanners and life-support lines like a monster in a bad holovid. They shifted Barak onto the table and hooked him up. Every line of the readouts plunged, and soft, tinny alarms began to sound.

Barak's face had gone a waxen gray. The table was already pumping stimulants and antishock into the boy's veins. Wover could see the initial diagnostic lines on the screen that ringed the antigrav personnel transport unit's sides.

No virus. No bacteria. No poison.

No foreign material in Koth Barak's body at all.

The lines dipped steadily toward zero, then went flat.

THE CRYSTAL STAR
by Vonda N. McIntyre
Setting: Ten years after *Return of the Jedi*

Leia's three children have been kidnapped. That horrible fact is made worse by Leia's realization that she can no longer sense her children through the Force! While she, Artoo-Detoo, and Chewbacca trail the kidnappers, Luke and Han discover a planet that is suffering strange quantum effects from a nearby star. Slowly freezing into a perfect crystal and disrupting the Force, the star is blunting Luke's power and crippling the Millennium Falcon. *These strands converge in an apocalyptic threat not only to the fate of the New Republic, but to the universe itself.*

The Black Fleet Crisis
BEFORE THE STORM
SHIELD OF LIES
TYRANT'S TEST
by Michael P. Kube-McDowell
Setting: Twelve years after *Return of the Jedi*

Long after setting up the hard-won New Republic, yesterday's Rebels have become today's administrators and diplomats. But the peace is not to last for long. A restless Luke must journey to his mother's homeworld in a desperate quest to find her people; Lando seizes a mysterious spacecraft with unimaginable weapons of destruction; and waiting in the wings is a horrific battle fleet under the control of a ruthless leader bent on a genocidal war.

THE NEW REBELLION
by Kristine Kathryn Rusch
Setting: Thirteen years after *Return of the Jedi*

Victorious though the New Republic may be, there is still no end to the threats to its continuing existence—this novel explores the price of keeping the peace. First, somewhere in the galaxy, millions suddenly perish in a blinding instant of pain. Then, as Leia prepares to address the Senate on Coruscant, a horrifying event changes the governmental equation in a flash.

The Corellian Trilogy:
AMBUSH AT CORELLIA
ASSAULT AT SELONIA
SHOWDOWN AT CENTERPOINT
by Roger MacBride Allen
Setting: Fourteen years after *Return of the Jedi*

This trilogy takes us to Corellia, Han Solo's homeworld, which Han has not visited in quite some time. A trade summit brings Han, Leia, and the children—now developing their own clear personalities and instinctively learning more about their innate skills in the Force—into the middle of a situation that most closely resembles a burning fuse. The Corellian system is on the brink of civil war, there are New Republic intelligence agents on a mysterious mission which even Han does not understand, and worst of all, a fanatical rebel leader has his hands on a superweapon of unimaginable power—and just wait until you find out who that leader is!

The Hand of Thrawn
SPECTER OF THE PAST
and coming soon,
VISION OF THE FUTURE
by Timothy Zahn
**Setting: Nineteen years after
*Star Wars: A New Hope***

The new two-book series by the undisputed master of the STAR WARS novel. Once the supreme master of countless star systems, the Empire is tottering on the brink of total collapse. Day by day, neutral systems are rushing to join the New Republic coalition. But with the end of the war in sight, the New Republic has fallen victim to its own success. An unwieldy alliance of races and tradi-

*tions, the confederation now finds itself riven by age-old
animosities. Princess Leia struggles against all odds to
hold the New Republic together. But she has powerful
enemies. An ambitious Moff Disra leads a conspiracy to
divide the uneasy coalition with an ingenious plot to
blame the Bothans for a heinous crime that could lead
to genocide and civil war. At the same time, Luke
Skywalker, along with Lando Calrissian and Talon
Karrde, pursues a mysterious group of pirate ships
whose crew consists of clones. And then comes the worst
news of all: the most cunning and ruthless warlord in
Imperial history has returned to lead the Empire to triumph. Here's an exciting scene from Timothy Zahn's
spectacular new STAR WARS novel:*

"I don't think you fully understand the political situation the New Republic finds itself in these days. A flash
point like Caamas—especially with Bothan involvement—will bring the whole thing to a boil. Particularly
if we can give it the proper nudge."

"The situation among the Rebels is not the issue,"
Tierce countered coldly. "It's the state of the Empire
you don't seem to understand. Simply tearing the Rebellion apart isn't going to rebuild the Emperor's New Order. We need a focal point, a leader around whom the
Imperial forces can rally."

Disra said, "Suppose I could provide such a leader.
Would you be willing to join us?"

Tierce eyed him. "Who is this 'us' you refer to?"

"If you join, there would be three of us," Disra said.
"Three who would share the secret I'm prepared to offer you. A secret that will bring the entire Fleet onto our
side."

Tierce smiled cynically. "You'll forgive me, Your Excellency, if I suggest you couldn't inspire blind loyalty
in a drugged bantha."

Disra felt a flash of anger. How dare this common
soldier—?

"No," he agreed, practically choking out the word
from between clenched teeth. Tierce was hardly a common soldier, after all. More importantly, Disra desperately needed a man of his skills and training. "I would
merely be the political power behind the throne. Plus the
supplier of military men and matériel, of course."

"From the Braxant Sector Fleet?"

"And other sources," Disra said. "You, should you choose to join us, would serve as the architect of our overall strategy."

"I see." If Tierce was bothered by the word "serve," he didn't show it. "And the third person?"

"Are you with us?"

Tierce studied him. "First tell me more."

"I'll do better than tell you." Disra pushed his chair back and stood up. "I'll show you."

Disra led the way down the rightmost corridor. It ended in a dusty metal door with a wheel set into its center. Gripping the edges of the wheel, Disra turned it; and with a creak that echoed eerily in the confined space the door swung open.

The previous owner would hardly have recognized his one-time torture chamber. The instruments of pain and terror had been taken out, the walls and floor cleaned and carpet-insulated, and the furnishings of a fully functional modern apartment installed.

But for the moment Disra had no interest in the chamber itself. All his attention was on Tierce as the former Guardsman stepped into the room.

Stepped into the room . . . and caught sight of the room's single occupant, seated in the center in a duplicate of a Star Destroyer's captain's chair.

Tierce froze, his eyes widening with shock, his entire body stiffening as if a power current had jolted through him. His eyes darted to Disra, back to the captain's chair, flicked around the room as if seeking evidence of a trap or hallucination or perhaps his own insanity, back again to the chair. Disra held his breath. . . .

Also from
TIMOTHY ZAHN
The #1 bestselling saga

STAR WARS ®

Join Luke, Leia, Han, Chewbacca, and
all your favorite *Star Wars* characters for a
rousing romp among the stars. . . .

"Zahn has perfectly captured the pace and flavor
of the *Star Wars* movies." —*Sunday Oklahoman*

"Moves with a speed-of-light pace that captures the
spirit of the movie trilogy so well, you can almost hear the
John Williams sound track." —*The Providence Sunday Journal*

"Chock-full of all the good stuff you've come to expect from
a battle of good against evil." —*Daily News,* New York

JOIN

STAR WARS®

on the INTERNET

Bantam Spectra invites you to visit their
Official STAR WARS® Web Site.

You'll find:

< Sneak previews of upcoming STAR WARS®
  novels.
< Samples from audio editions of the novels.
< Bulletin boards that put you in touch with
  other fans, with the authors, and with the
  Spectra editors who bring them to you.
< The latest word from behind the scenes of
  the STAR WARS® universe.
< Quizzes, games, and contests available only
  on-line.
< Links to other STAR WARS® licensees'
  sites on the Internet.
< Look for STAR WARS® on the World Wide
  Web at:

http://www.bantam/spectra.com

SF 28 5/98

Conquerors Saga

by

TIMOTHY ZAHN

CONQUERORS' PRIDE

A long era of peace and prosperity in the interstellar Commonwealth has suddenly come to a violent end as four alien starships, of unknown origin, attack humanity without provocation, destroying all they encounter. ___56892-2 $5.99/$7.50 Canada

CONQUERORS' HERITAGE

The Zhirrzh have recently won a temporary and welcome respite from their war against humanity, but now their most valued captive has escaped, their best bargaining chip lost. What now can prevent further bloodshed in an unwanted and unasked-for war...unless, as they have so long believed, it was *not* the Humans who started the conflict? ___56772-1 $5.99/$7.99 Canada

CONQUERORS' LEGACY

As both humans and Zhirrzh gird for an all-out war, a handful of individuals from both races discover the explosive catalyst behind the approaching holocaust--a misunderstanding so profound it has brought two mighty civilizations to the brink of mutual extinction. ___57562-7 $5.99/$7.99 Canada

---

Ask for these books at your local bookstore or use this page to order.

Please send me the book I have checked above. I am enclosing $ ___(add $2.50 to cover postage and handling). Send check or money order, no cash or C.O.D.'s, please.

Name _____

Address _____

City/State/Zip _____

Send order to: Bantam Books, Dept. SF 251, 2451 S. Wolf Rd., Des Plaines, IL 60018
Allow four to six weeks for delivery.
Prices and availability subject to change without notice.   SF 251 9/98